ACCLAIM FOR CAROLINE GEORGE

"Caroline George infuses an epistolary love story with a romance and charm that crosses centuries. Touching and inventive, it bursts with wit, warmth, and a blending of classic and contemporary that goes together like scones and clotted cream. *Dearest Josephine* is a delight."

—Emily Bain Murphy, author of *The Disappearances*

"*Dearest Josephine* is the type of story that becomes your own. The characters' heartaches worked their way into my own chest until I hurt with them, hoped with them, and dared to dream with them. This book is teeming with swoon-worthy prose, adorable humor, and an expert delivery of 'Will they end up together?' I guarantee you'll be burning the midnight candle to a stub to get answers. Step aside *Pride and Prejudice*, there's a new romance on the English moors."

—Nadine Brandes, author of *Romanov*

"*Dearest Josephine* is more than an immersive read. It is a book lover's dream experience. Josie's residence in a gothic English manor and her deeply romantic connection to Elias, who lived years in the past, is as chillingly atmospheric as Rochester calling across the moors. This story is George's treatise on the power of books and character to creep across centuries, to pull us close and invite us to live in a fantasy where we find love—literally—in the kinship of ink and binding. But it also acknowledges the dangers of letting ourselves fall too deeply when sometimes an equally powerful connection is waiting next door. This love letter to books, and the readers who exist in and for them, is a wondrously singular escape."

—Rachel McMillan, author of *The London Restoration* and *The Mozart Code*

DEAREST JOSEPHINE

OTHER BOOKS BY CAROLINE GEORGE

DEAREST JOSEPHINE

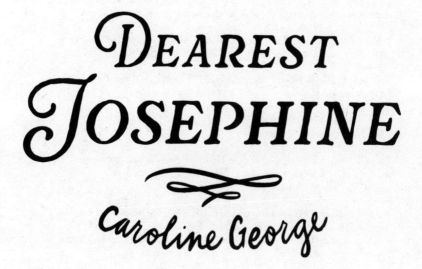

Caroline George

THOMAS NELSON
Since 1798

Published in Nashville, Tennessee, by Thomas Nelson. Thomas Nelson is a registered trademark of HarperCollins Christian Publishing, Inc.

Published in association with Cyle Young of C.Y.L.E (Cyle Young Literary Elite, LLC), a literary agency.

Interior design: Emily Ghattas
Map design: Matthew Covington

Thomas Nelson titles may be purchased in bulk for educational, business, fundraising, or sales promotional use. For information, please email SpecialMarkets@ThomasNelson.com.

Publisher's Note: This novel is a work of fiction. Names, characters, places, and incidents are either products of the author's imagination or used fictitiously. All characters are fictional, and any similarity to people living or dead is purely coincidental.

Library of Congress Cataloging-in-Publication Data

Names: George, Caroline, 1997- author.
Title: Dearest Josephine / Caroline George.
Description: Nashville, Tennessee : Thomas Nelson, [2021] | Summary: "Caroline George sweeps readers up into two different time periods with an unexpected love story that prompts us to reimagine what it means to be present with the people we love"-- Provided by publisher.
Identifiers: LCCN 2020032767 (print) | LCCN 2020032768 (ebook) | ISBN 9780785236184 (hardcover) | ISBN 9780785236191 (epub) | ISBN 9780785236207 (audio download)
Subjects: GSAFD: Love stories. | Epistolary fiction.
Classification: LCC PS3607.E6394 D43 2021 (print) | LCC PS3607.E6394 (ebook) | DDC 813/.6--dc23
LC record available at https://lccn.loc.gov/2020032767
LC ebook record available at https://lccn.loc.gov/2020032768

Printed in the United States of America

21 22 23 24 25 LSC 10 9 8 7 6 5 4 3 2 1

For Tessa,
Who believed in this story
before it reached the page.

And for everyone who's found
love within a book.

Streambank

South Ridge

Gorse Alcove

Smokehouse

Sheering Shed

East Wing
Gardens

Herb Garden
& Kitchen Yard

Stable

Orchard

A

C

E

B

D

F

Pastures

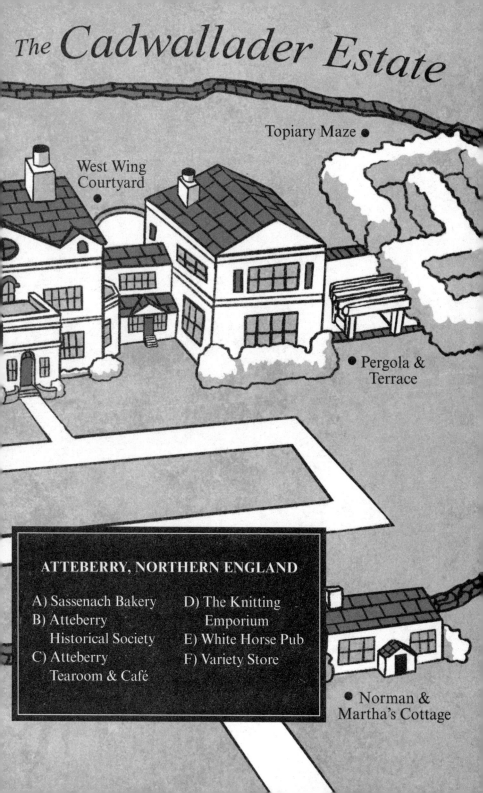

The Cadwallader Estate

Topiary Maze ●

West Wing
Courtyard ●

● Pergola &
Terrace

ATTEBERRY, NORTHERN ENGLAND

A) Sassenach Bakery
B) Atteberry
    Historical Society
C) Atteberry
    Tearoom & Café
D) The Knitting
    Emporium
E) White Horse Pub
F) Variety Store

● Norman &
Martha's Cottage

For a moment with you,
I wait an eternity.

ONE

JOSIE

From: Josie De Clare <JDeClare@mailbox.com>
Sent: Monday, June 20, 1:38 PM
To: Faith Moretti <Kardashian_4Life@mailbox.com>
Subject: Neil Is Rubbish – We Hate Neil

Hi Faith,

I did a thing. A big thing. And I'm not sure how to tell you without sounding like the rotten human being who abandoned her best friend for a boy. The rotten human being who reached out the moment she broke up with said boy. But surprise. That's what I'm doing. Reaching out.

Rashad and I broke up. Well, I broke up with him after he said we needed to cool down for a while. Maybe he broke up with me first. I mean, the whole relationship was a blurry mess.

You said he wasn't good for me. I should've listened. I should've gone to the school dance with you, taken you to the airport after graduation. Though you might not believe me, I haven't forgotten that during our first day at Stonehill Academy, we planned to end our thirteenth year by replacing all the headmaster photos with cut-outs of Leonardo DiCaprio. Epic prank idea. Headmistress Poston would've freaked.

I'm sorry for ruining your last year in England.

Guess my brain was scrambled by Rashad's chocolate-brown eyes and hair that always looked windswept, like he'd been on a motorbike. Ugh! And his gold chain. Laugh all you want, but chains on the right boy . . . (*kisses fingertips*) *perfecto*.

Rashad drove me to the bus station afterward. As I yanked my luggage from the trunk of his MINI Cooper, he said, "We need to break up, love. Your mood swings put a damper on my creativity." (Like my dad's death triggered his lack of artistic talent.) I told him we'd already broken up. Then I poured his cherry-lime energy drink onto his Fenty trainers.

Not my best moment.

Anyway, I decided to email you because (1.) I'm the wordiest person alive, and (2.) I have no idea how international calls or texts work. Part of me thinks I'll get a bill for two hundred pounds if I try to phone you. That's not an excuse for my lack of communication. I know I've been rotten and selfish—and you deserve to hate me. I can't even blame cancer.

You lost my dad too.

I want to be friends again. Remember our first slumber party at my house? Dad made the worst jam roly-poly, and we filmed videos of us singing karaoke. We promised to stay friends forever. Swore it. Heck, I think we did a friendship ritual to seal the deal.

Please forgive me, Faith. London is rubbish without you. I'm rubbish without you. Really, everything in my life seems destined to go wrong. I forgot to post my application to university and won't be able to re-enrol until the spring term. I ruined our relationship. Dad passed away, you returned to America, and Rashad . . . well, Rashad ended up being *Rashad*.

How did you put up with me for so many years? I can't even be alone for a couple hours without getting annoyed or wanting to dye my hair pink. That brings me to my second bit of news. I'm on my way to Atteberry—a village only an hour drive from Scotland's border. After Dad passed, I learned he'd purchased an estate in the town. He liked to renovate historical homes, but he never told me about the property. Maybe he wanted it to be a surprise.

Dad got a kick out of surprises.

I need to be alone (and hopefully not dye my hair) while I figure out what's next for me. I feel like a volcano about to explode, like I haven't breathed—really breathed—in months. I threw some clothes into a suitcase, texted my boss at the café, and left Dad's townhouse without even feeding the cat. (Don't worry. Mum agreed to care for Antoni while I'm gone.)

My first term at uni starts in January, which means I have seven months to decide what I want to do with my life. I'm seriously considering becoming a hermit with pink hair.

So far this holiday isn't off to a good start. My bus stopped at a petrol station not long ago. I went inside and had a mental breakdown while waiting to purchase tampons, jelly babies, and chocolate. Tears and snot everywhere.

The cashier gave me a pervert stare, you know, like the guys at Stonehill Academy. His lopsided name tag read: *HELLO, MY NAME IS NEIL*. He touched my candy with his tobacco-stained fingers and said, "One awful period, huh?"

All manners went out the shop's window. Instead of answering the question with a polite *NO*, I wiped my tears and yelled, "Neil, I'm having a real crappy day. Give me the chocolate." And that's how I managed to embarrass myself to a point of extinction.

My bus reaches Atteberry in a few minutes, so I must bring this monologue to a close. Overall, I want to tell you . . . I know I messed up. I messed up when I ignored your phone calls. I messed up when I didn't talk to you at Dad's funeral. I'm a mess. I've been a mess for a while. But I don't want to be messy anymore.

You don't owe me a second chance, but would you forgive me just the same?

If you ever want to FaceTime, let me know. I'll be at Cadwallader Manor for the next few months, so I'll have plenty of free time.

Cadwallader—sounds like a creature I'd fish out of a pond.

Yours truly,
Josie

(Sent from iPhone)

Josie: Bus reached Atteberry. Norman, the estate's caretaker, fetched me from the station. Headed to Cadwallader Manor now.

Mum: Thx for the update.

Josie: Any news from Dad's lawyers?

Mum: They advise selling your father's townhouse.

Josie: No! I want it. Plz don't sell.

Mum: Going into meeting. Talk later.

From: Faith Moretti <Kardashian_4Life@mailbox.com>
Sent: Monday, June 20, 3:16 PM
To: Josie De Clare <JDeClare@mailbox.com>
Subject: Re: Neil is Rubbish – We Hate Neil

Hey Josie,

Thanks for reaching out! I'll be honest. I stared at my laptop for a solid thirty minutes before I typed one sentence. And look at what I landed on!! Some corporate, autogenerated response that seems like I don't care about you. But I do care. I am glad you reached out.

I want to be angry and send you all the emails I typed up after graduation. I want to express how much you hurt me, that I thought Rashad was an idiot who used his good looks to manipulate people, that . . . I wasn't okay after your dad passed. I needed you like you needed me. I wanted to be there for you, to cry with you at the funeral, to get angry at God and life and growing up.

Maybe that's what hurt the most. Not being there.

During one of our last school lunches, I sat in the refectory with Hannah and Hope while you ate with Rashad. I watched you drape your legs over his lap and snicker at the faculty, and I got so mad because you weren't *you* anymore. I almost took the BFF slap bracelet (the one you gave me during our first year at Stonehill) off my backpack. I almost whacked you over the head with it. Not to hurt you. I just wanted to beat some sense into your thick skull.

All that said, I think I forgave you a long time ago. I'm not mad anymore. We promised to stay friends, right? Through all the good and bad. Even when it seemed hard.

So yeah, I'd like to give you that second chance.

Returning to New York was tough. I visited my family in Rochester before I moved to Brooklyn for college. My parents threw an Italian-style welcome party and invited everyone—my aunts, uncles, cousins, grandparents, godparents. (You would've loved it. So much food.)

After dinner I brewed a cup of tea while Mom served coffee. My uncle was like, "You fancier than us now, Faith?" He made jokes about England and my second family—what he called you and your dad. He talked about how my cousins went to public school and didn't need an expensive education to get into college.

Everyone at the table seemed to forget I got into Stonehill on scholarship and because Aunt Sylvia recommended me to Headmistress Poston during her stint as a science teacher. They looked at me like I was an outsider, and I realized I didn't fit in with them the way I used to, at least not the way I fit with you.

Time has changed me. I no longer snicker at Uncle Sal's jokes. I prefer tea over Mama's imported coffee. I wear designer clothes thrifted from online boutiques, not crop tops bought from the mall. Maybe I should've noticed the changes sooner, but I wanted to believe everything was the same—my family would be my family again. Still, as I sat at that dining table, I saw it plain as day. The changes. The differences. Why I couldn't pretend those years in England hadn't opened a gaping chasm between us.

We had lived apart from each other. We'd gone our separate ways, and en route I stopped wanting their dreams, like the law degree, husband and kids, moving next door to my parents. I decided to pursue a career in fashion, maybe launch my own store chain like the Kardashians. They think that's frivolous. I guess . . . my family is disappointed because they want the old Faith, and I'm disappointed because they want someone other than me.

Gah, I miss you so much, Josie. I miss eating takeout with you and your dad. I miss our Saturday strolls through Notting Hill. I miss your dad's movie commentaries and popcorn obsession. I miss every little thing.

Life seems so different now. I live in a crappy one-bedroom apartment and take summer classes. I eat frozen dinners, binge watch *Keeping Up with the Kardashians*. It's just . . . Home doesn't seem like home without Headmistress Poston's room checks, our plaid uniforms, and Chicken Tender Tuesdays. I still expect to see you reading upside down whenever I enter my room. And thanks to you, I crave Dairy Milk bars at nine o'clock every night.

We're not kids anymore, but we're not grown-ups, either. People said we were adults once we turned eighteen. Do you feel like an adult? I sure don't. I can't figure out how to reload my transit card or file taxes. Sometimes I think life would be easier if we could rewind time and do high school all over again. Maybe we'd do it better the second time around. No Rashad. No bangs and Converse. No fights over who'd play Sandy in *Grease*.

I'm still with Noah, by the way. We managed to survive two years of long-distance dating. He moved to Brooklyn, too, so we see each other all the time. Recently he's started talking about marriage, which terrifies me. I am NOT ready for more adulthood.

That's all my news! I guess the best way to conclude is to say you're forgiven, Josie. We're friends. Through messes, sucky boyfriends, bad haircuts, whatever—we'll stay friends. I hope you enjoy your time at Cadwallader Manor. Breathe. Learn to be alone. Figure out what you need to figure out, and I'll be here, ready to talk or listen or send memes.

Please tell me about Atteberry and your dad's secret estate. I need details!!

Faith

P.S. Let's stick to emails for now. I need to download a messaging app so my cell phone provider won't charge a fortune for international texts and calls.

Mum: Are you settled in?

Josie: Yes. Norman and Martha helped me unpack. Then we ate dinner at a restaurant in Atteberry. How was your meeting?

Mum: Fine. I'll chat with lawyers about townhouse tomorrow.

From: Josie De Clare <JDeClare@mailbox.com>
Sent: Monday, June 20, 11:37 PM
To: Faith Moretti <Kardashian_4Life@mailbox.com>
Subject: Cadwallader Manor

Faith, here is my detailed report, per your request.

Atteberry rises from kilometres of farmland, its sprawl nestled at the base of a grand hill. The town possesses a cosy sort of quaintness, almost like that porcelain village my grandmother

9

displays at Christmas. People wander its cobblestone streets and live in homes with thatched rooves. Very old-fashioned. Don't fret, though. I spotted a few restaurants and bakeries while Norman drove me to the Cadwallader estate, so I won't starve or lose my mind to the North England quiet. And according to a gentleman at the bus station, Atteberry houses the finest knitting clubs in the country. Would you like a scarf for your birthday?

Norman seems quite a character. He and his wife, Martha, take care of Dad's estate and inhabit a cottage on the property. One word to describe them: adorable. Norman served in the navy, then became a farmer once he retired. He dons a wool jumper and navy cap. Martha, on the other hand, resembles Headmistress Poston. Same bobbed grey hair and motherly smile.

The landscape here projects a vibrant gloom—beautiful and melancholy. Every coppice and patch of grass blazes green, and the overcast sky washes the world with a blue haze.

Did you consider London a dreary place? I used to love the city. Dad took me for picnics in Kensington Gardens. Once a month we had cream tea at a shop near Windsor. It must've rained then. But I only noticed the dampness when he got sick.

Mum doesn't understand. Granted, she left after the divorce and refused to join our outings. Oh, I need to tell you!! Dad's lawyers want to sell the town home. I won't let them. That house means the world to me—to us. (Your pyjamas are still in the guest room.)

Going to FaceTime you after I use the loo.

Josie

(Sent from iPhone)

From: Josie De Clare <JDeClare@mailbox.com>
Sent: Monday, June 20, 11:50 PM
To: Faith Moretti <Kardashian_4Life@mailbox.com>
Subject: Re: Cadwallader Manor

I saw your Instagram story, Faith. I know you're watching television with your dog. Do you like Netflix more than your friend? LOL

Whatever. I'll tell you about Cadwallader Manor, and I'll be extra wordy because I'm petty and have nothing better to do.

The house stands at the end of a gravel drive, built in the Gothic Revival style with buttresses and stone walls. Do you recall Thornfield Hall from *Jane Eyre*? That's where I now reside—within an eerie manor surrounded by moorland and fog.

I asked Norman about the estate and why Dad kept it a secret. This is what he told me:

Dad purchased the property at a private auction while I was at Stonehill. He planned to renovate the house so we could use it on holidays. But his cancer ended those dreams. Maybe he thought he'd recover and finish the project. Maybe not telling me was his way of holding on to that hope. Whatever his reason, he intended this place for us.

I'm not sure what to think or feel right now. To be here and see evidence of Dad—his sweater on the coatrack, the sparkling water in the fridge—reminds me of things I don't want to remember. Losing him. Getting swept away in the chaos that followed.

A few months of quiet will do me some good. Maybe I'll finish the renovations and have furniture appraised to complete Dad's project. He wanted me at Cadwallader. I cling to that truth now, while I huddle near my bedroom's fireplace with a cup of Earl Grey and an oil lamp. (The manor has electricity only on its main floor.)

Of course, Dad bought the creepiest fixer-upper in all of England. Too many spiders and drafts that seem to come from nowhere. I wish you were here to see it.

I wish you were here.

Email back as soon as possible! Your communication keeps me sane and less spooked by the creak of old wood and wind against shutters.

BTW, I planned to give you a virtual tour of the house. You missed out.

Josie

(Sent from iPhone)

Faith: Worth the international fees . . . I AM SORRY!!! I was watching Stranger Things and didn't realize you called. I'll respond to your email tomorrow. Love you.

Josie: Sleep tight. Don't let the Demogorgon bite.

From: Faith Moretti <Kardashian_4Life@mailbox.com>
Sent: Tuesday, June 21, 12:23 PM
To: Josie De Clare <JDeClare@mailbox.com>
Subject: Re: Cadwallader Manor

Josie, if you don't respond, I'll assume you froze to death in that creepy mansion, and my day will be ruined. JOSIE, RESPOND ASAP!!

Your description of Atteberry—although beautiful—makes the place sound lonely. I'm a full supporter of rest and self-discovery, but isolation can sometimes cause more problems. Please don't join a knitting club. But if you do, promise you won't become a hermit who collects yarn and wanders the moors and dyes her hair pink. Geez, I get nervous just thinking about you in that village with only Norman and Martha to keep you company. I mean, they're better than Rashad.

Pretty much everyone is better than Rashad.

I must know more about your first night at Cadwallader. Any ghost sightings? Or even better—did Mr. Rochester call on you? Oh, I wish I could visit and help renovate the house.

Your dad would have wanted you to finish his project, though.

OMG, your mom and lawyers better not sell the townhouse. That place belongs to you—your dad said so. Remember when we tried to slide down the laundry chute and you got stuck? I was so scared your dad would be angry at me when he saw your feet dangling out of the shaft, and I couldn't believe it when he just laughed and slathered you with vegetable oil to get you out. Didn't that stain the clothes?

I miss him too. He treated me like a daughter, and I needed that. I needed a family during my time at Stonehill. Did you ever hear about the skirt? During one of our weekends at your house, your dad overheard us talking about how I'd ripped my uniform. He went to the store and bought a plaid skirt, then put it in the guest room for me to find. He didn't say a word about it, but I knew what he'd done.

You both mean the world to me.

So yeah, I understand your reason for visiting Cadwallader Manor. Loss changes our perspective of the world, exposes its instability, and leaves us to gather the pieces of our broken selves and stick them back together. Your dad must've known that, Josie. Maybe he bought the house to give you a safe place—somewhere you could heal.

Explore the estate and let me know what you find.

Faith

Rashad: You misunderstood me, Jo. I don't wanna break up.

Josie: Wrong number.

Rashad: We had one fight. It's no big deal.

Rashad: Guess you're giving up on us, huh?

From: Josie De Clare <JDeClare@mailbox.com>
Sent: Tuesday, June 21, 4:01 PM
To: Faith Moretti <Kardashian_4Life@mailbox.com>
Subject: Weird Finds at Cadwallader

Good news, Faith! I didn't perish in the night and turn to ice. The fireplace warmed my bedroom to a comfortable temperature. I slept beneath a mound of quilts and didn't wake until Norman led his sheep past my window. Neither ghosts nor Mr. Rochester paid me a visit, which probably disappoints you. I can, however, report horrific texts from Rashad, but I won't waste time—or words—telling you about them.

I took your advice and explored the estate. First, I ravaged the kitchen and put together a breakfast of toast, eggs, and tea—like a genuine domestic. Martha left homemade butter and clotted cream in the fridge to liven up my meals. She even filled the pantry with canned soups. (I tell you this to prompt a craving for British food so you'll return to me.)

The weather seemed decent enough, so I took a pair of work boots from the cellar and went outdoors. I followed a stone wall around the property, then chased sheep onto the south ridge. Call me a child—I don't care! The air tasted like snow, and a frigid breeze clawed through my jumper. But I wasn't cold. Not for a moment. I felt something—something that didn't hurt—and I liked it. So, there I sat on the sod, scribbling in the notebook I carry around with me. I would've stayed for hours and watched mist swirl over the countryside, but a storm drove me back to the house. And that's when my day turned weird.

Granted, I find oddities in the simplest of things—you know this to be true. Case in point: when I spotted Headmistress Poston's star-shaped tattoo and invented an explanation involving spies, covert operations, and hidden identities. All that to say, I doubt my observations hold significance in the logical realm.

While roaming the house, I discovered a study in the manor's west wing. It overlooks the courtyard and contains a desk, chair, and shelves piled with books, each old and likely worth a small fortune. Above the fireplace hangs a portrait of a young man with dark curly hair and hazel eyes—and a chiselled jawline no person could forget. He looks about eighteen years old. Broody. Slender. Posed next to a horse and dressed in a tailcoat.

Our type of boy.

I've attached a photo. What do you make of it? Doesn't the guy resemble Ian Wyatt from third-period arithmetic? Same pale skin and angular features. But this boy looks mature, almost serious to a point of sadness.

He seems devastating in every way.

The portrait inspired me. I decided to write a few thoughts about him into my notebook, but my pen ran out of ink, so

I opened the desk to search for one. I pulled too hard, and the drawer popped off its tracks. That's when I found the weirdness—a bundle of unopened letters tucked behind the compartment, each addressed to a Josephine De Clare.

Should I read the letters? Dad might've left them for me. Probably not. I mean, they look rather dated. The paper is brown and brittle, and the handwriting is faded.

I want them to be from Dad. After everything that happened, I just want to make sense of the pain, understand *why* it happened to me. Maybe I need to find myself, or something cliché like that. But I feel lost at sea, and I'm not sure what being found even means.

Thanks for staying friends with me. I won't get oversentimental because tears—even a drop—might dissolve these letters. Just know Dad loved you. I love you.

Please tell me to read the letters.

Josie

P.S. I also found a box of old papers beneath the bookcase!!!

(Sent from iPhone)

Rashad: You obviously never loved me.

Rashad: Jo, I know these texts r reaching u.

Rashad: Are you with another bloke?

TWO

ELIAS

April 15, 1821

Dearest Josephine,

Not a day passes without thoughts of our fortuitous meeting. I think fondly of that night and the conversation we shared. Despite its brevity, our dialogue left an impression on me, which I cannot forget. I understand we have not engaged in an environment deemed socially appropriate. However, I feel the need to propose we begin a correspondence. Your wisdom and frankness lead me to believe only you can understand my situation. This was proven by your astute observations during our time together.

My father died a month ago. I barely knew him, yet I mourn him with a ferocity that makes little sense to me. I loathed his estate and his widow, hence my quick departure from it. Indeed, I disliked every aspect of him, from the smell of his library to the way he sliced his venison.

I now reside at Cadwallader Manor—my father's northernmost property. Arthur Banes, my closest friend, and his cousin Lorelai Glas join me here. Their company eases the ache of grief or loneliness—or whatever emotions linger after a parent's death. In truth, I thought myself immune to the loss of Father. I thought myself immune to most emotions, especially those attached to such a man.

The Roch fortune belongs to me—Lord Roch's bastard. Though not quite nineteen years of age, already I am considered the richest man north of Newcastle. The wealth should appease me, for I spent my childhood preparing for it. I attended Eton College and obeyed my father's commands. Not once did I rebel against his wishes. Even when my mother—who served as a maid in the Roch household—perished from winter fever, I remained at school in submission to Lord Roch.

Fortune has not satisfied me. Rather, it has created an emptiness. Perhaps I am ungrateful. The inheritance provides status and opportunities a bastard should not be allowed. Tell me—what do you think of my situation? I would appreciate your candour regarding this matter, for you are the first lady to address me with plain, honest speech. No practiced formalities. No wary application of the etiquette that governs relations between men and women.

Recently I have found myself in an ill humour far more disagreeable than my usual temperament. I suppose the moors have altered me. Cadwallader Manor, large and dreary, receives a great deal less sunlight than my father's home in the south. Cigar smoke from a previous owner clings to the walls. Candles burn tirelessly in a waged war against the darkness. Often I find the night more amicable, for at least the stars offer some consolation.

My housekeeper, Mrs. Dunstable, insists I replace my city clothes, which she starches and presses each morning, with wool garments. She fears my health declines, for I have not a dry head since my departure from the Roch estate, and my clothes remain in an almost-constant state of dampness. Outdoors the mud runs deep enough to swallow one's ankles. Inside, however, the fires burn smoky and weak. I must admit—a splash of brandy from time to time seems to best ease the chills.

At present, Arthur plays his violin in the parlour. He prefers to practice after breakfast, when Lorelai retreats to the drawing room for an hour of watercolour. His music echoes up the stairwell and fills my study with squealing notes. Rapturous songs do not appeal to him. Instead, he performs melancholic pieces, which magnify the house's already haunted ambience.

He and I became friends during our time at Eton. You may recall a few of the stories I shared, ones about secret parties in the boarding house and night-time trips to the local tavern. Arthur was involved in all misadventures. Of course I would like to blame him for our frequent punishment, but I must accept responsibility. I was rowdy and liked to anger the headmaster, for he treated me poorly due to my illegitimate birth.

Eton College prides itself on rearing boys from distinguished families. The school offers a superior education and lack of coddling—qualities which attracted my father. Lord Roch wanted me to grow into a strong man, not spend my youth in the servants' quarters, where people showed affection. Roch men, even the bastards, are expected to demonstrate their manhood through intellectual discussions and unsentimental conduct.

My reason for writing you must lie in the details of my upbringing. I find myself out of sorts, hardly the boy who climbed from his bedroom window and clowned at the pub. I feel as though my mind has imprisoned me, Josephine. You offered solace and friendship, and so I ask for your help. A gentleman should not request such advice from a lady, I realize.

Our acquaintance has not been conventional from the start. Why change that now?

Did you feel unlike yourself after the death of your father? I behave without the faintest trace of madness, but I feel it coursing through my veins. No one can know about it except you, for you are well acquainted—despite our limited engagement—with my sequestered notions of self and the world. Please know I am grateful for your tolerance.

Arthur has finished his violin practice, so I must conclude this reintroduction. He wishes us to venture into town for entertainment, which will likely consist of drinks at the public house followed by a visit to the hatter. Lorelai does not plan to join us. She prefers to go on walks and collect things for her art. Just yesterday I found her bird feathers scattered about the manor and dried flowers pressed between the pages of my books.

I pray the South agrees with you, Josephine. If you do

find yourself near Atteberry, I invite you to visit Cadwallader. Although my description of the estate does not merit enthusiasm, I promise to be an exceptional host and introduce you to the finest of Northern England.

With respect and admiration, I await your response.

Yours ever,

Elias Roch

P.S. I shall post this letter once I learn your address. Our quick parting left me without your information, and my contacts are not familiar with the De Clare Family. I have written to relations who live in London, Manchester, and Liverpool, in hope they might be acquainted with you—or at least know how to reach you.

April 17, 1821

Dearest Josephine,

If not for my wretched state, I would consider this letter and plea for correspondence an impertinence, daresay humiliating. I wish to preserve the sanctity of our meeting and your first impression. However, I believe only you can relate with my circumstance.

Arthur would consider my feelings a sign of derangement. Lorelai would lose all respect for me the instant I shared these thoughts swarming within my mind. They mean well, and they are dear to me. But those dearest to us cannot always understand what causes us pain.

I awoke in a panic last night, before morn smeared gold across the horizon, before the household staff began their chores. I had not a dream to frighten me, rather a weight that came from nowhere and settled on my chest. A weight I could not touch nor remove. It pressed until I struggled to breathe, and I sat up in bed, gasping at the gloom.

My thoughts went to Mother. I did not visit her during her illness, and I saw her only twice after I left for Eton. She contracted winter fever not long after I started my second year. Perhaps the weight I felt was nothing more than a reminder of her death.

Eton was not an amiable place in my experience. I considered its schoolrooms bleak, its recreations barely tolerable. Arthur's company helped me to survive the education, therefore allowing me to become the son Lord Roch wanted. I doubt I truly met Father's expectations, though. He anticipated a great deal from his heir, and I never seemed enough.

The past haunted me last night, and I sense it here still. I feel enclosed by a cage, but the bars are set wide. I could escape, and yet I choose to stay within confinement. Do you make sense of these scribbles, Josephine? Have I indeed lost my mind?

Arthur took me to the public house yesterday for amusement. The pub is small and noisome, its floor sticky with ale. Few candles glow within its rooms, perhaps for the best. Those who frequent the establishment are a far cry from Atteberry's respectable folk.

My friend brought his violin to the pub, for he relishes attention. He played a jig while I embarrassed myself by dancing on tabletops. Such behaviour came from my schoolboy days, when I clowned at the tavern more than thrice a week. I tell you this not with pride, rather to offer context. Arthur and I doth share a handful of reckless habits.

Patrons made wagers on how many rats the pub's cat would drag from the keg room. A foolish diversion, perhaps, but it lifted my spirits for several hours.

Exploits with Arthur tend to ease my moods. He is a genial person, the most reliable and loyal friend in my acquaintance. I consider him my brother, for we have known each other more than a decade. You would fancy him, I think. Although he does not possess the gift of eloquence, he makes up for all shortcomings with his knack for entertainment. In Arthur Banes's company, one shall never find oneself bored.

The outing refreshed me until I returned to Cadwallader Manor. One step into the entrance hall, and those feelings I had endeavoured to bury within the graveyard of my mind were exhumed. I went to my study and locked its door, the ale still fogging my head. I felt wrong. Even now I cannot explain the wrongness that swelled within me, its presence dark and despondent.

Arthur and Lorelai dine with me each night. We go on frequent walks across the moors, play games in the drawing room. I should not endure this sadness, for my guests are splendid company. They give this house purpose and strip away its shadows.

Lorelai seems most content here. She likes to paint the landscape and spend afternoons practicing her French. Not older than eighteen, she possesses an earnest countenance. Fun and games do appeal to her but in moderation—the opposite of her cousin. I suppose the best way to describe Lorelai would be by way of her fashion. She wears an ultramarine dress made from the thickest satin. It never loses its shape, like the bun that rests at her neck.

She and I get on quite well. A few days ago, she persuaded me to sit for one of her paintings. Arthur made jokes the whole time, which only provoked Lorelai into a rage. She lectured us both for over an hour, then conscripted Arthur to work as her assistant.

The portrait turned out to her liking. I rather loathe it, for it depicts my physique as lean and sharp. Her image of me has skin whiter than bone and dark curls that appear long, daresay true to life. I had best groom myself and request more cakes with afternoon tea. Perhaps a large dinner—white soup paired with lambchops and potatoes—will correct my spare build.

I need to resemble an adult if I am to lord over this estate.

Josie: CHECK YOUR EMAIL!

Josie: I'm reading the letters.

Josie: Not sure how international fees work, so don't text back.

Faith: You just spent a pound of your own money. LOL. Checking my email now.

Father left his entire fortune to me. I manage his properties and assets, represent the Rochs in society. I am a gentleman, not a gentleman's bastard, yet who am I without

Father's orders and disapproval? What shall I do with myself? Once, I mentioned my struggles to Arthur, and he laughed.

He wishes to talk only about Eton and gossip.

You must think me ungrateful. I have friends, wealth, and a large estate, yet I fill pages with complaints. I wish ardently to restore my wits so I may acknowledge the benisons of this world. Truly, if you find my words tedious, do tell me, and I shall cease all correspondence. Your good opinion means far more than letters.

I hope you are well. The night we met seems a lifetime ago, and I must confess that I miss you, perhaps more than one should after such a brief encounter. You are marvellous, unlike any woman in all of England. Please do not view my compliment as mere flattery. The repetition of accolades may dim their significance, but I state mine with sincerity.

Cadwallader Manor seems eerie today, more so than usual. I sit at my desk as a rainstorm pummels the land. Lorelai made wind chimes from old silverware and hung them outside the kitchen. They knell in the rain now.

Perhaps I should have moved into the Roch town home in Bath, enjoyed assembly halls and warmer temperatures. However, I felt drawn to Cadwallader, for its isolation suits my moods. I do crave brighter places, though. At present, wind claps the attic shutters. Spiders weave their gossamer tapestries in corners. And the maid dusts soot from my fireplace, stirring up a smog.

~~Did you fight for sleep after your father died? Were your thoughts and feelings jumbled like mine?~~ I shall not pester you with questions, but I wish to comprehend why I grieve a man I disliked, why I desire this pen and your company more than the persons downstairs.

Please write to me.

Elias

P.S. My friend in Liverpool confessed no knowledge of your location nor your existence. He claimed the only De Clare in his acquaintance is a clerk at a London bank. You must not be related to this person, for your apparel—what I remember—suggested distinguished birth. I shall continue to write as I search for you, in hope of one day posting my letters.

April 24, 1821

Dearest Josephine,

Writing to you calms me. I retreat to my study once everyone bids their good-nights, and I scribble until my thoughts steady themselves. I seem to write for several hours a day, either to you or no one in particular. The words inside me are so palpable and consuming they withhold rest until I let them out in the world.

My new habit vexes Arthur. He dislikes all pastimes that allow a sombre mood, except for his violin playing. To him, life should revolve around merriment and pleasure and avoid what causes discomfort. His intentions are noble, for he has seen me at my lowest. He found me in Eton's courtyard after

I received news of Mother's death. He embraced me—which breached our school's code of conduct—and said he would always be my family. From that day on, he has endeavoured to make life a bit easier for me. He was at my side when Father died.

He has been at my side all these years.

Arthur and Lorelai plan to stay at Cadwallader Manor until autumn. They want to enjoy Atteberry's social season. At least such is their claim. I suspect they fret about me. Lorelai seems to watch my every move. Arthur insists on keeping me company throughout the day. Neither of them asks questions, but they remain on alert.

I wish they would ask questions. Perhaps then I would find answers, and this loneliness I feel would subside. I am desperate to make sense of the fervour that plagues my thoughts, for it is full of contradiction. I suffer from isolation when surrounded by familiars. I want to be alone when I long for companionship. How strange. I live here, yet I am not here. I am somewhere else, entirely.

Do you ever get the sense that we are not where we ought to be, as if God made an error in our placement? I sound foolish, of course. Arthur and Lorelai have right to be concerned. Perhaps I should agree to Arthur's request and host a ball. He believes the event will make Cadwallader seem more like home. Strange enough, I am at a loss for excuses.

Lorelai refuses to enjoy an idle moment. She assists the servants with their chores, which baffles me, for most high-born ladies consider household work a violation of their class. Lorelai does not abide by those conventions. This morning she noticed a tear in my coat and took upon the task of mending it. She repaired the hole, then stitched my initials onto the sleeve.

She mothers Arthur and me in a gentle way, ensuring we stay out of trouble and do not visit the pub too often. After dinner we all gather in the drawing room for charades or chess, sometimes to hear Arthur play his violin. Lorelai talks but rarely about herself. She wants to know about the management of Cadwallader, a topic not usually of interest to ladies.

Is it horrible that the longer she stays here, the less I think of her as a girl?

Arthur and I spent the past few days hauling sheep from mud. A storm washed out some of the hills, trapping much of the estate's herds in mire. We laboured with groundskeepers, shepherds, farmers—anyone strong enough to rescue the animals. My body still aches from the arduous work. I pity Mrs. Dunstable the most, though, for she dealt with Arthur's and my mess.

She threatened to hand in her notice if I kept tracking sod through the house.

Due to the drudgery, Arthur demands I take part in the social season. He wants to attend dinner parties, host gatherings, and dance with young ladies who fancy his coquetry. Yes, I shall give him the ball to satisfy his need for amusement. Besides, an introduction to the local gentry may allow me to better integrate myself. I am Lord Roch, not a bastard schoolboy.

Illegitimate birth means little now that I have wealth and title, for money alters society's attitude. People once stared and whispered about my father's scandal. Not anymore. Because of my rise in station, they request my presence at their events. They curtsy and bow, introduce me to their daughters in hopes I might marry one of them.

When I told you of my circumstances, you did not even blink, and for that I shall always be grateful. Arthur once said those things we hate about ourselves are the same things others never notice, but I did not come into this world disliking myself. Rather, I was taught to hate by people who did notice.

Speaking of which, how are relations with your mother? I recall your mention of disagreements after your father passed. Have you reconciled? Also, do you plan to participate in the season? If so, I hope we have opportunity to meet.

To dance with you again as we did that night—I cannot think of anything I would enjoy more.

Cadwallader Manor will provide sanctuary while I toil to recover myself. From where I sit, the moors do not seem as desolate a place. Sheep graze across their slopes. Mist skirts the ridges and ravines. Yes, I shall endeavour to find peace here.

Rashad: Want me to apologize? I'm sorry.

Rashad: If u don't respond, I'll date someone else. Bet on it.

Josie: We're over. Do not contact me.

Rashad: Your dad's death sure did a number on u.

Behind the manor's east wing, where the smokehouse merges with a stone fence, resides an alcove fashioned from gorse and fallen rock. I write to you from that recess.

Atteberry forms a cluster in the distance. I ride my horse, Willoughby, there once a week to buy stationery, for I am quite particular about my paper and ink.

That said, despite my theatrics, life at Cadwallader is not a morbid plight. In fact, the estate's beauty needs no words to express itself, only the eyes of those willing to see it. I choose to see, and I will endure my troubles.

Worse things have tried to break me.

Josephine, we did not meet by accident, for no two people meet—especially not in the serendipitous circumstance that brought us together—by mere chance. I met you, and you knew me in a moment. For that reason, I state my request a final time. Would you write to me?

I shall not lose hope that we will meet again. Even the astronomers believe those destined to collide, whether they be stars or people, might cross paths and go their separate ways but eventually doth find themselves brought together once more. And so, I hope.

Yours ever,

Elias

P.S. Against my better judgement, I wrote to my father's widow and asked if she knew your whereabouts. I have yet to receive her reply. Each day, I question whether I should forsake this pursuit, for it seems childish. Then I recall how we talked and laughed, and I wonder if perhaps you wish to find me too. Such a notion compels me to continue my search.

Josie: I don't care—I'll waste my savings on texts.

Josie: A boy named Elias wrote the letters two hundred years ago! He knew a Josephine De Clare who lost her dad too. Weird, huh??

Josie: He didn't send the letters, though. I wonder if he saw Josephine again.

Josie: I found a stack of papers. Looks like a manuscript. Going to read the first chapter.

THREE

THE NOVEL

Sir Charles Welby, of Windermere Hall, in West Yorkshire, found himself the subject of gossip when his scullery maid bore to him a son. The child possessed Lord Welby's features, which confirmed all suspicions of paternity. Indeed, members of the household debated what best to do with the infant. They decided not to send him away, for news of his existence already plagued society, and the family dared not risk more scandal. However, to let him reside at Windermere Hall would surely prompt equal criticism.

"What fate could befall the bastard of a well-to-do gentleman?" Lady Welby said to her husband while occupying her hands, and frustrations, with needlework. She perched on a settee in the drawing room while Lord Welby concealed himself behind a shroud of cigar smoke. "Spare the babe our family name and let him live with the servants—and his mother. Once he is grown, you may provide him with a suitable position to appease your conscience."

Lord Welby parted the smoke with a newspaper and peered down his snout. "My son deserves the Welby name," he said. "I worry little about remarks spoken in idle conversation."

"I state my concerns to protect the boy, for men of good name require both fortune and well-thought opinions." Lady Welby maintained an expression of indifference, holding true to the belief that a woman with her age and appearance should look content in marriage, regardless of its offerings—or lack of. "Husband, you must admit a bastard does not merit the necessary well-thought. Consider your son's future. If you insist on forcing him into our way of life, send him to a boys' school. No Welby—even an illegitimate—should face the world unrefined."

After consideration, Lord Welby conceded to his wife's requests. He would send his son to Eton College—a boys' school located in Berkshire. Without the child at Windermere Hall, life could resume its decorous routine, and Lady Welby might forgive the affair. She deserved his compliance, for she'd accepted his adultery with the utmost grace. No other wife—especially one pronounced barren—would permit a bastard to roam the house in broad daylight.

"What will you call him?" Lady Welby glanced up from her needlework. She refused to meet her husband's gaze and instead stared at the portrait of her father, which hung above the fireplace. Were all men subject to immoral acts? Of course she would never ask, for etiquette and common decency considered it best to remain unaware of man's folly.

And to accept love in polite doses.

"My son may live with the servants until his eighth birthday. Then he will go to Eton for his education." Lord Welby stood from his chair and moved to a window overlooking the south yard. Near the rosebushes lounged the mother of his child—a young maid with the darkest curls he'd ever seen. Yes, he had violated his marriage vows and by doing so faced judgement, but the shame was his to bear. He would neither inflict further embarrassment on Lady Welby nor deny his son a proper upbringing.

The boy would one day inherit the Welby fortune.

"His name?" Lady Welby sighed. She drummed her fingertips on the settee's armrest, more so out of impatience than aggravation. Her sister planned to visit for dinner, which meant additional preparations. Already the clock's hands pointed at late afternoon.

Ever since news of the affair reached her family home in Sussex, Lady Welby's parents regarded her with amusement and traces of pity. She couldn't let her sister report another mishap. How else would she regain her respectability if not from a well-planned meal?

Lord Welby turned from the window. "Elias," he said. "We named him Elias."

∽

Windermere Hall belonged to an establishment of exceptional homes. It drew persons from across the country, all of whom desired to view the estate's gardens and galleries, Italian frescos, and modern furnishings. No house in West Yorkshire possessed the same grandeur—a fact in which Lord and Lady Welby took great pride. They enjoyed their resources, more so the privileges that came with deep pockets. They hosted dances and dinners to show off their good fortune, for society forgave all scandal in exchange for engraved invitations.

A bastard generated little interest compared to Windermere's silk wallpaper.

Elias, now a young man, hurried down the servants' stairwell. He made a sharp right, dodging a maid as she hauled bedsheets to the laundry. Upstairs belonged to the lord and lady, but downstairs a world of its own teemed with activity. Servants arranged flowers and polished shoes. The butler took stock of the pantry while footmen played cards in the dining room.

Lord Welby recommended Elias keep his distance from the household staff, but the servants' quarters radiated warmth, a sensation Elias had craved during his time at Eton College. He'd longed for the chambers while seated in draughty classrooms. He'd thought about the herbs drying from mantels, the clatter of pots, and the low thrum of conversations.

Downstairs was the closest thing he had to a home.

Elias rushed into the main kitchen, where oil lamps burned steadily and steam billowed from pots, running off the chill. He savoured the aroma of bread—rosemary sourdough, by the smell of it.

"Sorry I'm late. Father asked me to go riding with him."

Mrs. Capers, the cook, glanced up from her work and motioned to the tea spread. "Food's on the table. I made those biscuits you fancy." She tucked a strand of grey hair into her cap. "One of these days you'll eat us out of house and home."

"Won't that be an accomplishment?" Elias sat at the kitchen table across from Anne, the cook's daughter. He reached for a teapot and poured its dark refreshment into a cup.

"Better not let the mistress hear about your tea-time visits," Mrs. Capers said while flitting about the kitchen. She stoked the cast iron stove, then moved to a countertop strewn with poultry and herbs. Dinner would begin in a few hours, barely enough time to stuff the goose with apples and prunes, roast it golden brown, and send it to the decker's room.

"Lady Welby doesn't take kindly to intermingling," Anne said. She hunched over a wicker basket at the table's head, her arms wrist-deep in green beans.

"Intermingling? I was born in the servants' quarters. You're more my kin than anyone upstairs." Elias dropped a sugar cube into his tea and dissolved it with a few stirs of his spoon. He propped his elbows on the worn tabletop. A breach of etiquette. An ungentlemanly act. Indeed, the headmaster at Eton College would birch his knuckles for such behaviour.

Elias had become well acquainted with discipline over the years.

"Nonsense. You've grown into a fine lord." Mrs. Capers brought a tray of biscuits to the table. She placed the shortbreads in front of Elias, then pinched his cheek with her forefinger and thumb. "It's time you learned your place, Mr. Welby."

Her words caused a pang to ripple through Elias's chest. He didn't want to feel it, for all feelings stirred up emotions he'd waited years to settle. He sucked a breath to dull the sensation. He clenched and unclenched his fists. But the pain was a stone rolling into an avalanche.

It swept him away.

"Aye, you got much ahead of you, dear boy," Mrs. Capers whispered. "Your mum would be right proud." She dabbed her eyes with the hem of her apron, then waddled back to the stove.

Elias cleared his throat and looked down at the table. He blinked to keep his eyes from watering. Grown men didn't cry. The headmaster had drilled this lesson into Elias during his education.

"You think too highly of me," Elias said to lighten the mood. No, he didn't belong with Anne and Mrs. Capers. Neither did he belong with Lord and Lady Welby. He'd spent eight years of his life in the servants' quarters, then ten at Eton. Besides occasional visits to Windermere Hall for holidays, he had lived apart from all relations.

A gentleman's bastard didn't seem to belong anywhere.

"You'll be *Lord* Welby soon enough," Anne said with a wink. She snapped and strung beans, working faster as her lapel watch ticked toward five o'clock. If she failed to complete her tasks, Lady Welby would make her sleep in the coal cellar.

"Not for a good while." Elias raised a teacup to his mouth, its golden rim warm against his lips. He drank to loosen the knot in his throat.

Lord Welby had named Elias the sole heir to Windermere Hall and its assets, a yearly sum of ten thousand pounds. However, the inheritance was contingent on Elias's behaviour. He must become worthy of such a fortune. One misstep could render him penniless.

"Go freshen up for dinner," Mrs. Capers said. "You look a mess."

Elias tousled his dark hair and rose from the stool. He gestured to his attire, a cravat and navy tailcoat, his only non-uniform apparel. "Whatever do you mean? I'm fresh as a daisy."

Anne snorted.

"That hair of yours needs brushing. And look at your boots.

Muddier than pigs' hooves." Mrs. Capers sighed, her smile widening. "I'm glad you've returned to us, Mr. Welby."

"Until I eat all your snacks. Then you may change your mind." Elias bowed and moved toward the doorway. He winced, the pang in his chest now throbbing. Why couldn't he welcome sentiments from others? He was now a man, not a child weeping in the schoolyard, not a boy snivelling about his dead mother and unaffectionate father.

"Mrs. Capers . . ." Elias paused in the kitchen's threshold. He glanced over his shoulder and gave a nod. "I do know my place, and I daresay it's with you."

The statement was false, but it added a sparkle to Mrs. Capers's eyes. Of course, Elias wouldn't dare believe his own lie, but he wanted the statement to be true. His life would seem easier if he knew where and with whom he belonged. People took such certainty for granted.

Elias had accepted the nature of his birth. He'd embraced his responsibilities and Lord Welby's expectations. But accepting did not put an end to the wanting. It only made wanting all the triter.

He ventured upstairs, where chandeliers rather than oil lamps glowed. He shivered. The main floors seemed too empty for his preference. Their high-ceilinged rooms contained artwork and other valuables, most of them unused and unappreciated.

Such was the Welby way.

Elias wandered past the dining room. Already servants were preparing the table with glassware and silver. Three place settings. Two at one end of the table. A single at the other.

Lady Welby's voice drifted from the drawing room. "Must I look upon his face every day? Send him to London. Men his age enjoy the city. Perhaps he may return with a wife."

"The boy has no interest in London," Lord Welby said.

"Fine. Ship him off to France. I don't care where he goes as long as he's not here."

"He is my son."

"Your son. Not mine." Lady Welby moved toward the door, her silhouette casting a shadow into the hall. "We had an agreement."

"Elias just finished school. He's not been with us a month."

"An education does not reverse what he is," Lady Welby said. "Do us all a favour. Send him to live with your sister. If he's to inherit our fortune, he must find his place in society."

Lady Welby's tone caused Elias to stop dead in his tracks. She despised him, not for what he'd done, but for who he was—the aftermath of her husband's affair. Perhaps his face was partially to blame, for he bore a striking resemblance to Lord Welby.

Whenever the lady beheld him, she no doubt saw the man who betrayed her confidence.

Elias stepped toward the drawing room. He peered into the chamber, his breaths rasping as he watched Lady Welby pace. No other person—not even the headmaster of Eton—planted fear within him as this woman did. She seemed to tower over everything.

Her footsteps seemed to rattle the house.

"Very well. Elias will visit my sister," Lord Welby said while lounging in his favourite armchair. He waved to dismiss his wife, then opened a newspaper to its second page.

The harsh words blew through Elias, a gust that stripped him of the downstairs warmth and hopes of ever finding home. His father would force him to leave Windermere Hall, and for what—to appease Lady Welby's tantrum? It didn't make sense.

Elias was destined to inherit the estate. He'd spent weeks with his father learning about the property and family assets. Lord Welby had even taken him on a business trip to Leeds.

Elias withdrew. He clenched his jaw, a new pain blooming within his chest. He wanted to shout. But he'd learned to keep quiet. He wanted to beg his father to let him stay.

But a gentleman never begged.

"I'll write to your sister tomorrow." Lady Welby breezed into the corridor, her muslin gown dusting the tile. She looked at Elias as though he were a fixture. Her expression was blank, her eyes dull.

He found her indifference worse than resentment.

"Lady Welby exhausts me," Lord Welby said once Elias mustered enough grit to enter the drawing room. He flipped the page of his newspaper. "You would do best not to marry a woman for convenience, for a convenient lady replaces all ease with constant chatter."

"Father." Elias paused when Lord Welby glanced up from the print. His relation to the man was undeniable. They shared thin lips and diamond-shaped faces.

Their resemblance had dulled Elias's memory of his mother. He couldn't recall her appearance, only her eyes. He saw them whenever he looked in a mirror. Hazel. Haunted.

His eyes belonged to his mother, but he was his father's in every other way.

> **Mum:** Talked to lawyers. We'll lease the townhouse until you graduate from uni.

> **Josie:** Brilliant! Thank you.

Mum: I brought your cat to my flat. He seems to get on with Leopold.

Josie: Antoni likes dogs. :)

Mum: Is Rashad okay with your prolonged holiday?

Josie: We broke up a few days ago.

Mum: And I'm just now hearing of it? He seemed like a decent lad.

Josie: Nope, he's rubbish. Deserves his picture on a dartboard.

Mum: That's rather harsh. Relationships are two-sided, remember?

"Yes, it's true," Lord Welby said. He folded his newspaper and placed it on a side table. "You will visit your cousins. They live near Alnwick, at Cadwallader Park."

"In Northumberland?" Elias huffed. "What will I do there?"

"Take part in the social season. Make connections." Lord Welby rose from his chair and gave Elias's shoulder a hard pat. "I hope for impressive reports."

"Of course," Elias said with a nod.

"A gentleman settles for only the best," the lord said. He went to the fireplace and stirred its coals with a rod. "Do try to find some pleasure in your departure, Son. Only a fool possesses a distaste for the good fortune bestowed upon him."

Elias clasped his arms behind his back. He took his leave and went upstairs to pack his belongings, shedding not one tear, uttering not one complaint. He was a Welby.

And such was the Welby way.

Sebastian Darling lavished his presence on Windermere Hall for a brief time. He arrived by coach, his footmen dressed in scarlet uniforms trimmed with fringe. His grandeur, which inspired a gossiped reputation in France, drew a crowd from the manor. Lord and Lady Welby waved the carriage up the gravel drive while their staff arranged themselves on the front stoop.

The fuss seemed inevitable. Elias had overheard rumours about his cousin, of which the most admirable came from his father, who considered Sebastian the perfect Englishman.

The servants' conversations did not include the same level of flattery.

"One person for tea, and the lady requests a croquembouche and plum pudding," Mrs. Capers griped from her place next to Elias. "Oh, the nonsense of it all." Since dawn, she had laboured in the kitchens, preparing desserts.

"And you're surprised? Lady Welby requested a tiered cake when her sister came to visit." Elias cracked a smile. He faced the front lawn, where footmen waited to greet the carriage.

His relatives couldn't be worse than Lady Welby or the masters at Eton.

"Will you be gone long?" Mrs. Capers asked.

"I'll return when my father bids me," Elias said. He didn't wish to contemplate losing Anne and Mrs. Capers. Thoughts of farewell weighted to his shoulders, made him feel something he hated and feared.

Good-bye had taken his family. Years prior, he'd kissed his mother and shook his father's hand. He had climbed into a coach, waved to Mrs. Capers, then watched Windermere Hall fade into the distance. When life brought him back to the estate, his mother no longer stood on the front stoop.

"You are a kind and decent man, Mr. Welby," Mrs. Capers whispered. "Consider us your home, for we find only pleasure in your company."

Elias blinked to keep his emotions at bay. He wouldn't shed tears in front of Lord Welby. His feelings didn't matter. They couldn't matter. He needed to leave Windermere Hall for his future. For his inheritance. To please his father.

To prove he was more than a bastard.

Footmen rushed forward once the carriage rolled to a stop. They opened its door, revealing a young man with auburn ringlets.

"What a generous welcome," Sebastian said as he emerged from the compartment. He swept a tall hat from his head and fell into a bow. "I daresay I've not been received by such an audience since, well, my court date. Apparently celebration is a criminal offense."

"Good afternoon, Nephew. You look quite well." Lord Welby stepped from the lineup. He gave Sebastian a handshake.

"Quite well? Nonsense. I believe my looks fare a bit grander than *well.*" Sebastian grinned when one of the maids giggled.

"Will you join us for afternoon tea?" Lady Welby asked. Her mouth twitched into a sensible smile of the type Elias considered unattractive and, at times, frightening.

"Unfortunately, I must depart as soon as possible. My parents wish me back at Cadwallader by dusk." Sebastian dismissed Lady Welby with a turn of his shoulder, a discourtesy that caused Mrs. Capers to snicker. He motioned for Elias to enter the carriage.

"I suppose the lady will have plum pudding for dinner," Mrs. Capers said under her breath. She touched Elias's arm, perhaps to comfort him. "Godspeed, Mr. Welby."

Elias patted her knuckles. He left the front stoop, his heart racing as a footman strapped his trunk to the coach.

Lord Welby gave a nod, an acceptable good-bye.

"Cousin, we best leave with haste." Sebastian hurried to the carriage and scaled its step. "Tell me. Are you the snitch type?" he asked once Elias entered the coach. His amber eyes gleamed with mischief. His mouth lifted into a smirk.

"I mind my own business," Elias said. He knew several boys from Eton who behaved like Sebastian. Most of them had ended up with birched backsides and reprimands.

Sebastian flashed a smile, his body swaying as the carriage lurched into motion. "Good, good. I believe we'll get on, then." He reached beneath his seat and disinterred a bottle of cabernet sauvignon. With a tug, he removed its cork.

"Why do you ask?" Elias leaned toward the window to glimpse Windermere Hall before it vanished behind a coppice. He studied the limestone façade and its topiaries, the obscure silhouette of Mrs. Capers shooing other staff members indoors.

Sebastian chuckled and took a swig of the wine. "Tonight I begin your tutorage."

∞

The vacant country house rose from acres of farmland, its property basked in crisp northern air and scents of tilled soil. Although secluded, the estate offered pristine hunting grounds and quiet living. That is, whenever its owner dared venture from London.

45

Such isolation gave opportunity to the local and rather daring gentry. On nights when the moon shone through the gloom and flooded the hills with silver light, young people ventured from across the county to entertain themselves at the retreat.

Sebastian Darling refused to miss the clandestine engagements, for even the most witless noblemen understood the importance of attendance. He resolved to take his bastard cousin to the event, more so to keep the appointment than introduce Elias Welby to his companions. What could go wrong? His parents did not expect him to return until the following day. His cousin seemed tame enough. Besides, how could anyone distinguish their identities at a masquerade?

"I cut holes for your eyes." Sebastian shoved a burlap sack against Elias's chest and proceeded to fasten a capitano mask onto his own face. "I couldn't find an extra mask, so you'll have to make do. Remember. No snitching."

"Wasn't your family expecting us for dinner?" Elias slid the sack over his head and followed Sebastian from the coach. He peered through the crudely sliced holes at the front lawn, its overgrown flower beds, and torch-lit walkways.

"No, I fibbed. My parents don't anticipate our arrival until tomorrow," Sebastian said with a snicker. He led Elias to a bonfire located behind the main house. There, dozens of young aristocrats gathered, each person donning an ornate mask. They crowded buffet tables and danced to music played by a solo violinist.

"Who hosts the party?" Elias asked.

"Mr. Doyle owns the estate, but he only visits twice a year. His eldest son throws parties for those of us caught in the tethers of fine living. We do this in secret, so I ask you not to mention the event at breakfast tomorrow." Sebastian narrowed his eyes, perhaps to hint at a threat. "Stay here while I fetch us some pints."

"No, wait—" Elias groaned when Sebastian charged into the commotion. Of course his cousin had to be an unpredictable dandy with a penchant for alcohol. He couldn't have been related to a clergyman or someone civil.

Elias scratched his face, the burlap like nettles against his cheeks. He watched partiers mill around him. They stared at his apparel, and rightly so. No other gentleman wore a feed sack.

Granted, no other gentleman would've agreed to wear a feed sack.

"Sir, is your head too large for normal masks, or do you just appreciate the artistry of burlap?" A girl appeared beside him, clothed in a ruby-red gown with golden bumblebees trailing up her torso. She lowered her mask, exposing plump lips and slate-blue eyes set above a button nose. Her expression beamed a warmth that caused him to perspire.

"I'm quite shy," Elias said in jest, a flutter stirring within him as he watched the girl sway to the music. He towered over her, yet she didn't seem petite. On the contrary, she held herself with a confidence that added a meter to her height.

"Ah, I see." She laughed, her face scrunching to make space for a grand smile. "You need not feel shy around me, though. I'll be enough *not shy* for the both of us."

"You're too generous." Elias smiled beneath his shroud.

Their conversation defied etiquette. Without a mutual friend to introduce them, strangers were required to remain strangers. At least such was the rule taught to Elias. He had learned to maintain distance from all persons not in his realm of acquaintance.

"Or perhaps foolish. My father says I talk too much. He

swears I could befriend a rock." The girl curtsied and raised her mask. "Enjoy the party, Bag Head. I advise you stay away from men like . . . Mr. Darling over there. He'll get you into heaps of troubles."

Elias snorted. "That's my cousin."

"Really? Oh dear." The girl tucked a chestnut-brown curl behind her ear. "I shall leave you before I further embarrass myself."

Her rose perfume tingled Elias's nostrils as she waltzed toward the bonfire.

"I like when people talk," he called after her. "Very much so."

She twirled to confront him, her curved figure a spectacle beneath its satin gown. "Then you must ask me to dance later. I shall tell you all sorts of silly things."

Elias gave a bow, his skin tingling with a strange warmth. He'd met ladies during his stint at Eton, but none of them spoke like the girl in the bumblebee dress. There seemed a lightness about her. She belonged upstairs . . .

And yet she reminded him of downstairs.

"Cousin, your lessons begin now." Sebastian pranced from the buffet table with a pair of pints. He slurped from their rims to keep ale from spilling, his cravat already soaked with the amber beverage. "Drink one of these. You best learn the art of irresponsibility."

"Do you know that girl?" Elias asked when Sebastian forced a cup into his hand. He gestured to the girl in the bumblebee dress, who now stood with a cluster of ladies.

"Josephine De Clare? Indeed. Her parents keep company with mine." Sebastian guzzled his drink, then flung the empty cup over his shoulder. "Heed my advice, Elias. Stay away from Miss De Clare. The girl reads too many books."

"You dislike books?"

"They do not offend me," Sebastian said. "But I consider their effect on women most damaging. A well-read lady believes herself far too capable, daresay superior. Just look at Miss De Clare. The girl does not faint nor withhold her opinions. She denies the fragility of her sex—a treacherous violation of etiquette. I blame literature for her behaviour. A lady who reads too many words eventually feels the need to voice some of her own."

Sebastian gasped when a boy stumbled onto the dance floor and whirled with his arms outstretched. "Come, Elias. You must play spin-the-sot. I insist."

Before Elias could protest or drink his ale, Sebastian jerked him into the sea of dancers. Partiers formed a rotating circle around the drunk while he twirled. The game seemed juvenile, but Elias played along. He galloped in his place, his legs wobbling.

People orbited the intoxicated boy until he spun himself sick. His body collapsed with a thump, and he sprawled like clock hands, his arms pointing at opposite ends of the circle.

"Our sot chose his lovers," a girl yelled. "Now, they must kiss."

Fateful moments are few and far between, those life-altering instances where anything can happen—and anything does. Some call the occurrences destiny, coincidences, luck. Others joke about the turn of events because they seem predictable.

Elias processed all opinions when he noticed a finger aimed at him and another pointed at the girl called Josephine De Clare. He couldn't breathe. None of it seemed real. Perhaps he was drunk or dreaming. Perhaps the universe was playing a trick on him.

Josephine walked to him as the crowd applauded and begged for a kiss. Her eyes shimmered with firelight, and her hair swayed with the night's breeze—a sight that turned Elias to stone. "Let me kiss you, Bag Head," she said with a laugh. "Don't be shy."

He inched closer, his heart racing. No girl had ever kissed him. Throughout his school years, he had attempted to call on ladies. They'd overlooked him, especially once they learned of his inferior birth. But this girl—the one smiling at him—offered approval without conditions.

She gazed at him, not through him.

"You don't have to," Elias said. He paused near the bonfire and flinched when Josephine lifted the sack to his nose. "We haven't even been introduced—"

"I don't believe we meet people by accident," Josephine whispered. "Perhaps I'm foolish, but I think sometimes . . . *meeting* is enough." She glided her fingers across his jawline. Then, she stood on the tips of her toes and kissed him.

A release much like a sigh washed all fear from Elias's body, and in that second, his world consisted of her hands on his face, her lips fused with his lips, an entire universe freeing him from his prison of shadows. The night was bright. He was seen.

And she was everything.

FOUR

JOSIE

From: Josie De Clare <JDeClare@mailbox.com>
Sent: Tuesday, June 21, 8:21 PM
To: Faith Moretti <Kardashian_4Life@mailbox.com>
Subject: Elias Roch Is My New Boyfriend

Faith, I'm in love. Not really. But I fancy the idea of reading old
letters and falling head over heels for their writer (especially
if he looked like the guy in the painting). Elias Roch, the
Regency babe magnet, seems my type—well, as far as I can tell
from some letters and the first chapter of his manuscript. He
moved to Cadwallader Manor centuries ago, after his father
died. Strange coincidence, right? He wrote to a girl named
Josephine De Clare. She also lost her father, and she wasn't
close with her mum. Another coincidence.

51

Elias wanted to correspond with Josephine about his tragic past, Cadwallader, and their so-called serendipitous meeting. Pretty sure he had a crush on her. I mean, he wrote a book about the two of them. Maybe the story was based on his life. Who knows? I typed his name into a search engine, and nothing came up. The internet has no idea he existed.

I also searched for information about Josephine De Clare, but she, too, seems a ghost. No census records or family trees. Not even a birth date.

Something must've happened, because Elias never posted the letters. Perhaps he didn't learn Josephine's address, or they reunited at a ball. I hope they ended up together. Someone deserves to find happiness, and nobody I know—excluding you and Noah—seems content.

Our beautiful Elias Roch went to boarding school like us. He detested his headmaster and did stupid stuff with his friends. Sound familiar? Ugh, I wish he wasn't dead. We'd get along. In other news, Mum decided to lease the townhouse until I graduate from uni. She won't sell it. (Your pyjamas are safe!) I'm relieved because I didn't want to fight with her—again. We don't see eye to eye on anything, at least anything we talk about. And we don't talk much. Our conversations happen over text, and they're usually about boring stuff like dentist appointments.

Not that I want phone calls. I prefer our mutual indifference. If she talked more, I'd have to talk back, and I really enjoy not talking. Like, I don't hate Mum. I just don't trust her. There's a difference. Hate means I don't want her in my life.

Distrust means I refuse to let her guide it.

My counsellor at Stonehill told me to let go of grudges. She was like, "Forgive and forget, Josie De Clare. That's the Lord's way." I guess I was angry back then. Maybe I still am. It's just . . . We can forgive but we can't forget. Whoever says otherwise hasn't known true pain. Hear me out. Hearts are muscles, and muscles have memory. So, of course our hearts can't forget. They remember what hurts them. They remember so they can grow stronger. I think that's why we must remember. If we forgot the moment we forgave, we wouldn't receive the strength that comes from hurting. And something good must come from all the bad. Something. Anything.

Even the faintest good.

Mum was upset I didn't call her after I broke up with Rashad. But she left Dad and me, so why should I give her information about my personal life? She didn't take me bra shopping on my thirteenth birthday. I went with Dad, and yikes, that was a weird day. Mum didn't even know about Rashad until I made the relationship Facebook official.

I haven't forgotten all the years without her. Deep down, I must still be that thirteen-year-old girl, dying from embarrassment as her dad held bras to his chest. Whatever.

Screwed up is the new normal.

Tonight I did a bunch of oddball activities. What started as self-care turned into self-destruction. I made pizza pockets for dinner, then ate way too much of Martha's sponge cake. (She brings food at least once a day.) Then I painted my toenails, which took less time than expected. I got bored, and nothing good happens when I'm bored.

I decided to dye my hair, but I didn't feel like walking to the variety store. However, thanks to Dad's toddler-esque diet, I found a pack of strawberry Kool-Aid in the cupboard. Yep. I did what you're thinking. I soaked the ends of my hair in ancient pink Kool-Aid. Now I look like that Sindy doll my aunt gave me for Christmas six years ago.

Don't worry. The colour will fade in the next week or so.

Norman said he'd find a contractor to help me with renovations. I want to preserve Cadwallader's original features. Not sure how I'll manage it. This place is a disaster zone. The wallpaper has sprouted mould. A previous owner covered the drawing room's floor with shag carpet. And if that's not bad enough, I found an unkindness of ravens in the attic.

Google recommends scarecrows or CDs to get rid of birds. I might stuff my tiger onesie with newspaper and see if it'll de-raven the house. Say a prayer for me. I plan to start repairs tomorrow, and I'll probably injure myself. You remember what happened the last time I played handyman. I tried to change a light bulb in our residence hall and broke my wrist. The cast was cute, though. Lots of Tom Holland stickers.

Oh, Rashad phoned me! (I almost forgot to tell you.) He left several voicemails because I wouldn't answer his calls. The dummy thinks I stole his leather jacket.

Elias regarded his Josephine with respect. He was enthralled by her. All girls want that, I suppose—for a guy to see them and think, *Yep, she's the one*. Rashad wasn't *the one* for me. Not at all. I want a guy who cares more about our relationship than clothes.

I want a guy who writes to me.

The letters and novel make this place seem less vacant. I get the sense it was destined, that I was meant to visit Cadwallader and discover Elias's writing. Go ahead. Have a laugh. I understand how reality works, but it's fun to consider the what-ifs. What if fate, not my own breakdown, brought me here? What if Elias and I are somehow connected?

Those questions distract from the realer situation. That I'm alone in Dad's final project. That I have no idea what I'm doing with my life. That I stole my ex-boyfriend's jacket and am currently wearing it. Yeah, maybe I'll cling to my imagination a bit longer.

Talk to you soon.
Josie

P.S. I miss my cat.

(Sent from iPhone)

From: Faith Moretti <Kardashian_4Life@mailbox.com>
Sent: Tuesday, June 21, 11:14 PM
To: Josie De Clare <JDeClare@mailbox.com>
Subject: Re: Elias Roch Is My New Boyfriend

Sorry for my late reply, Josie. Shopping with Noah occupied the entire day. He wanted a new desk, so we took the bus to IKEA and spent hours looking at furniture. He isn't the most decisive person. Like, we ate lunch and dinner in the store because he couldn't make a choice.

We left around seven with a beanbag chair and no desk.

Your emails made the day interesting. Letters? A hidden manuscript? Wow. I expected you to find something from your dad, not messages written by a Regency era gentleman—a hot one at that. I looked at the picture you sent me. Dang, Elias Roch was model quality. With that jawline, he could've gotten jobs in New York and Milan. (Portrait does resemble Ian Wyatt from third-period arithmetic. Maybe we should tell Ian to pursue modeling.)

Keep reading!!!

I am relieved to hear about the townhouse (and my pajamas). Let's plan a two-week-long vacation for after we graduate. We can stay at the town home for a week, then drive up to Cadwallader. It'll be like old times, full of dance parties and movie binges. Maybe we can even visit your dad's grave. I'd like to go there with you.

Your mom doesn't understand. She doesn't see how the divorce and her leaving hurt you. A lot of parents don't get it, and cluelessness seems worse than if they intended to cause pain . . .

Because if they hurt us on purpose, then at least we'd feel seen.

My parents treat me like a stranger nowadays. When I first returned from England, they pretended I hadn't changed. I was still the kid with braces who collected Silly Bandz and One Direction posters. Over time they stopped trying to know me. They quit asking questions about you or Stonehill. They grew distant, and I blamed myself. I regretted accepting that scholarship. I regretted leaving them. But they'd wanted me to go. They were so proud.

Maybe they're embarrassed because they don't know me anymore. For example, Mama took me shopping, and I hated everything she picked out. She bought us deli sandwiches before I revealed my disgust for processed meat. I think she and Daddy gave up on me. Like, they decided I belonged to you and your dad, not the Moretti family. I'd become too modern with my impractical career dreams and fancy education. I'd lost the parts of me that came from them.

I wish they'd hurt me on purpose.

Yes, Noah and I are content. That seems a good word to describe us. I mean, we spend most afternoons together. We go to the laundromat, grocery store, and get takeout twice a week. Being in the same city has allowed us to find a routine. So yeah, we're content—we have this adult-ish relationship that pleases our families. It's just . . . I feel like Noah won't say what he wants to say, and whatever he wants to say is something I don't want to hear.

Does that make sense?

He has all these big dreams too. Like, he plans to study architecture in Barcelona and renovate a home in Jersey. His parents are rooting for us, so much so that his mom asked me about engagement rings the other day. I'm supposed to fit into

Noah's dreams. But what if his dreams don't align with mine? Why can't we enjoy our broke college days without planning?

I love him. I want us to last, you know, get the careers and house. My brain can't think about that stuff now, though. After what happened in England—losing you and your dad, leaving Stonehill—I need *easy*. Noah understands. Maybe that's why he won't say what he wants to say.

We're all living some messed-up coming-of-age story, right? Whether we're thirteen, bra shopping with our dads, or sixty years old, we're all trying to figure out who we are and where we fit. Nobody knows what they're doing. We just put our best foot forward and give life a go.

You're on the right track, Josie. Renovate the manor (or attempt it). Try not to hurt yourself. And get through the grief even if it requires Kool-Aid dye jobs and your ex's jacket. Also, please read more of the letters, because I need updates. LOL. Maybe you *were* meant to find Elias's writing. My nonno says God brings together people with similar pains so they can support each other. He met his best friend, Robert, after my nonna died.

I'm excited for you. Nobody finds two-hundred-year-old letters addressed to them. Doesn't happen. And yet it happened to you!

The coincidences blow my mind.

Gotta say good night and brew a cup of herbal tea (to hack my snack craving). Too bad we're not still roommates. I'd be elbow-deep in your chocolate stash by now.

Faith

P.S. I know you dislike the Kardashians, but Kim released the best at-home workout. I'll paste the link below so you can stay in shape while holed up at Cadwallader.

Rashad: I know u have my jacket. Post it to me.

Rashad: Did u take my sunglasses??

Rashad: What the heck, Jo? Answer me.

Josie: I'm blocking you now.

From: Josie De Clare <JDeClare@mailbox.com>
Sent: Wednesday, June 22, 10:21 AM
To: Faith Moretti <Kardashian_4Life@mailbox.com>
Subject: Re: Elias Roch Is My New Boyfriend

Good morning, Faith. I survived another night. Thoughts about Dad kept me awake, but what's new? I tossed and turned until the sun rose. Then I walked to Atteberry Tea Room & Café for breakfast.

I reread Elias's first chapter while I drank my tea. In the story, Josephine wore a red dress with golden bumblebee embellishments—a pattern that matches my old bedspread. I also had a bumblebee on my school notebook. And my laptop sleeve.

And the necklace Dad gave me.

The coincidences seem too intentional, like they couldn't just happen by chance. Elias knew a Josephine De Clare. The way he described her and wrote to her . . . It's like he knew me. I'm grateful for this find, whether it's serendipity or divine intervention.

Elias felt what I feel. Maybe that's the magic of all this.

Whenever I look at his writing, I get a pit in my stomach, this nagging sense I should remember him. Not in a time-traveller kind of way. (If I could go back in time, I would relive years with Dad, not visit the Regency period.) No, what I feel seems more nostalgic, like candy floss at the carnival or the smell of sunscreen. Maybe I heard about Elias a long time ago.

Maybe his words reflect my own experiences.

For the record, I do not think Elias wrote about me, nor am I using him as a rebound from Rashad.

His letters spur questions, though. I can't help but wonder if our lives are like motorcars weaving around each other, destined to collide. Take us, for example. You and I shouldn't have met. We grew up in different countries, separated by an ocean. You came from a large Italian family. I was raised by a single dad. And yet, despite the odds, we found each other. What if time works in a similar manner? What if we're all but a step away from colliding with history?

Another fun thought.

I better stop this babble and get to work. My to-do list seems a mile long. First on the agenda: unclog the kitchen sink. (Pretty sure Dad poured macaroni down the drain.)

Cadwallader will be a showplace once I'm finished with it. You must come for a postgrad holiday so I can boast about my newfound talent for renovations. ;)

Josie

P.S. Be honest with Noah. You won't know if your dreams align unless you share them.

(Sent from iPhone)

Mum: Heard from the university?

Josie: They received my paperwork. I start classes in January.

Mum: Good. You've lost enough time.

Josie: Lots of people take gap semesters. No big deal.

Mum: You'll need to work extra hard to catch up.

Mum: When do you come back to London?

Mum: Stay there a month. I leave for a business trip on Friday.

Josie: Fine.

Faith: Hey! Rashad tweeted a picture of him and some blonde clubber. Thought you should know your ex is still a trash bag.

Josie: Yeah, I saw the pic. Girl looks more like Rashad's type. Warmest regards to them.

Josie: OMG, I unscrewed a pipe, and black goo went everywhere!!!

Faith: Yikes! FaceTime me so we don't get charged for more texts.

From: Josie De Clare <JDeClare@mailbox.com>
Sent: Thursday, June 23, 10:07 AM
To: Faith Moretti <Kardashian_4Life@mailbox.com>
Subject: How to DIY a Hermit Life

I managed to clean up the goo, Faith. Took an hour of rigorous scrubbing (and a half bottle of bleach), but the stains are gone, the pipes are unclogged, and I avoided further plumbing disasters. That said, I'm right proud of myself. YouTube and Dad's boiler suit transformed me into a plumber—amateur but adequate. Maybe I'll start a pipe-unclogging business.

Renovations will continue later today. I want to pull up the shag carpet in the drawing room. It's a burnt-orange colour and reeks of cat urine. The sooner it's gone, the better. (I'm surprised Dad didn't tear out the carpet when he got here. He loathed 1970s design.)

Norman installed Wi-Fi in the drawing room yesterday, so I'm officially connected to the civilized world. He even hooked up an old television. It doesn't have cable, but it plays VHS tapes.

Where do I buy movies on tape? eBay?

I didn't want Norman to leave, so I begged him to stay for tea. He must've realized I was deprived of human interaction, because he talked with me for over an hour. Then he took me to the downstairs wardrobe and unearthed a box of Dad's belongings. Nothing spectacular. Only a shave kit, mobile charger, and wool jumper.

When I saw the box, I thought Dad might've left something for me, perhaps a journal or his ideas about Cadwallader Manor. I should've known better. He kept all his notes—shopping lists, reminders, thoughts—in his mobile. For someone dedicated to preserving historical sites, he was oddly hell-bent on living paperless.

He wasn't Elias Roch.

My seclusion has given me a creativity boost, hence my Kool-Aid hair. I came up with a television show idea titled *How to DIY a Hermit Life*. At first I considered naming it *Mad on the Moors No More*, but I figured the *M*'s were too confusing.

If you wish to view my program, check social media. ;)

Wi-Fi has dimmed Cadwallader's eeriness. Blasting music fixes the silence problem. And I occupy myself with crafts when I grow tired of repairs. Yesterday I used an online recipe to make soap. I took heather from the front lawn, crumbled the flowers into my lard-and-lye mixture. (Thanks to Martha for the supplies.) Then I added lavender essential oil. I won't ramble about the process. In summary, I made eight bars of soap, which you'll receive as a belated birthday gift, two scented candles, and a hot-chocolate blend—cocoa and rose petals. I've yet to try the cocoa, so I'm not sure how it turned out.

Evening dragged on. Horribly dull. I tweezed my eyebrows, which took a solid half hour. You're familiar with my—as you put it—regal brow. So, after I plucked myself to tears, I watched a BBC film on my laptop and found a cosy nook where I could read upside down.

Yes, I still believe a topsy-turvy posture boosts the absorption of literature.

Oh, I found the softest pair of socks in my bedroom's armoire. They're powder blue with embroidered daisies. Not sure who owns them. Finders keepers?

My hermit life won't end anytime soon. Mum told me to stay in Atteberry while she travels for business. (Not sure what she plans to do with my cat.) Although I'd expected to stay here a few months, Mum saying not to come home . . . I don't know what's the matter with me. The more I tell myself not to care, the more I do. Care. I care.

And caring hurts.

I feel a bit lost. Ever since Dad passed, I haven't recognized myself, and the shock of total change scares me as if I woke up and found myself in someone else's body.

Coming here magnified those feelings, but I wanted this clean slate because the choice isn't to move on—life moves whether I want it to or not. No, the choice is to look forward, not backward, to take a step, because refusing to move won't draw the past nearer—it only postpones better days.

Elias understood. He knew what it was like to live in this house, broken and desperate. He was afraid too. Of himself. Of letting people get close enough to see his pain. Maybe that's what happens when loved ones die—people realize the danger of loving and being loved.

I haven't opened more of Elias's letters, but I've reread the first three. His words keep me company and offer a guide to this place. Elias wrote about various spots in the manor. He disliked the drafts and shadows, the constant dampness.

Really, nothing unites people like a mutual complaint.

Dad and Elias stood in this house. For them I'll endeavour to restore it. One day the halls won't seem dark and draughty, the rooms will radiate warmth. That's how I will honour them—by turning the estate into the home they wanted.

Easier said than done. Right now the temperature indoors seems freezing cold, not at all like June should be. I built a fire in my bedroom and created a picnic spread on the floor. I even lit one of the candles I made. Smells awful. Rosemary and bergamot do not go well together.

Please email me once you wake up. I'd love to hear more about your classes and life in New York. Remind me of normal things like insurance so I don't lose my grip on reality. LOL

Josie

P.S. Download a messaging app! I want to text you without paying a fortune.

Faith: Uh, normal things . . . hair stuck in the bathtub drain, chipped fingernail polish, doctors with cold hands, clothes that hate boobs and hips.

Faith: Can't forget emotional breakdowns in petrol stations.

Josie: I couldn't forget even if I tried. HAHA.

Faith: Have you opened another letter yet?

Josie: Nope. IDK what's stopping me. I'm nervous for some reason. Elias's letters mess with my mind a little. His words . . . They add more shadows to this house.

Faith: What do you mean?

Josie: I get the sense I'm not alone.

From: Josie De Clare <JDeClare@mailbox.com>
Sent: Saturday, June 25, 6:41 PM
To: Faith Moretti <Kardashian_4Life@mailbox.com>
Subject: Re: How to DIY a Hermit Life

Faith, what happened to you? Are you okay?

Something changed yesterday. I woke up, and the manor sounded different. Its creaks and groans seemed like breaths, whispers. I tried to ignore the echoes by playing music. I paced the galleries, walked up and down the arched staircase. No matter what I did, the sounds grew louder. Of course I figured my seclusion had taken its toll.

Wouldn't anyone hear noises after five days spent alone in an old mansion?

Martha arrived with a pot of stew around noon. She went into the kitchen and said, "Lass, do you hear a draught?" That's when I knew the sounds weren't in my head.

Boredom fuels my imagination, right? Not a man who lived two hundred years ago. Not a book and bundle of letters with my name on them.

Josie

(Sent from iPhone)

Josie: Are you alive? I haven't heard from you in days.

Faith: Noah and I broke up.

Josie: Why? What happened?

Faith: We had a fight. Needed some time apart.

Josie: Do you want to talk about it?

Faith: Maybe tomorrow. I'm on my way to work now.

Josie: Sure. You know where I'll be.

FIVE

ELIAS

April 25, 1821

Dearest Josephine,

All this would be simpler if I were a man in a book, for stories, regardless of their trials, do find resolution and clarity in the end. Heroes complete their quests. Love draws people together despite impossibilities. And there is meaning to be found in agony and hope.

Perhaps stories are the best of us. Perhaps words are intended to capture our agony and hope and give them that meaning we so crave.

I wish to capture the plot threads that weave my own story, for if I can grasp them, then perhaps I can make sense of my life. I need resolution. I want to step out of this house, the monotony, and find a story that better suits me. Do you ever feel that way, like the story you're living is but a way station to something grander?

My world shrinks a bit each day. Cadwallader's halls seem narrower, the rooms more cramped. I must suffer from a bout of low spirits, for Arthur and Lorelai notice my altered behaviour. They insist I help them with menus and dance cards, tasks to keep me close by. As mentioned in a previous letter, we have begun preparations for a ball. Every respectable family in the county will receive an invitation.

I care not for events and large crowds. However, the anticipation of guests adds a pleasant vigour to the day-to-day. I assist Lorelai with decorations for the gallery. Arthur and I endeavour to construct a stage to accommodate our musicians. The constant hammering infuriates Mrs. Dunstable, so much so I gave her the day off.

Work should distract me, and yet my thoughts wander to Father, Eton College, and you. Indeed, I cannot prevent myself from considering what my story might have been if I refused to leave your company and come to Cadwallader.

None of my connections have yielded information about your whereabouts. It is as though you don't exist. Oh, why did I not ask for your address that night? I was an idiot for walking away.

Arthur took me to the public house last night, against Lorelai's wishes. He downed a few pints, then asked me why I seemed downcast. I told him about my struggles, but he appeared not to listen. Perhaps I lack the ability to translate my feelings into engaging speech.

Conversation often fails me, especially when it involves sentiments. I find it difficult to admit I am out of sorts, for my problems seem minor. Other people face worse miseries. A fortnight ago, the village tanner watched his house burn. My groundskeeper lost his son to consumption. Mrs. Dunstable received news her niece perished during the Scottish insurrection.

I loathe myself for aching while others ache more, but if a child falls and scrapes his knee, he does not say, "At least I didn't break my leg." He cries because pain causes discomfort regardless of its intensity.

All pains are equal and valid, and deserving of attention.

Lorelai discovered my art studio yesterday. I suspect she followed Mrs. Dunstable to the third floor and heard my palette knife scrape against wood.

Without a knock or greeting, Lorelai barged into the chamber and beheld my portraits. She remained silent for several moments, then said to me, "You're a romantic artist, Mr. Roch."

The statement was a compliment, but Lorelai spoke it with surprise as though she believed me incapable of creating art. I suppose she considered me a close match to her cousin, a man who yawns at the mention of Michelangelo and Rembrandt.

Lorelai peered over my shoulder and watched me guide a paintbrush across the canvas. She complimented my strokes, then studied the portrait, the dark hair and regal brow. I must confess to employing your memory as my muse.

Since Lorelai's arrival at Cadwallader, I had attempted to keep my studio and hobby a secret, for she knows a great deal about the fine arts, her expertise derived from her childhood in Bath and time spent abroad. I had wished to avoid her judgement.

After a brief chat about composition, Lorelai departed and soon returned with her own supplies. She perched on a stool beside me, then started work on her masterpiece, a painting of the moors. We continued our leisure and talked until Arthur summoned us for a picnic.

The conversation with Lorelai was more personal than my recent interactions with Arthur. She enquired of my writing, for she has caught me with stacks of paper on multiple occasions. She also mentioned her suitor, who teaches at the Royal Academy of Arts—a Mr. Francis O'Connor. Do you know of him? According to Lorelai, he is well connected.

I best conclude my ramble. The ball takes place in a few days, and I have yet to request ample provisions. My cook threatens to serve ham and stottie cakes if I fail to finalize a menu by tonight. Part of me wishes to see Arthur's reaction to such dishes.

Come visit us, Josephine, once you receive these letters. Your presence would surely lighten everyone's mood and restore Cadwallader to the proper home it should be.

Yours ever,

Elias Roch

Josie: Elias painted a portrait of Josephine, even mentioned her regal brow. What are the chances?

Faith: Now you're looking for things. Like when you dye your hair pink and then notice just how many people have pink hair. Shocker!

Josie: For the record, his subject had dark hair.

Norman: Ey up, Josie dear! Want to drive into town with me?

Josie: What time? I'm free all day. Just reading and doing chores.

Norman: Come to my barn around noon. We can leave after lunch.

Norman: Martha cooked a pot of soup. She insists you eat with us.

Josie: Okay! Need me to bring anything?

Norman: Just your darling self.

Norman: Martha wants you to drive. She says I'm too paggered from the morning load.

Norman: I told her a quick kip would set me right.

Josie: Of course I'll drive! You're in charge of directions. Agreed?

Norman: Well aye.

April 28, 1821

Dearest Josephine,

Lorelai found my letters today while assisting Mrs. Dunstable with chores. She cornered me in the parlour and waved the papers, a silly grin stretching her face. She yelled, "Elias Roch fancies a girl. How marvellous."

Forgive me for not hiding the messages. Of course, I plan

to post them once I learn your address, which means you will receive a bundle of letters eventually. They will likely come as a shock, for no one would expect to receive a pile of ramblings from someone they met once.

Arthur sprinted into the parlour and snatched the letters from Lorelai. He paraded them about, daring to read my words aloud. I tackled him to the floor. Lorelai laughed harder than ever, then beat me with a cushion. A peculiar turn of events. I would never have thought Lorelai capable of brawling.

Our skirmish ended with Arthur surrendering the letters. He begged me to send them, and I promised I would if he helped to find your address. What good are words if left unreceived? More so, what do I have to lose by expressing my desire to know you, Josephine?

Lorelai came to my study this afternoon. She apologized for betraying my confidence and offered to assist me with the letter writing. I refused her proposal, but I did inquire about girls and their views on romance.

Women live according to a different set of rules. At least, that's what I gathered from Lorelai's explanation. She told me ladies dislike men who express intentions too soon, but they also dislike men who refrain from expressing intentions. They want men to call on them but not too much. They want men to write to them but not too often.

They want a lot of things, and it all seems complicated.

Pardon me if I fail to abide by the rules. Men function more simply. For example, when Arthur and I quarrel, we punch each other and move on. Forgive and forget. And if I wish to befriend a gentleman, I comment on a sport and offer him a drink, and nothing more is required.

That said, I ask for your grace. I may express intentions too soon and write too often. I may not pen the right words or communicate with clarity. However, you must know I regard you with the upmost respect.

Yours ever,

Elias

P.S. I started drafting a novel last night. The writing itself is quite poor, but I enjoy the story. It was inspired by true events. Perhaps I shall become a novelist and my books will sit on shelves alongside Shelley and Austen. One can aspire.

May 3, 1821

Dearest Josephine,

I would like to report my excitement about tonight's ball. I do not wish to jump from my study's window, nor have I spent hours rehearsing dances in private. However, the parishioner claims lying is a divine offense. So yes, I did in fact practice my dance steps, and I considered fleeing the house. No party is complete without at least one escape attempt.

This morning Arthur and Lorelai agreed to join me on a ride to town. According to Mrs. Dunstable, my late nights have diminished the manor's store of candlesticks—a hundred of them to be precise. One cannot host a ball in the dark, though I would like to attempt such a feat. So I decided to venture into Atteberry and replace what I burned for these letters.

I fetched Willoughby, my white thoroughbred, from his

stall and saddled him. You would like Cadwallader's stable. It is one of my favourite places at the estate. If you climb into the loft and lie where the hay is thinnest, you can peer through the roof slats and watch the sky.

Arthur and Lorelai joined me on the front lawn. They looked smart in their riding clothes, while I wore breeches and a waistcoat. Eton did not teach me proper dress. While there, I learned philosophy and geography but not fashion. The school required a uniform, so I am accustomed to wearing the same attire each day. Indeed, I feel most accomplished if I change my cravat.

Mrs. Dunstable fled the manor, my overcoat waving from her arms like a battle flag. She reached the side of my horse and flung the garment at me, her chest heaving from exertion. Physical activity has never suited her frame.

I donned the coat to appease her, for to watch me gallivant across the county in improper dress causes her immense grief.

Arthur snickered at me. He sat atop his purebred, boots wedged in stirrups, a tall hat perched upon his scalp. Since our childhood, he has believed himself the definition of style. Even his uniform at Eton seemed finer than mine. He likes his caped greatcoat and embroidered handkerchiefs, the yields of his generous allowance.

He kicked his heels and galloped past Lorelai, who waited near the gates. She laughed at him, then followed in a charge toward Atteberry, riding side-saddle. They commanded me to race them, so I did. I steered Willoughby off the path and rode across grazing land. Lorelai called me a cheat but only because I won.

The race helped me to breathe, as if the movement relieved some of the tension in my chest. Several panic episodes have assaulted me since the night we met. Whenever they occur, I remember what you told me—to note my surroundings, to list all the small things that bring me joy. I think of you first. You are my happiness. Perhaps I am wrong to confess such a feeling, but people must select their own joys, because joy, if not chosen freely, isn't joy at all.

You are the joy I choose, Josephine. I confess it.

Arthur and Lorelai enjoyed Atteberry's moss-painted cottages and faded storefronts, idyllic qualities most appreciated by city folk. After we tethered our horses to a post, we wandered the streets. Arthur wanted to visit the haberdashery—he needed a button for his tailcoat—but we ended up at the market.

I thought I saw you in the crowd. I called your name and ran after a girl who resembled you. I smiled at her, believing my search was at an end. Her profile and hair were the same as yours, but she was not you. She did not even recognize your name.

Lorelai caught up with me. I believe she realized my mistake, for she hugged my arm and guided me to Arthur. She assured me I would find you, but I grow less certain by the day.

After Arthur purchased his buttons, we bought candlesticks and returned to Cadwallader. Now I hide in my study with a chair wedged against the door.

Father's widow responded to my letter. She told me she had not heard of your family, and she is versed in the who's who of society. I am beginning to wonder if you are a ghost.

Arthur hired valets to assist us tonight, which means I must let a stranger outfit me for the ball. Why do rich men need poor men to clothe them? Does wealth prevent one from dressing?

I suppose I shall find out.

Father added many poor men to his service. He liked the attention or perhaps the status of governing a large household. Whatever his reason, he collected maids, valets, footmen, cooks, butlers, and other titles. My mother, Victoria, joined the roster at age twenty. She worked for Lady Roch as a housemaid, a position that introduced her to Lord Roch.

Nobody knows the extent of what happened to Mother. I have kept the facts a secret, for the truth is raw, and people prefer their truth seasoned, marinated, and cooked medium-well. Such people do not deserve to know about her pain.

Do you think about me at all, Josephine? I cannot get you out of my head, not for a single moment. In my eighteen years on this earth, I have conversed with but one person who saw me, truly saw me. That person is you, so you must understand why I need you to be real. Even if I never see your face again, to know you exist would give me peace.

Over the past few days, I compiled a list of all the details I remember about you. I know you lost your father, you attended a boarding school, and your perfume smells like Paris in springtime. I know you love to dance and laugh and go on adventures. Your middle name is Emilia. Your eyes are slate blue. When you talk, you wave your hands.

I would rather seem too eager than spend my life wondering if you really found me that night. I was lost and broken, and I thought no one would care how I felt. My headmaster,

Father, and even Arthur have all told me to toughen up, be a man, drink an extra pint. I listened to them and made no mention of feelings. Then I met you, and I saw a glimmer of what living could be.

Please do not be a ghost.

Elias

P.S. My accountant leaves for London tomorrow. I shall ask him to make inquiries about you. Also, I have written more of my novel. 'Tis hardly a masterpiece, but I hope to share it with you one day.

Josie: He knew my middle name.

Faith: Who did?

Josie: Elias. He knew my middle name, eye colour, that I went to boarding school.

Faith: He wrote all that in his letters???

Josie: YES. I'm freaking out! Elias knew so much about Josephine—about me. He wanted her to receive his letters, visit Cadwallader, and read his novel.

Faith: What the heck is your life right now?

Josie: Elias couldn't find Josephine. He started to wonder if she was a ghost or figment of his imagination. Blimey. I don't want to ask the question.

Faith: What if Elias Roch wrote about you?

Josie: Impossible, right? I mean, he met his Josephine De Clare.

May 4, 1821

Dearest Josephine,

I have decided to forsake people, all of them. Arthur and Lorelai can stay at Cadwallader, but I wish to remain alone. My teapot seems good enough company. It refrains from hinting at marriage or coaxing me into the public's eye. Really, I consider my library the pinnacle of social interaction.

As you probably deduce, the ball did not go as planned. It was no disaster, mind you. Guests were polite, and the festivities lasted until dawn. Mr. Rose complimented the orchestra. Lady Seymore and her son praised the experience, which says a lot, for they are the most miserable people I have ever met. The trouble came from an unlikely person.

Lorelai Glas.

The night seemed varnished with a golden sheen. Carriages rounded the manor's drive, their horses pounding gravel as if to applaud the parade. One by one, gentry clothed in satin and velvet emerged from their boxes. They bid adieu to their drivers and flocked to the main house, glittering like jewels in the torchlight.

I watched the commotion from a second-floor balcony as the string quartet played a minuet. Guests drifted into the great hall, where candles and chandeliers shooed away the gloom. I might have greeted them at the front door, but I was delayed as my valet outfitted me in a tailcoat with a silk collar, a bloody awful design. I do not recall purchasing the garment. Surely Arthur ordered it from town to mess with me.

Before you blame vanity for my tardiness, let me add that the tailcoat was large and required alterations, for I am both tall and slim, as you know.

That said, I was late to my own ball.

Guests approached me once I entered the gallery. It would suit me fine if I never again engaged in small talk. How can one discuss weather for more than a minute? Northumberland experiences rain, fog, snow, and brief spells of sunshine in the summer. There. I have summarized the nation's environmental report for the next thousand years.

Arthur teased me when I reached his side. He snatched two cups of Madeira wine from a footman's tray and observed the dance floor, perhaps to select his next partner.

I followed him along the gallery wall, past my collection of sculptures. Older guests lingered near the artwork. They raised their ratafia and cigars to toast my good fortune. Indeed, my sudden popularity struck me as odd. I have attended countless parties over the years, and most of them included whispers about my birth, faux pleasantries, and gentlemen who ensured I did not speak with their daughters. How strange. I am now the most sought-after man in Atteberry.

My friend came to an abrupt halt, his stare fixed on Mary Rose, who stood alone while her husband prowled the card tables. He placed his empty cups on a bust of Julius Caesar, then marched toward the lady without so much as telling me good night.

The Banes Family cares little about their reputation. Mr. Banes earned his wealth from shrewd business. He married a bourbon heiress whom he met in Prussia before the French Wars. Their rise in high society involved politics and the worst of rumours. However, their popularity grew, for the public enjoyed gossip. Such behaviour encouraged Arthur to befriend me and to flirt with married women.

Not knowing what to do without Arthur, I moved toward the dining room. Dancers floated in a sea of ostrich plumes. Rainbows glistened on the marble floor, crawled up the partitions, and hovered above heads.

You would have enjoyed the party, Josephine. The whole night, I thought about dancing with you. I imagined us facing each other on the dance floor. Better yet, I remembered our horrid moves from the night we met, and I pictured us re-enacting them on the patio. A performance to give my guests a shock.

Lorelai drifted from the crowd as musicians played a waltz. She looked unlike herself, dressed in an emerald ball gown, her champagne hair no longer in its bun. At first, I did not recognize her, ~~for I have grown used to her fixed and rather plain appearance~~.

She asked if I would paint with her tomorrow.

Women speak in code, do they not? I try to decipher it, but I cannot manage. They mean what they do not say, and they say far less than what they mean.

In hindsight I now see how Lorelai blushed and batted her eyelashes. Instead, I asked her to dance. She needed a partner, and gentlemen were scarce. A waltz seemed harmless.

Lorelai smiled as we entered the whirlpool of dancers. She asked if I minded her prolonged stay at Cadwallader. I confess—I was not paying her much attention and do not recall my response. I gazed into space as we orbited the room like a planet within a candlelit solar system.

She touched my shoulder, her left hand clasped in my right. I twirled her across the floor, not once bruising her toes, thanks to my hours of practice. Then music slowed us to a turn, and our audience blurred into a kaleidoscope.

One face remained distinct.

A naval officer stood near the door with Lady Seymore. He caught my gaze, and in a flash of nostalgia I became a child peering into my father's study. This man used to visit Lord Roch.

Lorelai opened her mouth to speak, but I silenced her with the question: "Are you acquainted with that gentleman?" I motioned to the officer. My heart pounded as if to warn me, and my thoughts raced to memories of Father, his meetings, the names of his acquaintances. He dined with nobility and members of the militia. He welcomed friends, comrades, anyone with a decent title. Admiral Gipson visited most frequently.

The man's presence in my home filled me with dread. Father had warned me someone might challenge my inheritance. However, until that moment, I never considered my fortune in danger. But I sensed it. I knew. The admiral had come to Cadwallader to confront me.

I ignored the look of shock on Lorelai's face as I bowed and left the dance floor before the number ended. She chased after me and said, "Mr. Roch, I find myself happiest in your home. Although I am young, I'm certain I could not find a more blissful place." Her cheeks flushed, making the code quite clear. She wished me to declare intentions for her.

I could not have been more startled. What prompted her affections? I thought her view of me brotherly, not romantic. Indeed, we have become close friends, but she often speaks of Mr. O'Connor in London. She reprimands Arthur and me for returning from town at wee hours. Her behaviour is maternal, even austere. Not once have I noticed the faintest hint of attachment.

Besides, she is aware of my fondness for you.

I took her aside to prevent a scene. I said, "Miss Glas, you deserve a house less dreary than Cadwallader. A quiet estate suits me, for I find no pleasure in society, but you are far too accomplished to remain in Atteberry. London seems a better match for you."

Lorelai stared at me as though I had committed a crime. Her eyes filled with tears and her jaw clenched. Without a word, she turned and rushed into the crowd.

I did not mean to embarrass her or damage our friendship, but I couldn't voice feelings I do not possess. She should marry Francis O'Connor, move into a townhouse near Hyde Park, and paint on the Thames's bank. Such a life would bring her immense happiness.

The upsets with Lorelai and Admiral Gipson sparked another panic episode. I retreated to my study while the guests enjoyed supper, and I have remained here since. What am I to do, Josephine? If the admiral challenges my inheritance, I may lose everything. If Lorelai departs Cadwallader, I may not see her again.

My life hinges on the deeds of others, and it drives me mad. I wish to be content and loved, yet I find it poetic, even romantic at times, to be sad and alone. Truly, despair adds intrigue to my otherwise dull existence. If I could, I would shrink my world to a single room, a pile of paper, and an ink-dipped pen. I would write to you until my fingers grew sore, and then I would ask Mrs. Dunstable to scribe for me.

~~Lorelai's interest forced me to realize there cannot be anyone else, only you.~~

Elias

P.S. My great-uncle who dwells in Kings Cross sent word that he knows a De Clare Family. They reside in West London. He promises to investigate for me.

SIX

THE NOVEL

Cadwallader Park, located in County Northumberland, possessed an extensive and rather dull history. The great manor belonged to a lord who gambled it away to a courier of the Royal Mint, whose financial problems led to monastic occupation. After a series of unfortunate owners, the estate became home to the Darling Family.

Mr. and Mrs. Darling took pride in their modest lifestyle. They boasted about their humble country house, its sylvan charm and pristine gardens. Having come from a smaller yet far more prestigious London residence, the Darlings believed themselves simplistic to a point of superiority. Mr. Darling saw no reason to hire a full staff, a noble deprivation Mrs. Darling mentioned at her luncheons. Instead, he enlisted the help of several farmhands, a butler, maid, cook, and a valet who doubled as a footman.

Although rich from clever business dealings, Mr. and Mrs. Darling kept their purse strings tight and recorded all expenses. However, the Darling children lacked their parents' frugal nature. They preferred to bask in the grandeur society allowed them. Sebastian, the eldest son, built a reputation from his costly merriment and European tours. Kitty, the middle child, spared no pence on fashion, while the youngest, Fitz, desired only horses.

Life at Cadwallader Park seemed picturesque despite its owners' differences. Not a whiff of scandal travelled from the estate, that is, until Lord Welby's bastard came to stay.

∞

"Let me die, Elias," Sebastian said while pacing a stream bank. He shooed a team of ducks, his riding boots caked with mud. "I shall throw myself into the water and be lost forever."

"You seem more disagreeable than usual." Elias refused to look up from his book, a history of Northern England's great houses. Over his seven months at Cadwallader Park, he'd learned that Sebastian quickly lost interest in complaints and flitted to happier diversions. At least such was Elias's hope, for he needed to complete his reading before Mr. Darling's lessons.

Lord Welby had insisted Elias learn about the upper class from the Darling Family.

"Because I disagree." Sebastian groaned and cradled his top hat. He crouched in a tangle of knapweed, his juvenile face aged by side whiskers and a scowl.

"With whom?" Elias asked.

"Everyone. I am in a perpetual state of disagreement." Sebastian tossed a pebble into the brook, then sprawled on his back. He snorted when a gnat flew up his nose.

"How exhausting." Elias clamped his lips to hide a smile. He leaned against a tree trunk and flipped through the pages of his book. Despite his cousin's theatrics, he preferred to read outdoors rather than sit with Mrs. Darling and her yappy lapdog.

Nature kept time for him. Already September faded the landscape from green to brown in preparation for autumn. A chill blew over the ridges where sheep grazed, and withered summer flowers. Marigolds froze, cockles slumped, and ox-eye daisies shrivelled beneath a muted sun.

"Father thinks he knows best," Sebastian said with a huff. He rose to his feet and swatted the tree trunk with a branch, mere inches above Elias's skull. "I disagree."

"Blazes, Sebastian. I do need my head." Elias shielded his scalp with the history book. He glanced across the grounds, at the stream, coppices, and open land. The view put him at ease. Perhaps his father would confine him to the estate for years. Better yet, maybe his gentleman lessons would lead to a permanent residence with the Darlings. He liked Kitty and Fitz. He got along with Mr. Darling. Surely the family would not mind his extended stay.

"I want to pitch a fit, not act reasonable," Sebastian yelled. "I am not a reasonable man."

"Oh, really? I hadn't noticed." Elias laughed. He reopened the book, his attention drifting off its pages. Music seemed to echo around him. Workers laboured in the gardens, chatting as they tilled manure into the moorland soil. Kitty played her pianoforte in the main house, and somewhere in Cadwallader's sprawl, he imagined a maid hummed.

"Come. Let's go indoors." Sebastian returned his top hat to its perch.

"I'm reading."

"You *were* reading." Sebastian grabbed Elias's book and sprinted toward the manor, his legs flailing as he cut across the front lawn. According to the Darlings' governess, nobody hated the word *no* like Sebastian. He always managed to get his way.

"Bad form!" Elias rose with a sigh and followed his cousin to the main house. Since the bonfire party, he and Sebastian had developed a mutual toleration of each other. They weren't friends, but they got on well enough to spend time together.

Although most of their activities ended with Sebastian running solo into the distance.

Cadwallader Park gained popularity from its grounds. Besides pastures, the estate contained an orchard, topiary maze, and gardens that curved around the east wing. Such marvels distracted from the less impressive residence, a home built like a castle. It blended into the terrain, a fortress of chimneys, noticeable only due to the ivy that clung to its grey stone.

Elias had yet to grow accustomed to the manor's dreary chambers. He considered the windows too narrow, the ceilings too low. A hatbox compared to Windermere Hall. Still, the house seemed far warmer than Lady Welby's disposition.

Fitz met his cousin at the herb garden. "Would you play tag with me, Elias? Please? Miss Karel will not play." The nine-year-old abandoned his toy horse and governess, tackling a rosemary bush to block Elias's path. "Please."

"Sorry, Fitz. I must finish my lessons and dress for dinner. How about tomorrow? We can play games all afternoon." Elias ruffled the boy's copper hair.

"Hello, Mr. Welby," Stephanie Karel called from her blanket.

She waved a bundle of letters, notes written by a soldier in the militia.

"I hope you received good news, Miss Karel." Elias hid a smile, for he knew the governess spent more time writing poems to her suitor than educating the Darling children. He had edited her work on several occasions, even lent her books by Lord Byron. To his surprise, he rather enjoyed her sonnets. Perhaps Kitty and Fitz would become poets.

Elias saluted his young cousin, then hurried into the kitchen yard. He inhaled smoke and earthy aromas that reminded him of Windermere Hall.

"Master Sebastian ran upstairs." The valet pointed at a back door. He leaned against the house and sucked on a pipe. "You be lookin' for him, Mr. Welby?"

"Yes, well, he stole my book." Elias inched past a chicken and pig. Somehow the animals managed to escape butchery and wandered the yard, both caked with mud.

"Again? My, you best wear your books on a chain."

"Capital idea. Now to invent a chain that'll withstand Sebastian," Elias said with a laugh. He sneaked into the manor's scullery and climbed service stairs to the main floor.

Dinner preparations, a daily chaos, were underway. Mrs. Darling paced the main rooms, her ash-black hair tugged into disarray. She yelled commands at the butler, who followed at her heels and muttered a series of "Yes, ma'am," "Of course, ma'am," "Right away, ma'am." Kitty enhanced the commotion by playing her pianoforte in the parlour.

"We cannot serve baked apples for dessert. Are you mad?" Mrs. Darling marched into the foyer, ignoring Elias as she berated her butler. "What's next? Will you recommend porridge for the main course? No, go tell the cook to prepare blancmange. Baked apples . . . Ha!"

Elias straightened when Mrs. Darling glanced at him.

"Do not linger, Nephew. Go dress for dinner." She charged toward the parlour, shouting orders at everyone in earshot. "Cease the music, Kitty. I cannot think. Where is Mr. Darling? Has anyone seen my boys? Find Sebastian and tell him to wash. Fitz, you left your toys in the hall."

Mrs. Darling meant well. She adored her family, more so her role as wife and mother. Elias understood her enough to keep his distance. He knew his aunt cared about him, for she invited him to gatherings and forced his practice of the arts. Still, he'd learned that married women required space to mother their young and on occasion, their husbands.

"I'll find Sebastian," Elias yelled. He ascended the arched staircase and moved toward his cousin's bedroom. The manor, although smaller than Windermere Hall, contained dozens of narrow corridors. After weeks of getting lost, Elias had finally mastered the maze.

He passed the study lent to him by Mr. Darling. The room contained shelves packed with books, mostly volumes of historical text and fiction the Darlings no longer read. Still, Elias treasured the space. It made Cadwallader seem more like home, not a boarding school or prison.

Lord Welby still hadn't written. Each day, Elias checked the post for letters. He'd found messages from Mrs. Capers, a parcel of shortbreads from Anne, but nothing from the lord.

His father must've forgotten about him.

A wave of emotions rushed from somewhere deep and dormant, swelling until it sucked the air from Elias's lungs. He sagged against the wall and gasped. His father's lack of attention shouldn't bother him, for he knew only distance and stern approval. To have and then lose would give reason for feeling, but he'd never had, so he could not lose. Nevertheless, he felt loss. A deep loss.

Loss that brought tears to his eyes.

Such a response seemed dramatic, a lapse of gentlemanly behaviour. He should consider himself fortunate. Other children, even some of the boys at Eton, grew up with violent fathers. They suffered worse than a lack of correspondence.

Elias sighed. He rested his head against the wall, a memory lighting the back of his mind.

Josephine De Clare.

He thought about her all the time, as though her kiss had altered his brain. Of course, he wouldn't dare speak of the attachment. He barely understood it himself. What an embarrassment. A childish reaction. To grow fond of someone because she gave attention.

But she represented a hope still alive within Elias, that one day a person would look at him and not see a bastard. They wouldn't send him away or threaten to withhold his inheritance.

Elias needed to preserve all faith, so he clung to the memory—that bonfire dream—where he was kissed by the girl in the bumblebee dress. Still, over half a year later, she was the book he couldn't put down.

≈

The Darlings valued tradition as they valued afternoon tea. Each night before dinner they gathered in their drawing room to discuss the day's events. Mr. and Mrs. Darling played chess. Fitz wrestled the dog. Miss Karel inspected oil paintings and book-cases while Kitty sewed.

Routine bored Sebastian, but Elias rather enjoyed the pat-tern. He liked to huddle near the fireplace and listen to his cousins laugh. He smiled whenever Fitz coerced him into a game of charades.

Despite his longing for Windermere Hall, Elias found peace at Cadwallader. He was no longer a boy peering through cracked doors, rather a welcome guest.

And to be welcome seemed a novel concept.

Sebastian puffed an empty pipe. "Kitty has a knack for organ-izing dinner parties. However, she lacks the charisma needed to fuel its level of engagement." His father had banned tobacco from the estate, a mandate which sparked rebellion among him and the staff. Why should he behave like an adult if his parents refused to grant him liberty?

"I assume you believe yourself the source of such engage-ment." Elias rubbed his hands over the hearth. He shivered from the manor's dampness, a cold no fire could defeat.

"But of course. What is a party without Sebastian Darling?"

"You flatter yourself most profoundly." Elias tugged his cravat to loosen its noose. He'd asked Fitz to help him tie the neckband, a mistake which led to a great deal of wheezing.

Sebastian plucked a bottle of port from the mantel. "Care for a drink?"

"Liquor disagrees with me," Elias said.

"Same, but I enjoy the argument." Sebastian poured the amber liquid into a glass and guzzled it, his throat jerking with each swallow. He glanced at the doorway as if anticipating someone's arrival. Was he nervous? Elias rarely saw his cousin apprehensive, let alone distressed. Emotion did not suit Sebastian's ostentatious lifestyle. Quite the opposite—all feelings suffocated under smiles and false pretences.

Josie: Elias based his novel at Cadwallader. His descriptions gave the estate a facelift, but it seems about the same. Maybe he wrote the story to mirror what he wanted to happen in his life. I'm not sure. None of this makes sense.

Faith: Impossible things happen every day.

Josie: That's your explanation?

Faith: Until a better explanation comes along. LOL

Josie: His dad was like my mum. So much of his life was like mine.

Faith: To repeat what you said earlier . . . Maybe that's the magic of all this.

"Are guests joining us?" Elias asked. He'd dined with countless strangers, for the Darlings entertained guests from all over England. They hosted balls, formal dinners, and hunts. Such events forced Elias to prove his education. He spoke about politics and cricket, his time at Eton. Of course all conversation eventually veered to his birth and good fortune.

Gentlefolk wished to know why Lord Welby named a bastard his heir.

"Two of them," Sebastian said with a nod. "And they don't plan to leave."

Knocks rattled the front door, followed by the patter of footsteps. As if on cue, the Darlings rearranged themselves. Kitty and

Fitz stood at attention. Mrs. Darling hissed orders at Miss Karel, who then sprinted toward the dining room like a messenger with news from battle.

Elias had learned to tolerate the family's histrionics, but this occasion seemed different. He sensed a tension, the kind that made his hair stand on end. Who'd come to stay at Cadwallader Park? If the visit was significant, why did Sebastian ignore the frenzy and pour himself another drink?

"Calm yourselves. Let's not frighten our company." Mr. Darling rose from the chess table and hurried to welcome the guests. He paused in the drawing room's threshold, his broad frame hiding the newcomers from view.

"Who's here?" Elias asked.

"You'll find out soon enough." Sebastian plopped onto the divan and tucked his pipe beneath a cushion. He scowled at the floorboards while his mother paced.

"Nephew, come." Mr. Darling motioned for Elias to approach him. "I'd like you to meet our friends. They've heard quite a lot about you."

"Popular boy," Sebastian grumbled.

Elias rolled his eyes and left the hearth. As he neared the doorway, a lady breezed into view. She resembled a swan, her neck long, her elegant features untouched by age.

She wore a dress the darkest shade of grey.

"May I introduce Widow De Clare and her daughter, Josephine."

A lump clogged Elias's throat. He tensed, all voices fading until the atmosphere echoed his breaths. Josephine De Clare? At Cadwallader Park? No, he couldn't face her, not after months spent pining. And all because of what—a silly kiss?

The rustle of silk distracted him. He saw a flash of red, then golden bumblebees frozen in flight. He blinked, and his chest ached. Was she a figment of his imagination? No, she was there, in front of him, shimmering like a jewel held into firelight. Gloves ascended her forearms. Pearls roped her neck. She appeared the same as before, yet somehow brighter.

Elias averted his gaze. He panted, his cheeks burning. Indeed, Josephine wouldn't remember him, for he'd worn a bag over his head at the masquerade. Perhaps he might avoid embarrassment if he pretended not to know her.

"Ladies, this is my nephew, Elias Welby." Mr. Darling grabbed Elias's shoulder and drew him close. "He came for the social season, but we haven't been able to part with him."

Josephine glanced at Elias, and her eyes widened.

"A pleasure to meet you, Mr. Welby." Widow De Clare extended her hand and smiled when Elias kissed her knuckles. "Your uncle speaks highly of you."

"He perjures himself," Elias said. He looked at Josephine, and his voice faltered. How could he last an evening in her presence? Eton College had taught him to navigate conversations with formalities, but rehearsed speech could not express his thoughts . . .

And he thought so much about her.

Widow De Clare laughed. "You're too modest. Few people manage to raise their station. Your life attests to our ability to better ourselves, whether through education or connections."

"I am not so impressive, madam," Elias said with a bow. He cringed whenever someone treated his birth like an accomplishment, for a son did not choose his father.

A bastard didn't earn the fortune attached to his family name.

"Shall we go into the dining room?" Mr. Darling offered his arm to the widow. "My daughter created the menu for this evening. According to the cook, it is sure to impress."

Elias flinched when the adults moved across the chamber. He turned his chin so Josephine wouldn't notice his blush. He held his breath so her perfume wouldn't unravel him.

"It was you," Josephine gasped once her mother was out of earshot. She gazed at Elias as though to confirm her suspicions. "Not a word about the masquerade. All right?"

He nodded. "Consider it forgotten."

"That was so unlike me. I don't make a habit of *what happened*." She fidgeted with her purse, a rosy hue colouring her cheekbones. "Mother cannot know. She thought I was visiting my great-aunt, who is blind and deaf and likely wouldn't remember if I did visit."

"Your secret is safe with me," Elias said. He offered his arm, a flutter lifting through him when Josephine looped her fingers around his bicep. He'd dreamt about this moment for months. To see her again. To stand close to her.

He wanted to feel her lips pressed against his.

"Thank you, Mr. Welby." Josephine looked up at him as they walked toward the dining room. She flashed a smile. "Or should I call you Bag Head?"

Elias laughed. "Please do. I'll even wear a sack—"

"No, no, I think your face is much less terrifying." Josephine squeezed his arm, her nose scrunching to make space for a wider smile.

"Less terrifying? Brilliant. I'm pleased to know my face doesn't frighten you."

"I'm wretched with compliments. The worst." Josephine pinched her lips together, amusement shimmering in her eyes. "You have a fine look, sir. Perhaps you should go to London and become a stage actor. Crowds adore faces like yours."

"Until they witness my acting. I cannot even win a game of charades." Elias led Josephine into the dining room, where their families gathered. He wanted to banter with her all night, for she put a warmth inside him. She eased his nerves.

Indeed, she was the same girl he remembered.

Dinner involved a humble five-course meal, for the Darlings dared not flaunt their good fortune. Instead, they celebrated their estate's harvest in a room grand enough to seat the House of Lords. They adorned the table with flowers from their gardens. They displayed mutton and rosemary chicken— food indicative of their rural lifestyle.

"Sebastian, do you not wish to welcome our guests?" Mr. Darling asked once everyone took their seats. He sat at the table's head, his moustache twitching with frustration.

"Apologies." Sebastian glanced up from his plate and forced a smile. "I am thrilled by your presence, ladies. Your arrival . . . It fills me with . . . emotion."

Mrs. Darling cleared her throat when Sebastian slid down in his seat. She glanced to her right, at Widow De Clare. "Did you have a pleasant trip?"

"Oh, yes. I find the northern moors both eerie and evocative." Widow De Clare unfolded her napkin, then draped it across her lap. "Do you not agree, Josephine?"

"Yes. Eerie *and* evocative," Josephine said with a huff. She clutched her cup of tea, requested in lieu of wine. Her demeanour seemed tense, unlike her interaction with Elias. Had she not wished to visit Cadwallader Park?

Elias reached for the fork closest to her hand, his fingertips skimming her glove.

"Won't you miss the city, Miss Josephine?" Kitty asked from the opposite end of the table. She leaned forward, her auburn curls swishing over her food.

Widow De Clare answered instead. "Not at all! We've been living at our cottage in Morpeth, which is superior to the old town home. Besides, Josephine prefers the countryside."

"Really? Why?" Sebastian stabbed his knife into the table-top. He propped his elbows on either side of his plate, drenching his sleeves with potato pudding. Either the port had gone to his head or he intended to scare off the guests.

"Because it's eerie and evocative." Josephine delivered the response like a rehearsed line. She mustered a smile, one that appeared more spiteful than sincere. Had Sebastian offended her? What else could explain her sudden change of mood?

"Gracious, Sebastian," Mrs. Darling gasped. "Mind your manners."

"Yeah, Sebastian. Don't act like a pig." Fitz giggled. He squirmed in the chair next to Miss Karel and tossed peas onto Kitty's plate.

"Please do not make a sport of your dinner, Master Fitz," the butler said with a groan. He confiscated the boy's vegetables and replaced them with a slab of bread.

An easier cleanup.

The valet rushed to provide a second course of savouries and sweets. He balanced platters on his forearms, poured wine, and skirted the butler with careful steps.

"I want my peas back," Fitz yelled.

"When hogs fly," the valet said. He grabbed the boy's collar, forcing him to still. Mr. Darling nodded his approval.

Elias leaned toward Josephine, his heart racing when she met his gaze. "You shall have plenty of theatre here," he whispered. "Not an evening passes without entertainment. Take my word for it. Dinners would seem quite dull without Sebastian's tantrums and Fitz's pea cannons."

"Good. I like the theatre," Josephine said with a nod. She lifted her fork and guided a square of cheese into her mouth. Still, her expression remained despondent.

"This place looks gloomy, but it's not, really. Just mind the ghost upstairs. He doesn't like girls who joke around," Elias said in hopes of making Josephine smile. Perhaps her stay at Cadwallader would give him the chance to offer courtship. He possessed wealth and a good name. Surely Josephine wouldn't care about his birth.

"We were sorry to hear about your loss," Mr. Darling said as he sliced his mutton and doused it with gravy. "You have our deepest condolences."

"Thank you. My late husband's illness was a shock, but your kindness toward Miss De Clare and me has been more than generous." Widow De Clare dabbed her mouth with a napkin. "Please, let's not talk about the past. We should celebrate. Right, Josephine?"

"Celebrate. Yes," Josephine said, her bottom lip quivering. She reached for a teapot. Her elbow struck a soup bowl and tipped it to the side, dumping cream onto the tablecloth. "Oh, I'm sorry. I don't know what's the matter with me—"

"It's no problem. We make a lot of messes here." Elias pressed his napkin onto the spill. He refilled Josephine's cup with tea, a flutter stirring within him as her mouth tugged into a gentle smile. A smile that returned the light to her eyes.

A smile meant only for him.

"You're in good company," Elias said. He should've realized Josephine had lost her father. Was the tragedy responsible for her visit to Cadwallader?

He battled the urge to embrace her, for nobody had hugged him when his mother died. No one had scooped him into their arms and dried his tears. He'd broken alone and healed poorly, like an unset bone. Maybe he and Josephine could hurt together. Maybe the broken parts of him would fit the broken parts of her, and somehow, against all odds, they'd make each other whole.

"Pour the champagne," Mr. Darling said to the butler.

"What's the cause for celebration?" Elias spooned white soup into his mouth, the creamy broth soothing his hunger with tastes of veal and almonds.

"Did Sebastian not tell you?" Mrs. Darling furrowed her brow, perhaps shocked by her son's restraint. "He's engaged to Miss De Clare."

"Engaged?" Elias choked on the word.

"Betrothed," Widow De Clare said. "I could not hope for a better match."

"We finalized the arrangement months ago." Mr. Darling raised his champagne in a toast. "To Sebastian and Josephine—may you find happiness together."

The clink of glasses broke that hope still alive within Elias. He grew stiff in his chair and glanced at Josephine. No, she couldn't wed Sebastian. Why would she agree to the marriage? She despised him. And what about Sebastian's mood? He didn't love her. In fact, the betrothal explained his grumbles at the stream bank.

Elias wheezed. He braced his weight against the table. As he attempted to wrap his mind around the truth, something collapsed within him as if he had constructed a mansion of cards—a cathedral of dreams—and with a breath, it tumbled down.

Didn't Josephine want more than Sebastian and Cadwallader Park? She had prospects. She could experience the world. Of course, that was the beauty of potential—it liked to make itself useful, but it also enjoyed sitting idle and gathering dust.

"Tell me about the upstairs ghost," Josephine said with a sigh, her nose reddening. She looked at Elias as though to distract herself from the adults' conversation.

"Are you sure? It's a gruesome story . . . that I will invent just for you," Elias said. He tried not to look at Josephine, for candlelight blurred around her face like a halo.

The very sight of her made his chest ache.

"Do share your wicked tale, Bag Head. I wish to be frightened." She crossed her arms and motioned for him to commence his narrative.

Elias needed to stifle all romantic feelings. He knew better. He'd sworn never to want beyond his means. Even so, he felt an attachment binding him to Josephine, and the strands of his sanity hung loose.

He'd built a fortress around his emotions, then left the front door wide open.

After dinner everyone retreated to the drawing room. Mr. and Mrs. Darling entertained Widow De Clare while their youngest children played dominoes. Sebastian retired to his chambers, leaving Josephine to linger near the bookcase with her third cup of tea.

Elias pretended to read a novel. He mustn't further involve himself. If anything, he should avoid Josephine until his feelings dimmed. Nothing could happen between them. He'd be a fool to dream otherwise. Still, the sight of her standing alone twisted his stomach into knots.

He snatched a doily off a side table and walked to her side. "What did you think of my ghost story, Miss De Clare?" He draped the lace over his head and bowed.

"Bravo. I am scared out of my wits," Josephine said with a laugh. She relaxed against the bookcase and set her teacup on a shelf. "Will you stay here long?"

"Until my father summons me." Elias stuffed the doily into his coat pocket. He clasped his hands behind his back. He lifted his chin. "Father thinks I should behave like Sebastian."

"You're joking?"

"No, I'm serious. Father wants Sebastian to teach me the ways of high society. So far, my cousin has taught me to style my hair, spend money, and play spin-the-sot."

"All important lessons. How would you live without them?"

"I'm not sure. Like a normal person, I suppose."

Josephine launched off the bookcase and twirled to face him. "Try not to change, Mr. Welby. England doesn't need two Sebastian Darlings."

A new feeling breezed through Elias like wind from a horse race, like wings unfurling from their neat positions and stretching into full span. He grinned until his cheeks ached. Yes, he should put distance between him and his cousin's fiancée. Yes, he risked heartbreak and scandal.

But she gave him hope when the well of it ran dry.

SEVEN

JOSIE

From: Josie De Clare <JDeClare@mailbox.com>
Sent: Monday, June 27, 10:16 AM
To: Faith Moretti <Kardashian_4Life@mailbox.com>
Subject: Let's Talk About Boys

Hey Faith,

I read more of Elias's writing. I'll share thoughts about it later. Right now, I want to talk about Noah, Rashad, and all the crummy boys in our lives. I mean, Noah isn't crummy. But he's a boy. And boys scramble our senses because . . . well, they're boys, and we're girls.

Put aside your expectations for this email. I won't babble about Cadwallader or Elias Roch. I won't even mention the horrible weather (although it deserves a rant of its own).

Your breakup caused me to tumble down a mental rabbit hole. I can't stop thinking about my relationship with Rashad. For months, I thought he was this punky superstar. Not even David Beckham compared. I mean, Rashad walked into English class our thirteenth year, tattooed, pierced—a total cliché. And my dumb heart was like, "You need that anarchist energy in your life, Josie." Gah, was I lonely and desperate? Why did I think Rashad was a good idea?

It's not like he was bursting with decent traits. You said he had the personality of a rock, and you were right. Also, he treated me like a pet hamster. I'm serious. He fed me, gave me basic affection, and showed me off to his friends.

They called me Jo because Josie seemed too cute.

Dad's cancer altered my appearance, mood—everything. I didn't realize how much had changed until after he was gone. People told me what to expect regarding his illness. I went to the support groups and doctor's appointments. I knew early on how the process would go, but no one explained what that process would do to me.

When I met Rashad, I was angry at the world. I didn't want to cry anymore or be around people who cared. That's why I stopped talking to you. I knew you would empathize with me, and I couldn't handle it. Maybe that's why I dated Rashad. His indifference made all the bad stuff—the reasons for pity—disappear. He let me feel numb.

Rashad didn't love me, but he attended my school events. He distracted me while Dad went to chemo and radiation. That's all I wanted—to be angry with someone who liked me angry, to be broken and not feel obligated to heal. I relished being Jo . . .

Until I looked in the mirror and hated what I saw.

Until I returned to an empty house and realized everything I'd lost, including myself.

The past few days forced me to feel all the yucky stuff I've avoided for months. I pulled up shag carpet, painted walls, and phoned contractors. I was alone with Dad's project and Elias's letters, and I broke down because . . . they loved Josephine De Clare. They really loved her. And I decided I wanted to be loved again, like that.

From now on, I choose to let people care. I want to be Josie, not the girl who mocked teachers and cut her own fringe. (That might've been a worse mistake than Rashad.) I want to be a better friend to you. We promised to stay pals for the long haul, so I'm here. All in.

By the way, I have a crush on Elias. It's small and nothing. I mean, the guy lived two hundred years ago. Not like we can go out for coffee.

Remember when we made that checklist and profile of our dream guy? I don't know about you, but I spent hours analysing, strategizing, and searching for him. That's how my mind works, anyway. It tries to make sense of complex things like emotions, it puts the heart in a box and bosses it around. But what if logic cannot determine whether two people are right for each other? What if love is the simple realization: I was made for you, and you were made for me?

That's my argument for why crushing on a dead man isn't weird.

You're the most patient and level-headed person I know. Throughout secondary school, you put up with my clutter—the Dairy Milk bar wrappers, piles of clothes in my designated messy chair. You didn't request a new roommate when you found me attempting to tie-dye my uniform blouse. Despite all my antics and emotional roller coasters, you stayed. You loved me even when I was hard to love. So, I know you and Noah didn't break up on a whim.

I know you would've stayed if staying was possible.

Relationships are complicated because people don't stop evolving. They change over time due to circumstances, new dreams, whatever. And if they don't pursue each other, they drift apart. That's why Mum and Dad got a divorce.

Noah might not be a part of your future, and that's okay. Your relationship with him mattered. It was real even if it doesn't continue.

Make sure this is what you both want, though. I think people who drift apart can drift back together (with a lot of paddling, of course). I think some loves are worth fighting to keep because love—the real kind—doesn't come around that often.

That said, I support you no matter what happens. But if you love Noah and he loves you, please attempt to paddle back to each other.

Dad used to say if you love someone, let them go. I don't agree with him. If you really love someone, I think you have to take them back.

I remember those awkward phone calls, Faith. I heard your and Noah's conversations, all the *you hang up firsts* and other mushy stuff. You both survived puberty and years of long-distance dating. Some good-byes are inevitable, but if you and Noah can't last . . .

None of the romantics have a chance. ;)

Keep me updated! Your life seems like a proper romcom. I imagine you prancing through New York City, wind in your hair, Frank Sinatra blaring in the background. Granted, I learned about N.Y.C. from all ten seasons of *Friends*, so my knowledge is limited.

Holding out for your happily ever after.

A rainstorm keeps me indoors today. I plan to finish painting the entrance hall and bake an almond tart—Martha's scrummy recipe. (Blimey, I mentioned the weather.)

Josie

P.S. I downloaded that messaging app you recommended so we can text like normal people. I already have a series of gifs and memes ready to send your way.

From: Faith Moretti <Kardashian_4Life@mailbox.com>
Sent: Monday, June 27, 3:40 PM
To: Josie De Clare <JDeClare@mailbox.com>
Subject: Re: Let's Talk About Boys

Gotta keep this email short, Josie. My digital marketing class starts in a few minutes.

The fight with Noah was stupid. He wanted to go back to IKEA, and I exploded. Think apocalyptic proportions. I told him I felt suffocated—I wasn't ready to do boring adult stuff. I said I didn't want to get engaged or buy a house in Jersey. Everything I'd been thinking just came out, and the next thing I knew we were breaking up.

He walked me to the subway on Fourth Avenue. We kissed good-bye, and then we parted ways. I got on a train, and he returned to his apartment.

I couldn't give him an explanation, maybe because I didn't have one. Like, whenever I look at my parents, I see the future they want for me—the husband and kids, stable job, all things normal. Then I look at Noah. His future seems laid out for him too. He wants me to be a part of it. Everyone expects me to be a part of it. And that's what freaks me out. The expectations.

Noah supports my fashion career, but he doesn't know about the online boutique I launched a few months ago. Heck, I didn't even tell him about this opportunity I got to intern in Milan next fall. Now you are the only one who knows, because you know everything, and I've never felt the need to change myself for you. But with him . . . I can't really describe it. I'm just not *me* all the time.

At this point I'm not sure how to make amends or if I should try. Noah won't talk to me, and I'm fine with his silence. How is it possible to love someone and not mind their absence?

Maybe time apart will help us mature, figure out whether we're right for each other. Messy sometimes needs messy, but when two messy people are together, who cleans them up? Do they spend the rest of their lives in cluttered, mismatched pieces?

Yikes, my professor just walked into the lecture hall. He made eye contact with me.

NO! I'd be the worst romcom protagonist, like, Ryan Gosling would run through the airport but never find me because I went to the bathroom.

Professor yelled at me. Gotta run.

Faith

Josie: Dad must've slept in the old servants' quarters (near the kitchen) while he was here. I found our family photo in one of the rooms.

Faith: Are you okay?

Josie: The missing comes in waves, some more intense than others. I miss the toothpaste globs he left in the sink, how he'd watch the morning news while I ate breakfast. I miss crying on his shoulder, talking his ears off, being the first person to hear about his good days and the first to embrace him on his bad ones. I miss the small things more than the big things because the small things proved he was mine.

Faith: And how your dad made pancakes for us every Saturday?

Josie: He burned all of them.

Faith: But he drenched them with blueberry syrup.

Josie: To mask the burnt taste. LOL

From: Josie De Clare <JDeClare@mailbox.com>
Sent: Tuesday, June 28, 4:26 PM
To: Faith Moretti <Kardashian_4Life@mailbox.com>
Subject: The Hunt for Elias Roch

Hi Faith,

The weather resembled summertime this morning. I woke up to warmth. Sunlight cascaded through the manor's windows and flooded the hallways. Birds performed outside, singing at high volume. Such a pleasant surprise!

Elias mentioned various locations in his writing. I decided to take advantage of the clear skies and go on a scavenger hunt. I drew a map based on Elias's descriptions. Then I put on my daisy socks and work boots—the ones I borrowed. My chosen destinations: the stable loft, gorse alcove, studio, kitchen yard, herb garden, and the stream bank.

When I left the house, I tripped over Norman's sheepdog, Nan, who often naps on the front stoop. The Shetland must've felt sorry, because she followed me around all day. You would like her. She has a thick salt-and-pepper coat and copper streaks around her face. Maybe I'll persuade Norman to let me borrow her at night. I doubt he'd mind. He only needs her in the mornings and late afternoons. The manor would seem less eerie if I had a dog.

Nan escorted me to the stable. I'd hoped to climb into its loft and peer through the roof slats, but the structure was rebuilt years ago. So much for my hunt.

After that, I went around the east wing, to the ruins of a smokehouse. There I discovered the spot described in Elias's letters, a place where rubble merged with a stone fence. At first glance I didn't see the alcove, just rocks and gorse. But I crawled between the shrubs.

I found it, Faith.

Yellow flowers encircled the recess. Blue sky gazed down between the branches. And the air smelled like moss and wood. I almost cried at the sight. I relaxed against the fence, my toes pressed into cold sod, the sun hot on my cheeks. A breath caught in my throat because, for a moment, while Nan dozed beside me, I got the sense Elias was there too.

We sat on the same ground, centuries apart.

How could anyone hear about my situation and consider it a coincidence? Dad *happened* to purchase Cadwallader Manor. I *happened* to discover letters with my name on them. Elias *happened* to meet someone like me. No, this wasn't an accident. Life guided me to the estate for a reason. What if I was meant to find Elias Roch?

Once I left the alcove, I managed to visit the herb garden and kitchen yard before rain ended my hunt. Summer faded with the storm. Gone in a flash. Now I sprawl on my bedroom floor with Nan and a cup of Earl Grey. Norman and Martha invited me to eat dinner with them, so I need to bathe and detangle my hair.

Josie

From: Josie De Clare <JDeClare@mailbox.com>
Sent: Tuesday, June28, 10:03 PM
To: Faith Moretti <Kardashian_4Life@mailbox.com>
Subject: Re: The Hunt for Elias Roch

A quick update! Norman and Martha took me into Atteberry for dinner. We ate sausages at a place called White Horse Pub, then walked to Sassenach Bakery for dessert. They bought my food and wanted to hear me talk. Gracious, nobody had listened—like, really listened—since Dad died. I asked why they cared about me, and they gushed about Dad's kindness. Apparently he made sure they wouldn't lose their house or farming privileges after his death. What if Dad kept the manor a secret to lure me here so I'd meet them?

What if he planned for this place to become my new home?

The village grows on me. It has the quaintest shops. On my way to the bakery, I passed Atteberry Tea Room & Café and the Knitting Emporium. (I added a sketch of the town to my Cadwallader map so you'll understand my references. Photo is attached.)

Oh, I enquired about Elias Roch. Martha told me to visit the local historical society—they have records dating back to the 1400s. Maybe I'll go next week.

Final bit of news: I applied for a job at Sassenach Bakery. Of course, I don't plan to stay in Atteberry all year, but I need a reason to leave the estate and interact with other humans. Can't you imagine me in an apron, with flour on my cheeks?

Love, the future winner of *The Great British Bake Off*,
Josie

Faith: Please send pastries. Noah and I scheduled a coffee date for this Friday.

Josie: That's great!!!

Faith: Eh, it's a start. Pray I don't explode on him again.

From: Josie De Clare <JDeClare@mailbox.com>
Sent: Friday, July 1, 12:40 PM
To: Faith Moretti <Kardashian_4Life@mailbox.com>
Subject: I ALMOST KILLED SOMEONE

Faith, I threatened a boy with a sword—an actual blade from the nineteenth century. I'm not a violent person. Dad gave me a bottle of mace when I turned sixteen, but I never used it, not even when Trevor McGreevy scared me in the school carpark.

My time at Cadwallader must've changed me.

This morning I heard a noise—footsteps, a door slam, the occasional cough. Norman and Martha had gone to Durham for the day, so I assumed a burglar had broken into the manor. In retrospect, I'm not sure what I planned to do once I caught the culprit, but I jumped out of bed, shoved my feet into slippers, and crept down the hallway.

I pried an antique sword off the wall (Cadwallader possesses a lot of ornamental weapons), then snuck down the servants' stairwell. I held the blade like a cricket bat and charged into the kitchen, yelling, "Whoever you are, get out of my home."

Go ahead. Have a laugh. I already spent an hour facedown in my pillow, utterly humiliated. Just think about what might've happened if I had attacked first, asked questions later.

A boy stood near the furnace with an armful of firewood. He gawked at me—my sword and Donut Disturb pyjamas—and dropped the logs. He apologized, said his grandparents had told him I was at work. That's right. I almost killed Norman and Martha's grandson.

He introduced himself as Oliver McLaughlin, then claimed he'd noticed I was running low on firewood and had used Norman's spare key to open the back door. His outfit struck me as rather odd. He wore loafers, khaki shorts, and a thick, wool jumper *in June*.

Pause the narrative. Let me describe this Oliver person to you. He has a young face, but I suspect he's several years older than us. His expression seems one of perpetual amusement, as if he heard a joke and never stopped laughing at it. His hair sticks up like cowlicks, perhaps mussed from sleep. And OMG the colour. He must have dyed his black hair ginger months ago, because it's grown out, leaving him with a calico look.

Oliver knelt to gather the logs while I tried to fit my sword into a cupboard. He stacked wood near the furnace, and I rushed to make him a cup of tea like a good Brit.

He must've seen my empty Pot Noodle containers in the sink, because he smiled, his cheeks scrunching, his eyes sparkling as if he knew a secret about me. Maybe he noticed the giant pom-poms on my slippers or the interior design notes scattered across the kitchen table.

We talked for a polite amount of time. Oliver told me he studies medicine at the University of Edinburgh but took a gap semester so he could help Norman and Martha with the farm. He plans to stay in Atteberry until next year.

For someone who broke into my home, Oliver isn't so bad. There's a cosiness about him as if he should only wear overcoats and knitted scarves. He smells like patchouli, and he has a small anchor tattooed on his wrist. (I hope my description paints a vivid picture.)

Anyway, I felt less embarrassed when he spilled tea on his shorts. I might've even laughed when he tripped on a stray log. He laughed too. That's when I knew I didn't mind him. People who laugh at themselves make superb company.

How was your coffee date?

Josie

P.S. I talked to Norman about Cadwallader. He told me the Hawthorne Family bought the estate in 1892. They owned it until the late 1900s, which is why I can't find more evidence of Elias in the house. A lot can get lost in two hundred years.

EIGHT

ELIAS

May 21, 1821

Dearest Josephine,

I completed the first three chapters of my novel, therefore committing myself to the story and its exposition. Words—more so the authoring of them—demand our bareness, do they not? My headmaster once said we take from books what we bring to them, meaning books are but reflections of us. I share that belief now. For the sake of literature, I undressed on a page. I exposed myself in a quiet intimacy. Now I am seen and spent, and I have no more to show.

The novel reflects me, perhaps more than I intended.

Since the ball, my residing guests have seemed altered. Lorelai paints alone on the patio most days. She does not speak to me at length nor look at my face. In contrast, Arthur wants to talk, always. He forces me into conversations about his family whenever we go to town. He sparks discussions about women and travel. Indeed, after several pints, he becomes sentimental. Just last night he spent an hour reminiscing about our school days and cried when I mentioned the mouse we used to keep in a box under my bed.

I believe Mr. Banes has written to him and requested his return to Durham. Arthur hates the thought of working for his father. He wishes to study music in Paris and tour Europe. For the longest time, he even considered joining the navy. He is more tenderhearted than one might expect. Any change or worry, no matter how slight, traps him in a pit of nostalgia. He only seems to remember the good, though. His memories of Eton include recreations in the yard and our secret society gatherings, not the birched knuckles and tasteless food.

Arthur refuses to share what bothers him. Whenever I ask, he laughs and tells me to cheer up. He smacks the back of my head. He drinks another pint.

Writing has become my diversion from such things. I write so as not to fret about Lorelai, Arthur, and my inheritance. I write so as to avoid another panic episode.

The pastime seems like pouring wine into water. It improves the taste of my life but does little else. Where are you, Josephine? Each day that passes without news of you magnifies this sense—this ache—that I shall never hear from you again. I find my letters almost pointless.

Poets use countless words to describe their pain, but I need only three: I miss you.

Cadwallader is a palette of grey, coloured by black birds in the gorse shrubs and Lorelai's blue dress. I want more red and gold, more laughter and music. I want more of you.

After everything we have endured, I must cling to the belief that our stories will collide in the end. I need hope. And if I cannot hope in us, I shall lose hope in everything else.

Yours ever,

Elias

June 1, 1821

Dearest Josephine,

Be not alarmed on reading this letter, by the apprehension that it might renew the sentiments described in my previous messages. I wish not for your discomfort, only to continue the friendship we began weeks ago. Indeed, my writing is not a means to subject you to flirtation or declaration of intentions, which would, of course, be inappropriate.

Please do not allow my foolishness to prevent your correspondence.

Your friend,

Elias Roch

P.S. Both my accountant and great-uncle sent news from London. They met a Mr. Rupert De Clare who recently buried his brother. I plan to contact the family and enquire about you.

June 12, 1821

Dearest Josephine,

Arthur died yesterday. He fell off his horse during a hunt, an accident caused by too much ale. The doctor said Arthur bashed his skull on a rock and likely did not suffer. I disagree, for when I rushed to my friend's side, he was awake and struggling to speak. I lifted him into my lap and rode over the south ridge, but he passed on before we reached the house.

I am not sure what more to write. Etiquette requires me to soften this news with formalities, but I cannot muster them. Arthur Banes died in a blink. Now his body lies on the dining room table, swaddled by a wool shroud.

Lorelai refuses to leave her chambers. She will not eat, nor will she receive visitors. Mrs. Dunstable paces the halls like a distressed hound while my cook prays over Arthur's corpse. What a horrible word. Blame, is that all he is—nothing more than a dead creature?

I must send word to Arthur's family and request their presence at his funeral. I have grieved so much, but loss does not dim with practice. If anything, it gains momentum.

Yours ever,

Elias

June 13, 1821

Dearest Josephine,

This manor no longer seems a haven, rather a graveyard. Its eerie demeanour confines me to my chambers, where I huddle near the fireplace. Ghosts do not lurk in the corridors. However, they haunt my thoughts. I covet the fire's glow, so memories cannot claim me.

Arthur died two days ago. His body lies downstairs, washed and clothed, surrounded by flowers. The longer he stays above ground, the more unsettled everyone becomes. My cook will not visit the main floor. Mrs. Dunstable rents a room at White Horse Inn, for she refuses to stay at Cadwallader past nightfall.

Pray my letters reach Arthur's kin soon. They reside in Durham, a day's ride south. Lord willing, they shall come and allow me to bury Arthur in the estate's cemetery. I must put this tragedy behind me. I cannot sleep without reliving his death. Whenever I close my eyes, I watch him tumble off his horse. I hear the crack of his skull against stone.

Rest denies Lorelai too.

Last night I found her in the dining room, crouched beside Arthur. She held a single candle. Its flame wavered in the darkness, its wax forming lumps on her fingers. She did not react to the burns. Instead, she hummed a lullaby jagged with sobs.

She claimed the house was too silent.

She missed Arthur's music.

I knelt beside her and kept quiet, for words could not ease her pain. A gut-wrenching ache burrowed down my throat into my lungs.

The loss did not seem real even then. Arthur was sprawled in front of me, white as porcelain, yet my mind whispered, "He's fine. All shall be well tomorrow." I wanted to cry with Lorelai. I needed to get mad and sob and tell her I was sorry for letting him drink that day. I was so very sorry. But my tongue was still. And I could not shed a tear. I was porcelain, yet I was living, and my friend was dead. He was dead. Nothing would be well tomorrow.

Lorelai spoke about her relationship with Arthur, their childhoods, how she thought of him as a brother. She leaned against my shoulder and cried.

You told me everyone suffers anguish, yet we consider it a malady, something to conceal and medicate. You said we should talk about what pains us, but I believe there are some pains best left unspoken. Words give power to feelings, and not all feelings deserve power. Indeed, suffering together eases the isolation of grief. However, it cannot prevent the grief.

Sorrow is a sharable weight but a solo process.

When dawn flooded the room with blue light, I forced Lorelai to stand. A gentleman would have coddled and comforted, but exhaustion dulled my manners. I guided her to a back door and said, "Waste no more tears, Miss Glas. Arthur does not require our watch nor our lament."

Lorelai and I exited the manor. We moved through the garden to a pasture coated with dew. There, among the tall grass, we sat and watched gossamer clouds float across the horizon.

I invited Lorelai to stay at Cadwallader until she feels able to return home. Our exchange at the ball soured our closeness, but I still consider her a friend. We loved Arthur, and we lost him. What could be a more appropriate reason to mend our rift? Besides, I wish not to be alone in this house. Even the faintest creak sends chills up my spine.

Please do not go lightly into our separation, Josephine.

If I am to lose you forever, I best know soon, while these wounds, this anguish, are deep and fresh. Let me suffer the loss of you now, before I rise off my knees and endeavour a step forward. Let me grieve. Let me break. Or be real and let me speak to you once more. What should mean so little has altered me entirely.

My fire burns low. I must venture beyond these four walls to retrieve wood. Do wish me luck. No matter how bright the sunrises, this place remains a shadowland.

Yours ever,

Elias

June 17, 1821

Dearest Josephine,

We buried Arthur today. Lorelai arranged the funeral, a humble service in the estate's cemetery followed by a reception at the main house. The following people were in attendance: Lady Seymore, Edward and Mary Rose, the vicar of a local parish, and Arthur's relations. His parents and two younger siblings arrived from Durham yesterday afternoon, much to my staff's relief. ~~Six days with a dead man in the dining room had created a foul stench.~~

Pardon my indelicacies. I do not know the proper way to report a death. When my mother passed, the servants buried her without fuss, according to Father's cook. A vicar read scriptures before they lowered her into the ground. The housekeeper sang an off-key rendition of "When I Survey the

Wondrous Cross." Then everyone returned to the manor for afternoon tea.

I did not cry during Arthur's funeral. Mary Rose snivelled. Lorelai wept into a handkerchief. But I remained dry-eyed and stiff, every fibre of my body taut with rage or sadness—or the guilt of drinking with Arthur that day. If possible, I would have torn open my chest and crawled out of the hurt. I would have returned to the manor and dumped its store of alcohol into the kitchen yard.

Humanity knows not to take big things for granted. We understand the importance of loved ones, health, acceptance, but what about the billion other elements that define who we are? Big we see. For big, we toss and turn at night, fearing big loss. And yet the little things we overlook. Forgetting to savour life's details, such as the taste of fresh scones or the scent of books opened for the first time, is our greatest deprivation. Such pleasures are not subject to change. However, we change. Our hearts break, and pastries lose their flavour. Love dies, and our senses dull. By losing a big thing, we lose all the littles by default.

The funeral reception served currant scones flavoured with lemon curd. I took a bite, and the cake turned to ash in my mouth. All I could think about was Arthur's coffin.

If not for the guests, I would have emptied my stomach into a chamber pot.

Mr. Banes approached me while his wife mourned in the drawing room. He grabbed my shoulder and said, "It wasn't your fault, lad." His statement lifted a weight from my shoulders, but it did not absolve me. No, I was not to blame. Everyone knew of Arthur's reckless behaviour.

I blame myself, though.

The family plans to stay at Cadwallader until tomorrow morning. Lorelai entertains them downstairs while I sit in Arthur's former bedroom. His belongings—clothes, figurines, a cricket bat—clutter the space. Someone needs to pack the items into a trunk, but I cannot manage it.

Grief follows me, Josephine. Must I lose every person and thing I hold dear? Love and loss coincide, I suppose. Love teaches us how to live with, and loss forces us to live without.

We love so we can lose.

Elias

P.S. The De Clare Family in London replied to my query. They are not familiar with you.

NINE

THE NOVEL

Josephine De Clare seemed to pull light into Cadwallader Park. For an entire week, she and Elias wandered the estate. They put on plays with Kitty and Fitz, swapped ghost stories at dinner, and made fun of Sebastian's tall hats. Elias laughed until his stomach hurt. He smiled until he couldn't see Josephine without grinning. That's when he knew.

In other circumstances, she might have been his dearest friend.

Their outings and games only magnified Elias's affection, so he stopped participating in Josephine's escapades. He maintained a suitable distance, for his father had warned him about scandal. One bout of misconduct, even a rumour, might cause Lord Welby to disinherit him. A Welby bastard needed to be above reproach. No drunkenness or debauchery.

No relations with a cousin's fiancée.

Elias would not let his emotions outwit him. Why should

he risk his station when the future seemed certain? Josephine would marry Sebastian and become lady of the manor. She would forget him, and no amount of pining could prompt a different fate.

He must sever the friendship between them. Any communication—small talk, a glance at dinner—stoked the embers burning in his chest. He was fond to the point of being smitten. He was devoted until he was hers, completely.

The attachment frustrated him, for no amount of distance seemed to break it. He observed from an upstairs window as Josephine played cricket with Sebastian. He cracked open his door when she and Kitty raced down the hallway in their night-gowns, their arms filled with chocolate.

Distance was not enough. In seclusion he thought about Josephine, though he tried to distract himself with books and letters. Even his dreams swept him back to the bonfire party, where he kissed her again and again. He imagined that night until it drove him mad. Of course, *love* seemed too strong a word to use on a stranger. *Love* seemed foolish to waste on a kiss.

But that depended on the kiss.

It all sounded ridiculous to Elias. He could not love Josephine. Their few interactions constituted nothing more than amiable respect. And yet Elias was drawn to her like a moth to a flame. He did not love her. He was only infatuated. For certain his intense feelings would dim with time. He just needed to avoid Josephine until then.

October brought storms and contained the Darlings indoors. However, mist and mire could not stall Josephine's plans. She pranced across the moors until rain soaked her clothes. She created bouquets of heather and scattered them throughout the house. Was her constant motion intended to keep sorrow at bay? Did she laugh to conceal her pain?

Hope for unhappiness seemed cruel, so Elias retreated further into seclusion. Each morning, he parted his bedroom curtains and watched Josephine climb the south ridge to witness the sunrise. During meals he ignored her attempts at conversation. His rudeness would deter her attention, surely. His loneliness would suffocate all feelings eventually.

But isolation did not fade his emotions. Rather, it caused them to blossom like prickly thistles. He adored the girl for who she was, not who she was to him. Oh, why couldn't he recall a time before Josephine? And what life existed after her?

∞

The dining room quivered when its door flew open with a bang. Josephine, Kitty, and Miss Karel stumbled across the threshold in a whirlwind of giggles and ribbons. They clung to each other, dishevelled, breathless, tethered by laughter.

Elias dropped his toast. He straightened as the girls waltzed forward, their murmurs suggesting jokes and secrets. How did they appear so vibrant this early? And in their untidy state? Did ladies receive awards for such accomplishments?

"Good morning, Mr. Welby." Josephine patted her flushed cheeks, then lowered herself into the chair across from him. She glanced at Sebastian, who seemed too preoccupied with his newspaper to acknowledge her presence. "Kitty, Miss Karel, and I plan to go on a picnic—"

"We intend to weave flower crowns," Kitty said. She plopped into a seat and grabbed a ginger bun from the breakfast nosh.

Although younger than both her governess and future sister-in-law, she appeared the most dressed, her cotton muslin gown starched and pressed, her curls fastened on top her scalp with silver pins. Of course her mother had taught her well.

No member of the Darling Family would dare traipse about unkempt.

"Mr. Welby, would you care to join us?" Josephine filled her cup with tea. She plucked a honey cake from a tray, then looked at Elias, her smile widening. "Oh, please say yes."

"Josephine grows tired of my company," Sebastian said while flipping through *The Morning Post*. He lounged at the table's head like a royal, his cheeks stuffed with brioche. "Go with them, Elias. You need the fresh air."

"I best stay indoors and focus on my lessons." Elias tugged his cravat. He squirmed as Josephine's smile melted in disappointment. Did she mean to torture him with kindness? If she knew the extent of his attachment, how he battled himself to remain distant, how he clenched his fists whenever she laughed, perhaps she would have mercy and leave him alone.

Sebastian lowered his newspaper. "Your lessons? Nonsense."

"My teapot needs me," Elias said.

"Blazes, another excuse. Admit you intend to hide in your library." Sebastian scoffed and hoisted the papers into full spread. "Elias must hate women."

"Is that true?" Kitty spun toward him. She perched on her knees, a position which would have infuriated Mrs. Darling were she not away with her husband and Widow De Clare on a trip to town.

"No, Kitty. I like girls," Elias said.

"Prove it!" Sebastian crumbled *The Morning Post* and threw it across the room, his movement yielding aromas of ale and sweat, souvenirs from his night at the local pub.

"Stop teasing your cousin, Darling. He may do whatever he pleases." Josephine stirred cream into her tea and locked gazes with Elias. "Mr. Welby, I admire your dedication to literature. I think if I could live in your thoughts . . . your mind would seem a cosy place."

"More like a boring place," Sebastian grumbled.

"Never underestimate the artistry of human thought," Josephine said. Her dark hair draped her shoulders, loose and uncurled. Her attire included a handmade dress the colour of her eyes, which she wore daily. For all her extravagant qualities were equal simplicities, and she seemed more spectacular because of them.

"Please excuse me. I must greet our new kitchen staff." Elias stood and bowed his head, a prickly ache ballooning within him. He should travel somewhere distant, perhaps London. His uncle would not protest. Besides, he needed only to separate himself until the spring, when Sebastian would marry Josephine at the estate's chapel.

"Do let me know if you change your mind," Josephine said when Elias neared her chair. She lifted her chin, the curves of her neck an invitation. "You're always welcome."

"I won't change my mind." Elias flexed his fingers, battling the urge to lean down and kiss her lips. What a wicked doing, to greet her warmth with coldness.

But he needed to protect himself from all possible hope.

Elias left the dining room and rushed down the hall. His brusque exit seemed merited, for a cook planned to arrive before noon. The Darlings' previous employee had taken leave due to illness, forcing the family to hire a replacement. Fortunately, Elias knew a woman with impeccable culinary skills who desired to escape Lady Welby.

He entered the gallery, where oak buttresses and elaborate moulding showcased the manor's architecture. Fitz sat on the checkered floor, surrounded by an army of toy soldiers. His playmate was Mr. Darling's valet, a man who rather enjoyed boyish pastimes.

Their battle seemed best left uninterrupted, so Elias hurried to the servants' stairwell. He paused on the first step as heat drifted from the lower level, tinged with delicious scents. Then, with a sigh, he descended the stairs and followed a whitewashed corridor to the kitchen.

A bundle of heather caught his notice. He paused near a sideboard, where one of Josephine's bouquets wilted in a vase. Its purple buds scattered the counter, now dried to crisps.

Elias reached for the petals but recoiled. How could he starve his heart of Josephine if he filled his pockets with keepsakes? No, no, he would not take even a fragment of her.

"Good morning, Mrs. Capers," Elias said when he entered the kitchen.

Unknown: Hey! This is Oliver McLaughlin. Pop gave me your number.

Josie: Hi! Sorry for almost beheading you.

Oliver: No problem. You're welcome to my head. I'm not attached to it. LOL

Josie: Thanks for the firewood. Last time I ran out, I went outdoors and gathered twigs.

Oliver: No, no, that cannot happen again. What will the neighbours say?

Josie: Hmm. They'll probably bring me wood like you did.

Oliver: HAHA TRUE! I'm glad I met you, Twiggy.

Josie: Likewise.

Oliver: Next time I bring firewood, I'll knock on the front door.

Josie: Smart. This house is an armoury. There's no telling what pointy thing I'd grab next.

Oliver: Oh, please. Do your worst. ;)

A woman with grey hair stood near the stove. She looked at him, and her expression melted like butter on a skillet. "My, you're a sight for sore eyes."

"I brushed my hair for you. And look at my boots. No mud," Elias said as she hastened to embrace him. He hadn't realized his lostness until now, as if he'd misplaced pieces of himself and one gaze from a friend drew him back together.

"Dear boy, I've missed you." Mrs. Capers hugged Elias's waist, her small form scented with cinnamon and herbs, aromas that swept him back to Windermere Hall. She pinched his arm. "You're too slender. The other cook didn't feed you enough."

"Oh, Mr. Welby, hello." Anne emerged from the servants' hall and shooed a hen off the kitchen counter. "Please excuse the mess. Somebody left the back door open."

"Anne, I didn't know you planned to come." Elias beamed.

The past few weeks had messed with his mind, caused him to go too deep into himself. He'd started to feel cold. Not on his skin. Beneath. Like the main floors of Windermere Hall. But Anne and Mrs. Capers brought warmth. They knew him, and to be known in a world of unknowns seemed the greatest gift.

"The Darlings offered her a scullery maid position. Good thing too. She wouldn't last a day alone with Lady Welby." Mrs. Capers squeezed Elias's hand. "Stay here, and I'll prepare a spread of sandwiches. Want some tea? I'll make tea."

"I'm so glad you're here," Elias said. He rested on a wooden stool and tossed crumbs to the hen, who pecked the mud-smeared floorboards.

"Do the Darlings treat you well?" Anne fetched a tin of biscuits from the cupboard. She arranged shortbreads on a tray decorated with painted flowers, then offered them to Elias.

"They're kind to me," he said. "How's my father?"

"Unchanged," Mrs. Capers said as she flitted about the space. "Miss De Clare greeted us outside an hour ago. Quite a pleasant young lady. She invited us to afternoon tea."

"Yes." Elias cleared his throat. "She's betrothed to Sebastian."

"Poor girl." Anne snorted.

"They don't care for each other." Elias took a bite of shortbread and let it dissolve on his tongue. "Sebastian ignores her, which doesn't make sense to me."

"Blazes, Mr. Welby." Anne gasped and leaned against the counter, her eyes widening. "You love her. You're in love with Miss De Clare."

"What? No." Elias shook his head. He rose from the stool and inched toward the butler's pantry, his pulse racing. If Anne recognized his feelings, did other people notice his attachment?

"Retreating like a coward, are you?" Mrs. Capers followed Elias across the kitchen. She grabbed his chin and examined his face. "Tell me the truth. Do you fancy Miss De Clare?"

"How am I supposed to answer that?"

"See! He loves her. I knew it." Anne waved her finger at Elias. "Do be careful, Mr. Welby. My friend told me about a man who stole his brother's fiancée—"

"I do not love Miss De Clare." Elias pecked Mrs. Caper's cheek, then strode to the service stairs, trying to convince himself he spoke truth. "I'd better go. I'll visit again before dinner." His chest ached, for his heart had set off an avalanche, and there was no stopping it.

Elias went to the manor's west wing, a maze of forgotten chambers tucked behind Fitz's nursery. A previous owner had constructed the accommodations, perhaps to entice guests to stay for long periods. Now the rooms belonged to dust and disuse, furniture draped with sheets, and mice who frightened the maid. No one ventured down the narrow corridors, a fact which relieved Elias. He couldn't focus on his studies when Sebastian pestered or when Mrs. Darling's lapdog barked. And he needed to focus before he lost all sense.

He walked toward his study at full speed. The sooner he locked himself away, the better. In solitude his feelings wouldn't threaten his reputation.

His eyes couldn't reveal secrets from behind a closed door.

The same thoughts led Elias to this annex time and time again, for his mind reeled in a dreadful cycle—Josephine, self-loathing, and an emotion he categorized as bitter acceptance. At least his uncle cared enough to offer him a hideaway. The small library suited his moods with its dark wood panelling, the smell of browned pages and leather. He'd spent many afternoons lingering near the bookcases, tracing his fingertips across faded covers and worn spines.

Literature provided the purest form of companionship. It drew him into a safe place, where his worries floated like dandelion fluff. It preserved his sanity and let him dream. Of course he craved the library, for when he sat in his armchair and lifted a novel to his face, its pages acted like blinders. They masked him. Perhaps his dilemma could be solved with a thick book. He needed only to hide until Lord Welby allowed him to leave Cadwallader Park.

Elias reached the study and turned its brass doorknob. He entered the chamber but froze when he noticed legs draped over a velvet sofa, their shoeless feet swaddled by silk stockings. His breaths rasped as he absorbed the scene—a girl reading upside down on his settee. No, this room belonged to him, not her. She couldn't invade his one safe place.

"What are you doing in here?" he growled.

Josephine scrambled into an upright position. She gawked at him, her dress still bunched around her knees, her tangled hair a mess. "I saw the books and . . ." She wiped tears from her cheeks. "Forgive me. I didn't realize this study belonged to you."

Norman: Do you need a ride into town, lass?

Josie: No, I found a bicycle in the shed. Tires were flat, but I filled them with air. Bike seems to work okay. Should get me to Atteberry and back.

Norman: Stop by the cottage this evening. I'll add a basket to the handlebars.

Josie: Thanks! What do you want from the bakery?

Norman: Martha likes Bakewell tarts and pork pies.

Josie: (*thumbs up*)

Norman: It's official. You're our adopted granddaughter.

Elias flexed his fingers, trembling with anger or embarrassment. He should apologize for snapping at Josephine. He should push her into the hallway. He should do something, anything, make a choice, say a word. But all he could do was stare at her puffy eyes.

"I'll go." She climbed off the sofa and rushed to the door.

"No, no, please stay." Elias blocked the exit.

Cadwallader Park contained several libraries, all of them grander than his retreat. Had Josephine come here to escape attention? And what caused her to cry? Life's misfortunes or the book now abandoned on a cushion?

"What type of books do you like?" Elias asked. He stood close to her. Too close. His cheeks burned, perhaps to hint at what might happen if someone found him with Josephine.

"Fairy tales, mythology, novels with romance and ghosts. Really, I enjoy all fiction," Josephine said. She gazed up at him, her mouth stretching into a smile.

"You're welcome to borrow from this collection." Elias studied her features—the faint sunspots on her cheekbones, how her upper lip folded when she grinned. Indeed, she was beautiful, but like a rainstorm, not a piece of china.

Like a sprinkle of dried heather on a sideboard.

Josephine turned on her heels and meandered across the

study. With a sigh, she collapsed onto the sofa, her head lolling against the backrest. "I daresay you've been avoiding me, Mr. Welby. Because I am engaged does not mean we can't be friends, and I think we should."

"Be friends?"

"Yes," Josephine said with a nod. She grabbed a fistful of her skirt and proceeded to pluck thorns from the fabric. "Sebastian wants to discuss only parties and hunting. I doubt he's read a novel from cover to cover."

"So, you wish to be friends because my cousin bores you?" Elias rubbed his jaw as a smile tugged his face. He couldn't take his eyes off Josephine. She was magnificent and bold and uncouthly direct. No other girl compared to her, not in the slightest.

"We have fun together, don't we?" Josephine sat up straight, her expression reminding Elias of the afternoons they'd spent in Mrs. Darling's old clothes, practicing lines of Shakespeare with Kitty and Fitz. They were friends despite Elias's avoidance.

They'd been friends for quite some time.

"Mr. Darling arranged the betrothal," Josephine said. "He wrote to Mother a few months ago and proposed I marry Sebastian. Now, before you judge me—"

"I don't judge you." Elias perched on the chair across from Josephine. He leaned against his thighs, a knot twisting his stomach. Of course, money and station must've been involved in the arrangement, for no lady would agree to marry Sebastian without benefits.

"Are you pleased with the match?" he dared to ask.

"Girls don't get to be pleased, at least not in the real world." Josephine grabbed the novel she'd been reading before Elias interrupted her and flipped through its pages. "Books are kinder.

They allow girls to go on adventures and fall in love. I do believe literature holds the best of us . . . or perhaps it reflects the better versions of who we are." She hugged the volume, her voice faltering. "I'd like to live in a book."

"I know how we can manage." Elias rose from the chair and went to a shelf beside his desk. He wanted to beg Josephine to reconsider the engagement. He wanted to live in a book with her, about them, without Sebastian and Lord Welby. The notion seemed childish, but he was young and so was she. Neither of them should have to think about the rest of their lives.

Josephine followed him to the bookcase. She touched the embossed spines as he'd done countless times, and for a moment the library appeared to celebrate her. Golden beams poured between the curtains and framed her silhouette. Dust whirled around her in ashy tendrils.

The sight caused heat to ripple through Elias's body, the sensations expounding until he felt magnified and raw, until he burned from the inside out. He couldn't alter his and Josephine's circumstances, for society plotted their futures. All he could do was provide what she asked for—a friendship, a book, some afternoons of laughter before adulthood caught up with them. He wanted the whole story, but he'd settle for a chapter.

A little of her was worth the pain of losing her.

"Miss De Clare, I present you with a gift," Elias said. He removed a novel from the shelf and handed it to her. "A chilling ghost story."

"How chilling?"

"You won't sleep a wink tonight." Elias glanced down and shuffled his feet. "Also, I accept your proposition. Let's be friends."

"Shake on it." Josephine extended her hand. "My friend, Mr. Welby."

Elias wrapped his fingers around her palm. Their interaction defied etiquette, but he didn't care. He tried to care. He wanted to care. He listed all the reasons why he should keep her at a distance. But she stood close. She'd entered his safe place. Now no room was without her.

She was everywhere.

"Please call me Elias," he said. "Mr. Welby . . . It sounds too formal."

"Elias." Josephine spoke his name like a secret, each syllable careful and savoured. "You must call me Josephine, then. I insist."

"Hello, Josephine." Elias shook her hand once more. He laughed when she perched on her tiptoes and ruffled his curls as if he were still an Eton boy. For weeks he'd questioned whether the bonfire kiss fuelled his infatuation. He'd wondered if his feelings might've been different if he had met Josephine at the engagement dinner. However, each question led him to the same conclusion: Yes. Of course. No doubt about it. He would've loved her at any beginning.

He loved Josephine De Clare.

"Sorry. I don't know why I touched your hair." She covered her eyes with her fingers. "I embarrass myself all the time."

"I do too. A week ago I tripped and fell down the staircase, rolled all the way to the bottom," he said. "You . . . You're the least dislikeable person in my acquaintance."

"What a friendly thing to say." Josephine clutched the novel to her chest, its cover the same hue as her ribbon sash. "Thanks for the book. I shan't bend the pages or drop my tea—"

"Do what you like with it. The Darling Family doesn't read."

"Perfect. I'll use it as a coaster." Josephine curtsied, then ambled to the door. She turned and smiled at Elias one last time. "You make me forget why I was ever sad."

Elias bowed, his grin widening. That settled it—he wouldn't leave Cadwallader Park. He would suffer heartache. He would throw rice at the wedding. He would do whatever was needed to stay close to Josephine, for love was not based on whether the right girl ended up with the right boy. Love just was—was there, in one's chest, stubborn and certain.

Love wasn't something he could escape.

TEN

JOSIE

From: Faith Moretti <Kardashian_4Life@mailbox.com>

Sent: Saturday, July 2, 4:07 PM

To: Josie De Clare <JDeClare@mailbox.com>

Subject: Paddling Back Together

Hi Josie,

The coffee date happened. It seemed more like an interrogation
or standoff than anything romantic. Noah and I met at a coffee
shop on Bergen Street, ordered lattes, then went to a table in
the café's back corner. We sat across from each other. Stone-
faced. Neither of us wanting to say the first word.

I apologized for my outburst and gave an explanation. He
listened, but his mind seemed elsewhere. There was an

141

emptiness in his eyes, the same glaze that appears whenever someone talks about history or the stock market. I knew then we didn't have a chance.

He said we weren't kids anymore—we needed to think about our futures. He asked if I'd meet with him again in a few weeks. I promised I would. After that he gave me a hug and left.

Noah and I drifted apart, Josie. We paddled for an hour to see if we could draw ourselves closer, but I'm not sure we have the stamina (or motivation) to continue. Not everyone who loves each other ends up together, and that's okay. It must be okay.

Please don't try to make me feel less crappy. I've already eaten a pint of ice cream and cried in the shower. Any kindness might liquidate me into a puddle of my own tears.

I don't know if I'm to blame for the breakup or if it was inevitable. It hurts, though. I'm certain of the hurt. What if Noah is the one for me and I screwed up everything?

As humans, we reach the end of our metaphorical rope, and we discover more rope. We don't believe things can get better, but they do, and they don't.

I hope this is one of those *get better* moments.

Now to talk about Oliver McLaughlin. First off, your email about the sword and Donut Disturb pajamas made me cackle. Of course you couldn't meet a guy someplace normal. Is your firewood dreamboat in a relationship? Asking for a friend. (*wink*)

Second, I'm glad to know someone in your age bracket lives nearby. Maybe he will help you renovate, haul ladders around, guard the toolbox. A romcom in the making!

Did you get the job at Sassenach Bakery?

Faith

From: Josie De Clare <JDeClare@mailbox.com>
Sent: Monday, July 4, 10:31 PM
To: Faith Moretti <Kardashian_4Life@mailbox.com>
Subject: Re: Paddling Back Together

No feel-good sentiments from me, Faith. You may receive an ice cream delivery . . . but I had nothing to do with it. I also wasn't responsible for the peonies that appeared on your doormat or the Adam Levine poster that'll arrive today. (Love you forever and ever, pal.)

Sassenach Bakery hasn't contacted me yet. They said to expect a phone call sometime this week. I hope they give me the job. I need a break from Cadwallader, Elias's writing, and the constant repair projects. Already I've painted the entrance hall, de-shagged the drawing room, and cleaned as much as humanly possible.

A member of the Atteberry Historical Society comes next week to survey the manor and explain ways to preserve the original features. I met him today when I visited the AHS.

I biked into town around noon, once I reread Elias's letters and emptied a teapot. The landscape seemed fogged with chalk, as if Headmistress Poston had clapped her erasers. Mist blanketed the hills, warm like steam from a kettle. I didn't bother to wear a raincoat—a stupid decision. The weather soaked my clothes. I had to wring my socks.

A wee man greeted me at the society's front desk. He looked surprised when I enquired about Cadwallader Manor and Elias Roch. He led me into a back room that reeked of mothballs, then unearthed documents from a file cabinet. (I should've used the loo before asking questions, because the bloke chattered for hours.) Once he left, I studied the records until dusk, and then I met Norman, Martha, and Oliver at White Horse Pub for dinner.

Elias left a meagre paper trail. Records date his birth and death, where he was born, but not much else. I suppose no one cared enough to chronicle his life.

Documents confirm Arthur Banes (Elias's best friend) died June 11, 1821. His brother perished in the Crimean War, and his sister married a relative of Prince Albert. Oh, a family tree charts the Roch lineage back to Alfred the Great. However, somebody blotted Elias from the list.

My mind seems a hot mess, Faith. I can't stop thinking about Elias and Josephine. More so, I can't rid myself of the notion— which I cannot explain—that somehow Elias wrote about me. He knew I like to read upside down. He knew about my night-time chocolate habit. Sure, the matching name and description were a coincidence—the cute serendipity we all crave. But this?

Elias understood what hurt me, and he experienced the same pains. He knew about Mum and Dad, and that I talk too much, especially when I'm nervous. All the things I dislike about myself were the things he loved about Josephine. That must be why I feel the way I do.

I love that Elias fell for a girl like me.

Cadwallader enhances this feeling—this sense I'm close to Elias. I can't enter a room without expecting to see him, hence my desire to work in town. I cannot be alone without daydreaming about his letters, his story, what he sounded like. My imagination gets the better of me. Wishful thinking, perhaps. I do want someone to love me like Elias loved Josephine.

The deeper I go into his world, the harder it is to find my way out.

All this will make sense eventually. I'll continue to renovate Cadwallader and search for information about Elias. If I learn about him, maybe I'll find out whether Josephine was real.

I need answers.

Josie

P.S. Arthur Banes died at Cadwallader. His corpse sat in the dining room for days. You know I like ghost stories, but this . . . I get chills just thinking about it.

Oliver: Hiya! Pop needs razors and toothpaste from the variety store. I'm going to drive into town, maybe get a spot of dinner at the pub. Want to come? Please say yes. I'm desperate for conversation that doesn't revolve around sheep castration and WWII.

Josie: Darn. I love to talk about sheep castration.

Oliver: Pick you up in fifteen minutes? LOL

Josie: You're buying dinner, though. I blew my budget on 19th-century doorknobs.

Oliver: Because your mansion doesn't have enough doorknobs?

Josie: Wow, girls must love that charming wit of yours.

Oliver: Hence my entourage of adoring fans. Okay. Done with jokes. I will buy your dinner AND dessert. I'll even push the store trolley.

Josie: Deal. See you in 15 minutes.

Oliver: I'll ring the doorbell twice. Plz leave your sword in the cupboard.

Josie: Yeah, sure. I'll bring my flail and battle axe instead.

From: Josie De Clare <JDeClare@mailbox.com>
Sent: Tuesday, July 5, 8:52 PM
To: Faith Moretti <Kardashian_4Life@mailbox.com>
Subject: The Boy Next Door

Faith, you enquired about the boy next door, so here's an update . . .

Oliver and I went to the variety store a few hours ago. He picked me up from the manor, that boyish grin—his trademark—plastered across his face. He looked ridiculous, dressed in sweatpants, trainers, and a baggy The Strokes T-shirt.

I still can't get over his hair. It's a total mess, worse than my Kool-Aid dye job.

We ventured into Atteberry. (Oliver drives Norman's vintage motorcycle, which has a sidecar—a tin can of death.) After we bought stuff for his grandparents, we ate dinner at the pub. Bangers and mash with a side of chips, followed by sundaes. We're health nuts for sure.

Oliver is smarter than he appears. I mean, at first look he seems like an odd chap—the hipster jock sort who usually hangs out at the gyms in Kings Cross. You know the kind.

He reads a lot, though. Suspense novels and cult classics are his preference, but he does enjoy the occasional literature anthology and medical textbook. Did I tell you he's studying to be a doctor? Yeah, he wants to practice medicine in Atteberry once he graduates. He's super close with his grandparents and wants to live near them. (I can't figure the boy out. He's a paradox.)

A few days ago, I rode my bike to Norman and Martha's cottage. (Norman said he'd attach a basket to the handlebars.) Oliver was out in the pasture when I arrived. He must've seen me coming down the drive, because he sprinted across the field and hurdled a stone wall.

Somehow he crossed the barrier without injuring himself. The feat impressed him so much, he spent a half hour coaxing me to admit his trick was brill.

Oh, he just texted. I'll finish this update soon.

Josie

Oliver: What size helmet do you wear?

Josie: IDK. Do helmets come in sizes?

Oliver: Don't worry. I'll measure your head later. Pop told me to order a helmet for you, so I'm getting one with a unicorn. Ur welcome.

Josie: Emergency! I can't brush the knots out of my hair. Your grandfather's motorcycle gave me a rat's nest. I may have to cut it off.

Oliver: HAHA. You looked hilarious in the sidecar. Next time wear goggles and a scarf.

Josie: The perfect accessories.

Oliver: Well, I have a bruise on my forehead, so . . .

Josie: You thought it was a good idea to jump into the shopping trolley. Not me.

Oliver: But you pushed that trolley into a wall!!!

Josie: I slipped.

Oliver: First the sword, now this. You're a dangerous person, Josie De Clare.

Josie: What can I say? I live on the edge.

Oliver: (*wraps you in cling film*) Pop has the original Dracula on tape. Want to make fun of the special effects with me?

Josie: Tonight?

Oliver: Why not? I'll send Nan to fetch you. Oh, Granny says hello.

Josie: Hi!

Oliver: She made sure I typed the words and pressed Send. LOL

Josie: Okay, I'll come over for a bit.

Oliver: Brilliant. I'll make popcorn and find a barber kit.

From: Josie De Clare <JDeClare@mailbox.com>
Sent: Wednesday, July 6, 2:14 PM
To: Faith Moretti <Kardashian_4Life@mailbox.com>
Subject: Re: The Boy Next Door

Faith, I'm antsier than usual. I woke up in a panic this morning, and I don't know why. Nothing has changed, at least not really. I haven't talked to Mum in a while, so no stress there. Oliver and I are friends. His grandparents treat me like family. And renovations occupy my days.

Between hiring a contractor to repair the east wing and overseeing an electrician, I barely have enough time to read in Elias's study. I want to finish the construction project for Dad. I want to figure out what the heck is going on with the novel and letters and this attachment I have to Elias. The feelings grow stronger each day. I need to put his letters back in that drawer.

I need to remind myself why I came to Cadwallader.

The future will not wait for me to get my act together. In a few months, I'll go back to London and resume my life. Elias can't keep me in Atteberry, neither can missing Dad. I must focus. Please tell me to stop obsessing. It's bad, Faith. Really bad. Each night, I read across from Elias's portrait so I can pretend we're two people at a library, separated by books. I wander the manor and imagine his story playing out. And the dreams—oh, I have vivid dreams about him.

Oliver brought firewood (and a reality check) to the house this morning. He saw Elias's letters piled on the kitchen table. Being the nosey goof that he is, he asked me about them. I can't quite remember how the conversation went, but he ended up reading the opened letters and several chapters of Elias's novel. I think we might've created a book club.

The similarities between Josephine and me shocked Oliver. I haven't seen him so excited. It was as though he'd uncovered a mystery, like I was Nancy Drew and he was a Hardy Boy. He then wanted to see Elias's study, so I took him on a tour of the house.

He investigated every nook and cranny.

Afterward we visited the cottage and used Norman's printer to scan Elias's novel into a digital copy. Oliver plans to read it with me. That should help my sanity, right? I mean, treating the book like fiction should prevent me from thinking of it as a love letter to what might've been. Thanks for the care package by the way! I took one look at the *My Heart Belongs to Elias Roch* mug and laughed myself breathless.

Surely I won't fall in love with someone's words if I'm not the only one reading them.

Ugh!!! That's how I feel. One big UGH.

How's your life? Any news about *the one who won't be named*?

Josie

P.S. I've decided to study education at uni. I want to be a school-teacher. Mum will throw a fit when I tell her. (She doesn't think educators make enough money.) But the vocation seems a good fit for me. Even my dad thought I should teach.

Faith: Glad you like the mug! I designed it online.

Josie: You're the best. (*kisses*)

Faith: Love the idea of a book club!! Oliver sounds like a cutie.

Josie: I'll tell him you said that. He lives for compliments.

Faith: Noah and I haven't talked since our coffee

date. His mom called me, though. She wanted to know if we were getting back together. Awkward conversation.

Josie: Blimey, that sounds horrible.

Faith: Thanks for all the gifts, by the way. I hung Adam over my TV.

Josie: May he watch over you always. ;)

Faith: Proud of you for choosing a major! You'll make a fantastic teacher.

Josie: Baby steps. I still need to budget the money Dad left me so I can finish restoring Cadwallader and pay for uni. Oh, want to see my to-do list? It's become a scroll.

Faith: No wonder you feel out of sorts. Take a day off! Relax.

From: Josie De Clare <JDeClare@mailbox.com>
Sent: Friday, July 8, 3:47 PM
To: Faith Moretti <Kardashian_4Life@mailbox.com>
Subject: Plot Twist

Faith, I hope you're sitting down. If you're not, please find a chair. I'd hate for you to read this email and collapse. Perhaps I should begin with the least shocking news—I got the job at Sassenach Bakery! Good thing too. Not sure I could last another full day at Cadwallader.

My hands won't stop trembling, so I apologize if my words are jumbled. I considered waiting until the panic subsided, but . . . I must tell you what happened.

This morning I resumed my scavenger hunt. A giant mistake. I should've gone outside and pressure-washed the front stoop, but mist hovered thick on the moors, and I didn't want to suffer the cold. Instead, I looked for Elias's studio. I went to the third floor and peered into each room. Someone had emptied a lot of the chambers, so I didn't expect to find anything. However, I noticed a door beside the staircase. It blended into the panelling, its knob the only giveaway.

Obviously, I opened the door.

Grey light spilled into the room from a single window. Easels crowded the space, and paintings dotted the walls. I coughed. Dust clung to the air like smoke. No one had entered the studio in years, proven by the undisturbed layer of grime that coated the floorboards.

I wandered among the artwork until I reached the fireplace. That's when I saw it—the portrait of Josephine from Elias's letter. It hung over the mantel, discoloured and smeared with soot.

But its likeness was unmistakable.

My heart skipped a beat. I stumbled backward and knocked over a painting—a blonde girl in a white frock. The room seemed to shrink around me, narrowing into a tunnel with a face at one end, a door at the other. I couldn't breathe, so I fled the studio.

He painted me, Faith. It was me on his wall. How is any of this possible? How did a man from two hundred years ago know about me?

And why do I have this feeling I'm supposed to know him too?

Josie

Faith: WHAT?! No way. Elias didn't paint a portrait of you.

Josie: Sending a picture now.

Faith: OMG. Excuse me while I go question everything I know about reality.

Josie: Looks like me, right?

Faith: Near identical. Maybe he knew your doppelganger.

Josie: Who had my name and personality? Who also lost her father?

Faith: Just trying to create an explanation that doesn't involve . . .

Josie: What?

Faith: I don't want to say it. (*wide-eyed emoji*)

From: Josie De Clare <JDeClare@mailbox.com>
Sent: Friday, July 8, 6:22 PM
To: Faith Moretti <Kardashian_4Life@mailbox.com>
Subject: Re: Plot Twist

Elias met a girl with my name and face. He wrote about her, and the character he created resembled me too. He wanted to post letters to her, but something happened.

He never found her address.

I can't wrap my mind around this situation. Whenever I type Elias's name into a search engine, nothing comes up. When I look for information about Josephine Emilia De Clare, I find only details about myself. The old Josephine doesn't appear in any public databases.

Our suspicions cannot be true. I refuse to believe Elias loved me, because I'm here and he's not. Letting myself hope seems foolish. I mean, nobody rational expects to find their Mr. Darcy. As girls, we know what kind of love we're allowed. Our men flock to the pubs and watch rugby with their mates, not write us letters filled with phrases like "I'm ardently yours."

Why search for Elias Roch in a world of Rashads?

Josie

Oliver: Hey! One of my mates at uni works at the School of History, Classics & Archaeology. He may be able to scrounge up some info on Elias Roch.

Josie: That would be AMAZING!!

Oliver: I'll ring him this afternoon. It may take a few weeks to get the information. My friend works at the speed of a sloth—an elderly, blind, legless sloth.

ELEVEN

ELIAS

July 4, 1821

Dearest Josephine,

I find myself in an impossible predicament, and no amount of civil behaviour can save me. Society will not rest until my station unravels. They come for the Roch fortune like hounds ready to devour all I have left. Besides the fact my wealth and title will not withstand their efforts, I fear Arthur's death has weakened me. I cannot be prevailed upon to feel anything but fatigue.

At present I write to you from my coach. A lantern swings from the ceiling, and damp air gusts between curtains. My driver shouts at the horses as we travel the moors at a reckless speed. Perhaps I should request a gentler pace, for the carriage rattles, and my penmanship suffers.

Nothing could tempt my strength, not after tonight's affairs. I accepted Lady Seymore's invitation and spent the evening at Bletchley Place. The visit began without incident. Lady Seymore introduced me to her guests, all of whom embraced my presence with conversation.

Dinner included fifteen dishes, my favourites being the white soup and stuffed partridges. Lady Seymore gave all guests a tour of the main floor prior to the meal. She talked about her late husband's fascination with French design, hence the abundance of Parisian furnishings. She led us into chambers with satin wallpaper and gilded fireplaces. Really, if I had known what awaited me in the dining room, I would have attempted to prolong the jaunt.

As luck would have it, I ended up at the farthest corner of the table, seated across from a clergyman. Lady Seymore's mother sat to my right, her age encouraging bouts of slumber.

I might have enjoyed the companionship if not for Admiral Gipson's arrival.

He joined the party as footmen served beef and mutton. His presence, more so his navy uniform, demanded attention. Everyone paused conversation to inspect his decorated blazer.

The admiral kissed Lady Seymore's wrist and apologized for his tardiness. He sat in the chair to my left, his clothes reeking of tobacco and Bay Rum. Without looking at me, he said, "I read in the paper about your friend's accident. My condolences."

I nearly spilled my drink at his impertinent unwillingness to introduce himself to me before conversing. The remainder of the evening confirmed his refusal to acknowledge me as Lord Roch.

Admiral Gipson straightened his ornaments, perhaps to flaunt his proficiencies. He enquired as to whether I planned to occupy my family home in Durham. I told him I preferred Cadwallader Manor, and he said, "You had good sense to move into that place. Indeed, a bastard does not merit the right to manage a prominent estate. Perhaps you should relinquish—"

Lady Seymore interrupted with a question about news from town, thus diverting the dialogue to matters of gossip and entertainment.

It was just as well. Shock rendered me speechless. I did not finish my dinner, rather I stared at the table's centrepiece like a fool. Admiral Gipson desired me to spurn my inheritance, but why? What could he gain from my rejected title? And who would dare strip me of it?

The festivities ended an hour later when Lady Seymore's mother fell asleep in the drawing room and shattered a bottle of ratafia. Guests used the accident as a reason for their departure and escaped the clergyman before he read his sermons.

Why did Admiral Gipson bother to attend the party? He lives in Dorset, a two-week's ride from Atteberry, unless he is staying nearby.

Josephine, I feel the truth, but to give it words is to breathe life into it. Regardless of how I wish to perceive intentions, Admiral Gipson's motives appeared quite clear. He came to Atteberry for reasons involving me.

Father bequeathed his heir ten thousand pounds per year, money derived from the Roch aristocratic lineage and success in trade. The sum puts a target on my back.

I am not afflicted with false modesty, so believe me when I say I am unable to endure another tribulation. My vigour fades like a covered flame, shrinking from gold to muted blue. If relatives come to brawl for my fortune, I may very well give it to them.

Lorelai went to stay with Mary Rose for several weeks, claiming my house reminded her too much of Arthur. She promised to return by August, but I think she may venture south instead, perhaps to visit Mr. O'Connor in London. Cadwallader does not seem a kind place, especially now. I expect to see Arthur whenever I enter the dining room. I sit in silence, waiting for his music to echo up the stairwell. Each day without him drives me closer to madness. Lorelai must sense that darkness too. She would do well to leave Atteberry.

Without her presence, I can barely tolerate the house. I paint alone. I eat alone. I go downstairs to the servants' quarters and play cards with Mrs. Dunstable so I won't die from boredom. Even reading and writing seem more solitary than before.

The carriage slows, which means we're nearing Cadwallader. I best conclude this letter before my driver finds me crouched on the floorboard, surrounded by stationery.

Elias

P.S. I am inclined to saddle Willoughby and ride to where I met you. Of course, you will not be there, but I must do something. I have spent months in pursuit of your address. I have written to people all over England, and no one seems to know your whereabouts or if you exist.

Josie: I read another letter. Elias contacted people all over the country, and no one knew about Josephine. He wrote about meeting her, so she must've been real.

Oliver: Unless . . .

Josie: Unless what?

Oliver: He was bonkers. Lots of writers were/are. Take Edgar Allan Poe, for example.

Josie: Elias wasn't like Edgar Allan Poe. He wasn't even a real novelist.

Oliver: What constitutes a real novelist?

Josie: I asked for this, didn't I?

Oliver: (*clears throat*) A novelist is someone who . . . writes a novel.

Josie: Mansplain to me one more time, and I'll revoke your book club privileges.

Oliver: Sorry! I couldn't help myself. Plz don't kick me out of the club.

Josie: Admiral Gipson showed up again. He's going to make trouble for Elias.

Oliver: Dang. Our boy couldn't get a break. FYI, I finished reading chapter 3.

Josie: And??

Oliver: You are Josephine De Clare.

July 19, 1821

Dearest Josephine,

A messenger called this morning. He brought a letter from the town courthouse.

One glance at the wax insignia confirmed my suspicions. I tore open the letter and removed a summons. Apparently my cousin Thomas Roch has contested Father's will, alleging I forced Lord Roch to sign the document and thus committed fraud. He also claimed Lady Roch did not sign as a witness, which poses another reason to nullify the terms. Now, according to common law, I must hire a solicitor and appear before a judge.

Surely Admiral Gipson encouraged my cousin to pursue legal action, perhaps for a portion of the inheritance. I assume they believe a court will rule in their favour due to my illegitimate birth. If they secure the right judge, their notions may prove correct.

My cousin believes himself the rightful heir to the Roch fortune. Pray tell, should I concede before the trouble begins? I could leave Cadwallader once and for all, maybe purchase a cottage near the coast. I like the sea, and a change of scenery may put the past behind me.

No, I cannot yield. Admiral Gipson and Thomas Roch declared war against my honour, so I must fight for what is mine. I will not be snuffed out.

Yours ever,

Elias

P.S. I completed the fourth chapter of my novel.

July 23, 1821

Dearest Josephine,

Yesterday I rode Willoughby into town and met with a solicitor whom Lady Seymore recommended. He promised to hire a top-notch barrister to vouch for me. Still, with two months until the first hearing, I seem to have no advantage. The circuit court plays favourites.

I am hardly anyone's favourite.

Mother feared this day might come. She took me aside one Christmas morning when I was six years of age. I do not know what prompted her concern, but she said, "When you're older, somebody may try to steal from you—to hurt you—because Lord Roch wants to give you a good life. Promise you'll treat them with kindness, for the moment you strip someone of their humanity is the moment you lose your own."

She encouraged me to live beyond reproach despite our circumstance. I tell a happier story in my book, but reality was not so gentle. Mother and I suffered, and through it all she forgave and clung to faith. Her words echo within me now as I prepare for the trials to come.

Admiral Gipson and Thomas Roch believe the case a sure win. However, I am not without connections. I'll write to my father's lawyers and request their legal advice. Who knows? Perhaps I'll manage to gather enough proof to support my claim.

In other news, Lorelai returns tomorrow. Her letters say Mary Rose lifted her spirits, and she plans to travel home in a fortnight. I've yet to tell her about the court case, though. She tends to stick around when there's trouble.

Yours ever,
Elias

July 26, 1821

Dearest Josephine,

Lorelai returned to Cadwallader. Upon arrival, she rushed to my study and entered without a knock or greeting. I suspect Mrs. Dunstable informed her about the case, for she gazed at me with tears in her eyes, her lips pinched into a scowl. She fussed at me for not sending word. Then she enquired about my health and what needed to be done.

Nothing I said pacified her. She rolled up her sleeves and went to work, sorting through documents, ordering the staff to open windows and bring in flowers. She claimed the manor was too dark and musty, so she asked Mrs. Dunstable to purchase new curtains and lamps.

I suppose Lorelai does care about me.

The news spread through Atteberry. Again, I blame Mrs. Dunstable. Locals visited the house to pay their respects. I did not think people noticed my residence at the estate, but they brought food and wished me well. Some of the farmers even gathered to say a prayer. Indeed, they are so good-natured. I cannot imagine what I did to earn their regard.

Lorelai asserts I need to better receive affection. She cornered me yesterday and said I was foolish to assume myself negligible. Our friendship has mended. We paint in the evenings and visit Arthur's grave. Not once has Lorelai mentioned what occurred at the ball. Instead, she wishes to know about you, how we met, and if I plan to declare intentions.

She insists I contact the directory in Bath. Apparently lots of young ladies go there during the social season for its assembly rooms. Lorelai believes you may reside in the city until September and wants me to make inquiries. My unsent letters seem to fascinate her, so much so that she advises me what to write. Now we both hope to find you, Josephine.

Without Arthur here, Lorelai spends a great deal of time with me. She doesn't appear bothered by possible rumours. During our last conversation, she mentioned her scheme to visit London prior to her return home, for Mr. O'Connor has expressed interest in courtship. She anticipates a marriage proposal.

At present I write to you from the gorse alcove. I sprawl on a patchwork quilt of leaves and scribble without disruption. The shrubs are in bloom, their blossoms a bright yellow and smelling of tropical fruit. How could I feel despondent in such a place?

Nature heals like a ginger tonic. It fixes the parts of me no physician can see.

My thoughts seem changed now. Since infancy I have endeavoured to be worthy of the inheritance. I allowed other people to determine what I wanted and how I lived. Then Father died, and the money was placed in my hands. I hated it, truly, for the wealth did not give me satisfaction. It failed to confirm Father's affection or to transform me into someone I admired.

The court case has presented an opportunity for me to wipe the slate clean. I could rid myself of the Roch title, cast aside expectations, and start anew. However, these past few days proved I am not my father. I decide the path set before me, and so I shall face Thomas Roch and Admiral Gipson. I shall not relent, for this fight belongs to me. It is mine to win.

My future is not contingent on the whims of others. I want a real home and family, and I believe such things attainable. Of course, one's belief cannot be allowed to suffocate under the tyranny of small minds, for hope itself does not hinge on the faith of the masses, rather the singular soul.

And I hope most ardently.

Lorelai begs me to write my feelings with directness, for she knows I have withheld a certain sentiment from these letters. Although I risk offense, I wish you to know my intentions and the emotions that compel my pursuit. I love you, Josephine.

I have loved you from the moment I laid eyes on you.

After I learn your address and this legal matter ends, I would like to solicit an audience with you and suggest a courtship. Our separation has confirmed that my attachment is more than mere infatuation. I miss you. Each letter I write reminds me of your distance. I need a day with you, then another. I need an infinite amount of last days with you because none of them, no matter what we do, will be good enough to encapsulate how much I love you.

Please do me the honour of considering my request. I shall not surrender hope until I know whether you share my affection. For a moment with you, I wait an eternity.

Yours ever,

Elias Roch

August 13, 1821

Dearest Josephine,

The court date approaches like the storms that spool black over the moorland ridges and progress in a slow creep. I cannot escape its looming presence. Mrs. Dunstable marked every calendar in the house to encourage communal support and insists the cook serve my favourite soup to, as she lovingly puts it, improve my wounded morale. She and Lorelai do their best to calm my nerves, but they hover like anxious parents, always checking on me, asking if I need more tea and firewood. Yes, I appreciate their efforts, but I would not mind less attention. They watch as if I am dying but they cannot bear to tell me.

Lorelai refuses to leave Cadwallader until after the trial. Every morning, she comes to my study and helps sort through the documents Father's lawyers posted to me. She thinks I shall gather enough proof to support my case. I want to share her enthusiasm, but just last week I rode to Newcastle and met with my barrister, and he seemed uneasy.

Thomas Roch's claims revolve around hearsay. No one can prove fraud, and the will includes signatures from two witnesses. However, if my cousin finds a judge who dislikes bastards, I stand no chance. The nature of my birth seems a great offense.

In a month's time, I shall enter the courthouse and plead my case. I cannot determine what happens to me. I can only control how I respond to it.

Josephine, I shall write to you again soon. My solicitor and barrister wish to meet with me, so I return to Newcastle tomorrow. Pray they bear good news.

Yours ever,

Elias

P.S. I wrote to the directory a fortnight ago. A lady by the name of Miss Catherine Wood responded and said a Josephine De Clare was reported at 11 Great Pulteney Street.

September 23, 1821

Dearest Josephine,

I went to court today, and not a thing went right. I stood in a whirlpool of angry voices, the room tight and reeking of bodies and urine. Some poor bloke soaked his trousers, and I understand why. Barristers waved their fingers while a judge perched above me. They posed questions until the air seemed to evaporate. I could not breathe. I still cannot breathe.

The assembly reconvenes tomorrow, but I fear I am ruined. Thomas Roch will inherit Father's assets. He must loathe me, for at the hearing he refused to acknowledge my presence. Yes, blood is thicker than water, but what is thicker than money?

Without a farthing to my name, I cannot purchase that seaside cottage or make you a suitable offer of marriage. I shall be fortunate if I secure a position

Josie: Elias didn't finish his letter! He stopped midsentence. What if he died?

Oliver: Maybe he took a bathroom break or wanted to give you an intermission. Old things tend to fancy intermissions. Do you have more letters to read?

Josie: Um, crisis averted. (*hides under blanket*)

Oliver: LOL. Did Admiral Gipson cause problems?

Josie: Yep. Elias went to court to fight for his inheritance. Also, he learned a Josephine De Clare was staying in Bath. Maybe it's THE Josephine.

Oliver: You're not a time traveller, right?

TWELVE

THE NOVEL

Sebastian marched across the entrance hall with a rifle propped against his shoulder. "Look alive, Elias," he said while smacking his cousin with leather gloves. Like all Darling men, he relished the wee hours of morning, especially when hounds barked outside.

"Must we leave so early?" Elias squirmed in buckskin breeches, a garment lent to him for the occasion. He rubbed grit from his eyes and followed Sebastian to the vestibule.

Cadwallader Park seemed to buzz with activity as its staff prepared for the hunt. Mrs. Capers's clattering echoed from the kitchens on the lower level. The valet polished shotguns while the maid beetled from room to room with breakfast trays.

"I daresay you care more about sleep than entertainment," Sebastian said.

"Sleep is my entertainment." Elias smirked, his stomach grumbling for more breakfast. He accepted a thick wool coat from the butler and buttoned it over his jacket.

"Promise you won't be dull. If you complain, I'll make you sack the grouse." Sebastian grabbed Elias's shoulder and dragged him onto the front stoop. Their breaths whirled like smoke as they beheld the landscape's blue haze, its gossamer webs that glistened with dew. Even the fog seemed hesitant to rise for the day.

Elias shivered and pocketed his hands. He shouldn't put himself in this situation. Anne and Mrs. Capers had warned him not to flaunt his new friendship. They'd recommended he fake illness to avoid the hunt—advice he'd considered until Sebastian barged into his bedchamber an hour ago. Somehow he'd ended up in riding clothes, his belly half full of porridge.

"Best get a move on," Sebastian said. "Don't want you to catch a chill."

The estate appeared frozen, its topiary garden crystalized by frost, its outbuildings iced like gingerbread. Five horses waited on the lawn. Their hooves created U's in the verglas as Mr. Darling wove among them, attempting to quiet his pack of hounds. He blew into a whistle. He shouted obscenities, which startled the onlooking women more than his dogs.

"Gracious. Any earlier and I would've come in my night shift." Josephine entered the cold, wearing only her slate-blue dress and boots, her unbrushed hair baled with a ribbon.

"Ah, my lovely fiancée. You look . . . fit for the outdoors," Sebastian said. He snatched Josephine's hand from her side and pecked her knuckles, perhaps to appease his mother and future mother-in-law. The women seemed to watch him like hawks.

Elias smiled, his face warming against the wind. "Did you finish the book?" he asked Josephine once Sebastian joined Mr. Darling on the lawn.

"Yes. I read until midnight, but then I was too afraid to sleep. What marvellous fiction. You must lend me another novel, perhaps one with more ghosts. The last didn't have nearly enough." Josephine beamed at him. She tucked a strand of hair behind her ear, its tip caressing her rouge-smeared cheekbone. "How did Sebastian entrap you in his plans?"

"I owed him a favour."

"For what?"

"I'm not sure. He claims I owe him a great deal." Elias laughed and stepped into the manor's doorway. "Perhaps I'll sneak inside—"

"No, no, you must come." Josephine gripped his sleeve, her thumb grazing his bare wrist. She drew back. Her cheeks flushed. "I won't press you, though. If you decide not to join us, I'll tell Sebastian you're unwell. At least one of us should be able to escape this madness."

Without another word, she hurried toward the hunting party.

Elias sighed and rubbed the spot her fingers had touched. Every thud of his heart seemed unrequited, but he couldn't walk away. He couldn't preserve himself. He needed to stand close to her, for the sight of something wonderful—like a first snowfall or Vauxhall Pleasure Gardens—seemed better than nothing at all.

Ice crunched beneath his boots as he strode across the front lawn. He waded through Mr. Darling's pack of dogs, their coats smearing mud across his breeches.

"Are you warm enough, Elias?" Mrs. Darling asked. She and Widow De Clare observed from a distance, both swaddled by cloaks and shawls.

"Satisfactory," he said. His teeth chattered from the bitter wind. His cheeks grew numb. Still, he dare not ask for more clothes and subject himself to Sebastian's mockery.

"You're the responsible one, Nephew. I trust you'll guard my boys from misadventure." Mrs. Darling mustered an affectionate smile. She pivoted toward the main house and glared at Fitz, who peered from his nursery window. Poor lad—the hounds must've woken him.

"I shall do my best," Elias said. He reached his steed and adjusted its stirrups. His legs required ample slack, more than the stableman gave him.

"Josephine, you look indecent. Did you not consider your attire?" Widow De Clare yelled. "No one of importance will attend your wedding if you damage your reputation."

"I disagree, Mama," Josephine shouted in response. She grabbed her horse's reins and snickered. "Scandal engenders popularity. A woman of little propriety may not receive the public's respect, but she will gain their attendance."

Widow De Clare scowled, her jaw set. She removed her cloak—a wool tartan—and motioned for her daughter to take it. "At least wear my shawl."

Josephine crossed the lawn, her boots creating divots in the frost. She draped Widow De Clare's garment over her shoulders, then returned to her stallion, where Mr. Darling lectured on rifles and game. He must've told a joke, for she tilted back her head and laughed at the grey sky.

"Do keep an eye on her, Elias. I expect she'll fall behind once the hunt begins," Sebastian whispered as he tightened his saddle's girth. He glanced at Josephine and huffed. "Oh, just look at her. She cannot manage proper dress, let alone behave with the faintest intrigue."

"You still don't like Miss De Clare?" Elias grew stiff, his fingers still clasped around a stirrup's buckle. He knew Sebastian did not care for Josephine, but the churlishness ignited hope within him. Perhaps his cousin would end the engagement.

"I know dozens of more accomplished, better-suited ladies." Sebastian slid his hands into leather gloves, then swiped an auburn curl from his forehead. "My parents wish me to settle down so I won't cause further damage to the family name. They arranged a marriage to the first girl that came to mind. You and me . . . I suppose we're not so different. We both live at the mercy of our parents, and we fear reputation because of what it may cost us."

"The hounds are restless," Mr. Darling yelled as dogs nipped his thighs. He fought through the pack and blew his whistle, signalling for everyone to mount their horses.

"Reputations take only what we give them," Elias whispered. He wedged his foot in a stirrup and swung himself into the saddle. "For approval, we gamble ourselves away."

"And yet we do it happily," Sebastian said with a chuckle. "Come on, Elias. Don't be dreary. You must admit my fiancée demonstrates vulgarity of manners."

"You consider yourself a worthy judge?" Elias snorted.

"Of good manners? Hardly." Sebastian grinned and mounted his steed. "But as someone versed in the art of indelicate behaviour, I consider myself an expert on all matters vulgar. Josephine De Clare does not merit a high score from my judging, and I swore to marry either a true lady—the type who sits indoors all day—or a sterling imp."

"Please tell me you're joking."

Sebastian tipped his top hat. "Oh, how I dream of wedding

an imp." With a laugh, he kicked his heels and lurched into motion, leading the party in a charge across Cadwallader.

Hooves slung frozen sod. Dogs yipped and yapped as they raced toward the hills, their ears flapping like wings. It all seemed regal—skylarks flitting from their heaths, air drenched with the metallic scent of rain—as if the northern land bore English pride.

Elias hovered above his seat, the worn leather rocking between his legs. He clutched the horse's reins and leaned forward to let the wind roll down his back. Since childhood, he'd exercised his riding to please Lord Welby. He'd galloped around Windermere Hall, jumped hedges and gates. Such practice gifted him with exceptional balance. Granted, he couldn't rely too much on his proficiencies, not when the world blurred around him.

Regardless of skill and caution, one blunder could result in a bashed skull.

Mr. Darling veered onto a path while his dogs traversed the moorland brush. "A good day for sport," he yelled. "I predict a generous yield—"

"I daresay my gun agrees with you." Sebastian fired a shot at the clouds. He glanced over his shoulder and laughed at the valet, who bounced in his saddle. "Did you forget how to ride?"

"You shall make yourself sick if you don't change stance," Mr. Darling added.

"I already did, sir," the valet said, his complexion tinted green. He leaned off the cantle and braced his knees against the horse's sides. His adjustments must've satisfied the masters, for they raced on, slicing through mud, chasing invisible game.

Norman: Ey up, Josie dear! I can't find Nan. Is she with you?

Josie: No, I let her outside an hour ago. Want me to search the grounds?

Norman: Don't worry yourself. She'll turn up. The ole girl fancies her morning stroll.

Josie: We have that in common. :)

Norman: Be careful where you wander, lass. Folk get lost on the moors.

Josie: I stay near the main house nowadays. Got the sniffles last week from a rainstorm.

Norman: Aye, that's best. The damper weather will make you lurgy.

Josie: Tell Martha I have a bag of hot cross buns with her name on them.

Norman: Cheers.

Elias fell behind when the party ascended a hillside. He matched pace with Josephine and steered his horse up the grassy slope.

"What is it we're hunting?" Josephine asked. She rode side-saddle, her mother's tartan wrapped around her neck like a cowl, her dark hair a billowing pennant.

"Birds, I think," Elias said.

"On horseback? With hounds?"

"Perhaps foxes, then."

Josephine laughed. "The Darlings are the worst countrymen

I've ever met. I wouldn't be surprised if they opened fire on a herd of sheep."

"Give them a keg of ale, and I assure you anything's possible." Elias smiled. Now that he thought about it, he couldn't recall a time when the Darlings brought home more than a single bag of grouse. His relatives must've used the sport as an excuse to gallivant across the county.

"Hmm, today just became interesting," Josephine said with a shimmer in her eyes. She kicked her heels and galloped onto a ridge, her skirt bunching to reveal a petticoat and blue-threaded stockings. She was not vulgar. No, she possessed a raw elegance, like the heather scattered across the kitchen sideboard.

Elias rode at her side, moving toward silhouettes now obscured by fog. He lifted his face into the cold and listened for barks. He swayed with the horse's movements, relaxing as wind combed through his curls. What if he endeavoured to prevent the wedding? Sebastian did not wish to marry Josephine, nor she him. Elias could end the ordeal with a few planned remarks. Already the words entered his mind like nightshade, poisoning him with dark possibilities.

That was a line Elias would not cross. He refused to sacrifice his honour in selfish pursuit, for love gained through deceit was no love at all.

"I cannot breathe," Josephine yelled over the pound of hooves against soil.

"What's the matter?" Elias glanced to his right, but Josephine no longer rode beside him. He twisted in the saddle and spotted her a few yards back, halted like a bannerman. Her skin was pale, her breaths jagged.

Elias pulled the reins, trotting to where Josephine sat frozen.

He removed his overcoat and wrapped it around her shoulders, more to provide comfort than warmth. "You'll be well," he whispered. "Sometimes we tell our minds not to worry, but our bodies don't listen."

"I don't know why I'm like this," Josephine gasped, her voice crackling like dried wood in a bonfire. She gazed at the horizon with haunted eyes as if something, perhaps a realization, had drained her vigour. "I'd made peace with it all, so why can't I breathe?"

"Peace with what?"

She waved her arms at the bleak terrain. "Is this my life now? Hunting? Oh, I need to—I don't know—scream or run or . . . curl up in a ball. Please. Let's do something else."

"Sebastian will notice," Elias said. His excuse seemed ridiculous, for the party charged ahead without regard for his and Josephine's delay.

"Not for a while," she pleaded, her nose reddening.

The desperation in her voice gutted Elias, for he'd felt similar emotions the day Lord Welby sent him to Eton. It was a desperation that confirmed his life didn't belong to him. He was trapped between expectations, responsibilities, and his own need for acceptance. That same desperation had caused him to break down in the upstairs hallway before the engagement dinner. It compelled him to hide behind closed doors to avoid Josephine. Indeed, he understood her pain, so he couldn't say no regardless of what yes might cost them.

"Okay. What do you have in mind?"

Josephine tapped her heels against the horse's belly and bolted toward a ridge shaped like a citadel. She rode hard and fast, her green tartan waving like a flag.

Elias joined the race. He grinned as they bolted across the moor, through wavy hair grass and crowberry clusters. He wanted to remember the moment until his dying breath, how golden plovers fluttered out of shrubs, the way hills rolled across the landscape like waves casted in clay. If possible, he would've made camp in the memory and dwelled there forever, with Josephine riding beside him. She was soaring, and his heart was falling. Being alone with her was dangerous, but anything else seemed impossible.

The horses snorted and huffed as they climbed a hill. Daylight had melted the frost, making the ground soft, a torment for hooves.

Josephine dismounted once they reached the pinnacle. She folded her mother's shawl and placed it on a rock, then marched to the slope's edge. "I need to roll down this hill," she said with a nod. "It'll make me feel better."

"Are you mad?" Elias slid from his saddle. He couldn't let her tumble down a steep drop. Sebastian would blame him if she got hurt, and what would people say if she returned to the estate with muddy clothes and a man who wasn't her betrothed?

"Come on, Elias," Josephine said as he crawled over boulders to reach her.

"No, no, you'll break your neck—"

"I won't break my neck."

"Or I'll break my neck, and you'll feel terrible."

She grabbed his wrist and dragged him to the brink. "Look. It's not *that* steep."

Fifty yards below, the hillside eased into a crevice lined with gorse. No doubt the descent would hurt, but it appeared moderate, not the deathtrap Elias had first imagined.

"But I have terrible luck." He looped his arms around Josephine's waist and tugged her away from the edge. Their closeness violated several rules of conduct, but they were young. They were friends.

"You need to roll down this hill too." Josephine smiled and ruffled his hair, combing the dark curls over his eyes. "When the world seems dark, we must look for a bright spot, to *be* bright. We choose our joys." She gazed at him for a moment, and her message became clear. The hillside was her happiness. It was freedom.

Elias nodded, a sigh rasping in the back of his throat.

"You're going to roll down this hill with me, Elias Welby. And if we die, then . . . at least we died laughing." Josephine nudged him with her elbow. "Are you with me?"

"I'm with you," Elias breathed. He wanted her fingers tangled in his curls and his arms wrapped around her waist. Always. He wanted her. In this moment. Always.

He wiggled out of his jacket and tossed it aside. The cold air burned his skin, cutting through his waistcoat and shirt. Of course, Mrs. Capers would call him a fool once she heard about his actions. He might even agree with her, but for Josephine, he'd catch pneumonia, lose a toe to frostbite, or roll down a mountain. His feelings didn't make sense. They were a mystery.

And the more he felt, the less he could explain.

Josephine put his overcoat with her shawl, then crouched on the hilltop. She gazed at the landing below, her face glowing with new colour. Did she fight her emotions like Elias battled his? Oh, how he ached to scoop her into his arms and tell her brokenness wasn't a crime. Sometimes that was all a person needed—permission to fall apart and a safe place to rebuild.

"On the count of three," Elias said with a huff.

Faith: You okay, Josie? I haven't heard from you in days.

Faith: Noah and I went on another date. Let's FaceTime. I have news.

Faith: You were active on Instagram yesterday.

Faith: Hello? Did you die? I'm panicking.

Josie: I'm alive! Sorry for not responding.

Faith: What the heck is going on? Talk to me.

Josie: All this stuff with Elias . . . I don't want to get into it right now.

Faith: Do not cut me out of your life. Please. Not again.

Josie: I'm not cutting you out! I just need to be left alone for a while.

Faith: That's what you said last time.

"Three!" Josephine flung herself down the slope. She tumbled sideways, rolling like a spool of thread, her squeal echoing across the heathland.

"Wait, Josie . . ." Elias crossed his arms and dove headfirst, which seemed a poor decision as the world spun around him. He bounced down the incline, whirling with sensations—dirt in his eyes, bile stinging his throat, and a dizziness so violent, he saw stars.

The hill would flatten soon. He needed only to last a few more seconds. But the pain grew stronger, the knocks and blows more extreme. He cried out and gasped for air. He choked on a mouthful of sod. If this was a fistfight with the mountain, the mountain was surely winning.

Elias went limp. A fuzzy blackness filled his eyelids like ink, and when it subsided, he found himself sprawled at the hill's base, surrounded by gorse and heather. He groaned, an intense ache pulsing through his body. The fall had bruised him from head to toe. He likely wouldn't be able to get out of bed the next day, which wasn't the worst fate. Mrs. Capers would insist on a remedy of white soup, warm blankets, and plenty of rest.

"Josephine?" Elias sat up with a start. He spotted her an arm's length away, her clothes painted with mud and trampled grass. "Are you all right?"

She clutched her stomach and laughed, tears streaming her cheeks. "No, but I can't stop smiling. I can't unfreeze this horrible grin. I want to show just how *not all right* I am, but my body is too broken . . . or perhaps it's so tired of pain and sadness, it decides to exist in denial. I don't know. All I can tell you is I'm not all right. I want to cry."

Her confession ripped through Elias, freeing the emotions he'd struggled in vain to forget. He wasn't all right either. He wanted to be whole and undamaged, for other people seemed immune to the pain he felt. Then again, no person had expressed their feelings like Josephine. She put her sufferings—her father's death, the engagement to Sebastian—into words.

And she wasn't ashamed to expose them.

Elias crawled to her side, his elbows sinking into mud. "You seemed content—"

"Let me assure you I have been deeply unhappy." Josephine twisted onto her back and dried her eyes. "Sorry. I'm prone to these dark moods from time to time."

"You're the most vibrant person I've ever met," Elias

whispered. He placed his hand near hers to feel the prickle of warmth from her skin.

"My father told me that . . . to live, one does not need to be strong and courageous, just awake. He claimed the world is like a deep pool, and the bottom of it is covered with seashells. Some blend into the sand. Others sparkle and shine. And the bright shells—those are the ones people treasure. They prompt joy because they dare reflect light in a gloomy place." Josephine's body relaxed into the ground. She turned her hand so her knuckles rested against Elias's little finger. "I wish to live a bright, waking life."

The hurt that carved into her voice made Elias tremble. He understood Josephine chose her joys to save others from pain. She endeavoured to reflect light when the world cloaked her in darkness. She was awake, and she was hurting. She was a bright shell, yet sands of sorrow buried her, crushing her beneath the pressure.

Elias had lost his sheen years prior. He'd let the gloom dull him, and he'd lived in its shadows ever since. What could he do to help Josephine? He couldn't resurrect her father, nor sever her engagement to Sebastian. He couldn't even summon a proper response.

"Do you miss your mum?" Josephine asked. She rolled onto her side and studied Elias's expression, her lips parting like a rose in bloom. How did she know about his mother's death? Sebastian must've told her. The bloke couldn't keep a secret if his life depended on it.

Elias nodded.

"Missing someone is the same as breathing, I suppose. It continues until the end." Josephine sat up and hugged her legs.

"When my father died, I promised myself I wouldn't crumble to pieces. Mum didn't seem upset, so I pretended not to hurt. I found that if I smiled and only celebrated the good, I forgot the bad, at least for a short time." She rested her dirt-smeared cheek against her knees and sighed. "What makes you happy?"

"Books, the outdoors . . ." Elias scooted to a cluster of gorse. He reached into a shrub and plucked a blossom, then handed it to Josephine.

"You like yellow flowers?" She cradled the bud in her palms and snickered, a grin scrunching her face into a display of white teeth and jewelled eyes.

"Gorse," he said with a nod. "It's thorny and overlooked—"

"Like you." Josephine stroked the flower's petals. She gazed at the blossom while a breeze gusted through the vale and ruffled her tangled hair.

"I daresay I'm not thorny," Elias said with a laugh.

"No, that's not what I meant." Josephine blushed as if she knew about the times Elias had ignored her when he'd wanted to kiss her, the glances he'd stolen before looking away. "I meant humans often fail to acknowledge the beauty around them, but their lack of notice doesn't determine a thing's value. Gorse does not require an audience to grow, and neither do people. We aren't who we are because of what others see or say."

Her response sent chills through Elias's body. Did she think him a handsome man, a beautiful thing gone unnoticed? His heart raced at the thought, for she sat beside him, dirty and shivering. And somehow she was lovelier than everything else.

Elias combed his fingers across the turf. He lolled against his elbows and watched birds swoop from the surrounding hills. "When I was a child, I sneaked out of the servants' quarters and ran as far as my legs could carry me. I reached a pasture lined with gorse and stone," he said, his voice barely above a whisper. "I didn't want anyone to find me, so I crawled beneath a shrub and watched its flowers sway in the breeze. For a moment I felt safe."

Josephine smiled.

"To this day, gorse reminds me of that feeling, that sense of home. Strange how a small thing can mean so much." Elias tensed when she tucked the flower behind her ear. "It suits you."

"I want to find my safe place." Josephine collapsed onto her back.

"You're welcome to borrow mine," Elias said.

She glanced at the shrubs and wrinkled her nose. "Looks a bit snug under there."

Elias laughed. He stared at her puddle of hair, the golden flower pressed against her temple, and the small thing that meant so much suddenly meant even more. "I'll make room," he said. "I bet Sebastian has a pair of hedge clippers—"

"Yeah, the ones he uses to trim his side whiskers." Josephine rolled onto her side. She met Elias's gaze, and her expression softened. Did she detect his connotations? Was she aware of how the situation could damage them? They were alone, too close. They sprawled on damp soil in a state of undress. If anyone questioned their honour, they would lose a great deal.

Josephine flinched when the sharp trill of a whistle echoed across the moor. She groaned and squeezed her eyes shut. "They noticed after all."

A knot formed in Elias's stomach, tightening as the hunting party called their names from higher ground. He and Josephine could ignore the shouts. They could hide among the shrubs, talk until the sky turned pink, and pretend they weren't scared and broken.

They could find their own safe place.

"Come on." Elias rose to his feet with a grunt. "You're going to climb that hill with me, Josephine De Clare. And if we die—which I think is probable due to our lack of conditioning—then at least we'll die wheezing. Laughing. I meant laughing."

"You might be the dearest friend I've ever had," Josephine said, her nose reddening.

"Are you with me?" Elias offered his hand. Despite his want to stay near Josephine, he wouldn't prevent her from returning to Sebastian. He'd do what she needed, be who she wanted, forget himself so she could find her own joys. That was the love he chose.

Love that did what was right even when it hurt.

Josephine laced her fingers around his palm. She looked at him in a new way, and his resolution faded into the background. Attraction was not seen—it was sensed. And Elias sensed it like coming rain. He'd need to prove himself worthy of her, overcome countless obstacles. But hope drew back the curtains of his gloom and let the light shine bright again.

Josie: No, no, that cannot be the end!! Oliver, I finished chapter 4 of Elias's novel, and the whole book just stopped. No more pages. Elias must've written another draft.

Oliver: The manuscript only contains four chapters?

Josie: Yes! Elias wouldn't have left the story unfinished. He cared too much.

Oliver: Weird. Did you search the study?

Josie: I turned the entire house inside out. I rummaged through every piece of furniture, looked up chimneys, even felt the walls for hidden compartments. No manuscript.

Oliver: The Hawthorne Family might've discovered it. You told me they sold a lot of the original furnishings. Who knows? Maybe they found Elias's book and donated it to a museum or historical society. Want me to phone my mate at uni? His department might be able to track down the book if it was donated.

Josie: YES. I need to know how the story ends. I can't spend my life wondering.

Oliver: Wondering about what?

Josie: Whether Elias and Josephine ended up together. For some reason, I have this feeling the book holds answers. And if I don't read it, I may never learn the truth.

Oliver: We'll find the book.

THIRTEEN

JOSIE

From: Faith Moretti <Kardashian_4Life@mailbox.com>
Sent: Thursday, July 20, 1:10 PM
To: Josie De Clare <JDeClare@mailbox.com>
Subject: DID YOU CUT ME OUT?!

Josie, I called you, like, a gazillion times. I thought about faking my death so you'd feel horrible. But I couldn't stay off social media long enough. And Noah said I was overreacting—what most dudes say when they want their girlfriends to murder them. Oh, we're back together. You would've known that a week ago if you'd answered my texts, calls, FaceTimes, and DMs.

I don't understand why you need space from me. We had plenty of space until you asked for less space. Then we became friends again, and I still respected your space. Heck, there's a whole ocean of space between us. What's going on? Please talk to me.

You promised to let people care about you, so I can't fathom why you'd push me away, especially after what happened last time. You knew what you did hurt me. You apologized, and I forgave you. But here we are, back where we started.

Did I tell you how I learned about your dad's passing? You didn't call or text me. No, I heard the news from Headmistress Poston. She came into our residence hall. (I was alone in our room. You'd returned home weeks before that.) She informed all the girls of Mr. De Clare's death and asked us to pray for you. Don't you understand how that made me feel? Your dad was yours, but I loved him too. I didn't get to say good-bye. You took that from me.

At this point I'm not sure whether to yell at you via voicemail or be worried. If I had Oliver's phone number, I would call him. Already I searched for his profiles on social media but couldn't find an account. Josie, email me so I know you're all right.

Please don't cut me out.

Noah and I went on a date last Wednesday. He took me to a building near Radio City Music Hall with the best rooftop view. We sat in metal lawn chairs—the super redneck kind—and drank blue raspberry slushies while the city flickered. New York resembled a million television screens, each displaying a sitcom of someone's life.

We seemed like ourselves again, maybe because the location was so informal. Noah said he wanted a future with me. He asked if we could dream together, find common ground, and I said yes. Our plan is to finish college before we consider marriage.

I wanted to share the news with you that night. I expected to call you and hear the excitement in your voice. But you didn't pick up the phone. And I felt robbed. Maybe I am overreacting. I mean, Noah thinks you're busy or got sucked into the whole Elias drama.

Let me care, Josie. Please respond.

Faith

(Sent from iPhone)

From: Josie De Clare <JDeClare@mailbox.com>
Sent: Thursday, July 20, 9:22 PM
To: Faith Moretti <Kardashian_4Life@mailbox.com>
Subject: Re: DID YOU CUT ME OUT?!

Elias wrote about me, Faith. I see myself up close, but he saw the bigger picture. He loved me before I knew me. He understood the emotions I feel but cannot put into words.

For years we envied the girls in romcoms. We hoped guys would look at us like that—like we were beautiful and one of a kind. You found Noah, but I had no one. Until now. Now I'm *that girl*, and I won't pretend it doesn't matter. Something fantastical happened to me. Two hundred years ago, a man fell in love with someone, and that someone—or at least her twin—found his letters centuries later. Elias and I were meant for each other. I must continue to search for his book even if you think I'm crazy because . . . I feel him like a sharp pain in my side.

This past month, I spent every afternoon in his study. I examined his letters, rummaged through his belongings. I fell asleep in his reading chair, and I heard his voice in the dead of night. But it wasn't him. It was the wind. And I cried because his absence felt like loss even though I never had the pleasure of calling him mine.

His manuscript ended after the fourth chapter. Oliver contacted a friend at the University of Edinburgh who may be able to locate the full story. We haven't heard back yet, but we're on a mission to find the book. Elias wouldn't have left it unfinished. He would've brought his character and Josephine together, given them a happy ending.

I need to read the whole manuscript.

Do you remember when I threw up on Dr. Kleinman? I pretended to have the flu so I could dodge classes. The embarrassment was too much, worse than when I accidentally flashed my knickers at the school recital. I didn't want to show my face anywhere.

Not talking to you wasn't because of you, Faith. I'm sorry for repeating my mistakes and hurting you all over again. I don't know what's the matter with me. I can't seem to avoid messes, dysfunction, or spreading pain. Elias's Josephine was different in that respect. She chose joy and made people see the best in themselves. Not me. I feel dark like Elias.

Maybe books do reflect the better versions of us.

I was embarrassed to tell you the truth—that I'm attached
to someone who no longer exists. I was embarrassed to
admit I'm losing all sense. Like, how could I expect anyone to
understand? I don't even understand. I just feel what I feel,
and my feelings say Elias wrote to me. Perhaps I'm wrong.
(The logical part of my brain knows I'm mistaken.) But I can't
walk away. My feet seem glued to Atteberry and Cadwallader
Manor.

This place supplements all the missing elements of my life.
I started work at Sassenach Bakery as a cashier and novice
baker. (The pâtissier doesn't trust me with complicated recipes,
so I make scones and biscuits.) I fancy the job, more so the
shop. It's located in the centre of town, has blue windowpanes
and a Tudor rose insignia. Quite a lovely place. It smells like
fresh bread and coffee, and the owner insists we play singer-
songwriter music.

On Wednesdays an elderly woman with pink hair, Lucille,
comes to purchase snacks for her knitting club. She
wears round glasses and a camouflage parka. Last week I
complimented her outfit, and she invited me to visit her group.
I've yet to give her an answer.

All that to say, I have a life here. I'm part of the community
now. People know my name. They pop into the bakery
and say hello. (Some of them remember Dad.) On the
weekends, Oliver and his grandparents come over for
afternoon tea.

They invite me to eat dinner with them at least twice a week.

You deserve to be mad at me. I'm mad at myself, not just for my behaviour this past week, but for how I cut you out of my life when Dad got sick. I'll always regret that. You should've been at hospital. You should've heard about his passing before everyone else.

Since his death, I've felt a bit detached from the world. Living here changes that, connects me to Dad and Elias, lets me feel like I belong somewhere again. I've grown used to being alone at Cadwallader. Right now I'm inside the west wing study, nestled on a velvet sofa. Nan lies at my feet, twitching from a dream. Elias watches us from the wall.

And I am perfectly content.

Please keep an open mind for this next part. I won't go into detail. I'll just type my bigger news and press Send so I won't persuade myself otherwise.

I decided to stay in Atteberry until Christmas.

Josie

P.S. I'm happy to hear about your mended relationship with Noah!

Faith: WHAT?! No, you can't stay at Cadwallader until Christmas.

Josie: There's nothing for me in London, not until January.

Faith: Is this because of Elias? He might've written about you. Regardless, you can't time travel. You won't find him in your kitchen, hunched over a cup of tea. Sure, you're allowed to love a boy from a book (or letters), but you can't live in the pages with him.

Josie: I need to stay at Cadwallader.

Faith: Why? Being there won't change anything. You can fix the manor, but restorations won't bring Elias or your dad back.

Josie: Until I make sense of all this, I can't leave.

Faith: Your father died, Josie. You're grieving.

Josie: Thanks for reminding me. I forgot.

Faith: Please listen. I think sometimes we love things we can't have because knowing we'll never get them protects us from wanting too much. Or maybe we use those unattainable things as a distraction because we're afraid to open our hearts to what's right in front of us. That's the biggest risk—choosing to love something we could lose.

Josie: See! I knew you'd respond like this.

Faith: You're my best friend. I don't want us to be mad at each other, but I love you enough to speak the truth. Your detachment worries me.

Josie: It shouldn't.

Hi, Faith! Just checking in to see how you're doing. Are your summer classes treating you well? Any news in the Noah department?

Our last conversation ended poorly, and I hate when we're on bad terms. I'm usually to blame. (I have a Hulk-sized destructive vein.) We'll be okay, right? I mean, we survived the Bra Debacle of 2017, among other things. I'm confident we can get through this rough patch.

Some updates: The electrician finished wiring the upstairs floors, so Cadwallader has electricity. Workers came and patched the roof. No more leaks!

Mum phoned yesterday. She has a new boyfriend—a bloke half her age. They met at a charity auction in Brighton. I forgot his name, but it's something horrible like Ernie or Thad.

Blimey, I hope I don't end up with a Stepdaddy Thad.

In other news, July brought warmer weather to Atteberry. I ride my bike into town and wear those jumpsuits you gave me, except when I help Oliver with farm chores. (Martha lent me overalls and Wellingtons because I step in sheep dung at least once a week.) Nan stays with me at night. She sleeps at the foot of my bed and snores louder than the manor's creepy noises.

How can I convince you I'm all right? Remember when I first asked why you left America? You told me sometimes it takes letting go of everything to get something worth having. You detached from your world, and look at what happened.

Elias understood misery better than he realized. That or he just knew how to write about it. His letters prove he wanted someone to guide him through grief, but loss isn't a textbook process. It's different for everyone. Yeah, we want advice and steps—anything to shorten the pain. But grief can't be hurried or pummelled with self-help. It's just there.

The only way out of it is through it.

I'm getting through my grief, Faith. So what if I need a manuscript and love letters? People have found solace in literature for centuries. I'm no different. I mean, a book is but a stack of paper until someone reads it. And when someone reads it, they build a house within its pages, so whenever they return to that book, they feel right at home.

Let me have this home.

Josie

Josie: Any word from your friend? It's almost been a month.

Oliver: The chap is a sloth. I'll text him and see if he can hurry the process.

Josie: Thanks! Everything okay? I haven't seen much of you recently.

Oliver: Pop and I were shearing ewes all week. We're bushed.

Josie: Do you need help? I can swing by the farm after work.

Oliver: Yeah, come on! We finished shearing, but Pop needs someone other than me to listen to his stories. Please eat dinner with us. You'd be doing me a mega favour.

Josie: One condition. You must refer to me as My Hero all night.

Oliver: (*gags*) Fine, My Hero.

From: Josie De Clare <JDeClare@mailbox.com>
Sent: Wednesday, August 9, 11:09 PM
To: Faith Moretti <Kardashian_4Life@mailbox.com>
Subject: Re: Life Updates from Cadwallader

Faith, rest assured I've taken steps to mend my imagination.

Last night I dreamt I climbed out of bed and wandered into the hallway, where Elias waited for me. He smiled and whispered my name, his tall form traced with candlelight. I collided with his chest. I embraced him while he combed his fingers through my hair and kissed a line across my forehead. For what seemed like hours, we held each other. Then, I woke up in an empty room with his scent—a blend of fresh wood and ozone—on my pyjamas. Even now I remember his warmth, the feeling of his lips against my brow.

The dream frightened me, so much so that I decided to visit Lucille's knitting club. Human interaction seemed a cure for such things.

Lucille's club meets at the Knitting Emporium on Glebe Street. They gather in a back room filled with inventory, sip tea, and gossip. They're a pleasant bunch, hardly the old folk I expected. Members include Lucille, Dorrit, Clare, Margery, and Stuart.

Dorrit immigrated from the Scottish Highlands. She speaks with a thick accent. Really, I don't think anyone understands her, but they all play along. Margery doesn't look older than forty. She wears colourful bandannas and pins back her curls with knitting needles. Stuart is Lucille's younger brother. He's retired, but he volunteers at the local radio station. And I can't forget Clare—the eldest of the group. She's charming, truly a precious lady. Her parents died in the Blitz when she was five years old.

I went to the club after work. (My boss insisted I stay late to bake tarts.) A bell chimed when I entered the emporium. Lucille rushed to greet me, her wardrobe more eclectic than usual. She wore a furry jumper, lilac trousers, and bedazzled trainers.

Social media would fall in love with her.

Once I purchased red yarn and a pair of needles, Lucille walked me to the back room, where everyone sat in a circle. They introduced themselves, then asked what brought me to Atteberry. I told them about Dad, the estate, Mum's new boyfriend. Perhaps I should've withheld my personal woes, but they didn't seem to mind. They rose from their seats and surrounded me in a group hug. Not a pity hug. A sincere welcome. And for a moment I felt at home, like they wanted me to be a part of their mismatched family.

Stuart placed a foldout chair between Clare and Dorrit. I joined the circle and wound my yarn into a ball while Margery joked about her ex-husband. Clare taught me basic knitting stitches. (I may finish a scarf by Christmas.) Lucille gave an overview of the last romance novel she read and explained how to make the perfect steak-and-kidney pie.

The club meeting steadied me. I plan to go back next week. Yes, Cadwallader Manor still creaks and groans, but I feel better. Elias may sneak into my dreams. (I almost want him to find me in that hallway.) But who cares if I fancy a dead author? I have Oliver, Norman and Martha, a job, the knitting club, and I have Elias.

My existence seems rather balanced now.

Josie

P.S. Please talk to me!! I've had a taste of my own medicine, and it's bitter.

Oliver: You did good today. Pop was impressed with your pen-building skills.

Josie: "Good" shouldn't be used to describe a girl in any way. There are good books, good food, but not good girls. ;)

Oliver: Fine. You weren't good—you were perfectly adequate.

Josie: Careful with those compliments. I might get a big head.

Oliver: Let's go somewhere. Fancy a drive to Alnwick? We can tour the castle and pretend we're characters from Harry Potter.

Josie: Wish I could buy a subscription to your stream of consciousness.

Oliver: You'd want a refund. LOL

FOURTEEN

ELIAS

September 24, 1821

Dearest Josephine,

I write to you from a corner table within Atteberry's public house. Night dims the bustle to smouldering conversations. Patrons bask in the amber glow from oil lamps while imbibing both ale and poor company. At this late hour, no one bothers to approach me, which seems a comfort after such a horrid day. I wish to write and sip my tea in absolute peace.

Please forgive the abrupt end to my previous letter. Mrs. Dunstable barged into my study while I wrote to you, her intrusion forcing me to stuff the papers into a drawer. I am not ashamed of my attachment to you. However, my housekeeper seems keen on me finding a wife. She demands her participation and introduces me to every young lady in her acquaintance. Although I value her opinion, I wish to avoid further involvement.

The court reconvened this morning and debated for hours. Barristers argued. Thomas Roch yelled accusations. Admiral Gipson watched from the audience, smirking as though my opposition has already won the case. His expression taunted me. It resembled the arrogance of my headmaster at Eton, the gentlefolk who called me a "leeching bastard," and Father on multiple occasions.

All my life, someone has looked at me the way Admiral Gipson did today. I am done with it—the whispers and sneers, being treated as a pawn. Indeed, in that moment the need for an end swelled within me until I could've burst from it. I washed my hands of the silence.

I wanted to fight.

My barrister addressed the magistrate and pleaded my case. His words echoed through the room, muted by the audience's murmurs. I could not bear to let another person speak on my behalf, so I cleared my throat and stood. My sudden willingness to address the court caused surprise, for everyone grew quiet. Even the admiral leaned forward in his chair.

The judge motioned for me to speak.

I said, "Your Worship, I refute the accusations made against me, for they were issued by an avaricious relative with whom I first made acquaintance in this very room. Mr. Thomas Roch did not attend family gatherings, nor did he offer his condolences after my father's passing. In fact, I was unaware of the man's existence until I received a court summons. He wishes to profit from my father—his distant uncle—by charging a bastard heir with fraud.

"Regarding the disputed matter of illegitimacy, I am a Roch, the only son of Lord William Catesby Roch. I was born in Durham and have resided in Atteberry for almost a year. My cousin wishes you to believe me the uneducated child of an improper union. With little civility, he attempts to slight my honour and reputation by resting his charges on my birth.

"Sir, I am an Englishman and the named heir to William Roch's fortune. I beseech you to consider the charges against me without discrimination. I will not challenge your verdict, nor will I restate my defence. May the court judge me fairly."

Objections rose from the crowd, followed by shouts of protest from Thomas Roch. My barrister forced me to sit and mumbled obscenities while the magistrate commanded order.

A verdict shall be announced tomorrow. I cannot predict the ruling, nor will I curse the outcome with a guess. If I am meant to live without fortune, I shall quit Atteberry and visit the Glas Family until I secure employment. Perhaps I shall offer myself as a teacher.

Lorelai believes Mr. O'Connor would offer me a position at the Royal Academy.

Blazes, I should get some rest before my mind stoops to dark places. I have not slept a full night in weeks. Lorelai gave me a valerian root tonic, but I doubt the remedy will help while I am anxious and horizontal on a strange bed. Against my better judgement, I rented a room at the public house so I can meet with my barrister in the morning.

I shall be fortunate to manage an hour of uninterrupted slumber.

I do not regret what I said in court, but my decision to speak posed threats to my case. For weeks my barrister told me to stay quiet and thus prevent surprise obstacles. I disobeyed him, and I may lose everything because of it. Whatever happens, at least I know the life that resides beyond this legal matter is mine, not the one Father designed for me. If I am to be penniless, then I shall earn my own wage.

Father's expectations will not control me anymore.

Of course, without title and fortune, I cannot make you an offer of marriage. You deserve to find happiness with someone who possesses a home and decent means, for no lady should compromise her welfare. I refuse to prevent your comfort, so I shall withdraw my proposal if the magistrate rules against me. I want the inheritance for many reasons, most of which involve you.

I sent a message to 11 Great Pulteney Street. You may receive it. At least such is my hope. Our continued friendship surpasses my desire for courtship. I love you, and love surpasses all want in such a way that I could never have you and still feel at peace.

Your correspondence is my greatest aspiration.

We have found ourselves in an unusual predicament. I confess attachment to someone I met by chance, and you are likely reading my letters, a bundle written over months of searching. Thanks to you, I feel more confident in my ability to express such feelings.

Perhaps there was no moment in which I fell in love, rather a series of trips and tumbles.

Or perhaps you were a part of me since the beginning.

I best draw this report to a close and surrender my table to another patron. The public house appears busier than usual, perhaps due to the visiting militia. Arthur would have fancied the crowd, for he viewed such as an audience. He would have played his violin and ordered me to clown. I miss him, though not the headaches that followed our exploits.

He would have commended my efforts today, I'm certain.

Do not worry about me, Josephine. I shall carry on despite my misfortunes. I've read too many novels to believe in finality, for at the end of the story, there is a lot more story.

Yours ever,

Elias

October 1, 1821

Dearest Josephine,

The court ruled in my favour. Thomas Roch did not receive a penny of my inheritance, and neither did Admiral Gipson. Both men departed Atteberry, and I doubt they will return, for the locals seem vexed at them. Mrs. Dunstable reports a general displeasure among the townspeople in connection with my accusers. Granted, I do not bear any ill will. I am only glad to be liberated from the dispute. More than anything, I am pleased to renew my proposal for courtship.

Father's wealth and properties belong to me. Never again shall a person question my claim, for the laws of England have deemed me the legitimate heir. I can now offer myself as a suitor without hesitation. Would you consider me? Although we are not well acquainted in the traditional sense, I find myself irrevocably devoted to you, so much so I cannot fathom a match with anyone else. To love you is to believe a dream, and what a tremendous risk—to give myself to a hope, an inclination that we were designed for each other.

I implore you to regard my proposal.

Without legal matters to address, my life seems close to normal. I write in my study, go on long walks, and read by the fire. Not much has changed at Cadwallader besides extra chores. I have spent the past few days shearing herds with the estate's farmhands. We must finish the job this week so the wool has time to regrow before colder weather sets in. I also want to start lambing in a few months. Such a process dirties the wool if we fail to gather it prior.

Father would laugh if he saw me labouring in the shed, but I rather enjoy the work. It is honest and useful. The shepherds are decent men, and they treat me well. I wish to toil alongside them, not lord over them. Perhaps I am not a real gentleman after all.

Lorelai plans to leave Cadwallader once she makes travel arrangements. She intends to visit Mr. O'Connor in London despite her parents' concern, for she expects an offer of marriage. She will stay with the Banes Family to avoid impropriety, a precaution which seems laughable.

Arthur's relatives view decorum with the upmost indifference.

Since the court case, Lorelai has seemed in high spirits. She invites the farmhands to picnic with us and hosts dinner parties. When she tires of the house, she ventures to the shed. My foreman taught her to shear ewes. A poor decision. Now all Lorelai wants to do is help with the shearing. Indeed, Mrs. Glas would lynch me if she learned of her daughter's new habit.

Mrs. Dunstable and Lorelai refuse to admit they have formed an alliance, but I am sure of it. Yesterday, when I returned from the pastures, they forced me to bathe in the kitchen yard, claiming my stench would ruin the house. Lorelai brought ice water and soap from the scullery, then laughed as I attempted to wash behind a bedsheet.

I shall miss her company, for the estate seems large and desolate when I am alone. Perhaps I shall travel next year. Edward and Mary Rose invited me to tour with them for the social season, attend parties, stay with affluent connections. I am inclined to accept.

No reply has arrived from 11 Great Pulteney Street. I check the post each afternoon, hoping for news of you. Lorelai tells me not to worry. She believes I shall receive a response despite the social season's end. Oh, how I pray you are the Josephine De Clare in Bath.

Yours ever,

Elias

P.S. I still wait for you.

October 11, 1821

Dearest Josephine,

There's a stack of letters in my desk drawer. It grows a bit higher each month, the papers various sizes, all sealed with red wax and addressed to you. Although no word has arrived from Bath, I cannot help but wonder if sending the letters, reintroducing myself in such a manner after nearly a year apart, is a wise decision. You may have forgotten our meeting or secured an appropriate match.

~~Beyond those concerns, I worry you will not fancy me. I am not a brawny man, nor do I speak how I write. If you recall, I am rather diffident, perhaps even comical at times. Arthur and I got on for that reason. I muck about more than I should. Truly, my pen gives me a bold persona, but I am known for being quiet and sarcastic. I would never dare make these sentiments known if not for what you said that night. Indeed, unrequited emotions best suit me.~~

I cannot sleep, hence my sudden apprehension. Not even a spot of brandy calms me. I crouch on the floor of my chambers, surrounded by papers and books. For hours I worked on my novel, but the story only magnifies this ache—this desperation—within me. I fear you will deign to consider my proposal, but I also cannot stomach the notion of never speaking to you again.

You have haunted my thoughts for months. I think about your wild hair and your ridiculous laugh, how you spoke as though we have been friends since childhood. I still remember the patter of your feet as you grabbed my hands and forced me into a country dance.

~~My life revolved around formalities until I met you. Then, I met you, and my heart was yours. Completely. In a moment. I was yours.~~

Shakespeare mastered the art of romantic declaration, but I am quite poor at it, and no amount of practice seems to mend the inadequacy. Instead of endeavouring to craft an orotund sentiment, I shall state myself with plainness.

Josephine, regardless of my faults, I have one detail in my favour. I love you most ardently. If you accept my offer of courtship, and if we find ourselves inclined to marry, I promise to stand by you all the days of my life, to be your friend—the boy who kept you company that fated night—first and foremost. Upon these words, I swear it.

We met for a reason, one that must extend beyond this lopsided correspondence. Some opportunities present themselves but once, and if not seized, they are lost forever. I cannot miss this chance, so I will post the letters. Yes, I have made up my mind.

A place is only good if we keep good company there. No amount of rain or fog could dim that goodness, for the *good* is not contingent on circumstance, rather on the people who fill it.

I want Cadwallader to be a safe place for us, where we can grow old and be happy. I wish to show you the gorse alcove, take you on walks across the moors.

Even if you refuse my proposal, you are welcome here.

The autumn weather has caused me to develop a cough. I feel ill, another reason for my lack of sleep. Mrs. Dunstable claims my late nights will prolong the illness and prompt listless behaviour. She is likely correct. I should retire.

My novel keeps your memory close, Josephine. I hope you might read it one day. Whenever I sort through its chapters, I am reminded we are on the same page in different books, together in spirit despite our separate lives.

I anticipate a day when our stories collide again.

Yours ever,

Elias

October 13, 1821

Dearest Josephine,

I am most unwell. My body rebels against me, shivering as if cold pierces my skin. I lie near the study's fireplace, wrapped in quilts, for I cannot seem to get warm.

Rain beads on the windowpanes, and a blue haze spools between curtains, brightening the gloom like cream poured into a cup of black tea. I can almost see the cerulean pigment swirling above me. Indeed, to perish from illness while surrounded by books seems fitting, for I am more ink and paper than skin and bones.

I fear this letter may be my last. I cannot stop coughing or shaking. Earlier today Mrs. Dunstable brought me a bowl of white soup. I could not eat it, not even a spoonful. Mother experienced these same symptoms when she contracted winter fever. She struggled to breathe for two weeks until her lungs filled with bile.

I may join Arthur and my parents soon.

Lorelai packed her trunks and hired a coach to take her to London. She departs tomorrow. I do not wish to further postpone her travels, so I fake good health in her company. The charade grows challenging to maintain, for I cannot walk more than a few steps without fatiguing.

She may detect my sorry disposition when she bids farewell. What then? Will she forgo her plans to look after me? No, no. I shall not subject her to further impropriety. Perhaps Mrs. Dunstable will devise an excuse for my poor state.

Already I implored her not to say a word about my illness. I told her about the letters in my desk.

Mrs. Dunstable promised to send them to 11 Great Pulteney Street if I die.

Although no one has confirmed your presence in Bath, I do not wish my letters to go unread. Maybe the Josephine De Clare at that address can help my messages reach you.

You deserve to know my feelings regardless of my end.

I do not wish to go, for I feel close to the life I want. All my hopes and aspirations seem a mere step away. But I may not reach them, and that scares me. After so much loss, I thought my luck would change and I would know what it's like to *have*. To have a home.

To have a moment with you.

Please come to Cadwallader after my death, that is, if the fever does claim me. You shall find a manuscript under my bookcase. It is yours. Do what you like with it.

Until my last breath, I promise my arms will always welcome you. My soul will never grow cold toward you. My safe place, my home, is yours also, and regardless of where you go, who you love, I will adore you endlessly.

Here is to hoping for more breaths.

Elias

Oliver: Good news! My friend located a PDF of Elias's full manuscript. The Hawthorne Family found the book and donated it to Oxford University, who then scanned the pages into a digital copy. Want me to email you the rest of the novel?

Josie: OF COURSE!! I'll clear my schedule so I can read all afternoon.

Oliver: Book club meeting tomorrow? I want to hear your thoughts.

Josie: Six o'clock. Bring Nan and chocolate cake.

Oliver: Twiggy, I can't keep baking for you!

Josie: Why not?

Oliver: Fine. I'll make Elias's favourite soup to stay on theme. Deal?

Josie: You might be the dearest friend I've ever had.

FIFTEEN

THE NOVEL

November wreathed Cadwallader Park in fog so thick the Darlings refused to leave their property. They wore thick garments and sipped elderberry wine as their staff prepared hot baths, bed warmers, and a surplus of lanterns. The days seemed dark, the nights darker.

And yet laughter swept through the house.

Elias and Josephine spent the weeks in a series of fine conversations. No one batted an eye at their togetherness, so they remained side by side, occupied by their own diversions. They played cricket with Sebastian and the valet. They explored the estate, smuggled chocolates from the kitchen, and read in Elias's library until the candles burned low.

Being with Josephine drew Elias into plain view. Her friendship warmed him like a cup of tea, but it never grew cold, nor did it run dry. He craved the sound of her voice, the way she looked at him when he made her smile. To know and love her heart seemed the greatest pursuit, so he woke each morning with that single goal in mind. He finished his lessons.

He rehearsed the spiel intended for his relatives.

Love felt by one could easily go unrequited. However, when that love was returned or even given hope of return, it seemed impossible to stay silent. Elias had sensed affection from Josephine. He knew his feelings were felt by her also, and such unity of heart whispered possibilities that once seemed beyond reach.

Josephine was betrothed to Sebastian. Etiquette interdicted his pursuit of her. Still, if neither she nor Sebastian desired the union, and if Mr. Darling found another lady to fill her position, could not scandal be avoided? Engagements were contractual agreements, but such were voided all the time. And love seemed too paramount to overlook.

The obstacles Elias perceived grew smaller by the day. He no longer fretted about scandal, for he could avoid dishonour by merely speaking to his relatives. He didn't pay mind to matters of his illegitimacy, for his wealth more than compensated. Indeed, everything that had deterred him from declaring his sentiments now dissipated.

Elias would petition Sebastian and Mr. Darling. He would inform Josephine of his attachment. Of course, his efforts could prove futile—he almost expected disaster—but when fear gnawed at his will, courage was the quiet voice saying, "You might fail, but why not try?"

∝

The fog subsided one morning, a mere week before Saint Andrew's Day. Such an opportunity could not be missed, for the murk would undoubtedly return. Everyone gathered in the entrance hall to bid farewell to Sebastian and Widow De Clare, both of whom desired to visit London until mid-December. Mrs. Darling issued commands while the butler and valet hauled trunks out the front door to the awaiting carriage.

Elias stood with the kitchen staff to avoid his relatives' fuss. He leaned against the staircase bannister and made faces at Fitz. The lad appeared bored out of his mind.

"I'll return once I finish business. Do try to have fun without me," Sebastian said. He kissed Josephine's hand, then hurried to say good-bye to his siblings.

"Ah, is that what they're calling it these days?" Anne scoffed and crossed her arms. She met Elias's questioning look with a shrug. "We know very well the gentleman enjoys his follies and vices. I daresay his business includes excessive merriment."

"He should be ashamed of himself, the miserable little sot," Mrs. Capers said. She eyed the adjoining corridor and fidgeted with her apron. Mrs. Darling had insisted she abandon her buttered apple tarts for the departure. At any moment smoke could plume from the stairwell.

"Do you think Miss De Clare knows?" Anne whispered.

Josephine lingered beneath the family crest. She observed the commotion from a distance, her demeanour polite and subdued. Sebastian had gifted her a royal blue redingote and white muslin gown after the hunting incident, perhaps to replace her threadbare dress. She wore the clothes now, her hair pinned at the nape of her neck.

"Yes, I believe she does." Elias clutched a history book to his chest. He'd woken before dawn to finish his lessons so he and Josephine could spend the day outdoors. Nothing cured heartache like fresh air and open spaces, for nature shrank problems to scale.

"And she plans to marry him? Why?" Anne tugged Elias's sleeve to capture his attention. "You're wealthier and more respectable than your cousin. Why doesn't Josephine marry you?"

Elias sighed. "Ask me that question in a few weeks. Perhaps I'll have an answer."

Widow De Clare buttoned her fur-trimmed pelisse. She donned gloves and a feathered bonnet, her dark curls dangling around her face like streamers. "Will you fare well without me, dearest?" she asked her daughter while rummaging through her reticule.

"I'll get on." Josephine glanced at Elias. She flashed a smile, a glimmer at the bottom of a deep pool. In her eyes sparkled weeks of inside jokes, playtime with Kitty and Fitz, and races across the front lawn. She was undimmed. And one look from her swept Elias back to the bonfire, where she'd cupped his face and kissed him as if they were two people with all possibilities in reach. She did not care about his illegitimate birth. She had to love him. What else could explain her desire for no other companionship but his?

"Your aunt wishes me to visit only a fortnight. I shall return before the Christmas ball." Widow De Clare pecked Josephine's cheek, then followed the butler out the front door.

"Take care of your future mother-in-law." Mr. Darling gave Sebastian a firm handshake.

"Yes, yes, I'll ensure she reaches her destination." Sebastian flitted about like a bird anxious to leave his cage. He strode toward Elias, his mouth twitching into a smirk. "I'll see you in a few weeks, old chap. Pray I return with good stories."

"Don't make a fool of yourself," Elias said. "Consider your fiancée—"

"Entertain her, would you? I mean, you've done such a great job. She hasn't bothered me one bit." Sebastian smacked Elias's shoulder and winked. "I owe you a night at the pub."

"Please, no."

"Fine. I owe you a stack of books or a new tailcoat—or buckskins for your next roll down a hill." Sebastian tipped his hat. "Until next time."

Once the carriage set off, Miss Karel led the children to their schoolroom. Mr. and Mrs. Darling headed toward their private sitting chambers, Mrs. Capers dashed to her tarts, and the staff resumed their duties. Within a matter of seconds, the hall emptied, leaving Josephine and Elias alone on the checkered floor.

Elias cleared his throat. "My cousin travels south at least twice a year."

"I'm not daft. I know what Sebastian intends to do in London," Josephine said. Her expression hardened until it resembled stone. "You must wonder—"

"You don't owe me an explanation." Elias clasped his hands behind his back. He stood across from her as if ready for a dance. "It's not my business to make assumptions."

"But you do. We all do." She tiptoed forward, each step clapping her soles against marble. She tilted back her head and gazed at Elias's face, her neck so exposed, he ached to slide his thumb along its ridges. "When my father died, he left us with his debt. Mother and I sold our lands to pay the sum, but it wasn't enough."

"Josephine . . ." Elias squirmed. Her financial circumstance was not his business, at least not yet. He planned to petition Mr. Darling once Sebastian returned. Then he would know for certain whether he and Josephine stood a chance at togetherness.

"The Darlings own my family home," she said. "They acquired it after Father's death."

"What, you'll wed Sebastian for a house?" Elias clenched his fists and scanned the hall's faded paintings. A chill infiltrated his bones. An empty cold that stripped him of Josephine's warmth. No, he couldn't stand idle and let her marry Sebastian to salvage her father's assets.

"I'm destitute. I have my good birth, that is all," Josephine whispered. "If I marry into the family, Mr. Darling will allow Mother to live in the town home that was once my father's."

Elias grabbed her shoulders, his arms shaking. "Let me help. I'll purchase the estate from my uncle. You can have it back—"

"I need more than a house." Her voice cracked, letting the truth shine through. She had agreed to marry Sebastian for the security and station he'd provide. A penniless woman, even one of noble birth, would struggle to find a gentleman husband. And society thumbed its nose at poor spinsters, for those who were alone reminded everyone else of their loneliness.

"What do you require? Tell me, and it's yours." Elias crouched to her level and breathed in her perfume, a spellbinding aroma of rose, bergamot, and pear. He waited for her response. He stared at her mouth, hoping and praying she'd ask him to propose. He could give her wealth and title, return the De Clare home. And she loved him. He was sure of it.

"People like us . . . We cannot afford to be romantic," Josephine said. She touched his wrists and mustered a smile, her pert nose reddening. The silence that followed suggested she knew his intentions. She knew, yet she did not accept them. She gave a nod, perhaps to both commend his efforts and call them pointless.

Elias stepped backward. He blinked to blur the realization, but it did not stand before him, dressed in another man's clothes. No, it stood within his shoes.

He was to blame for his and Josephine's separation.

"The Darlings wish Sebastian to avoid further scandal by settling down," Josephine whispered. "They do not care about my lack of wealth. I have a respectable pedigree, so as far as they're concerned, I am a suitable match. I'm grateful, really. Few gentlemen would deign to marry a woman of little means, for society promotes constant betterment."

A breath jerked Elias's chest. He turned his face so Josephine wouldn't see his pain. Of course she was right. Most families desired their children to rise in station through matrimony.

Lord Welby was one of those families.

"Sebastian will not break our engagement. His parents offered him an increased allowance for marrying me. Isn't that flattering?" Josephine wiped her eyes. "I shall marry him, and you'll find someone who pleases your father. We must do what's expected of us."

Elias shook his head, a mixture of disappointment and grief coursing through him. He had believed the engagement divided him from Josephine, but it was his need to earn Lord Welby's approval. Him. He was the obstacle. And he couldn't rise above himself.

Josephine moved toward the staircase. She paused beneath the chandelier and glanced over her shoulder. "Please do not pity me, Elias. A loveless marriage is far better than poverty."

"But what is living without love?" He loathed himself for asking the question. It seemed flowery and insincere, unlike a man's thoughts.

Josephine held his gaze, her figure slight compared to the grand room. "Love must reside in your safe place—among the gorse—with all other fanciful things I cannot have."

Elias struggled for air. He wanted to change their situation with a few words, but he could not propose without risking his inheritance. And what use would he be to Josephine without funds? Their lives hinged on the purse strings of others. Elias served Lord Welby. Josephine depended on the Darlings. Indeed, they were slaves to the roles given to them, caught between what they wanted and what they had to want.

"Let's not pretend we can reverse our decisions," Josephine said. "I was aware of Sebastian's nature before I accepted the proposal. We attended the same parties, had the same friends. Remember that night you and I met—"

"Of course, Miss De Clare, but I fear mention of it would trifle with feelings I have struggled in vain to repress." Elias bowed and left the room. He'd made peace with the prospect of heartbreak, yet it came for him with a vengeance.

It clawed through his body and made him sick.

He wanted to shove his fist through a wall or abandon Cadwallader Park. He wanted so many things, none of which compared to the girl he could not choose. Still, with all hope resting in his gut as sharp fragments, he knew one thing for certain.

There was no moving on, not from her.

A letter arrived days later. It was addressed to Mr. Darling but contained news involving Elias. According to its contents, Lord Welby had found a potential bride for his heir—a lady from royal stock, destined to inherit an annual sum of nine thousand pounds. She would attend the Darlings' Christmas ball, where Elias would make his intentions known.

Mum: Want to visit your gran for Christmas? She misses you.

Josie: Maybe. I won't get back to London until Christmas Eve, though.

Mum: You haven't seen her since your dad's funeral.

Josie: Why don't I meet you in Nottingham? We can drive to Derby from there.

Mum: Fred wants to spend the holiday in France. I agreed to go with him.

Josie: Who the heck is Fred?

Mum: My boyfriend. I told you about him.

Josie: Oh, I thought his name was Thad. What a relief.

Josie: Wait. You want to send me to Gran's house?! So, you can drink French eggnog with your baby boyfriend?! THAT IS LOW, MUM.

Mum: He's twenty-eight. And stop with the drama. You're a big girl.

Josie: I'll spend Christmas with Norman and Martha. Problem solved.

Lord Welby's command did not invite debate. He desired the match, so it must be. Elias could devote his heart to Josephine, swear to love only her, but he would marry someone else. There was no avoiding it. His responsibilities demanded an advantageous marriage.

Mr. Darling reminded him of these facts. He listed all the reasons why Elias needed to obey Lord Welby and wed for money, status, and whatever else drew the public's attention. Reasons that included the words *bastard* and *scandal*.

Josephine had been right all along. Still, Elias refused to feel less, for moving on from her wasn't an option. He would learn to live without, and perhaps loving from a distance—being Josephine's friend—would make his father's will bearable.

Or perhaps it would ruin him completely.

"Hurry before she catches us." Fitz bolted from Josephine's bedroom. He slid into the hallway and tripped on a carpet runner, slamming his small body against a table. "Dickens!" He rubbed his elbow and grinned, showcasing the gap between his two front teeth. Injury seemed his comrade, proven by the bruise beneath his left eye, his scabbed knees, and dirty fingernails.

"Oh dear, Fitz. Don't say that." Elias stepped out of the chamber and eased its door shut. He plucked a yellow petal off his waistcoat.

"Why not? Our valet says it all the time." Fitz inspected his limbs, perhaps to ensure the accident did not damage his clothes. Mrs. Darling refused to purchase him new outfits, for he soiled and ripped his garments on a regular basis.

"Because he's not a gentleman like you," Elias said.

"I don't want to be a gentleman." Fitz groaned, squirming when Elias grabbed his collar and dragged him down the east wing corridor. Their scheme had occupied the entire morning, which prevented Fitz from building forts with Kitty. He hadn't minded the sacrifice when Elias let him sneak around, but no number of secrets and surprises could surpass the thrill of playtime.

"What do you want to be, then?" Elias glanced over his shoulder. No one had seen them enter or exit Josephine's bedroom, and they'd been careful not to leave a mess. What could ruin the gesture? More importantly, how would Josephine respond to it?

"A pirate." Fitz punched Elias's stomach and sprinted ahead, his feet drumming the floorboards. He screamed when Elias chased after him.

"Get back here, you rascal, or I'll give you to Mrs. Capers," Elias yelled. He dashed past frosted windowpanes and rooms that filled his nose with scents of starch and potpourri.

"Capital! Mrs. Capers gives me sweets." Fitz raced through a gallery toward the manor's west wing. His copper hair danced like flames, and his stomps rattled the house. Despite his and Elias's previous caution, their presence could no longer be unnoticed.

"Hello?" Josephine's voice drifted from the nearby annex.

"Don't squeal." Elias tossed Fitz over his shoulder and ducked into a linen room. He lowered the boy onto a stack of sheets. "Keep quiet. We can't let Josephine find us."

"Because of the surprise?" Fitz scrunched his nose.

"Yes. Don't say a word about it." Elias peered into the passageway, a flutter sweeping through him when Josephine appeared, dressed in a white muslin gown and her mother's shawl.

"Kitty and I built the fort," she yelled.

"I want to play in the fort." Fitz kicked Elias's shin and reached for the door.

"Shush." Elias clamped his hands over the boy's mouth. He watched Josephine approach, his mind flashing to the memory of her in the entrance hall, alone on the checkered floor, like a single dancer on a vast stage. That morning had changed them. Their conversation had altered the very nature of their friendship, and they were forever different.

"Fitz, is that you?" Josephine stopped. Her gaze lingered on the linen room as if she sensed the boys' presence. She would discover them eventually. How could they explain their behaviour without revealing the secret?

"Pretend I'm not here." Elias shoved his cousin into the hallway. Everyone knew about the boy's shenanigans—how he hid in obscure places and frightened the staff. Another scare attempt would raise no suspicions.

"Oh, hello." Josephine gawked at Fitz. "What were you doing in there?"

"We're playing hide-and-go-seek," he said. "I lost."

"Have you found Elias yet?" Josephine eyed the cracked door. She lifted the boy's chin and examined his face. "Were you really playing a game, Fitz?"

"Will you get mad if I lie?"

"I'm right here," Elias said with a groan. He stepped out of the room and clasped his hands together. "All right, then. Let's go see that fort."

Josephine grabbed his arm. "You're up to something."

"Me? Never." He smiled, his cheeks burning. In a few hours, she would enter her chambers and behold his gesture, all his emotions gathered, strung, and displayed like bunting.

"Do not fib, Mr. Welby. Set a good example for your cousin."

"I don't mind," Fitz said. "Besides, *not talking* isn't fibbing."

"Right you are, Fitz. Thank you." Elias winked at Josephine. "I'm *not talking*." He liked to tease her, for she gave theatrical responses—she touched him, she gazed into his eyes as if he were a pool filled with bright things.

"You're cheeky. I do not fancy you at all," Josephine said through a grin. Her fingers slipped off Elias's forearm and fell to her side. A week had passed since Sebastian and Widow De Clare left for London, but Josephine had yet to act like herself. She remained indoors. She declined Elias's invitations.

Elias understood her distance. For days he'd paced his study and wondered if he should leave Cadwallader Park after Christmas. He'd written his father and asked to travel south. But he'd changed his mind. Again. Because he knew he could love Josephine and not end up with her. He could make her happy without fending for his own happiness.

"Oh, really? You dislike my company?" Elias sighed. "Blazes, I was convinced you adored me. How embarrassing." He pocketed his hands and sauntered toward his study while Josephine laughed. Yes, he would pursue his father's approval, and she would marry his cousin. They would live apart, but for this moment, they were together. And a moment seemed enough.

"Run on ahead," Josephine told Fitz. "I put tea and biscuits in the fort."

"I daresay you've won his affections," Elias said once the boy sped down the corridor.

"He would like you, too, if you stopped flinging him around."

"Fitz likes me." Elias scoffed. "He likes to be flung."

Josephine held Elias's gaze, her face beaming. She retreated to his study and leaned against its door frame, then motioned for him to enter the room. "Promise not to have a fit."

"Did you rearrange my furniture, again?" Elias stepped into the chamber and froze, his body cloaked in warmth from the fireplace, the aromas of spiced biscuits and evergreen.

Between the desk and bookcase, Kitty lounged in a fort constructed from blankets and novels. Paper chains drooped from the ceiling. Candles dotted the shelves. No longer did the chamber resemble a library. Josephine had transformed the space into a wonderland.

> **Oliver:** Have you read the next chapter, yet? I need to talk about it.

> **Josie:** I'm reading at work. Nobody has visited the bakery in hours.

> **Oliver:** And the Employee of the Month Award goes to . . .

> **Josie:** Don't judge me. I'm bored. And if I don't read, I eat scones.

> **Oliver:** LOL. What?!

> **Josie:** Yeah, I attack the baked goods when I have nothing to do.

> **Oliver:** Maybe you should—I don't know—mop the floor or something.

> **Josie:** Want me to read or not?

> **Oliver:** Never mind. Keep reading. Where are you in the chapter?

> **Josie:** Josephine found Elias and Fitz in the linen room. They're headed to the study now.

Does Elias confess his love anytime soon? His unrequitedness gives me anxiety.

Oliver: Patience, young grasshopper. (*giant wink*)

Josie: He makes a move? On which page? I'll scroll ahead.

Oliver: DON'T YOU DARE.

"What do you think?" Josephine pranced to the room's centre and twirled. She had volunteered to entertain the Darling children so Miss Karel could spend the day with her suitor. Without the governess's supervision, and with Mr. and Mrs. Darling visiting a neighbour, the children's playtime could refrain from sensibility.

"You're a superb governess," Elias said. He wouldn't forget the sight, for perfect moments were rare, and they never repeated themselves. They came like snowflakes. Soon this moment would melt and his study would grow dim.

"Sit next to me, Elias." Kitty patted an embroidered cushion. She giggled as he ambled toward the fort. "I think Miss De Clare is a pixie."

"Of course. If we ask nicely, maybe she'll fly around for us." Elias crawled beneath the quilted canopy and collapsed onto a pillow.

"Is this our new playroom?" Fitz asked. He sprawled on the velvet settee with biscuits piled on his belly. "I like it better than the nursery."

"No, all this shall disappear at midnight, so we must endeavour to enjoy ourselves." Josephine climbed onto the desk as if it were a stage. "Do you want to hear a story?"

"I don't like stories," Fitz said.

"Nonsense. You just haven't heard the right story." Josephine tossed her shawl to the floor and marched across the desk. "Close your eyes. You too, Elias."

He buried his face in a cushion to make the children laugh.

"What do you see?" Josephine whispered.

"Darkness," Kitty said.

"Use your imagination."

"I see a pirate ship and yellow flowers." Fitz cracked open his eyes and snickered when Elias glared at him.

"Open your eyes. We're now on a pirate ship covered in yellow flowers." Josephine hopped off the desk and retrieved a paper hat from a bookshelf. She perched it upon her head, then yanked Fitz from the settee. "Captain Darling, what is our destination?"

"Uh, we're sailing to Antarctica." He pointed at Elias. "Get off your bum, First Officer Welby. We need to stop the polar bears before they eat the princess."

Josephine cackled—the way she laughed was pure magic. She looked at Elias, and her expression softened. Did she ache the way he ached? Was she overwhelmed with the same happiness and sorrow? Oh, if she felt his chest, she'd know she had bewitched him, for his heart raced in her presence. He could not love by halves. He was hers in full.

"Should we use the polar bear nets, Captain?" Elias scrambled out of the fort and joined the enactment. For hours he played with Josephine and his cousins, participating in sword fights and tea parties. He wore a paper hat. He danced with Kitty. He and Josephine smacked each other with pillows until one burst, snowing goose feathers.

The library once held Elias captive. Now it set him free.

Its darkness gave way to dozens of candles. Its silence became laughter. No more hiding. He was seen.

"You're my horse, Elias," Kitty said. "Get on your hands and knees." She wrapped her arms around his neck and tackled him to the floor.

"Why can't I play the sleeping princess?" He squirmed across the rug until his arms fatigued. "Dismount. This horse needs rest."

"Pirate attack!" Fitz leapt off a chair and pounded Elias with a cushion. It exploded like the others, spraying feathers across the room.

Josephine extended her arms as fluff rained from above. "I'll clean up the mess, First Officer Welby." She sat next to Elias and plucked feathers out of his hair.

"Don't bother. I think the room looks better this way, like a slaughterhouse party." He grinned when she threw a handful of feathers into his face. Indeed, she was his dearest friend too. She knew him. She was downstairs and upstairs, and a whole other world.

He couldn't imagine a day without her.

At half past six, Anne brought dinner to the library and created a picnic spread. Then, around nine o'clock, the children fell asleep in their fort, nestled between Elias and Josephine. The candles burned low, masking the day's chaos with shadows.

Elias draped his jacket over Fitz and glanced at Josephine, who seemed enthralled with the dying fire. She would find his gift soon. What could he say to preface it? All week he had wanted to speak with her, pretend their conversation in the entrance hall never occurred. Now he sat beside her, and his words seemed lost among the feathers, empty chinaware, and paper hats.

"Let's get them to bed," Josephine whispered. "Carry Fitz, would you?" She woke Kitty and guided her across the study, into the hallway.

"Wake up, lad." Elias lifted Fitz from a mound of pillows, but the boy remained asleep, his body limp like a rag doll. How did a nine-year-old manage to act obnoxious in slumber?

Elias followed Josephine down a dark passageway. He slung Fitz over his shoulder and listened to the house, but it did not creak or groan. It stood still. No one spoke except for the maid and valet, who chatted downstairs, perhaps waiting for Mr. and Mrs. Darling to return.

Once the children were asleep in their respective chambers, Josephine said good night and headed toward her bedroom. Elias watched her move down the hall, his breaths quickening. He tapped his foot when she entered the boudoir. He rubbed his temples as time passed. Did his surprise offend her? Was it so insignificant she thought it did not merit a response?

Seldom did people express their hearts, for sincere love was the indelicate sort. Elias had forgone propriety to convey his fondness and in doing so made himself vulnerable. What a tragic error. He should've concealed his emotions until they no longer bore weight.

Josephine rushed from her bedroom. She froze in the hallway and stared at Elias as if she saw him for the first time. Her chest rose and fell, and tears spilled down her cheeks.

Elias nodded, his bottom lip quivering. He had spent the past two nights in the larder, stringing gorse blossoms onto thread. He'd smuggled the garlands into Josephine's bedroom and hung them from the ceiling, furniture, across windowpanes. The gesture seemed minor, perhaps childish, but Elias wanted her to know his arms would always welcome her. His soul would never grow cold toward her. His safe place—his home—was hers also, and regardless of where she went, who she loved, he would adore her, endlessly.

She was the joy he chose.

The gloom pulled them closer until they stood face-to-face, barely apart. Elias tilted forward and pressed his forehead against hers. He combed his fingers across her hand.

"I can't." Josephine placed her palms on his chest to keep him at a distance. She looked up, her gaze lingering on his mouth. Nothing could happen between them. Elias wouldn't risk her honour. He wanted to kiss her, but if he kissed her once, he'd kiss her again, over and over, until he forgot how to stop.

Josephine clutched her mouth. She cried as they lingered in the glow from her bedroom, each sob a confession. Elias rested his chin against her hairline. His body hurt, but to know his feelings were returned eased the anguish of being divided from her.

"Good night, Miss De Clare." Elias cupped her hands and kissed them. He stepped backward, his vision blurring with tears. The gorse was his vow. He would stand next to Sebastian at the wedding altar. He would visit Josephine at holidays, play with her children, pretend what happened tonight, in the darkness, was nothing more than an old reverie.

She was the breath in his lungs. He drew her close. Then he let her go.

Josie: That was heartbreaking!! :(

Oliver: Oops. I must've read ahead.

Josie: How far ahead?

Oliver: I stopped after the ball scene. Keep reading! You'll thank me later.

Josie: Is it worth staying at the bakery an extra hour?

Oliver: YES. Don't eat any more scones, though. I'm making soup for our club meeting.

SIXTEEN

THE NOVEL

Sebastian and Widow De Clare returned from London a week before the Darlings' holiday ball, a tradition anticipated by local and exotic gentry. They bestowed the finest wares. Sebastian gifted his mother a straw hat covered in silk and taffeta, his father a box of cigars. He gave Kitty and Josephine embroidered shawls, Elias and Fitz buckskin breeches. Widow De Clare also supplied presents but ordered their recipients not to open them until Christmas Day.

With preparations for the ball underway, Cadwallader Park regained its intrigue. Mrs. Darling bought wreaths and garlands, crates full of candlesticks. She issued commands until her voice went hoarse. Such behaviour merited empathy, for all women understood the benefits of hospitality, especially when extended to titled persons. And what better way to establish amiable connections than to offer merriment and all its follies?

Invitations were sent by messenger. Menus were decided,

much to Mrs. Capers's displeasure. She and Anne laboured in the kitchen from sunrise to sunset, preparing turducken seasoned with sausage meat, pike stuffed with pudding, and dishes of equal complexity. Of course, baked goods were also needed for the party. Elias helped Anne make scones garnished with apricot jam, a surplus of lavender shortbreads, and Mrs. Darling's favourite stollen cake.

For guests' amusement, the Darlings further abandoned their humble lifestyle. They hired a full staff, along with performers and musicians. However, their loose purse strings could not augment the event's appeal, for the traditional extravagance already drew the upper class thither.

Lord and Lady Welby arrived at the estate two days before the ball. Upon their advent, Lady Welby complained of a migraine and retired to her chamber. Lord Welby occupied himself with hunting while the household fretted over table settings.

People arrived. Hours passed. Work consumed all time for sentimentality. Elias welcomed the distractions. If not for his checklist, he might've taken offense at his father's lack of greeting or spent hours mulling over that night in the hallway when he had admitted his feelings to Josephine. Nowadays he passed her in the same hallway as a stranger. He muttered polite nothings at dinner and exchanged meaningless glances during afternoon tea.

Boundaries protected them, or so Elias told himself. He needed to finish his lessons and think about his future, not pine for a girl engaged to his cousin.

Their separation wouldn't last forever. He and Josephine had agreed to resume their friendship once emotions dulled. Still, doing the right thing made him feel wrong.

With Christmas Eve came flurries and opulence. Partiers

arrived after nightfall, their presence accompanied by the squeal of string instruments and Mrs. Darling's last-minute alterations. Everyone put on their best behaviour, that is, the best one might expect.

∞

"Attractive women at every turn. Oh, how I envy you," Sebastian said. He promenaded through the garden, beholding his guests, ladies clothed in the finest muslin and satin, adorned with fur stoles, feather plumes, and ropes of pearls.

"Me?" Elias smirked. He followed Sebastian down a gravel path lined with torches, his nose tingling with scents of roasted nuts and cider.

As expected, the Darlings had transformed Cadwallader Park into a pleasure garden. Full-length mirrors glistened between topiaries, offering lavish reflections. Vendors scattered the grounds and served treats while performers juggled, twirled fire, and contorted their bodies into knots. Indeed, the event resembled a circus more than a ball.

"Why, yes. You may have your pick of them. I, of course, am no longer an eligible bachelor. My heart belongs to Miss De Clare," Sebastian said with a sigh. He paused in front of a looking glass to retie his cravat.

"You changed your mind about her?" Elias clenched his fists as snowflakes drifted from the heavens and dusted his tailcoat.

"London enlightened me, dear cousin. What an education. I have abandoned my childish ways for good." Sebastian chuckled, his eyes squinting to imply mischief. "The city taught me an important lesson, that we are never without options. Even what's expected of us comes with . . . customization." He finished adjusting his necktie. "I assure you I'm quite altered."

"Good. I'm glad to hear it." Elias mustered a smile and clasped his arms behind his back. He shivered as they explored the maze of mirrors, his chest aching with a pain so acute he struggled to remain upright. What had caused Sebastian's new-found affection?

More so, what had taken place in London?

Elias halted when they passed a gilded mirror. His reflection stared back at him, stoic and startling with pale skin and a furrowed brow. He had trimmed his hair for the ball, leaving the dark curls to rest evenly against his forehead. The cut seemed a poor decision, for it made his features more pronounced. His jaw curved with sharp, chiselled edges. His body appeared long and angular in the fitted clothes Sebastian had given him.

The man in the glass didn't match Lord Welby. He was new.

"You may benefit from befriending a smile, Elias. Women dislike sour-faced chaps." Sebastian grinned and waltzed toward the main house, his breaths curling upward like smoke.

Elias straightened his jacket and moved through the whirl of snow. He stomped his boots against the icy gravel, each step relieving some of the pressure within him. He didn't want to admit his ill will toward Sebastian, nor did he want to imagine Josephine with another man. But the feelings and thoughts poisoned him.

It all seemed odd—Sebastian's confession, his sudden change of heart. Whatever had occurred in London gave him a plan. He intended to do something that involved Josephine.

Of what nature, Elias couldn't be sure.

Shrubbery grew scarce as the path snaked out of the topiary maze into a garden dotted with stalls and performers. Elias quickened his step. He joined the river of guests as they floated between flower beds, their forms hidden beneath wool cloaks and hooded capes.

The cold seemed different tonight, almost hospitable. It did not pierce Elias's clothes or burn his skin. It transformed Cadwallader Park into a frozen oasis. Icicles dangled from rosebushes. Torchlight shimmered across the thin layer of snow while steam plumed from vendors' cauldrons, rich with the smell of cocoa.

Elias smiled. He should fetch a cup of hot chocolate for Josephine. She fancied the drink with cream and cinnamon, made thick enough to leave a milky moustache on her upper lip.

He stopped dead in his tracks.

Josephine stood beneath a frosted arbour a few yards to his left, surrounded by aristocrats. She borrowed three balls from an entertainer and cradled them in her gloved hands. Then she tossed the objects, fumbling to juggle them. One by one, the balls landed in the snow. Her audience cheered. She curtsied, laughing so hard her eyes squinted.

A lump clogged Elias's throat. He watched Josephine catch snowflakes with her tongue. He remained a static onlooker as she captivated people with her antics. He didn't want to spend his life *here* when she stood *there*. He belonged at her side. He belonged with her.

Fire billowed from a performer's mouth, the flames sizzling as they collided with the air. Elias flinched. He glanced at Josephine, his stomach lurching when she met his gaze. Her expression softened. She gave a half smile and waved.

Their lives would continue like this, parallel, never intersecting. Josephine would become Mrs. Sebastian Darling. Elias would assume his father's title. They could smile and wave as if not destined for heartbreak, but nothing would ever be the same, nor would it be what they wanted. Elias understood. He needed to sunder from her.

Better to hurt now than suffer later.

Josephine followed a group of girls to the hot-chocolate stall. She wore her bumblebee dress and a green cape, her curls pinned up with golden clips. She laughed again, and he recognized her laughter was medicine, but it was also rebellion. It broke down barriers.

It made the worst pains bearable.

Elias resumed his trek to the manor. He climbed onto a terrace and entered the ballroom through a set of patio doors, his neck prickling with sweat as warmth greeted his cool skin.

Guests filled the chamber, pressed shoulder to shoulder. They danced across the mosaic floor and congregated near the orchestra, all glittering and gleaming like firelight on snow. Elias squeezed past them. He savoured aromas of spiced wine and perfume, the earthy musk of evergreen. Indeed, the ball was unlike any party he'd experienced.

The air itself seemed tinted rose and champagne.

"Mr. Welby," Anne murmured from the dining room's threshold. She held a platter of mincemeat pies, her new uniform starched and pressed. The butler had agreed to let her bring dishes from the kitchen because the footmen were needed to serve drinks. Such inclusion seemed a great honour, for her scullery-maid duties confined her to the servants' quarters.

"Save me a pie," Elias said with a wink. He made his way to the dance floor. Until tonight, he hadn't noticed the ballroom's ceiling. It arched into a dome, its mural depicting a gateway to heaven with cherubs painted blush and gold, all nestled among lavender clouds.

Mrs. Darling had decorated the space below with candelabras, silk paper bunting, and wreaths made from holly and laurel. Garlands entwined bannisters and hung from doorways, along with mistletoe, which the maids and young ladies avoided.

Lord Welby emerged from the sea of faces and greeted Elias with a quick nod. "Our relatives take pride in their hosting, do they not?" His countenance remained inscrutable.

"Indeed," Elias said as he observed extravagance in a stupor. His ears purred with a cello's thrum, the whoosh of skirts against marble. He scanned the crowd and spotted Sebastian near the orchestra, conversing with Mrs. Darling and Widow De Clare.

"You've matured into quite the distinguished gentleman, Son. Your uncle finds you well suited for your title." Lord Welby lifted his chin, the muscles around his mouth tensing. He resembled a monarch with his silvering chops and the pendants fastened to his tailcoat.

"I'm obliged to him." Elias flinched when his father gestured to a dancer, a girl with mousy hair and mature features. He'd nearly forgotten about the prospective bride.

"Have you made yourself known to Miss Wood? I daresay she's a fine match for you," Lord Welby said. "She comes from royal blood, and she's set to inherit a substantial fortune. Together you would make the Welby Family a pillar of high society."

"Not yet," Elias admitted. He hadn't given the girl much thought until this moment. His mind had occupied itself elsewhere, perhaps juggling balls or drinking hot chocolate.

"Ask her to dance with you. I insist."

"I've grown attached to someone." The words breezed from Elias before he could cage them. They whooshed like skirts and thrummed like cellos. They clung to the air like evergreen.

Lord Welby cocked his head. "Really? Is her family established?"

"Very much so." Elias drew a breath. He knew his father would disapprove of Josephine, yet a small part of him wondered if he was incorrect. "However, the lady is betrothed."

"Betrothed? Ha!" Lord Welby leaned forward, his breath warming Elias's cheek. "You cannot afford to taint yourself with ill repute. Such behaviour may suit your cousin, but you are not afforded the luxury of misconduct. Already your position in this world threatens to unravel. I hold you together with my title and promise of inheritance. Without me, however, you are nothing to society but a rich man's bastard. Look around. I wish to protect you from these ravenous dogs. If you heed my advice, I'll make someone of you—"

"What if she were not betrothed? Would you consider her then?" Elias dabbed sweat from his brow, a sharp pain rippling through his abdomen. He didn't want to marry someone for the sake of title. Indeed, his father had warned him not to marry a woman out of convenience.

"Make yourself known to Miss Wood. If you find her disagreeable, then I permit you to search for a wife of equal grade. She must come from a notable family and be without scandal."

"Do you require her to possess a certain sum?"

Lord Welby didn't appear to hear the question. He gave Elias's shoulder a hard pat and stepped toward the patio. "Return to Windermere Hall in the spring. I have work for you to do."

Faith: Would you knit a set of doilies for me?

Josie: I'm not senior enough to attempt a doily. May I interest you in a dishrag or partial sock? You could pretend it's a doily, hide it under a plant.

Faith: Ooh, enticing. What is a partial sock?

Josie: Something that resembles a sock but cannot be worn.

Faith: Like a mangled quilt square?

Josie: Hmm, maybe. Think of a dream catcher.

Faith: You better keep it, then. Maybe it'll catch Elias. LOL

Josie: I'm sorry, Faith.

Faith: Yeah, me too. I shouldn't have ghosted you. That was petty.

Josie: I deserved it.

Faith: Any news about dear Mr. Roch?

Josie: Oliver's friend located Elias's full manuscript. Would you like to read a sample? I have a PDF of the last few chapters.

Faith: Sure! I'd love to see what all the fuss is about.

Josie: I'll email it to you!

"After my cousin's wedding," Elias said with a nod. Lord Welby disappeared into the multitude and Elias stepped closer to the dance floor.

Tension festered within him like an embedded splinter. He watched Sebastian and Mrs. Darling join the dance lineup, his senses numbing to the party's splendour. Music grew dense and indistinct within his ears. The aromas made his stomach churn.

He loathed something, perhaps a lot of things. He disliked his own temperament. He resented Lord Welby for not caring about him as a father should. He despised his need for connections and reputation, the pettiest of necessities. What did he expect to happen once he completed his rise to lordship? People would still see him as the bastard.

Society preferred disappointment, for complaints led to exceptional conversation. Mrs. Capers had said it best, that no topic sparked discussion like general displeasure, for speaking of sunshine seemed dull when life offered so much rain.

Elias tugged his cravat, the air thin in his lungs. What if Lord Welby did accept Josephine? The man's criteria had included respectable family and repute, both of which Josephine possessed. Of course, Elias would need to persuade the Darlings to void the engagement, which presented risks to his reputation.

Most people did not think highly of men who stole their cousin's fiancée.

Regardless, Elias couldn't let decorum prevent him from taking his one chance. He would have to marry someone eventually. His father expected it. And who could replace Josephine? No lady bore even the slightest resemblance to her, not in manners nor disposition.

She was the only girl in the world.

"Move, Elias!" Kitty and Fitz sprinted toward the dining room with Miss Karel in pursuit. They shoved through the crowd, passing in a whirlwind of limbs.

"Slow down," Elias yelled. He sighed and shook his head. All evening the children had played blind man's bluff, except they'd forgotten to use a blindfold. Their game consisted of stampedes through the house and their unfortunate governess endeavouring to catch them.

If they weren't careful, Miss Karel would one day drop dead from exhaustion.

With a violin's sharp trill, the song concluded. Dancers bowed and curtsied, prompting an exchange of participants. Guests hurried onto the dance floor to claim their places. They formed two lines, men in one, ladies in the other.

Elias stood his ground as women gathered around the floor. They giggled, their smiles begging for partners. He should ask Miss Wood to dance. Perhaps a quick trip around the dance floor would please Lord Welby and make Elias appear less taciturn.

Josephine, now without her cape, stepped through the patio doors with her friends. She dusted flurries off her skirt and beelined to the dining room. Her ruby gown shimmered in the chandelier's glow. Her curls drooped from their pins, framing her face with snow-caked strands.

Elias's mind went blank. He moved toward her, crossing the dance floor as if in a trance. His heartbeat grew louder, stronger, until he felt it in the tips of his toes.

Lord Welby wanted him to find a suitable wife, but there was no one more suited to him than Josephine. Everything he wasn't, she was, as if they were created together but pulled apart.

He couldn't stay away.

"Miss De Clare . . ." Elias nodded to her companions, whom he recognized from the bonfire masquerade. "Pardon my intrusion."

"Yes?" Josephine turned, her smile vanishing. She gazed at him with a panicked look in her eyes.

"May I have the next dance?" Elias asked. His voice wavered as though to warn him. Such a request threatened to circulate his attachment, for if Lord Welby beheld Elias and Josephine together, would he not form a realization?

'Twas a great danger for Elias to break his sworn distance with Josephine, especially before discussing matters of engagement with the Darlings. A dance could very well smother the impossible hope still burning within him.

But the world grew from impossible things.

Josephine let out a breath. "You may."

Elias bowed and returned to the dance floor. Within minutes, he stood across from her, positioned in a line of gentlemen. Sweat painted lines down his temples as guests observed from the side-lines, batting the sultry air with fans, whispering into each other's ears. They seemed intrigued by yet another country dance, all except for Sebastian. He remained near the orchestra, now amusing a young woman with peacock feathers in her hair.

Josephine curtsied as music flooded the ballroom. She turned and extended her arm. Elias placed his hand beneath hers, the silk of her glove caressing his knuckles. He took four steps forward, three steps back, then pivoted to face her.

"Are you altogether pleased with the ball?" he asked as they wove around each other like plaited dough, moving back and forth, spinning until the room blurred.

"Quite." She lifted her chin, refusing to meet his gaze. "Why did you seek my company? I'm certain other ladies would have appreciated your invitation."

"I would've been remiss not to offer myself as a partner," Elias said when they formed a circle with other dancers. "Your fiancé seems otherwise engaged."

"He enjoys meeting new people." Josephine sashayed a few beats. She locked hands with Elias, the music guiding them into a standoff of silence and touches. Her formality struck him like ice water. It sent a shiver up his spine. It chilled him to the bone.

Never had she treated him as a mere acquaintance. Despite his reserve, she'd always greeted him with warmth. He adored that warmth, how she had raced into his study with the scent of outdoors on her clothes, the way she arranged his furniture so she could read upside down near the window. Their relationship had bloomed like a seedling beneath the sun.

"We must keep to our agreement," Josephine said when the music reached a crescendo. She twirled back to her place in line, her expression hardening.

Elias winced. Keep to their agreement? No, he didn't want to stay apart, hold his tongue, choose Lord Welby's prudence in place of his own will. He loved Josephine more than he believed possible, and that love compelled him forward. How could he turn a blind eye to Sebastian's misdeeds? More so, how could he justify not pursuing the girl before him when a solution lingered in reach? The betrothal didn't sunder them. Lord Welby seemed keen to accept a lady of good standing. In truth, there seemed but a conversation dividing Elias from Josephine.

He could alter their fates. Yes, Lord Welby may disapprove, the Darlings might express outrage, but Elias felt less inclined to care. He no longer desired to emulate his father, not when so much hinged on this choice. And he chose Josephine.

Until the stars dimmed to black, he would choose her.

Without saying a word, Elias left the dance floor and walked to the patio doors, hoping his sudden exit would prompt Josephine to follow him. He abandoned the room's champagne glow, all heat dissipating from his clothes the instant he stepped onto the ice-glossed terrace.

"I can bear this no longer," Elias said when Josephine emerged from the house. He trembled, not from the wind and snow, but a feeling so rich it stole the air from his lungs.

Josephine stared at him. Puffs of white released from the gap between her lips. Flurries kissed her bare neck, melting into droplets that shimmered on her skin like diamonds.

"For years I thought my life would get better once I made something of myself. I stood in grand rooms like that one. I went to the best school, obeyed my father's commands, all without considering what I wanted. Being a bastard . . . It seemed to drown out everything else until that's all I was—the unwanted son who had to prove his worth." Elias clenched his jaw and shuffled his feet against the ice. "Blazes, I was forced to leave my home, and I didn't shed a tear or complain. Nothing. And you know why? Because it wasn't my home. I never had a real home or family or anything until I came here, until I met you. *You.*" His voice cracked, waning into jagged gasps and the gentle patter of snow. "Don't marry Sebastian."

"Elias—"

"No, hear me out." He crossed the space between them and leaned forward until her cocoa-scented breath whirled across his face. "I don't want you. I love you, and that love surpasses all want in such a way I could never have you and still feel at peace. I could throw rice at your wedding, hold your firstborn, watch you live without me . . . and I'd handle it all perfectly well because love—this tether binding me to you—would endure."

Josephine looked up, her eyes glistening with tears.

"But I'd rather not do those things," Elias whispered. He cupped her cheeks, anchoring his forefingers behind her ears. "Don't marry Sebastian."

The words coursed with ease as if they'd been inside him all along. He should've spoken them months ago, before that moment in the hallway, before each attempt to distance himself.

"How dare you burden me with this," Josephine wheezed. She grabbed his wrist and dragged him into the shadows, away from the ballroom. "Do you expect me to break my promise to Sebastian and his family? I gave my word—"

"You're a pawn to them," Elias said. "They don't care about you."

A sob grated in the back of her throat. She tensed, her lips pursing. "Do not pretend you're any different. If someone else had kissed you at that party, you—"

"What? You think me so easily won by a kiss?"

Josephine crossed her arms. She gazed at the sprawl of hills and gardens, her eyelids drooping from exhaustion. Was she enraged by his confession or that he'd waited until now to give it? Did she feel the same about him?

"You must know," he whispered. "What I feel for you isn't founded on a kiss. I'm certain, because I spent weeks thinking about what might've happened if it hadn't been us that night. I debated and contemplated, but then I looked at you and all logic melted away. It wasn't the kiss that changed me. It was you, Josephine, when you became my friend."

Elias sagged against the manor's stone exterior. He shivered.

A new cold with teeth seemed to infuse the air. It chewed through his tailcoat, stung his nostrils, and nipped at his skin. It filled his mouth with a bitter taste.

The landscape appeared menacing from where he stood. Winter smudged the estate into a chalky smear. Gentlefolk prowled the maze of mirrors, their merriment echoing like parish bells. But where the torchlight ended, a savage darkness began, coating the moors with a gloom blacker than tar. If someone ventured beyond the fire's glow, they might not find their way back.

Josephine sighed when a dull melody vibrated from the house. She turned to face Elias, her expression begging him not to quarrel with her anymore.

"I'm sorry for waiting until now," he said.

"You're sorry?"

"Please, Josephine—"

"No. No, you can't say all this and expect me to . . . I don't even know what you want from me. We spent weeks together. You could've told me about your feelings a long time ago, but you didn't. You let me go on pretending that I didn't loathe Sebastian, that I'd happily become Mrs. Darling, when all I wanted—and *despised* myself for wanting—was you. But you were my friend. I understood you couldn't marry me. I accepted our situation—"

"Josephine." Elias launched off the wall. He grabbed her shoulders and drew her close, his arms shaking. "I'm sorry. I am."

She opened her mouth to speak but stopped when guests emerged from the ballroom, all laughing at high volume. Elias motioned for her to follow him beneath a pergola of ivy and icicles. They hurried into thicker shadows, where ribbons of torchlight sliced through foliage.

Josephine leaned against a lattice and watched Elias pace. "Do you mean it?" she whispered, her bottom lip quivering. "You love me, then?"

He nodded. "I love you, then."

"And you want to marry me?"

"Yes." Elias walked forward until their shoes touched. He propped his forearm on the lattice, curving over Josephine, close enough to feel the heat radiating from her body. "When I look back at my life, all the good moments . . . you're in every one of them. And I'd rather face a thousand bad moments with you than experience one good with anyone else."

"What about your father? He won't accept me—"

"I think he might."

Josephine sniffled and reached for Elias's hand. She laced their fingers, her grip tight as though she feared he'd leave. "Time doesn't work in our favour, does it?"

"No, time understood what it was doing," Elias said. The hoping, the longing, every twinge of heartbreak had changed him for the better. It had brought him and Josephine to this moment despite the odds. That's how he knew . . .

They would be together at the end.

"You haven't asked me." Josephine drew a breath and held it captive. She tilted back her head, the pergola's shadows like a mask on her face.

"Should I ask you?"

"What would happen if you did?"

He smiled, his heart racing out of control. "If I asked and you said yes, I'd talk to Sebastian and beg for his blessing. I would explain our situation to my aunt and uncle. Then, regardless of what followed, I would marry you."

A weight lifted from Elias's chest. Until now he had focused on practicality, whether his decisions would lead to wealth and acceptance. He needed Lord Welby's approval but not if it cost him a life with Josephine. Yes, he would marry her, for any other fate seemed cursed. Regardless, he would stand by her side.

"I'm not accustomed to this," Josephine said with a gasp.

"To what?"

"Feeling happy." She wiped the sides of her eyes, her smile growing. "Go on. Ask me."

"You'll have to end your betrothal to my cousin."

"Gracious. What a dilemma." She laughed hard—Elias's favourite laugh. Her eyes squinted. Her nose scrunched above the grandest smile. "Mum will throw a fit."

Elias pressed his forehead against hers, his vision hot and blurring. "Josephine De Clare, I promise my arms will always welcome you. My soul will never grow cold toward you. My safe place—my home—is yours also, and regardless of where you go, who you love, I will adore you endlessly. I was yours before I even knew your name." He lowered to one knee and gazed up at her. "Please do me the great honour of accepting my hand."

Josephine laughed and cried and nodded. "Yes."

His mouth crashed into hers like a wave greeting the shore. He kissed her over and over, and she kissed him. Her fingers combed across his scalp, resting at the base of his hairline. They were no longer two kids dancing around a bonfire, swapping books, or building forts in his study. They were more, everything, a culmination of all time spent waiting.

Her kiss tasted like . . . *finally.*

SEVENTEEN

JOSIE

From: Josie De Clare <JDeClare@mailbox.com>
Sent: Thursday, August 17, 1:28 PM
To: Faith Moretti <Kardashian_4Life@mailbox.com>
Subject: Being Honest with You

Faith, no amount of chocolate and Earl Grey can fix me. I know because I ate a whole bag of mini candy bars and guzzled enough tea to worry an alcoholic. Whenever I look at Elias's letters, his unfinished manuscript, I think about how I'm here and he's there.

I'm lonely for him. I'm lonely because I know who I'm missing.

Try to understand—you look for the right person in coffee shops, at parties. You start thinking no one could understand you, and you should just settle for second best to avoid being alone. Then you find someone who changes everything, someone who fits you like a puzzle piece, and you want that person more than you ever believed possible. But you can't have that person. No, that person moves on like a ship passing in the night, and you're on the shoreline, out of reach. You must watch that person live without you, and all you can do is wave as they cruise toward a better horizon. Can't you relate with that? Sure, you don't love a guy who lived two hundred years ago, but you know how it feels to love and lose.

Yes, I admit it. I'm falling for Elias.

Cadwallader Manor breathes his name with every creak and groan. I eat breakfast alone, and he's at the table with me. I dance to music in the gallery, and my heart flutters because, for a moment, as I spin, I get the sense he's holding me.

I must reach him. He seems close, like he's standing just out of view. I wander the house as if I expect to find him, as if each draft that whispers down the halls could lead me into his arms. I visit his alcove and lie among the gorse. I sleep with his letters on my nightstand.

Time appears to lead us apart, but what if it's a stitch pulling us together? I understand my theory goes against science and reason. I tell my heart not to grow too fond of someone who doesn't exist. And yet I'm attached.

Elias wanted me to visit Cadwallader and find his manuscript. He knew this would happen somehow, and I have a gut feeling that if I figure out what happened to him, something will click like gears in a vault, and we'll reach each other.

Our stories must collide in the end. That's what he said.

Faith, you wish to find your place in this world, but I just want to grip hold of it. My future seems a dark abyss. But here, in this house, I feel my heart knitting itself back together. I have something good for the first time in a long time, and I need to keep it. I want to be Elias's Josephine because she makes sense to me. His story makes sense. Maybe I'm pathetic for needing to be the girl he loved. Maybe I am detached and all that stuff you said.

This is me being honest with you.

No one else knows about my love for Elias. Oliver and I discuss the book and letters, but he thinks it's all a fun mystery, not some fated encounter. I behave as though my life doesn't hinge on whether a dead author wrote about me. I act normal on the outside—go to work and knitting club, de-wallpaper the servants' quarters on the weekends—but I'm messed up inside.

Mum decided to spend the Christmas holiday in France without me. She doesn't care whether I return to London, so maybe I'll stay in Atteberry. Of course I want to attend uni and become a schoolteacher, but I'm tired of feeling dark.

Here books always leave a light on.

Please read the chapters I sent you. You don't have to support my theories, but maybe you'll understand why I feel this way. Oliver and I are still waiting to hear back from his friend. We requested information about Elias from the University of Edinburgh.

Josie

P.S. I visited the knitting club again. Stuart and Margery spent the whole hour debating how to best cook turnips. Lucille quizzed me about my love life. Really, I'm surprised I managed to knit twelve rows of my scarf. Everyone seemed to prefer chatting over crafting.

Faith: You were right. It's you. He wrote about you.

Josie: Uh, okay. Care to expound on that?

Faith: I read the whole PDF, and I'm convinced now. You don't understand. You will once you finish the book. It's just . . . He knew how you like your hot cocoa. He knew the way you act when you're sad. He knew the things I know about you, the things I love about you, and I AM FREAKING OUT because he shouldn't have known what I know.

From: Josie De Clare <JDeClare@mailbox.com>
Sent: Monday, August 21, 8:57 AM
To: Faith Moretti <Kardashian_4Life@mailbox.com>
Subject: Re: Being Honest with You

Faith, what changed your mind? You said I'll understand once I finish Elias's book. I'm afraid to finish it, though. There's an emptiness within me. My heart knows what it wants and my mind knows I can't have it, but I keep looking for it anyway.

I'll forever be without a piece of myself.

Cadwallader Manor proves time isn't divided into past and present, rather here and there. I'm here. Elias is there. We're separated by years and paper, a barrier thin like spider web. I try to break through that barrier by dreaming about him. I go to bed early, drink apple juice, and read his letters before I turn off the lights. I repeat his name in my head until I fall asleep.

He hasn't returned.

This house seems otherworldly when I'm alone. I like its shadows more and more, maybe because they're not just around me. They're inside me.

Sometimes I sit in the upstairs hallway late at night. I close my eyes and listen to wind hiss down chimneys, the moan of aged wood. Perhaps I do it so Elias may find me. His presence fills these rooms like air. I can't see him, but I know he's here.

I look for him in places he could never be.

My thoughts have split, divided between Elias's world and mine. It's as though someone draped the manor's furniture with bedsheets, locked the front door, but trapped me inside. That's how I feel, like a frantic bird stuck within an empty home.

Elias felt that way too. I want him. He's the part of me I always sensed but never understood. Is it possible to love someone before you know them?

Scratch that. Is it possible to love someone after they know you?

Don't worry. I treat our emails like a journal, so I sound crazier than I am. It's just . . . When you know what you want, nothing else seems good enough.

I should launch a biweekly newsletter to keep you informed on all matters Atteberry, Elias, and Cadwallader Manor. You'll get busier once your fall semester begins. I don't want to bug you with emails, and my life doesn't change a lot in fourteen days.

An update every two weeks should suffice, right?

The latest news: I'm an official member of the knitting club. (Lucille gave me a certificate that reads: Josephine De Clare, fellow of the Atteberry Knitting Society.) Aren't you proud? My scarf is near done. I hope to start on a hat soon.

Last week's meeting was quite the event. Stuart and Margery sparked a debate about hair dye, which lasted over an hour. Clare fell asleep, and Dorrit—oh, that sweet, baffling woman— mumbled Scottish nonsense until Lucille ended our session by yelling, "Get out, you nitwits!"

I like them. Our gatherings remind me of family reunions. Stuart is the weird uncle. Margery is the fun aunt. Clare is the beloved grandmother. Dorrit is the distant relative, maybe a cousin. And Lucille—she's the great-aunt who runs family affairs like a business.

At present I sit at Elias's desk with my laptop and breakfast. (I made your favourite—sausage, eggs, beans, and roasted tomatoes.) Nan prowls the manor as if to make sure it's safe. I'll let her outside in a few minutes. Norman and Oliver need her to herd their sheep.

Well, I better sign off. My boss wants me to open the bakery soon.

Please email me!!

Josie

Faith: Hey! I'll respond to your email when I get home.

Josie: No rush. After my shift, Oliver and I plan to drive to the Cheviot Hills.

Faith: Tell me about this Oliver guy. You seem to spend a lot of time with him.

From: Josie De Clare <JDeClare@mailbox.com>
Sent: Tuesday, August 22, 9:40 PM
To: Faith Moretti <Kardashian_4Life@mailbox.com>
Subject: Oliver McLaughlin, aka Firewood Boy

Yes, Oliver and I hang out a lot. Don't get excited, though. We're just friends. He's a ridiculous person. He dances in shopping aisles, and he can't hold a tune. If my life depended on his ability to sing "Twinkle, Twinkle, Little Star," I would certainly die.

Oliver gets emotional about corgis. Really, his voice rises an octave whenever he sees one of those dogs. He sounds like a flute or choir boy addicted to helium. And he loves podcasts, but not the self-help or political kind. He listens to podcasts about espionage and true crime, anything that involves conspiracy theories. (You can't stalk him online. He doesn't have social media, probably because the podcasts freaked him out.)

Unlike me, he's tidy and responsible, a communication expert. I'm not sure how we're friends. He's the most reliable person I've ever met. Ridiculously reliable. Just ridiculous.

He's obnoxious too. He walks around with a half smirk on his face as if the entire world is amusing. And he teases me ALL THE TIME. Ugh, I wouldn't care for him if he didn't balance the teasing with ridiculousness . . . and kindness. He's kind. He keeps my house stocked with firewood, and he brings me lattes when I'm at work.

You'd like him. He's your type—smart, cultured, witty. I would play matchmaker if you weren't dating Noah. At least you have a backup plan. Kidding!

Oliver is brilliant at baking. Just yesterday he made puff pastry filled with cream. He's also close with his family, which makes sense because they're not screwed up like mine. His dad and brother serve in the navy, hence his anchor tattoo. He phones his mum every day. He calls Norman and Martha his best friends.

I enjoy spending time with him, except when he forces me to watch classic movies. He's pretentious about films. I thought Dad was posh about cinema, but his reviews pale in comparison to Oliver's analyses. (Spoiler alert: I don't care about *Citizen Kane*.)

Hope you enjoyed this comprehensive overview of Oliver McLaughlin.

Josie

From: Faith Moretti <Kardashian_4Life@mailbox.com>
Sent: Wednesday, August 23, 11:09 PM
To: Josie De Clare <JDeClare@mailbox.com>
Subject: Re: Being Honest with You

Josie, I finished the chapters. They left me in tears, like, ugly crying. I reread them word for word the next day. That's when I felt it—whatever you've been feeling.

I knew Elias had written about you.

Gah, I'm not sure where to start or if I should tell you what I think. You asked what changed my mind, but I can't answer that question without giving away everything.

You were right about Josephine, so you may be right about other things. Who knows? Maybe Elias's writing will bring you both together. However, until that happens, I recommend you tone back the . . . sitting alone in dark hallways and trying to induce hallucinations. Like, if someone did that for a living, boy, they'd seem nutty as a fruitcake.

I agree with you about the biweekly update. My fall semester begins next week, and I'm already up to my neck in work and relational drama. Oh, did I mention Noah put marriage back on the table? Not a distant table. A *right here* table—one that was

258

set picture-perfect with movie nights and lunch dates. (*sends table to Goodwill*)

What's the matter with me, Josie? Why can't I put my fears aside? Noah wants marriage because he loves me, no strings attached. That's just it—we shouldn't love someone for what they give us, but because they are. We just love.

And if I love him, shouldn't I want marriage too?

Maybe I'm afraid something bad will happen. I don't want to get hurt, and when you love someone, you choose to be hurt by them. You give consent to the pain.

You open your heart and let the break inside.

On a lighter note, your knitting club sounds like my worst nightmare. I went to dozens of family reunions when I was a kid, and they all ended with Uncle Sal drunk-singing Mariah Carey. I'm proud of you for knitting a scarf, though.

Whoa, I didn't notice the time. I need to wake up in six hours.

Good night, Josie. Text me when you learn more about Elias or if he makes a miraculous appearance. And finish reading his novel. It may surprise you.

Don't forget the real people.

Faith

Oliver: May I visit your club this week? I desperately want to meet Dorrit and Lucille.

Josie: My knitting club? Sure, you're welcome to come. Don't sit next to Margery, though. She'll interrogate you until you forget your own name.

Oliver: Challenge accepted. My podcasts have prepared me for this moment.

From: Josie De Clare <JDeClare@mailbox.com>
Sent: Wednesday, September 6, 8:41 PM
To: Faith Moretti <Kardashian_4Life@mailbox.com>
Subject: Re: Oliver McLaughlin, aka Firewood Boy

I think Oliver likes me, Faith.

Last night I went to Norman and Martha's home for dinner. They live in a stone cottage surrounded by garden boxes and pastures. It's a lovely house, the kind that makes you want to wear a soft jumper and drink milk tea. The whole place smells of fresh wood and scones. Ivy clings to the stone exterior. A ribbon of smoke always curls from the chimney.

Martha greeted me at the front door and led me into their sitting room—a low-ceilinged chamber with armchairs and a roaring fire. Norman sat near a bookcase, reading a hardback on World War II. He motioned for me to sit next to him. After a few minutes of hearing his stories about Oliver, I laughed so hard I couldn't breathe.

Oliver leaned out of the kitchen and begged his grandfather to stop. He smiled at me, then returned to his cooking. He made the entire meal—Lancashire hotpot, which consisted of lamb cooked in rich gravy and covered with golden potatoes, followed by a treacle tart for dessert. Blimey, his tart was scrumptious. (It was shortcrust pastry with a lemon-ginger filling.)

We gathered around the dining table like a family. Martha and Norman talked about my father, their children and grandchildren. Oliver mentioned our efforts to collect info on Elias Roch and looked at me with the faintest smile. That's when I knew.

He doesn't see me as *just* a friend.

Ugh, I'm such a fool. I should've noticed the way he grins when I enter a room or how he goes above and beyond to help me. I mean, he brings firewood to my house every morning. I have so much firewood. Stacks and stacks of firewood.

On the weekends, we do renovations or road trips to various castles. We visit the pub once a week. Sometimes Oliver pays the tab.

I've led him on, Faith. What should I do? I don't want to lose his friendship, but I don't view him *that way*. He's nice-looking and perfect by most standards . . .

Just not perfect for me.

Why can't I do one thing right? I'm a mess. A lovesick, emotionally disturbed mess who hurts everyone she touches. Did I tell you about my recent madness? I strung gorse into garlands and draped them from my bedroom ceiling. I took the portrait of me from Elias's studio and hung it downstairs like a self-obsessed heiress.

Oliver cares about me. He attended the last two knitting club meetings, perhaps to show his interest in my affairs. First time, he brought Martha's needles and a steak pie. He charmed everyone with jokes as Clare taught him different stitches and Stuart raved about the food. No wonder Lucille begged him to return. He's like a knitter version of Cary Grant.

To answer one of your questions, nothing is wrong with you. Explain your feelings to Noah. If he doesn't understand, then perhaps you aren't right for each other.

Elias fell in love with Josephine after one meeting. Norman and Martha have stayed married for over forty years despite their differences. I guess love isn't time. It's not past or present, here or there. It doesn't rely on convenience or agreement.

Love—the real kind—outlasts the hard days.

Cadwallader Manor seems restless tonight as if something disturbed it. I sit on the main staircase while Nan snoozes in the foyer and floorboards creak overhead.

OMG. Nan stood up and started barking at the drawing room.

I'm scared.

Josie

(Sent from iPhone)

EIGHTEEN
ELIAS

November 8, 1821

Dearest Josephine,

Winter fever came for me with a vengeance. It drained
the life from my body until I stood at heaven's doorway,
a mere step from Mother and Arthur. Somehow I did not
cross the threshold. I defied medical prognosis and survived.
However, the illness did not depart without repercussions.
It left me weak and short of breath. Even now I struggle to
hold my pen.

Lorelai discovered me unconscious near my study's fireplace. She and Mrs. Dunstable managed to carry me to my
bedchamber despite their slight builds. They sent word to
Atteberry's doctor, who came post-haste. He feared I would

not recover, for my lungs were flooded with bile, and no amount of coughing brought relief.

I spent weeks in a feverish sleep, my respiration so impaired my fingernails turned blue. According to Mrs. Dunstable, Lorelai decided to prolong her stay at Cadwallader Manor until I convalesced. She remained at my bedside. She washed me, gave me water. In truth, I am mortified by her attention, more so that a guest in my house administered such care.

No lady should feel obligated to bathe a gentleman or empty his chamber pot.

Four days ago, I regained total consciousness. My fever broke, and my breaths grew deeper. The doctor said I shall not fully recover for a month or so, but I am fortunate to be alive. Few people who contract winter fever regain their health.

Faith: DID NAN SEE A GHOST?!

> **Josie:** IDK. She bolted into the drawing room and pawed the bookcase.

Faith: Spooky. Did you ask Oliver to come protect you?

> **Josie:** No comment.

Faith: You did?! I thought you wanted to avoid him.

> **Josie:** I just asked him to check the rooms for intruders.

Faith: Did he linger afterward?

> **Josie:** I made him a cup of tea.

Faith: OMG, you are the worst.

Josie: You're telling me! I'm the president of the JOSIE IS AN IDIOT club.

Oliver: Um, did you turn on a light in the study?

Josie: No. Why?

Oliver: I went outside to water the sheep and saw a candle glowing in the study's window. Stay where you are. I'm on my way.

Josie: Elias is coming back.

I must draw this letter to a close, for my hand trembles with fatigue. I cannot sit up for long periods of time. Even the simplest movements exhaust me.

Josephine, the fever played tricks on my mind. I saw you at my bedside and heard your voice. I dreamt of you whenever the illness trapped me within sleep. Once I saw you reading in my alcove. I called your name, but you did not hear me. In that moment I wondered if death would end our separation. I inched closer to that promise of peace.

My agony seemed endless. I shook with chills. I ached and gasped, the pain so intense I experienced it even in slumber. And yet the more I suffered, the more vivid you became. I touched you, felt your cheek against my fingertips.

Truly, I would repeat the illness if it meant I could hold you again.

A letter arrived from Bath. Josephine De Clare no longer

resides at 11 Great Pulteney Street. According to the current resident, Miss De Clare travelled north to her family home in Morpeth. The village is but a half-day's ride from Cadwallader. Once I am well and liberated from this dismal bed, I shall venture there and determine whether Miss De Clare is you.

I pray you're in Morpeth.

Elias

November 20, 1821

Dearest Josephine,

I grow stronger by the day. Although I cannot walk more than a few steps, I sit up and eat on my own. The progress satisfies me, for I loathe constant attention.

Lorelai continues to tend to my needs. This past week she helped me eat, drink, and perform other human functions. The doctor told her such care was unsuitable for a lady. However, she disagreed and continued to nurse me, stating that sensibility, when chosen before the needs of others, resembled impudence. Mrs. Dunstable even offered to relieve her so she might wash, but Lorelai refused. I must credit her—she has more gumption than I believed possible.

Mrs. Dunstable and the maid brought a chaise lounge into my room. Each morning they guide me to the chair so I can lie near the window. Sunlight does wonders. It brightens my mood and keeps the chill away. For hours I bask in its warmth and watch blackbirds swoop across the grey sky. I gaze at frost as it paints small silver branches on the windowpane.

Lorelai reads to me until I doze. Then she needlepoints or watercolours. She prods me awake for afternoon tea and forces at least two scones down my throat, claiming I look gaunt. We share memories of Arthur and discuss literature until dinner.

Nothing could repay her kindness. When I thrashed with fever, she slept on my bedroom floor. She filled a vase with heather and put it on a side table to lift my spirits.

I owe her a great deal.

She cried when I first regained consciousness, then made me promise not to die. Now, before I retire each night, she visits my chambers and refuses to leave until I restate that promise.

Her sister died from consumption at age thirteen, a tragedy which resulted in Lorelai's aptitude for caregiving. She worked as a nurse until the disease caused her sister to waste away. Indeed, life and loss go hand in hand.

The weather seems pleasant from my window. I sit with a quilt tucked around my legs and a pillow nestled against the small of my back. God willing, my strength will return before Christmas. I should like to host a gathering, perhaps invite the Glas and Banes Families.

Lorelai just entered the room with a tea tray. She insists I finish this letter and eat a scone before I—as she lovingly puts it—shrivel into an emaciated raisin.

Yours ever,

Elias

November 26, 1821

Dearest Josephine,

I went outdoors for the first time in ages. Lorelai and Mrs. Dunstable helped me descend the staircase, an endeavour which consumed half an hour. They guided me into the herb garden, to a bench situated among rosemary plants.

My legs shook from the exertion. Since the fever I have walked no farther than a few yards at once. Sweat poured down my face, and a dull beat sounded in my ears. However, the discomfort faded once I submerged myself in the crisp breeze and idyllic quiet.

Winter arrived during my illness. Ice glossed the estate. A dusting of snow coated the ground, making the hills appear as though they were powdered with confection sugar.

Lorelai sat with me while I enjoyed the fresh air. She mentioned her family, no more upstanding than my own. Her brother lives in London with his slew of improper relations. Her parents reside in Dover and prefer social functions to the companionship of their children.

I was not the only child exiled by his father. At seven years old, Lorelai was sent to live with the Banes Family so her parents could travel abroad.

When we are children, we see our parents as moral authorities. We believe them all-knowing and unafraid, perhaps even blameless. But as we get older, we realize our mothers are just girls with babies, and our fathers are boys who do their best.

All children bear the collective weight of their parents' behaviours, their upbringing, every praise and criticism. We are moulded by our circumstances, but we are not our parents' mistakes.

We are not the errors inflicted upon us.

The past few weeks have opened my eyes. All this time I sulked and brooded though joys surrounded me, waiting to be chosen. I overlooked the blessings in my life, for they were not the blessings I desired. I thought myself alone, but I had Lorelai and Mrs. Dunstable.

My existence seemed dreary until I let the light in.

Elias

December 1, 1821

Dearest Josephine,

A coach will arrive tomorrow and take Lorelai to London. She must leave Cadwallader before her presence elicits rumours or alludes to an offer of marriage, which I have not made. Her prolonged presence at my home may encourage gossip or mislead her into thinking I share her affections.

Mrs. Dunstable and I organized a dinner party to bid Lorelai farewell. We asked the cook to prepare a meal of boiled fowl with gooseberry cheese, a repast that we agreed demonstrates a cordial amount of care. Edward and Mary Rose came to dine with us, their company more than amiable.

I moved without assistance, for the doctor has given me a cane, a smart-looking wenge shaft with a burlwood handle. Although my pace belonged to someone triple my age, I walked unaccompanied and greeted the Roses no longer frail and bedridden.

Faith: What the heck? Did you see Elias?

Josie: False alarm. I must've forgotten to blow out a candle.

Faith: Huh? Did you light a candle?

Josie: I don't remember.

Faith: Yikes. That's dangerous . . . and eerie.

Oliver: Pop's Scottish cousins invited us to a ceilidh. Want to come?

Josie: What's a ceilidh?

Oliver: A party with folk music, dancing, and loads of traditional food. You must try haggis and neeps—and cranachan!

Josie: I'm a wretched dancer.

Oliver: No problem. I'll teach you the steps. Pop taught me when I was a wee boy.

Josie: Will you wear a kilt?

Oliver: If that'll persuade you to come. LOL

Lorelai met us in the dining room. She looked rather overdressed compared to our guests' simple attire. Her ensemble included a silk evening gown the colour of dried lavender, its design frothy and fussy with ribbons, frills, and extravagant sleeves.

She elected to sit next to me. I should've noticed her closeness, how she touched my arm with her elbow, the way she laughed when I attempted a joke. In truth, I was too clueless and distracted to recognize her flirtation.

We finished dinner and retired to the drawing room for tea and a game of cards. The Roses left around midnight, after Edward pried a weepy Mary from Lorelai's arms.

Farewell seemed a tiresome affair.

I said good night as Mrs. Dunstable snuffed candles. I climbed the staircase and shuffled toward my bedchamber, the cane adding a third step to my stride.

Lorelai called my name. She crested the staircase and raced toward me, bunching her skirt in one hand. "Ask me to stay," she whispered once she reached my side. "Please ask me to stay." Her chest heaved, and her eyes watered. She gazed at me for what seemed like hours, perhaps anticipating a response I would not give.

A lump clogged my throat. I leaned against the cane and asked why she wanted to extend her visit at Cadwallader. The answer to my question etched her face, but I needed to hear it.

"I love you," Lorelai said with a gasp. "I've loved you a long time." She grabbed my hand and pressed it between hers. She tilted back her head as though desiring a kiss.

The confession rippled through me like a punch. I freed my hand and stumbled back a step. I could muster no decent response, so I remained silent and watched heartbreak shatter Lorelai's expression. Of course, I never forgot that moment at the ball when she expressed interest in a possible union. However, I assumed her attachment had faded due to Arthur's death, her involvement in my pursuit of you, the court case, and illness.

Love? No, no, I did not think her feelings so advanced.

In retrospect, I should have discerned her affections. She had shown love in the smallest and biggest ways. She helped me in times of trouble, stayed at my side through sickness and health. But what about Mr. O'Connor? I believe she expected a marriage offer from him.

"Forgive my imprudence, Mr. Roch. I shan't burden you with another outburst," Lorelai said through clenched teeth. She turned on her heels and retreated down the hall.

She has already piled her luggage in the foyer.

I wish to part with Lorelai on good terms, but I cannot give her what she wants. Indeed, she must understand. She knows I love you, for she has seen the letters and read my book.

No other woman could find the slightest bit of happiness with me, for I have not the ability to halve myself. I am yours, Josephine. My love belongs to you and you alone. Why should I toy with a girl's emotions when I know the truth? I am depleted of romantic offerings, the openness needed to form an attachment. Pretending otherwise seems cruel.

It is right that Lorelai quits this place before I inflict more pain. She will thank me one day, when she's married to a respectable gentleman and well off in society. She will realize her love for me and Cadwallader was foolish at best, for every girl deserves to marry a man who loves her in whole, not pieces. Every girl deserves to be someone's first choice.

You are mine.

Elias

P.S. I plan to visit Morpeth next week.

NINETEEN

THE NOVEL

Josephine smiled at Elias from across the ballroom. She loitered with her friends in a champagne haze, beaming like the candelabras. Her expression seemed a reprise, the repetition of music once mournful, now triumphant. She wouldn't marry Sebastian or spend her life indebted to the Darlings. She'd become Mrs. Welby, Lady of Windermere Hall.

Elias inched toward the dining room, his lips still tingling with Josephine's kiss. He met her gaze with a crooked half smile. Until his final breath, he would remember this night, how mulled wine and evergreens infused the air, how the girl he loved had agreed to marry him.

Dancers performed La Boulangère as Elias squeezed through the intoxicated crowd. He elbowed and shoved, his body urging him to stride across the dance floor and kiss Josephine. His want to kiss her felt like hunger consuming his thoughts. He wanted to draw her close and glide his thumb across her cheek. He wanted to press his mouth against her forehead, the bridge of her nose, the puff of her bottom lip.

His face warmed at the thought. He needed to act normal, pretend as though his life hadn't changed. No one could know about the engagement until he spoke with the Darlings.

After that, Elias could inform Lord Welby of his proposal.

The festivities dragged on for hours. Elias sat with Fitz at the dining table, where the boy nested in a mound of cakes and candies. They built gingerbread houses until candles burned low, music faded, and the last guest stepped into a carriage.

Servants hurried to clean the rooms before dawn painted magenta lines across the horizon. Mrs. Darling prostrated herself on the drawing room settee. Mr. Darling sipped port and wandered the house while Miss Karel lugged an unconscious Fitz up the staircase.

Cadwallader Park seemed dead without its horde of partiers. A dense quiet settled within the manor, conclusive like stage curtains drawn together after a performance. The Darlings praised their staff, then bid good night to their residential guests.

Elias waited until everyone retired to their chambers, and then he sneaked up the servants' stairwell. Josephine met him in the east wing corridor. They squeezed into a niche to avoid being seen.

"You won't change your mind?" Josephine lolled against the moulded wall, her figure a dark silhouette. She grabbed Elias's lapel and pulled him close.

"Not a chance." Elias leaned forward and kissed her slowly as though to memorize her lips. He closed his eyes, a shiver washing through him as her fingers traced the back of his neck.

"I'm not easy to live with," she whispered. "I can be rather messy and scatter-brained. Sometimes I leave chocolate smears on furniture. Mum hates it. Really, I try to clean up after myself but . . . I'm not sure how it happens. The chocolate seems to come from nowhere."

"We'll hire a good maid," Elias said with a laugh.

Josephine perched on her toes and kissed him again. "I love you," she breathed. "I didn't say it earlier, but I do. You're ridiculous—"

"A common misperception."

"Shush." Her smile widened. "Can't you see I'm trying to be sincere?"

"Oh, I thought you were stalling so I wouldn't kiss you again." Elias snickered. He liked their banter, more so who he became in her company.

"Believe me. I've wanted to kiss you since the first time I kissed you." Josephine rested her cheek against his chest. Her words seemed unreal, too good to be true. But they were true. She loved him. One day she'd marry him. Elias wouldn't throw rice at the wedding—he would run through it. He would hold their firstborn, live alongside Josephine.

And he would handle it all perfectly well.

"I'll speak with Sebastian." Elias pecked her cheek and stepped out of the niche. He glanced up and down the hallway to ensure their solitude. Regardless of the late hour, someone might emerge from a bedroom and see them.

"Now? It's four in the morning," Josephine said with a groan. She reached for Elias's arm, perhaps to draw him back into the nook.

"The ball put Sebastian in high spirits. He may respond well if I talk to him now," Elias said. "I want to go about this in an honourable fashion. The sooner I settle matters with my family, the sooner we can announce our engagement."

Josephine nodded and tiptoed from the shadows. "Elias . . ." Her voice cracked. "Kiss me in the morning so I'll know this wasn't a dream."

He smiled, his eyes prickling with tears. "Every morning. For all my mornings."

∾

The east wing corridor seemed peculiar to Elias, elongated like one of the footpaths that snaked across the moors. He crept toward Sebastian's bedchamber, careful to muffle his footsteps on the carpet runner. Any sound might alert his aunt, who suffered bouts of insomnia.

Moonlight trickled into the passage from a window, criss-crossing the floorboards with lattice shadows. Beyond the pane, snow fell in giant flakes. At least the storm had withheld its fury until after the ball. Due to the ice and drifts, no one would be able to leave Cadwallader Park for days unless they departed on horseback. Even that seemed a risk.

Elias lifted his chin and sucked in a breath, his eyelids dipping from exhaustion. He reviewed his spiel—the monologue he prayed would persuade Sebastian to release Josephine from their betrothal. Surely Sebastian would jump at the chance to escape his parents' wishes. He could return to London, marry an impish lady who enjoyed his misbehaviour. Despite what he'd said in the mirror maze, he didn't care about Josephine.

No man in love ignored the girl he loved.

A wave of nausea swept through Elias when he reached the

room. Once he made his intentions known, he would have to live with the outcome no matter the cost.

Voices drifted from the chamber. Elias froze, his body paralyzed by the sound. Who had Sebastian welcomed into his bedroom so late at night?

Elias nudged the door ajar.

Sebastian stood near the wardrobe, still clad in his evening wear. A woman lingered close to him, whispering, her gracile arms draped around his neck. She fingered his auburn curls and glanced over his shoulder, her gaze settling on the cracked door.

Elias staggered backward. He shook his head. No, no, there had to be an explanation. What he saw didn't make sense.

Oliver: Pop wants to leave for the ceilidh around noon. You coming?

Josie: Only if you wear the kilt. I need the incentive.

Oliver: I'm already wearing it. Super cute. Navy-green tartan with a little tassel bag in the front. You'll want to borrow it for sure.

Josie: Please don't ever call your man skirt cute!!!

Oliver: I'll pick you up at eleven thirty. FYI, you make the best faces. I created a photo collage of pictures I took when you weren't paying attention. It's my new screensaver.

Josie: Creepy much?

Oliver: I laugh whenever I look at it.

Josie: Two can play that game. (*calls Martha and asks for your baby picture*)

Oliver: Fine with me. I was a cute baby. Can I call myself cute?

Josie: I don't recommend it. BTW, I have a bad feeling about the post-ball chapter.

Oliver: Yeah, it gets intense. You should use the loo before scrolling to the next page.

Josie: Sebastian doesn't have an affair with the maid or governess, right?

Oliver: There's one way to find out.

Josie: Give me a hint. Does he scheme with Lord Welby?

Oliver: KEEP READING.

Widow De Clare looked at Elias as though she'd seen a ghost. She resembled Josephine in the face, but her eyes bore a wicked gleam. Indeed, she was beautiful in a dangerous sort of convention, one that could be hidden beneath grey-and-black clothes.

A breath grated in the back of Elias's throat. He hadn't paid attention to Widow De Clare at the ball. If he had, he would've noticed that instead of mourning clothes, she wore a sage-green ball gown adorned with lace and embroidered flowers. The garment must have cost at least six pounds, an expense too great for a destitute widow.

Josephine wore her red dress to all gatherings, for she couldn't afford a new frock.

"Tell me it's not true," Elias wheezed. He stared through the doorway, a frame around the portrait of a woman and her daughter's fiancé.

Sebastian rushed to block the door. "Do not breathe a word of this," he growled. His eyes flashed a threat before he shut the panel and snapped its deadbolt into place.

Elias panted as darkness grew thick around him. He tugged his cravat. He sagged against a wall and slid to the floor. All the times he'd seen Sebastian talk with Widow De Clare, the glances shared between them, what Sebastian had said in the garden—it made perfect sense now. They'd betrayed their families, Josephine, even themselves.

Regardless of their plans, they had brought scandal to Cadwallader Park.

Had their relationship started in London? Did they intend to marry, or would they continue their liaison behind closed doors? What about Josephine? Widow De Clare must know the affair would damage her daughter's social standing.

She must know this would break Josephine's heart.

Elias rose to his feet. He wanted to kick open Sebastian's door. He wanted to beg the couple to mend their wrongs. But his chest ached. His eyelids dipped.

Nothing could reverse this harm, so Elias went to his bedroom and cried.

∽

An eerie stillness invaded Cadwallader, silencing all creaks and groans as if snow had frozen the manor into a deep slumber. Even the smouldering fireplaces seemed to beg for rest, but Elias didn't sleep. He paced his room until the black of night lightened to grey, then blue.

Mrs. Capers would be toiling in the kitchen by now, concocting a Christmas breakfast spread to satisfy post-ball stomachs. Perhaps she could tell Elias what to do next, help him decide whether he should keep his mouth shut or expose Sebastian and Widow De Clare.

Elias changed his waistcoat and jacket, then dabbed his neck with cologne. Still, he reeked of sweat and stale breath. He needed to bathe. He needed to crawl under a blanket and sleep the day away. Fatigue settled in his gut like a brick, nauseating him.

He sat on the bed and leaned against its headboard, his shoulders relaxing into a pillow. He must tell Josephine what he'd witnessed. She deserved to know about the affair before news of it spread. But how could he deliver the news without causing her immense pain?

No arrangement of the truth could ease what her mother had done.

By the time Elias awoke, the morning had turned from blue to gold. He rolled off the bed and rushed to the door. Breakfast would've been served by now, which meant Elias wouldn't be able to speak with Mrs. Capers before he laid eyes on Sebastian. The Darlings expected him to attend the meal. Such was a Christmas tradition. Indeed, he would have to control himself, for a surge of emotion might cause him to throw a punch at his cousin.

Elias went to the dining room and stopped dead in his tracks.

Kitty and Miss Karel sat at the table while Fitz wormed across the floor. They dined alone, surrounded by platters of steaming food.

"Where is everyone?" Elias asked, his heart racing as he surveyed the spread of untouched plates and silverware. Whatever had caused the adults to skip breakfast left behind a stench—the nagging sense of catastrophe.

"Ladies went to the drawing room," Fitz said as he wallowed on the rug, his pantaloons bunching around his knees. "Papa and Uncle Welby left hours ago."

"They're searching for Sebastian and Widow De Clare," Kitty said. She turned in her chair and looked at Elias with puffy eyes. Her expression confirmed his fears.

Sebastian and Widow De Clare had run off together.

"Dimwits. They won't get far, not in the snow." Miss Karel hunched over a dish of porridge. She clutched her forehead, perhaps suffering the delayed consequences of too much wine. "Pass the sugar, would you?"

Kitty handed the governess a sugar bowl. She glanced at Elias again, her nose reddening. "Sebastian ran off with the widow," she whispered. "He claims to love her."

Elias clenched his fists. "How do you know?"

"He pinned a note to his bedroom door." Kitty lifted a teacup and sipped from its rim. She appeared out of sorts, her curls unbrushed, her face pale and splotchy.

"Josephine," Elias gasped. "Where is Josephine?" He blinked to refocus himself, but his mind swirled with memories of Sebastian and Widow De Clare.

"Mother took her into the drawing room," Fitz said.

"She knows?" Elias winced as pressure flooded his chest.

Josephine had received the news with everyone else. She'd woken this morning, perhaps content from the night before, only to learn her mother had run off with her betrothed. The information must've been a shock—an agonizing blow. Indeed, Widow De Clare did not know about Josephine's relationship with Elias. She had permitted an affair with Sebastian, believing her daughter would marry him. How could a mother be so cruel?

Elias turned and bolted down the hallway. Each step blurred the house into a tunnel where Sebastian stood at one end, grinning as he whispered, "You should've seen this coming." Of course, Elias should have realized the couple would attempt to flee. He might've been able to prevent this madness if he hadn't kept quiet.

Mrs. Darling perked in her chair when Elias entered the drawing room. She and Lady Welby sat across from Josephine while a maid flitted about the space, plucking evergreen needles from the carpet. "Did you hear?" she asked.

"Yes." Elias crouched next to Josephine, who sat on a chaise lounge, stiff as a board. He examined her face—the dark circles beneath her bloodshot eyes, her vacant expression. The news had broken her spirit.

How devastating, for she was the most complete person in his acquaintance.

"Sebastian makes a sport of my nerves," Mrs. Darling huffed. She propped her feet on an ottoman and fanned herself with a book. "How could he do this?"

"That *woman* took advantage of him," Lady Welby said, her eyebrows lifting into sanctimonious peaks. "Widows prey upon young men, especially those with fortune. I read about similar cases in the newspaper. Just last year, Mr. Beauchamp's widow eloped with a gentleman not quite twenty." She pursed her lips with disapproval. "Indeed, do not blame your son, for men cannot resist the lure of mature women."

"Oh, I do blame him, that wretched boy." Mrs. Darling dabbed her nose with the hem of her apron, snivelling as Lady Welby stoked the fire. "I don't understand. He was betrothed to dear Josephine. Look at her. She's delightful."

Josephine crushed a handkerchief between her palms. She gazed at Elias and wheezed, her shoulders drooping. "Where have you been?"

"Not where I should've been," he whispered. His lungs burned as if there was an ocean of silence between him and Josephine, and he was drowning in it.

She reached for his hand.

Elias curled his fingers around her knuckles. Mrs. Darling and Lady Welby would notice the touch, but Elias didn't care. He didn't need to care. Sebastian had broken the engagement, which freed Josephine to marry whomever she desired.

"We must remain hopeful," Mrs. Darling said with a sigh. "Perhaps our husbands will discover Sebastian and Widow De Clare before—"

"I fear it's too late. They could be married by now." Lady Welby glanced at Elias, her expression harsh and indignant as though she blamed him for the affair.

Josephine shivered.

"Move closer to the fire," Elias said. "I'll get you something warm."

"Stay." Josephine gripped his arm, her fingernails cutting into his sleeve. She looked at him with tears in her eyes. "Please don't go. I'm fine, really. Just a chill."

In the pain, in the loneliness, sometimes all one needed was to feel seen.

Elias nodded and gestured to the maid. "Would you ask

Mrs. Capers to make a fresh pot of tea? And blankets—would you fetch a warmed blanket for Miss De Clare?"

The maid curtsied, then hurried to complete the tasks.

"Sebastian better not return with *her*," Mrs. Darling said with a scoff. She waved her forefinger at the room's exit. "I shan't let her through the front doors."

"Your son will inherit this house—"

"Not until Mr. Darling rests in a deep grave!"

Josephine stood and wandered toward a window. She parted its curtains with a jerk, her gaze drifting beyond the frosted glass. No longer did she beam joy and brightness. She seemed like firewood reduced to ash.

"Poor girl," Lady Welby whispered. "This will ruin her."

"What do you mean?" Elias rose from his crouched position. He sat on the chaise lounge and stared at Josephine's back, her neat bun and wrinkled muslin gown.

"Scandal makes spinsters of the loveliest girls," Mrs. Darling said.

Elias clutched his mouth and released hot breath against his palm. He wished to ignore Mrs. Darling's remark, but her words implied a universal fact, that reputation served as currency. It could not be purchased, yet it bought one's place in the world.

Josephine had used her family's reputation to navigate the upper class despite her lack of fortune. Without it, she possessed only manners and charm—traits which Lord Welby deemed insufficient. No gentleman would make her an offer of marriage. No respectable family would seek her company. In the eyes of society, her mother's affair had become her own.

The scandal couldn't ruin Josephine. Elias refused to let Sebastian and Widow De Clare come between them, for they were so close to forever. Perhaps his father would understand. Perhaps news of the affair wouldn't spread, and Josephine would be spared from shame.

Lord Welby had experienced such dishonour, however, and by his own doing, hence his astute opposition to matters of impropriety. No, of course he would not favour Elias's affection for someone tainted with ill repute. Instead, he'd once again recommend Miss Wood as a suitable match, for she was well disposed and without spurned parents.

Elias wouldn't marry anyone but Josephine. He promised himself. He resolved before God to follow through with his proposal. Lord Welby might disapprove, but he had only one heir. Would he really disinherit Elias for marrying a De Clare?

After years of boarding school and gentleman lessons, Elias had learned society was a game in which everyone played their best cards. Each person fought to win, to rise in station, reach the top—because if one did not climb, one fell to the bottom. And those who dwelt at the bottom were forgotten like pebbles tossed into a lake. But another game was also played. The game between fathers and sons, lords and heirs. 'Twas a game Elias knew well.

He was ready to play his best cards.

When the maid returned with a tea tray and blanket, Elias called to Josephine. She didn't respond. Instead, she leaned her head against the window, her breath fogging the pane. Was she afraid her mother's wrongdoing abrogated Elias's proposal? Or was she paralyzed by shock?

Elias went to her and said for her ears alone, "I won't change my mind." He wanted to rescue her from the pain, remind her of when they raced across heaths and rolled down hills. He longed to fill the room with gorse garlands to prove his feelings were unaltered. He loved her. He intended to marry her. Reputation wouldn't divide them again.

For hours they waited in the drawing room. Mrs. Darling and Lady Welby embroidered while Elias tried to coax Josephine from the window. Not long after nightfall, hooves pounded up the estate's snowy drive, the sound like music after such a quiet day.

Everyone rushed to the foyer. They congregated near the front door, a hush descending over them as Lord Welby and Mr. Darling entered the house.

"Did you find them?" Mrs. Darling asked.

"Yes," Lord Welby said as he removed his coat and gloves. "They're married."

"God have mercy." Lady Welby clutched her mouth.

Elias struggled to breathe, his face beading with sweat. He could've stopped Sebastian and Widow De Clare from eloping. His few hours of silence had allowed the marriage.

He turned and studied Josephine, but her expression was unreadable, a wall of stone. She lifted her chin and blinked.

"We discovered them at a public house in Rothbury," Mr. Darling said. He stomped to knock the ice from his boots. "Sebastian sends his regards."

"That hateful child!" Mrs. Darling burst into tears. "Does he not realize what this will do to us? We'll be laughingstocks."

"Papa, did you find Sebastian?" Kitty and Fitz raced down the staircase, tripping over each other to reach their father. "What happened, Papa?"

"Your brother disgraced our family." Mr. Darling rubbed his neck, perhaps stiff from riding in the cold. "I'll speak more on the subject later. Right now I need a bath." He groaned and staggered across the entrance hall, trailing melted snow.

The women turned to Lord Welby for information.

"A vicar married them not long before we arrived," Lord Welby said. "They leave for London tomorrow." He gave his outerwear to the butler, then strode toward the drawing room with a procession on his heels.

"Did you give them money?" Lady Welby asked.

"Not a penny. They intend to use Sebastian's allowance for their honeymoon." Lord Welby went to the room's fireplace. He plopped into a chair and pried off his boots. "Blazes, I cannot feel my legs. Bitter cold out. Snow up to my knees."

Josephine muttered something under her breath. She clawed at her chest and drifted out of the chamber as though in a trance.

"Josephine?" Elias left his place by the fire. He stepped into the corridor and searched for Josephine in the gloom, but she had vanished. His chest grew tight. Bile rose to his throat, and blood pounded in his ears.

The front door flew open with a bang. Flurries whirled into the entrance hall and dusted the marble floor. Wind screamed through the house, snuffing candles with a sizzle.

"Josephine!" Elias ran to the doorway and squinted against the blast of snow. He spotted her in the distance. She paddled through drifts as if they were ponds. She dashed toward the moors, her silhouette fading into darkness.

"Is she mad?" the valet yelled. He joined Elias on the threshold and held a lantern to the night. "She'll get lost out there. Storm will freeze her solid."

"Josephine, stop!" Elias sprinted from the house and crashed into snow. He shivered with a fear so vast and penetrating, it consumed him until he felt nothing . . .

Until he was the fear.

Nobody expected betrayal from the person closest to him. Such pain changed everything. It rendered trust null and void. It made hearts sceptical. Perhaps the worst part of betrayal wasn't the act itself, rather becoming the victim of someone who called themselves a friend.

Perhaps the worst part was loving someone who didn't love back.

"Where are you?" Elias yelled as the blizzard swirled. "Call out to me!"

Cadwallader Park glowed in the murk. It hovered within the grey expanse, flickering an amber glow. The light would guide Elias and Josephine back to the house.

"Josephine!" Elias trudged forward, the drifts swallowing his calves. He gasped as wind stung his face and shoved him sideways. The cold had teeth, but the storm had fangs. It chewed through his clothes and froze his skin.

It breathed snow into his lungs.

He coughed and shielded his eyes. He shouted until his voice went hoarse, his mouth like cotton. If he didn't find Josephine soon, they might both freeze.

Elias wouldn't let Josephine perish. He would search the moors until he found her. Then he'd squeeze her tight and tell her to break but not to stay broken, to let the tears fall so she could find joy again. Indeed, grief was a solo process, but one needed a friend to set their broken pieces so they could heal whole, not crippled.

A gale parted the snowfall, revealing her sprawled in a

nearby drift with her knees drawn to her chest. "Josephine!" He collapsed and pulled her body into his lap. He scraped his numb fingers against her dress, brushing snow from the thin fabric.

"I'm ruined," she cried. "I'm ruined."

"You're safe. Everything will be fine." Elias kissed a line across her frigid brow. She was dear to him. In sanity and madness, she was forever dear.

"Why did Mum run off with him? She knew what it would do to me. She knew . . . and she did it anyway," Josephine said between sobs. Her body shook. Her teeth chattered.

Her skin was ice, but her eyes were boiling.

"Let's get you indoors." Elias wiggled out of his jacket and wrapped it around Josephine's shoulders. He cradled her against his chest, pain engulfing him until it became a friend, then an ally, the only thing keeping him from total despair.

"You don't understand." Josephine pulled back, weeping, her cheeks burned red with snow. "Your father won't let us marry now."

"Nonsense." Elias lifted her from the drift and headed toward the manor's glow.

Josephine cried into the crease of his neck. "You didn't kiss me," she wheezed. "This morning . . . You didn't kiss me." Her body relaxed, drooping from his arms like a bundle of blankets. She drew a breath and released it as a trickle of vapour. "We were a nice dream."

TWENTY

JOSIE

From: Josie De Clare <JDeClare@mailbox.com>
Sent: Friday, September 22, 6:40 PM
To: Faith Moretti <Kardashian_4Life@mailbox.com>
Subject: About Elias Roch and Life Stuff

> Faith, I predict Lord Welby won't be thrilled about Elias
> and Josephine's engagement. Maybe he'll present an
> ultimatum—Josephine or the inheritance. Isn't that how
> most Regency romances go? Rich boy must sacrifice
> everything to be with the girl he loves. Clichés exist for a
> reason, I suppose. People must either fantasize about them,
> or they really do happen.
>
> Wouldn't that be nice—to live a life full of clichés?

Knowing our dear Elias, he will abandon his wealth and marry Josephine. They'll live happily ever after. And me . . . Well, I'll be here in this draughty old house, miserably left out.

We agreed to biweekly updates, but I don't have much news. Work seems about the same. (My boss lets me ice cakes now.) I still go to club meetings every Wednesday despite the fact recent gatherings consist of Lucille and Margery fawning over Oliver. They love him. Really, really love him. I shouldn't be surprised, though. He's a brilliant knitter. He knitted a red stocking cap for me, even made a pom-pom for the top.

He forces me to wear it at least once a week.

A few days ago, I went to a ceilidh with Oliver and his grandparents. It was a social event for Scots, held at a community centre in the hamlet north of Atteberry. As expected, Oliver and I were the youngest in attendance. That's not a complaint. I rather enjoy old folk. They make superb food, tell interesting stories, and they give loads of compliments. Now I'm not saying I like elderly people because they tell me I'm pretty. Maybe that's true, but I'm not saying it.

Oliver taught me traditional Scottish dances, a feat which should've earned him a medal. He looked hilarious in his kilt. (I attached a photo to this email.) We danced for a while, and then he persuaded me to eat haggis. Awful stuff. I didn't like it one bit.

We are mates. That's all. I know he likes me, but he hasn't mentioned any non-friend feelings. So I'll pretend I don't notice and carry on with our escapades. Maybe I'm wicked to keep my mouth shut. Maybe I should tell him I'm in love with someone who no longer exists.

But I'm afraid he'll leave once he finds out.

He makes Atteberry seem less dreary with his cowlicked hair and ridiculous smile. We laugh a lot when we're together. On Wednesdays we drive the motorcycle to knitting club, then stop by the café for dessert. Sometimes we organize Norman and Martha's living room into a makeshift cinema, and we screen vintage movies.

Faith, I only have a few more letters to read, and I'm nearing the conclusion of Elias's novel. Part of me needs to know what happens because . . . I still believe I'll meet Elias somehow. But if I finish the book, all this comes to an end.

FaceTime me when you get the chance.

Josie

P.S. Mum is dating a young bloke. Coincidence?

Josie: I bought my costume for the Halloween party!

Oliver: Let me guess. You're going as Elias Roch?

Josie: Nope. I couldn't find a Regency era tailcoat in my size. ;)

Oliver: What's your costume, then?

Josie: (*drumroll*) I'm going as Audrey Hepburn!

Oliver: Why??

Josie: The costume was on sale. LOL

Oliver: Solid reason. I'll probably wear Pop's clothes and say I'm a sheep farmer.

From: Faith Moretti <Kardashian_4Life@mailbox.com>
Sent: Saturday, October 2, 8:37 AM
To: Josie De Clare <JDeClare@mailbox.com>
Subject: Re: About Elias Roch and Life Stuff

Josie, I'll begin with the less spectacular news.

My fall semester includes a lot of classes, homework, and midnight trips to the gym. Last night I saw my Mass Media and Society professor on the elliptical and fled to the locker room so I wouldn't laugh at him. He wore spandex and a sweatband. Total babe magnet.

A new bookstore opened on my block. It has three floors and a spiral staircase. Pretty sure I keep its coffee bar in business. If you ever visit New York, I'll take you to the shop, and we can sip lattes while perusing the aisles.

Do me a favor and sit down for this next part.

Noah came to my apartment yesterday out of the blue. I answered the door while wearing a nose-peel thingy. Like, the kind used to tear out blackheads.

He apologized for pressuring me about the engagement and presented a peace offering of Starbucks coffee. We chatted for a while. Noah said he'd pushed for marriage because he wanted to spend his life with me and didn't see the point of waiting.

But he swore he'd wait until I was ready.

At that moment I thought about you and Elias, how you'd give anything for ten minutes with him. I mean, I can go on dates with Noah, talk to him face-to-face. He lives down the block, not two hundred years in the past. Okay . . . so yeah, I kind of broke up with Noah. Don't freak out. (I'm imagining your expression. Jaw dropped. Brows raised. Eyes all buggy.)

The breakup wasn't bad like last time. I think we both realized we still have a lot of growing up to do. Believe me. We love each other. And who knows? Maybe we'll get back together one day, after we do our study abroad trips. Yep. That's right.

I'm going to Milan for that fashion internship.

Please don't act grim and sympathetic. This is a good thing, Josie. I'm excited for the first time in months. When I moved back to New York, I struggled to decide what I wanted from life. My family hoped I'd get married and settle into this future they'd dreamed up for me. Noah had wants too. And I felt guilty for loving him but not wanting him.

I broke up with Noah for that reason. He wasn't my first choice. Each time I think about my future, I picture my own store and clothing line and *maybe* a family. *Maybe* Noah. *Maybe* that house in Jersey. And he does not deserve a *maybe* life.

Really, I think my happy ending right now isn't getting the boy. It's doing what I'm passionate about, moving forward in a direction I choose.

Lots of girls believe they'll be happier once they find Prince Charming, but marriage isn't a fairy godmother waving a wand to change a pumpkin into a carriage. It doesn't instantly transform people into better versions of themselves. Instead, it brings couples together and asks them to use love as a reason to become better. It's hard. It sure as heck doesn't make life easier.

Maybe one day I'll be ready for the challenge.

Not everyone will understand my reasons for breaking up with Noah. (I've already received half a dozen calls from our parents, voicemails from his sister, and an opinionated Facebook message from Uncle Sal.) But that's okay. We each must live our own story, like you said in your email. This story belongs to me.

Despite the breakup, I'm glad Noah and I dated. Our relationship shouldn't have lasted so long. We met at a middle-school dance. We dated via FaceTime while I was at Stonehill. I must say the miracle wasn't that we ended up together. It was finding each other in the first place.

We'll stay friends and see what happens.

There. You have my news. Now I want to talk about you and your boy problems. First off, I'm glad you're reading the chapters, but your predictions aren't one hundred percent correct. Keep reading. The book's conclusion may help you make sense of your situation.

Please don't hate me for saying this . . .

I want you with Oliver. The fact he knitted you a hat gives me all the feels. Yeah, I know you don't *like* him. He deserves to know where you stand, though.

Your updates put a smile on my face. I'm happy to know you aren't hiding in your mansion, attempting to conjure spirits. Has anything strange happened since the candle incident? What did Elias say in his letters? We talk about his novel, but I want to hear about the notes.

Keep me posted.

Faith

Josie: I AM SO HAPPY FOR YOU!!

Faith: Thanks! I'm still in shock—the good kind.

Josie: May I visit you in Milan? We can road-trip across Italy and have the best holiday. Dad's coworker did that, rented a caravan and everything.

Faith: Of course! You better hurry with your renovations, though. I'm coming to Atteberry. I want to meet Oliver and his grandparents, your knitting club, everyone.

Josie: When?!

Faith: Are you free the second week of January, before your classes start?

Josie: YES! YES! YES!

Faith, I messed up. I didn't say what I needed to say, and I don't know what to say now to fix my *not saying*. Last night seemed great until my *not saying* happened. Well, it started to get awkward when Oliver pulled me aside. Scratch that. I'll start at the beginning.

Oliver and I went to an early Halloween party at the Knitting Emporium. Lucille had decorated the shop with yarn made to resemble spider webs. Margery had created a witch's brew punch—a mixture of ice cream and ginger ale. Really, the festivities took me by surprise. Who would've thought a group of knitters could be so fun?

We played charades and a murder mystery game until our senior members' bedtime. Oh, I wish you could've seen the costumes. Dorrit and Clare wore kitty ears. Stuart arrived wearing a Batman suit. Lucille wrapped her body in toilet paper and called herself a mummy. However, the winner of my silent costume contest was for sure Margery. She'd knitted herself a Tinkerbell outfit complete with a dress, slippers, and a yarn wig.

Oliver and I hugged everyone good night. We left the shop and strolled to where he'd parked the motorcycle. Atteberry seemed quieter than usual, almost deserted. No one walked the pavement or drove their cars down the main street.

I saw the words on Oliver's face before he spoke them.

He told me he wanted to be more than friends. He said he'd liked me since the day I almost killed him with a sword. (That's what gets the boys—threatening to behead them.) My heart dropped. I didn't know what to say, so I stared at him like a halfwit.

We drove to Cadwallader in silence. I thanked Oliver for the ride, then went indoors and drowned my nerves with chamomile tea. I messed up, Faith. I should've told him about Elias. I should've explained myself. Tell me what to do!

Josie

(Sent from iPhone)

Oliver: Hey! I'm sorry for what I said the other night. I made things weird between us. Blame my stupidity on too much sugar. (I ate three of Lucille's Chelsea buns.)

Oliver: Okay . . . I know it's only been four days since we last talked, but I miss you like crazy. The variety store isn't fun without you. Really, nothing is fun without you.

Oliver: Did my last text make our situation even worse? I'm an idiot.

Oliver: Josie, I left firewood near your back door. Give me a ring if you need more.

Oliver: Hiya! I saw you when I passed the bakery this morning. Didn't know if you wanted to see me, so I kept walking. Hope you're doing well. Granny and Pop talk about you all the time. Pretty sure they like you more than me.

Josie: Hey! Yes, I would've loved to see you. And no, you didn't make anything weird. I just don't handle those kinds of situations well. I get super awkward.

Oliver: It's okay. I knew I was taking a risk.

Josie: You mean a lot to me. I don't want to lose you as a friend.

Oliver: No need to worry about that, Twiggy. I'll stick around.

Josie: Good. Want to get a spot of dinner at White Horse Pub?

Oliver: I can't tonight. Maybe next week.

Faith: Plz tell Oliver about Elias.

From: Josie De Clare <JDeClare@mailbox.com>
Sent: Friday, October 22, 3:16 PM
To: Faith Moretti <Kardashian_4Life@mailbox.com>
Subject: Re: I Messed Up

Faith, I texted Oliver a week ago, but I haven't seen him since the Halloween party. He leaves firewood on my doorstep while

I'm at work. He goes to the shed whenever I visit Norman and Martha. I need to explain what happened that night, why I'm unable to return his feelings.

But I can't get a moment alone with him.

An ice storm has trapped me at Cadwallader Manor. I've enjoyed the solitude under the circumstances. During the day I retile the kitchen and rummage through boxes I found in the attic. Nan stays with me at night. Martha visits on occasion.

You asked if I'd experienced strange happenings. Yes, I have witnessed peculiarities within this house. For example, the other night, I carried a candle to the second floor. (The storm had caused the electricity to go out.) As I walked down the hallway, a draught came from nowhere and extinguished my candle. I stood frozen, my heart beating so fast, I almost passed out. That's when I heard it—a faint whisper. It breezed across my neck, sultry like an exhale.

I almost peed my pants.

What if Elias is in this house? I mean, why would fate bring me to Cadwallader if not to unite Elias and me? What's the point of all this if we don't end up together?

Records do not reveal where Elias was buried. The manor doesn't possess evidence of his later life. It's as though he vanished.

I will find him.

Josie

TWENTY-ONE

ELIAS

December 2, 1821

Dearest Josephine,

Scribble these words onto a scrap of paper and tuck them into your pocket. Recite them to yourself when you feel despondent, and please do not forget me. Remember I adore your funny expressions, how you furrow your brow when you laugh and smile, when you are cross. I fancy your quickness to tease me and your giggle, that sound you make when you are happy for no specific reason. I love that you argue your opinions even when you know they are wrong.

I love every detail of you.

Our souls belong together. Perhaps at the beginning of time, when God paired His creations two by two, He placed us at each other's side. I like to think we were meant for more than separation, that a mistake was made. However, I do not believe God makes errors, which means He intended us to live apart. Mind you, I have not surrendered hope in our togetherness, but I have reached a crossroad and must decide which path to take.

A coach arrived this morning. Its driver hauled trunks from the house while Lorelai bade my staff farewell. She thanked me for my hospitality, then strode toward the carriage with her chin lowered, blocking me from view with her bonnet's brim.

I stood on the front step with arms crossed behind my back, no better than Lord Roch when he sent me away from his home. Indeed, I have turned into my father.

Lorelai spun around once she reached the coach. She gazed at me with tears in her eyes and rushed forward, her shoes crunching gravel until we stood face-to-face.

With her chin now lifted, Lorelai told me she wished to preserve what little remained of her self-respect, yet she felt possessed to speak. She said I was a wretched man—I believed myself undeserving of affection, hence my attachment to someone I could not locate. She claimed I had proven my love for her through our friendship, which she did not consider platonic or temporary. She then admitted her lack of interest in Mr. O'Connor.

I opened my mouth, but Lorelai hushed me. She restated what I had said at the ball and told me I had offended her by presuming to know what was in her best interest. She said, "How dare you cast preconceived notions upon me. I know my own mind. I decide what brings me happiness. And despite your ignorance and dismissal, I am certain of my love for you."

She revealed she had loved me since our arrival at Cadwallader. Nevertheless, she refused to wait another day, for I had proven my inability to view her as anything more than a friend. She vowed neither to nurse my devotion to you nor stay where she was not welcome.

Her declaration and, frankly, her insults rendered me speechless. I closed my mouth. I stared at her face, spotting hints of you, not in her features, rather in the steel that supported them. She understood how I worked, saw me like gears and cogs behind a clockface.

We had become such dear friends.

Lorelai acknowledged my bond with you. She said, "I do not wish to replace her in your heart, rather join her there. People cannot love everyone the same, for no two loves are the same. Love her the way you need, but I ask—and I humble myself with these words—if you could love me in a different way. I think you do, but regardless of your feelings, I pray you will remember what I have said. I pray you will realize you are worthy of good things."

Memories seemed to awaken within my head, gaining a fresh slant. I recalled the afternoons I had spent with Lorelai in my study, how she read on the settee while I wrote. I remembered the way she peered over my shoulder as I painted your portrait, our quiet evenings in the drawing room when we played cards and told stories. From the moment she and Arthur first entered my house, she lingered nearby, waiting for me.

I daresay we were contented all that time.

Lorelai turned to leave, but I stopped her. The idea of loving someone other than you seemed like heresy, and yet I asked her to stay. I am not sure about love, but I know I am not indifferent toward her. Indeed, much can grow from lack of indifference.

This event appears the denouement of a lifelong quest. I am not sure where to go from here or if I made the right choice. At present I sprawl within my gorse alcove while Lorelai unpacks her trunks indoors. She will stay at Cadwallader, and I will ponder what best to do.

Her family will expect an offer of marriage soon.

I shall not propose to Lorelai unless my feelings change, for the girl deserves someone who returns her affections in full. I will endeavour to make amends, however, during which time I'll cling to the hope that one day, after such a strenuous wait, I shall hold you in my arms and whisper against your lips, "My dearest, you were worth every second."

Yours ever,

Elias

P.S. I shall ride to Morpeth tomorrow.

TWENTY-TWO

The Novel

News of Sebastian and Widow De Clare's elopement left Cadwallader Park in a sullen humour. The manor's occupants sulked about. They dined in their chambers. They whispered about Josephine's health, for her flight to the moors had caused quite a stir. Their mood infused the house with a frigid dampness, its presence enhanced by the ash-grey dimness of a winter sun. Indeed, the Christmas ball seemed deep in the past, buried under snow and ice, snuffed by a sense of dread.

Elias ascended the staircase and wandered toward his study. He buttoned his jacket over a white waistcoat, his breath like steam in the corridor. He despised the cold, for it reminded him of Josephine's shivering body, her final words as he carried her across the snowscape. Only a few hours separated him from that memory. A few hours of waiting and praying. A few hours spent in darkness, then at a vacant breakfast table.

A kindled fire and cup of tea would revive him.

He entered the west wing as Mr. Darling's valet attempted to haul a portmanteau—a chest embossed with the letter J—to the servants' stairwell.

"What are you doing with Miss De Clare's trunk?" Elias asked.

"Lady Welby told me to carry it downstairs." The valet tilted backward to balance the luggage on his chest. He staggered forward, ramming against a door frame.

"Downstairs?" Elias tasted the word's connotations. He cleared his throat and waved at Anne, who crouched on the floor with a bucket and rag. "Do you know what's happening?"

She rose onto her knees and dabbed sweat from her brow. "I overheard Josephine tell Mrs. Darling she plans to return to her mother's cottage in Morpeth."

"What?" Elias tensed. Josephine wouldn't leave Cadwallader, not when she was engaged.

"The girl hasn't recovered from the shock of . . ." Anne resumed her scrubbing, perhaps worried the butler might find her idle. "Talk to Miss De Clare. She's in your library."

Elias hurried to the annex. He barged into his study, the door swinging open with a clap.

Josephine sat at his desk, clothed in her mother's grey bombazine gown and black velvet pelisse. Mrs. Darling had insisted she wear the clothes, for the heavy fabric provided more warmth than muslin.

"You're leaving?" Elias said.

She looked over her shoulder and nodded. Her skin was like the moon. Her eyes were veined with red. "There's nothing left for me here," she whispered. "I must go someplace else."

"But we're engaged." He crossed the room, where they'd built forts and talked for hours on end. His chest ached as though to warn him of coming pain.

Josephine rose from her chair. She gazed up at Elias's face, her nose reddening. "Your father won't let you marry me—"

"I'll speak with him." Elias cupped the back of her neck. He wanted to beg her not to lose hope, for they were but a vow away from togetherness. They were so close.

A tear spilled down her cheek and splotched her neckline.

"Stay," he breathed. "I'll go talk to my father."

Josephine squeezed Elias's wrist, then returned to her chair. She sank into a puddle of inky fabric and stared out the window. Her expression darkened as if she'd accepted the fate Widow De Clare had sealed. She would become a spinster, alone and destitute.

"I'll kiss you in the morning," Elias said. He left the study, his heart racing when he realized her touch—the squeeze of his wrist—was no consolation.

Her touch was tragedy.

∞

Elias went to the parlour located behind the dining room. He peered into the chamber, where Lord Welby lounged on a sofa, flipping through *The Morning Post*.

"Father, may I speak with you?" Elias asked. He stepped over the threshold and beheld the room's silk wallpaper and pianoforte. At this time of day, Kitty liked to use the space for her music lessons. Perhaps she had postponed her practice due to yesterday's upset.

Lord Welby glanced up from the newspaper. "Of course. Do

come in." He smacked the pages as Elias walked to an armchair. "Have you seen *The Morning Post*? Ghastly stuff."

"Not yet." Elias sunk into the chair. He coughed and bounced his leg to ease his nerves. "Do you recall our conversation at the ball? About marriage?"

"Indeed. You expressed interest in a lady engaged to be married," Lord Welby said with a smirk. He folded the newspaper and placed it on a side table.

"Yes, well, that lady . . . She is no longer involved." Elias slumped forward as bile shot up his throat. He couldn't afford to lose his composure or be sick on the rug, for the next few minutes would determine his and Josephine's future.

The next few minutes could ruin everything.

Lord Welby grew stiff with realization. He stared at Elias, his jaw clenched and nostrils flaring. "Have you made your intentions known?"

"Yes," Elias said with a nod. "We'd like your blessing."

"Are you mad?" Lord Welby snapped. He rose from the sofa like a snake, uncurling into a tower of pale skin and fine clothes. "You wish to marry Josephine De Clare?"

"I love her." Elias gripped the chair's armrests. He needed to make his father see sense before an ultimatum was made.

"Tush," Lord Welby sneered. "She is your cousin's former betrothed, now his stepdaughter. Consider the scandal you'd bring upon our family."

"Josephine is innocent—"

"No one is innocent in conversation, not when speculation offers amusement. People wish to believe the worst, for the wickedness of others dims their own sins." Lord Welby paced the room, fuming. He shook his head. "For years I fought to make you more than an illegitimate son. I gave you the Welby name, an education, and sent you into society to find your place. All my hard work shall mean nothing if you marry the daughter of a penniless trollop."

"The public will not reject Josephine. She'll have my name to protect her," Elias yelled.

Lord Welby paused next to the pianoforte. He studied Elias in silence, his demeanour less hostile. "I have nothing against Miss De Clare. In fact, I sympathize with her predicament. Your uncle and I plan to provide her with a yearly sum of one hundred forty pounds—"

"She doesn't want your money!"

"Then who will put food on her table? It shan't be you. I forbid it." Lord Welby waved his hand as though to dismiss Elias. "Go to London. Find yourself a respectable bride."

"Do you think my feelings shallow, that I'm able to purge myself of attachment?" Elias trembled, his breaths quickening. "I am not like you and Sebastian."

Lord Welby laughed. "Come now. The moment a prettier girl looks your way you'll forget about Miss De Clare."

"Is that what happened to your wife?"

"Watch your tongue. You understand the responsibilities that come with your position. Regardless of your emotions, you must do what's best for your family. You're a Welby. Your offspring will be my grandchildren. They'll inherit from you what I give to you. Do you wish to sacrifice your future—*their* future—for a passing fancy?"

"Are you threatening me?" Elias stood at attention and met his father's gaze with a scowl. He panted, his vision blurring with heat as he realized the game was over. He had lost.

"My heir will not marry someone of disreputable pedigree." Lord Welby clasped his hands behind his back and strode across the room, his footsteps rattling a tea stand.

"Do you not recognize the hypocrisy of your words? We are no better than Josephine and Widow De Clare," Elias yelled. "I am your bastard. You cannot expect—"

"You're set to inherit Windermere Hall and ten thousand pounds a year. Women shall throw themselves at you," Lord Welby said. "I expect a great deal from you because *I can*."

"I've done everything you've asked of me—"

"And you shall continue to do so." Lord Welby paused in the doorway and held Elias's gaze. "Be wise about your decision, Son."

"You would disinherit me?" Elias wheezed. He was Lord Welby's only child, the sole heir to the Welby fortune. His father wouldn't bequeath the sum to a stranger.

"Josephine will leave Cadwallader Park this afternoon. I suggest you let her go," Lord Welby said without a trace of compassion. He vanished from the threshold, his words lingering like a bitter aftertaste.

Elias collapsed onto a chair. He clutched his mouth and wept, a gut-wrenching ache burrowing down his throat, into his lungs. How could he provide for Josephine if Lord Welby estranged him? He was reliant on his father's generosity. Without the inheritance, he possessed the clothes on his person, nothing more. Indeed, the household staff earned a higher wage.

Josephine would gain more support from his relatives if he broke off their engagement.

The realization made Elias sob. Anguish shook him, each sputter and gasp an explosion of hot pain within his torso. If possible, he would tear open his chest and crawl out of the hurt. He'd become someone no longer tethered to approval, someone who didn't have to choose between love and family. The choice was made, though. He couldn't marry Josephine without forcing her into poverty. He couldn't inherit his father's estate unless he allowed Josephine to leave Cadwallader Park.

Forsaking love meant survival for them both.

With a groan, Elias dried his face and staggered to the door. He didn't want Kitty to find him in such a wretched state. The girl would ask questions. Questions with dreadful answers.

He went to the entrance hall and froze beneath an unlit chandelier.

Josephine stood at the top of the staircase. She gazed down at Elias. Her eyes flickered with understanding as if she knew what had transpired between him and Lord Welby.

She gave a nod, then disappeared behind a wall.

"No, Josephine . . ." Elias sagged against a bannister and struggled for air. He needed her to cry or yell, not accept their fate without a word. He needed her to shed tears and resent him, for any response would prove she'd believed in their relationship.

But she had known this would happen. She knew the rules of society's game.

All along she had predicted they would lose.

❧

Elias followed the inhabitants of Cadwallader Park outside, where they intended to give Josephine a sober send-off. He stepped onto the gravel drive and pursed his lips as church bells echoed from the parish, as blackbirds soared from the manor's gables. At least the landscape had enough decency to dull its lurid features. Any warmth from the sun might shatter the wall Elias had built around his emotions. He refused to cry in front of his relatives.

He wouldn't let his father see him suffer.

Josephine emerged from the house. She lowered a bonnet over her plaited curls and tied its ribbons beneath her chin. The Darlings' carriage would take her into town, where she could hire a stagecoach. Fortunately, the snow had melted enough to allow transportation.

Lord Welby maintained a stone face as Josephine bade her farewells to Mr. Darling and the household staff. He glanced at Elias as though to ensure his son wouldn't attempt to interfere. Was he pleased with the outcome of his ultimatum? Did he find satisfaction in separating a young couple, who loved each other, for the good opinions of strangers?

"My son is a fool," Mrs. Darling said as she pulled Josephine into an embrace. She kissed the girl's cheek and mustered a smile. "I wish you well, dear."

Josephine nodded and stepped toward Kitty. She drew a breath, perhaps to hold back tears. "I shall miss you, Kitty Darling."

"You must visit us again." Kitty snivelled and reached for Josephine's gloved hand. She laced their fingers. "Perhaps when your mother returns."

"Perhaps." Josephine sighed and moved on to Fitz, who mewled like a babe. "Cheer up, my little pirate." She crouched in front of him and thumbed his chin. "I am certain Miss Karel will entertain you better than I ever did."

"She's not you," Fitz said with a sniffle.

313

"Indeed, but you must try to behave for her. Not everyone gets along with pirates." Josephine straightened, her gaze resting on Elias. She inched toward him and curtsied.

Elias trembled. He wanted to pull her aside and explain why she was better off without him. He wanted to kiss her until his heart ceased its torment.

"Time doesn't work in our favour, Mr. Welby." Josephine leaned closer to him and brushed her fingers against his wrist. "Write to me," she breathed, her eyes welling with tears.

He panted as she walked toward the carriage. Letting her go felt wrong. His veins filled with wrongness. But in a world governed by such things, even the right choices weren't right.

TWENTY-THREE

JOSIE

From: Josie De Clare <JDeClare@mailbox.com>
Sent: Saturday, November 6, 10:22 PM
To: Faith Moretti <Kardashian_4Life@mailbox.com>
Subject: I Told Oliver

Faith, I told him.

Oliver brought firewood to my house this morning. I opened the
back door right before he knocked and invited him inside. He
looked at me like I was a serial killer, like I planned to lure him
indoors so I could tie him to a chair and rip off his fingernails.

After a long stare, he stepped into the kitchen. He dropped
his wood near the furnace, then plopped onto a stool without a
word. I was nervous. Tremendously so. I kept fiddling with my
braid and tugging the flower decals on my jumper.

I babbled for several minutes. About what, I'm not sure. All I remember is Oliver's expression when I said, "You better not say I'm mental after I tell you this. One silly face, and I'll throw you outside." Then I told him I was in love with Elias.

His eyes widened as I mentioned all the similarities between Josephine and me, that I fell head over heels for Elias while reading part 2 of the manuscript. I kept talking. I told Oliver everything—about you, Rashad, Mum and Dad, Stonehill, why I came to Cadwallader.

Being honest seemed like stripping myself naked. I didn't want Oliver to see what lived beneath my jokes and ridiculousness. I didn't want him to see the vulnerable parts of me, because no one has ever liked those parts, that is, besides you.

Rashad called me vain when I complained about the stretch marks on my thighs. Mum said I was dramatic and wanted attention, hence my frequent breakdowns. Hearing those comments from people I thought loved me . . . They made me seal up like a carnivorous plant. I thought if I shared my true self with someone, they wouldn't accept me anymore.

I expected Oliver to leave. I figured he'd laugh and say I had an overactive imagination. But he did none of those things. He just looked at me as if he saw all my expectations and fears, as if he understood. He stood up and wrapped his arms around me. I couldn't decide if I needed to cry or fake a smile—or let him embrace me for as long as possible.

Oliver put a kettle on the stove, then spent the next hour asking me questions. Not critical questions. The thoughtful sort—the kind people ask when they want to be a part of your life. That's when I realized I wasn't just a girl to him. He didn't like me for my quirkiness and cute expressions, what might happen if he stayed my friend long enough. He just liked me.

To know a boy cares like *that* gives me faith in mankind.

On an unrelated note, I called it! I knew Lord Welby would give an ultimatum. Please tell me Elias goes after Josephine. He doesn't play the martyr and sacrifice his happiness for money, right? I mean, no one wants to live in poverty, but isn't love more important? I did research. In Regency times, a couple needed an income of only two hundred pounds per year to live well.

Mr. Darling could hire Elias to manage his assets.

Fine, I'll stop my commentary and finish reading the book. If it ends with an epilogue of Elias reuniting with Josephine after twenty years only to find she's married, she named her son after him, or something trite like that, I will throw a royal fit. You said the novel's ending will help make sense of my situation. I am hoping for a romantic gesture, a dazzling instrumental soundtrack, and a kiss that turns my heart to putty.

In his letters, Elias invited Lorelai to prolong her stay at Cadwallader. He seemed tempted to propose, which makes zero sense to me because he didn't love her.

Yikes, I sound jealous.

All this will come to an end soon. I have two more letters, one chapter, and an epilogue to read. After your visit, I leave Atteberry and start classes at uni. How will I manage to say good-bye to everyone? More so, how will I muster the courage to bid farewell to Elias?

I need a miracle *now*.

Josie

P.S. Say a prayer for me. I plan to phone Mum next week.

Oliver: Are you still interested in a pub dinner? Maybe bangers and mash followed by a treacle pudding? IDK, I feel adventurous tonight. Might order a shepherd's pie.

Josie: That's your adventure? Shepherd's pie? Wow, you need to get out more.

Oliver: Okay, I'll take my invitation a step further. Dinner AND a movie?

Josie: What a novel concept! (*applauds creativity*)

Oliver: Thank you. Thank you. I'll accept my Nobel Prize at dinner.

Josie: I've missed you.

Oliver: Blimey, Twigs. Don't get all sentimental.

Josie: Wait. Did you just give me a nickname for my nickname?

Oliver: Appears that way. My autocorrect hates me. So, yes to dinner?

Josie: Of course. ;)

From: Faith Moretti <Kardashian_4Life@mailbox.com>
Sent: Sunday, November 7, 1:46 PM
To: Josie De Clare <JDeClare@mailbox.com>
Subject: Re: I Told Oliver

Gotta keep this email short, Josie. I'm commuting to the Upper West Side and need to change trains at the next stop. Lots of creeps in my subway car. One guy has a ferret in his hoodie pocket, and it keeps staring at me. A woman is leaning against the doors. Low-key afraid the panels will slide apart and suck her onto the tracks. (Sorry for the violent mental image.)

For the record, I love Oliver. He sounds perfect for you. Like, if a Build-A-Boyfriend store existed, I would custom-make you an Oliver clone. I know you love Elias, but I'm worried he won't appear in your house and you'll be heartbroken.

I'm worried you will spend your entire life waiting for someone who can't show up.

Over the past couple weeks, I've thought a lot about love and boys—and other mushy stuff that makes me feel like a middle-school girl at church camp. The breakup put me in a contemplative mood, so much so I'm acing my philosophy class.

When people go through dark times, they look for crutches to support them. They want to keep themselves from falling apart, so they try to compartmentalize pain or replace it with distractions. Maybe it sounds dumb, but after we stopped talking and your dad passed, I thought if I changed myself, the grief wouldn't hurt as bad. I found new friends and pretended like your silence didn't bother me. Still, at the end of the day, I was the same broken person with the same grief, just without the people who really cared about me.

You seem like yourself again. You have a job, friends, even an adoptive family. I mean, who would've thought so much pain could result in good?

I believe Elias wrote about you. (He needed you as much as you needed him.) But there comes a point in all our lives where we must choose how we're going to move forward, whether to long for what we don't have—to lean on our crutches—or embrace what's already around us.

There comes a point where we must close the book.

Next stop is approaching, so I better conclude this longer-than-expected message. I guess my point is . . . I think you already have what you're looking for, and I want you to see it.

You could spend your whole life searching for love with your eyes closed.

Faith

(Sent from iPhone)

From: Josie De Clare <JDeClare@mailbox.com>
Sent: Monday, November 15, 5:09 PM
To: Faith Moretti <Kardashian_4Life@mailbox.com>
Subject: Mum Says Hi

Faith, I rang Mum earlier today. She answered the phone, which surprised me. I usually leave several voicemails before she gets around to returning my calls. We talked about Dad and the divorce. We fought because I mentioned her lack of parenting. Then she said, "I love you" and "Let's talk again soon," and we hung up. The conversation didn't change much, but I'm glad it happened. I feel this sense of relief, like a weight was lifted off my shoulders.

Oliver and I ate dinner at the pub last week. We seem back to normal except for the occasional Elias question. I'm chuffed that you fancy him, and you're right—he is perfect for me. Perhaps if I'd met him years ago, I would've had an open heart.

You're wrong about Elias, though. Maybe he started as my crutch, but he's more than that now. I love him. I can't stop loving him. Do you really want me to shut the book and move on as if all this didn't matter? I realize we can't love everyone the same because no two loves are the same. And I know we can love somebody and not end up with them. It's just . . . I feel like if I let go of Elias even a little, I'm admitting that I'll never meet him.

Holding on makes the impossible seem necessary, like God will have to bring Elias and me together because I refuse to loosen my grip.

I did the same thing with Dad when he was sick. I pretended my life wasn't falling apart. I waltzed into the hospital every day, wearing outrageous clothes and offensive smiles. I brought cupcakes to the nurses and watched sitcoms with Dad for hours. I acted as if he would get better and the whole cancer mess would fade into the past. I wouldn't acknowledge the truth because it hurt. I wouldn't let go, not even when I stood at Dad's grave.

To be honest, I think part of me never left that hospital room, and I've been waiting all this time for my life to begin again.

Searching for Elias gives me hope. It makes me wonder if miracles do happen. I mean, what if Dad's death led me to Cadwallader for a reason? What if someone can love me and not leave? What if "happily ever after" does exist?

Faith, I'm scared to open my eyes. Atteberry has given me so much, but I'm afraid of what'll change or be lost when I stop waiting.

I'm afraid to close the book.

Josie

TWENTY-FOUR

ELIAS

December 3, 1821

Dearest Josephine,

I did not go to Morpeth. When I awoke this morning, the trip seemed wrong. It created a knot in my stomach, added an extra weight to my legs. I just knew I was not meant to search for you in that village, perhaps because you are not there. Perhaps my soul sensed your distance. Perhaps my heart was afraid to search and not find, to love and not be loved in return.

Whatever the reason, I remained at Cadwallader. I sent a messenger instead, and I spent the rest of the morning with Lorelai. She wished to help my farmhands herd sheep into the north pasture.

Confusion plagues me. I tell myself to wait for you, but

what good is waiting if you are not approaching? I wish to yell, "Come back to me," but you have never come at all.

Oh, I must know you exist in this world. If you are a ghost, then haunt me. If you are a figment of my imagination, do appear once more, for I long to hear your voice. I need evidence of you, so I still hope for news, a day when I can post my letters.

I hope to receive your response. Truly, if you told me to wait another day, I would wait a lifetime. I would continue to write, for it was through words I found you. Through words, I reach you. And through words, I beg to keep you close.

But perhaps some loves must remain on the page.

Nothing could dim my memory of that night. We were destined to meet, for no other encounter has left me so changed. Regardless of what occurs hereafter, I want you to know why I fell in love with you, how that night—those few hours—restored my faith in the future.

Arthur and I left the Roch estate soon after Father's death. We travelled from Durham, intending to meet Lorelai at Cadwallader. The journey was most unpleasant. Our driver elected to travel back roads riddled with holes. The carriage bounced. Then a storm came and spooked the horses. We had no other choice but to stop at a public house in Ryton.

Once we rented a pair of rooms at the inn next door, Arthur and I went to the tavern, ordered beer and meat pies, for such was our habit. He played his violin. I draped a feed sack over my head and danced to earn a few laughs. Something happened to me, though. My vision blurred, followed by a ringing in my ears, then a drumming in my chest. I yanked off the sack and stumbled toward the pub's exit. I could not breathe. The air seemed thick in my throat.

My absence went unnoticed. Arthur continued to play his music as patrons laughed and toasted their ale. To this day, I can still hear the fuzzy echo of his merriment accompanied by my jagged breaths, the grating thrum of my heartbeat.

I turned down a corridor and ended up in a vacant assembly room. The hall was dark, illuminated by ribbons of moonlight that streamed through four large windows.

Memories struck me like waves breaking against a cliff. I saw Mother's name engraved on a headstone and Father's coffin lowering into the earth. I remembered Widow Roch's veiled face, the hiss of her voice when she whispered, "You got your wish, little parasite."

The images harrowed me, and I tried to run from them. I had shut the hall's door, however, its lock clicking into place. I joggled the handle. It would not turn. Then your voice echoed through the room, saying, "Sir, I do believe you trapped us in here."

By sharing this report with you, I wish to prove my attention to even the smallest detail. Indeed, you saw a boy at his wits' end, but I beheld the most brilliant girl, who became so very dear to me. One glance at your face, and I knew there could be no moving on from you.

Such an attachment seems illogical, but when has love ever made sense?

You stood near the farthest window, dressed in a muslin gown embroidered with gold and red threads. The garment surely cost a substantial amount of money and hinted at your high birth. You also wore a crimson redingote with lopsided

buttons, obviously handmade, a testament to your unpreten-
tious nature. A bumblebee brooch adorned your lapel, and
your hair dangled loosely above your waistline, damp from
the rain.

The sight of you paralyzed me. You had been crying.
Tearstains dotted your collar, and your eyes were puffy. Still,
even in the dimness, you appeared more interesting than
anyone in my acquaintance, not merely beautiful, rather
astonishing.

To be alone with you threatened our reputations, so I
turned and pounded the door. You joined my efforts, shouting
for help, beating your hands against the panel. After a while,
you retreated to the hall's centre and said, "Aren't you the man
who had a bag on his head?"

Your question caught me off guard, for it defied all formality. I grinned—I had not done that in months—and told
you about my exploits with Arthur. You laughed and introduced yourself as Josephine De Clare. Then you shocked me
with a handshake. "What's your name, Bag Head?" you asked.
"And what brings you to the pit of despair?"

For over a decade, I had kept such feelings a secret even
from Arthur. But you were different. You behaved as though
we had been friends for years.

And I loved you for it.

You moved with a bounce, like the world was a stage
and you were the featured performer. Your facial expressions
filled me with warmth, for they reflected you, your fun and
sincerity. Of course I must also comment on your manner
of speaking. You talked so much. The words flew from you.
Brilliant words. Hilarious words.

And I loved you even more.

We sat on the assembly room's floor and chatted for ages. I told you everything, about my parents, Eton, and the inheritance. I mentioned my recent panic episodes, and you said you suffered them too. You shared about your father's passing, your estranged relationship with your mum, and your aspiration to be a schoolteacher rather than a titled lady.

You confessed that grief had driven you to the assembly room too.

The hall was enormous compared to us, but it felt like home as I sat across from you. We played noughts and crosses in the floor's dust. We swapped embarrassing stories, mine being far more humiliating than yours. Then, during our second hour of captivity, you cupped your mouth and shouted for help. No one came to our rescue, for Arthur's violin drowned out all sounds.

I stood and offered you my hand, and you flashed a smile. Next thing I knew we were positioned across from each other on that massive dance floor.

Music filled the chamber, its melody dulled by the closed door. You snickered as we followed the notes into a country dance. Rightly so. We were bloody awful. I bumped into you at least twice. You gave up halfway through the routine and improvised your own steps, twirling, looping your arm around my waist, ruffling my hair when I bowed.

We endeavoured to make the most noise possible. You stomped and jumped, your heels pounding the floorboards. I tilted back my head and screamed. The sound amused you, to put it mildly, for you laughed so hard, you collapsed into a puddle of skirts.

The music stopped, yet no one came to our aid. I found out later Arthur stumbled back to the inn in a drunken stupor without me.

Another hour passed. We sprawled on our backs and gazed at the rafters, imagining constellations in the darkness. The room was ours—our kingdom, where decorum no longer mattered, a gap between your life and mine.

You said this, and I shall not ever forget it: "Nobody talks about the other loss, the loss that happens within us. We lose people and things, but we also lose parts of ourselves. We grieve those missing parts too. We grieve them, and we grieve us. But I think losing those parts creates space. For newness. For understanding others' hurts and welcoming them into our free spaces. There is no shame in brokenness, Elias. Maybe we met tonight because God knew we needed to be broken together. Maybe wholeness comes not from healing, but from being together."

I slid my hand across the floorboards and touched your wrist. You laced our fingers, your grip firm with resolve. At that moment propriety did not exist. Neither did Widow Roch or the inheritance. Everything faded into a dark room where I sat alone with you, holding your hand, surrendering the weight I had been carrying for years.

The proprietor liberated us around midnight. He and another gentleman managed to break open the door. Apparently your travel companion finally noticed your absence when she visited your room at the inn. She went to the pub and demanded a search.

Our parting happened in an instant. You were there beside me, and then you were out the door. We stood face-to-face before distance, timing, and whatever else separated us. I held you in my arms, but then I made a mistake. I hesitated. I let you walk away, and I told myself we would see each other again.

Arthur and I departed Ryton the next morning. I asked the innkeeper to give you a message, but he said you departed before dawn. And such was our good-bye.

You were my bright spot in a dark place, Josephine. I fell in love with you then, for you were everything I lacked—a sense of belonging, the freedom to feel and break and laugh regardless. We were young. We are still young.

But I shall love you always.

The past few months have forced me to evaluate what I desire from life. No longer am I lost, for I have friends and a home to call my own. Having met you, I feel whole for the first time.

Perhaps meeting you was enough.

My letters may yet find their way to you. If so, please heed this advice. Forgive your mum for her neglect. Let your pain yield to brighter days so you can flourish wherever you are planted. And live always with the wind against your cheeks and buds of gorse tucked into your hair.

Live always, and never forget where you belong.

Yours ever,

Elias

December 20, 1821

Dearest Josephine,

The messenger did not find you in Morpeth. He visited the De Clare estate and learned a Josephine—perhaps you—had returned to London. He brought me an address. Now I must decide whether to post my letters or put an end to this pursuit.

Breathing comes easily to me now. I no longer require a nurse or cane, for I am in good health. I ride Willoughby and take walks with Lorelai. Our relationship seems mended. At present, she plays the pianoforte downstairs while Mrs. Dunstable hums in the annex.

I have not proposed marriage. However, the notion seems less foreign now. Weeks ago Lorelai said people cannot love everyone the same, for no two loves are the same. I must agree. The affection I have for Lorelai is unlike what I feel for you, but it is here, within me.

She has been my constant friend since our arrival at Cadwallader.

A groundskeeper made known the bog outside of Atteberry has frozen over, causing everyone within a five-league radius to flock the glassy banks. I invited Lorelai and the household staff on an expedition to the quag. They seemed eager for recreation. At this time of year, my estate offers little amusement. One can find themselves quite bored.

Lorelai purchased skates from a village shop and distributed them among the staff. We took a carriage and sleigh across the countryside, a light snowfall adding to our enjoyment. Mrs. Dunstable made us all sing a chantey. The cook distributed fairy cakes, potted paste sandwiches, and syllabub flavoured with nutmeg. A festive outing, indeed.

We reached the bog around mid-afternoon and joined the crowd of people on its shore. At first I refused to skate, for I am not versed in the art. Lorelai persuaded me otherwise.

She helped me onto the ice and held my arm as I wobbled across the frozen surface.

She glided in circles until snow plastered her fur stole. Then we locked arms with Mrs. Dunstable and the farmhand, and we skated across the bog in a single line. I only fell thrice.

My knees and backside are moderately blue.

Life has not been gentle with me, Josephine. I have lost a great deal over the past nineteen years. Through it all, I have learned to appreciate the wonderful days. I want more of them, to know what it is like to live alongside people who care about me.

Words provide splendid company, but they cannot love.

Perhaps I shall post the letters.

Elias

TWENTY-FIVE

THE NOVEL

It had been four months since Josephine left Cadwallader Park. The Darlings remained at the estate, for its seclusion offered haven from Sebastian and Widow De Clare's scandal. Of course, society grew bored with the affair and substituted it with more relevant headlines. All impropriety seemed to have been forgiven or forgotten, whichever came first.

And the memory of the girl damaged by the indecent elopement fell by the wayside.

Elias did not witness the reinstatement of normalcy. He returned to Windermere Hall soon after Josephine's departure and occupied himself with Lord Welby's assignments. He had only resided at the house a fortnight before Joshua Heyworth came to call.

Mr. Heyworth practiced law in Durham. A revered barrister, Heyworth had managed to grow his income to thirteen thousand pounds per year, an accomplishment which earned him notice from the country's nobility.

The barrister took a liking to Elias and invited him to join his travels, for he found the road dull without intelligent conversation. Elias agreed. He wished to learn from Mr. Heyworth in hopes of securing a position with the man's practice. An income of more than one hundred forty pounds would allow him to renew his proposal.

Josephine might resent him, though. He had not written to her despite her request. Whenever he lifted a pen, his mind went blank. He could not muster a cordial greeting without balling the stationery and tossing it to the floor.

Elias despised himself for letting her go. Over time the self-loathing poisoned him like strychnine, withering his body into someone he didn't recognize. His skin looked whiter than porcelain. His eyes appeared matte and lifeless. Perhaps his worst alteration was his expression—a chiselled grimness much like Lord Welby's.

His father swore he would forget Josephine, for his heart was young and malleable. Elias considered such remarks a grave insult. He could not forget her any more than he could forget a knife in his side. Indeed, he was young, but even the young felt pain.

And they felt it the longest.

Josephine figured prominently in his dreams, her bumblebee dress fanning around her legs as she twirled across a dance floor, as snow drifted from a fictitious sky. Elias craved the sight of her face. He could live without her, but he wished not to, for living without her was like living in a world without colour, like eating a meal without taste.

She was his world's vibrancy.

Before his departure from Cadwallader Park, Mrs. Capers told him prosperity involved a balance of love and fortune. Neither element possessed in isolation provided the least bit of satisfaction. Elias realized Lord Welby's ultimatum had crippled him. He accepted that he and Josephine would not secure prosperity without each other.

Money would feed their stomachs while their hearts grew thin.

∞

The Mowbray Family invited Mr. Heyworth and Elias to dine at their home in Consett. News of the barrister's travels went ahead of him, prompting gentlefolk to offer their generous reception. Such invitations seemed a relief. Elias preferred to take more delicate meals with others who would engage Heyworth, for the food of public houses unsettled his stomach, and he could no longer devise new topics of discussion.

One more conversation about King George IV would surely bore Elias to death.

"Mr. Welby, what brings you to Consett?" Mrs. Mowbray asked. She perched on a chaise lounge and sipped ratafia from a crystal goblet. Her milky complexion gave her a youthful appearance, quite unsimilar to her husband, who showed premature age.

Elias straightened in his seat. He glanced around the drawing room—a chamber decorated with Chinese wallpaper and oil paintings. A portrait of Mr. Mowbray hung over the fireplace. Its artist had taken liberty to give the man an athletic build.

Heyworth answered for him. "I hate to travel alone, so

Mr. Welby offered to accompany me. I am a social creature. Without conversation, I go quite mad." He lingered near the hearth and puffed on a cigar. "Welby, you must tell Mr. and Mrs. Mowbray about our adventures in Sunderland. I believe they would find your account of the assembly rooms quite amusing."

"Yes, do tell." Mr. Mowbray sat next to his wife, the panels of his waistcoat gaping to make room for his large gut. "We like to hear about society, especially when it's a bit wicked."

"Perhaps another time." Elias massaged his temples, a dull ache pulsing behind his eyes. Months of travel had left him unwell and put him in a distasteful mood. He could not prevent his rudeness. It seemed to pour from him like water from a broken spigot.

Knocks rattled the front door, followed by indistinct chatter within the entrance hall. Elias recognized the voices. He tensed, his heart racing.

"I hope you don't mind, Mr. Welby. We invited your cousin and his wife to join us," Mrs. Mowbray said. "I had the pleasure of meeting the new Mrs. Darling in town this morning. Of course, I felt the need to extend a dinner invitation."

> **Oliver:** My friend emailed me a file packed with information about Elias!
>
> **Josie:** Really? Have you opened the documents?
>
> **Oliver:** Yes! I need to show you something. Free tomorrow around noon?
>
> **Josie:** I'll be waiting outside with my umbrella.
>
> **Oliver:** Or I could ring your doorbell. LOL

"Oh, Elias . . ." Sebastian froze in the drawing room's threshold with Widow De Clare on his arm. He wore a velvet frock coat, his cravat tied into an intricate knot.

Elias lurched to his feet. He hadn't seen Sebastian or Widow De Clare since discovering them in Sebastian's chambers.

"Blazes, what a nice surprise. I thought you'd returned to Windermere Hall," Sebastian said through a forced smile. "Are you not going to congratulate us?"

Pressure tightened Elias's chest until he panted like a horse. He couldn't decide whether to speak or tackle his cousin to the floor.

"I am pleased to see you in good health, cousin," Elias said as the couple greeted their hosts. He clenched his fists, his fingernails cutting into his palms. "Are you staying nearby?"

"No, we're passing through." Sebastian held Elias's gaze as though daring him to misspeak. He cleared his throat. "We're traveling to Cadwallader. My bride wishes us to settle down for the season." His speech exuded confidence and civility, yet he seemed nervous. Beads of sweat formed on his brow. Colour drained from his face.

"Congratulations to you, Mr. and Mrs. Darling," Heyworth said, perhaps to ease the tension. "I trust you had a nice honeymoon."

"Yes, indeed." Widow De Clare nodded, her cheeks flushed. She removed a brisé fan from her reticule and batted the air beneath her chin. "London was most agreeable."

"We hope to purchase a town home near Hyde Park," Sebastian said, his stare fixed on Elias. He escorted his wife to a sofa and commented on the Mowbrays' fine rooms. Both newlyweds donned expensive fashion, proof they likely spent the past few months promenading through city parks and taking afternoon refreshments at the Tea Gardens.

They would enjoy such grandiose activities for as long as God permitted. Sebastian would flaunt his impish wife at dinner parties. Widow De Clare would live in luxury while her spinster daughter grew old within a cottage, invisible to the upper class.

Elias lowered onto his chair and studied the floor's scroll pattern. He trembled with a rage so complete, it almost seemed to revive him. He wanted to shove Sebastian against a wall. He wanted to yell until his voice went hoarse.

Mrs. Mowbray invited her guests into the dining room, where footmen served more than seven dishes. Everyone took their seats and engaged in polite conversation. Sebastian spoke of his and the widow's elopement, their experiences in London, and plans to have children. No one appeared fazed by the circumstance, that a couple who had damaged their families with scandal now lived as distinguished members of society.

"Does your daughter reside at Cadwallader Park, Mrs. Darling?" Heyworth asked.

Widow De Clare dabbed her mouth with a napkin. She glanced at Elias, perhaps worried he'd share the intimate details of Josephine's departure. "No, she resides in Morpeth."

"Such a modest place for a young lady," Mr. Mowbray said. "Is she married?"

"Do you mean to interrogate our guests?" Mrs. Mowbray laughed. Her eyes flashed a warning, as if she knew what had occurred between Sebastian and Josephine.

"No, she is not married."

Elias stabbed his fork into a square of cheese. He couldn't

eat. His stomach churned. He bunched his napkin beneath the table.

"Our situation was most unfortunate," Sebastian said as a footman refilled his wineglass. "Of course, I feel tremendous guilt for breaking my engagement to Josephine."

"Consider yourself lucky." Mr. Mowbray winked and raised his cup in a toast.

"Indeed. Why marry the copy when you can have the original?" Heyworth chuckled. He turned in his chair to face the widow. "Mrs. Darling, you are from the heavens."

She mustered a polite smile. "I must confess my daughter was not keen to marry Sebastian. She thought him too bold a person. I daresay I did her a favour."

"How noble of you," Sebastian said with a laugh. He took a bite of roast beef, then addressed the table. "It is true Josephine showed more affection for my cousin than me." His grin shrank to a smirk, one that stripped all gallantry from his expression.

Heyworth looked at Elias. "Is it true? Did you return Miss De Clare's interest?"

Elias clenched his jaw, anger boiling within him. He glared at Sebastian with as much venom as he could summon.

"Indeed. He was madly in love with her," Sebastian said with a snicker, his eyes gleaming with mischief. Perhaps he wished to lure attention from his misconduct. "Yes, my cousin seemed quite enthralled with Josephine at the Christmas ball—"

"That's enough," Elias yelled. He slammed his palms onto the table and stood, his movements rattling the chinaware. "You are a man without honour. I am ashamed to share blood with you."

"For heaven's sake." Heyworth scoffed. "Calm yourself."

"I mean it." Elias gestured to Sebastian and Widow De Clare. "You sit here unbothered by your misdeeds—your blatant treachery—while Josephine suffers. Where is the justice?"

Sebastian sipped from his glass, the wine staining his upper lip. All along, he had known about Elias's feelings for Josephine, and he'd never said a word. What cruelty possessed him? How did he find joy in the misfortunes of others?

"I want no part of this." Elias dropped his napkin onto the table and raised his hands in surrender. He stormed out of the room, each step like a breath of fresh air.

"Welby!" Heyworth rushed from the dining room and followed Elias to the entrance hall. "Stop right there. Where do you think you're going?"

Elias snatched his coat from a hook and opened the front door. He looked at Heyworth, a sigh breezing from his mouth. "Tell my father I've gone to Morpeth."

∽

The choice was simple. Elias would go after Josephine regardless of her distance. He would find her and beg her to forgive him. No fortune was worth their separation. He would discover a way to provide without his inheritance. He'd labour for Mr. Heyworth or ask his uncle for work. He would do whatever necessary to build a life with Josephine, for time hadn't groomed him to take hold of his dream. It had prepared him to give it away for someone better.

He should've made this decision months ago, before Lord Welby presented an ultimatum, before Josephine bid her good-byes. He once thought happiness required many things. Now he realized it needed only one.

Elias rode all night, his back and shoulders aching from the strain. He reached Morpeth as dawn painted a blue haze across the horizon.

A shepherd directed him to the De Clares' cottage—a small property located a league from town. The house sat on a hillside, surrounded by tended gardens and pastureland. Wisteria clung to its stone walls, and smoke curled from its chimneys.

The cottage was a far cry from the hovel Elias had imagined. Mr. Darling and Lord Welby's stipend must've allowed Josephine to hire a groundskeeper. Would she give up the financial aid for Elias? He would promise to weed the garden and prune the rosebushes. He'd attempt to cook meals, chop wood, do whatever task was needed.

Elias dismounted once he reached the property's fence. He opened its gate and walked his horse up a grassy path, the morning dew soaking his pants legs. He should have tidied his appearance, for the long ride had left him in a sorry state. His clothes were dishevelled. His breath tasted stale, and his nostrils tingled with his own musk.

No lady would find him the least bit appealing under the circumstances.

He stopped in front of the cottage, where chickens meandered and clucked for their feed. His heart raced when Josephine appeared in an upstairs window. She peeked between curtains, her eyes widening at the sight of him.

Love was not based on whether the right girl ended up with the right boy. Love just was—was there in one's chest, stubborn and certain. But sometimes the right girl did end up with the right boy. Sometimes their love won.

Josephine emerged from the house moments later, dressed in nightclothes and her mother's tartan. She gazed at Elias as if she couldn't decide whether he was real or a dream. She approached him with careful steps, her bare feet imprinting the grass.

Elias dropped the horse's reins and moved forward. He looked at her, and he loved her. That was all he wanted to be— the boy who saw a girl and never stopped seeing her, the boy whose love never grew stagnant.

She halted at a safe distance. Her brow furrowed as she regarded Elias's appearance. Indeed, she was beautiful even at this ungodly hour. Her chestnut hair tumbled over her shoulder in a single braid. Her complexion seemed to shimmer like dew.

"You'll lose everything," she whispered. The words drifted from her mouth like a gasp as if she knew Elias's plans. She read him like a book.

He rushed forward and drew her face against his. He kissed her like it was the end of the world, and he didn't mind if she was his last breath. He kissed her for every month they had been apart. He kissed her for every *I miss you* and *I love you* he had wanted to say. If they could hold each other now, after long waits and countless mistakes, then surely anything was possible.

Her kiss was the only home he would ever need.

Josephine hugged Elias's neck as he lifted her off the ground. She laughed and kissed him again, her sigh washing all doubt from Elias's body. In that second, his world consisted of her hands on his jaw, her lips fused with his lips, an entire universe freeing him from his prison of shadows. The day was bright. He was seen.

And she was everything.

TWENTY-SIX

JOSIE

From: Josie De Clare <JDeClare@mailbox.com>

Sent: Thursday, November 18, 4:53 PM

To: Faith Moretti <Kardashian_4Life@mailbox.com>

Subject: What Happened to Elias Roch

Faith, I know what happened. Oliver's friend sent us the information about Elias. You should be glad we aren't FaceTiming because I can't stop blubbering. My keyboard is wet, and my face is pink and blotchy. Nan won't even come near me.

Earlier today Oliver and I drove outside of Atteberry to a graveyard set upon a hill. I saw the headstones, and I couldn't breathe. I refused to go near them until Oliver hugged me and said I needed to know the end of the story. He led me to a plot surrounded by gorse.

I started crying before I read the markers.

The inscription said *Sir Elias Catesby Roch: Beloved Husband, Father, and Friend.* He was buried with Lorelai Roch, his wife of fifty-five years.

Oliver told me Elias married Lorelai and moved to the coast soon after their wedding. They had five children, twenty-one grandchildren. Elias lived for eighty-six years.

He grew old without me.

Maybe I should be happy for him. I mean, he got what he wanted—a home, people who loved him, a full life. I'm not happy, though. Quite the opposite. I'm miserable because I know he didn't need my love as much as I need his. I'm miserable because he spent his life with someone who wasn't me. Am I the worst person ever to wish Lorelai had fallen off a cliff?

I knew this day would come. Even when I sat in that hallway and prayed Elias would find me, I knew we wouldn't meet on this side of eternity. Yes, I'm glad he didn't wait. (I'll tell myself that until I believe it.) I wasn't meant to end up with him but to know him.

Knowing the right person changes everything.

Elias met Josephine De Clare. Perhaps she was real, and their encounter was nothing more than serendipity. Regardless, Elias brought so much good into my life. We didn't get our *happily ever after* moment, but our love won just the same. It won because we tried.

Oh, what I would give for a kiss good-bye.

The final chapter was cliché, and I liked every bit of it. I don't see how it makes sense of my situation, though. Elias hasn't ridden through Cadwallader's gates or swept me off my feet.

Maybe I'll gain clarity once I read the epilogue and his final letter.

The novel gave me a life with Elias. In those pages I belonged to him, and regardless of time and place, I'm confident he was mine. Perhaps we never stop loving someone. We just learn to move forward. To live without them because of them.

Perhaps we let go to hold on.

I must start the next chapter of my life. No more crutches. I'm on my two feet. A little wobbly but standing.

Oliver invited me to go into town with him and his grandparents tonight, so I need to mend my blotchy face. In conclusion . . . I think I'm ready to close the book.

Josie

ELIAS

January 1, 1822

Dearest Josephine,

This message shall end my correspondence, for I have decided to quit Atteberry and forsake these letters. I will not finish my novel, nor will I continue the pursuit of you. All my words shall remain in Cadwallader's study, where they will gather dust and pay tribute to the redemption that occurred. Meeting you changed me. Writing to you added to my wholeness.

Perhaps these letters brought you to me despite our distance.

Forgive my abysmal penmanship. I find this task more than difficult. Never would I have thought myself capable of parting with you by choice. Indeed, I believed our lives so intimately woven together, fated to result in more than one evening at a public house. My soul was made for your soul. A love like that cannot be forgotten.

Lorelai visited my study not long ago. She perused the bookshelves and insisted I hang her portrait of me over the fireplace. When I agreed, she mentioned the farmhands, how she wished to give art lessons to their children. She asked if we could host a party for the estate's workers to thank them. At that moment I realized I loved her in earnest, for she thought of others, she found joy in the simplest things. I understood my love for her was gentle and steadfast, one of admiration. Maybe the revelation would have come sooner if I had welcomed it.

I married her yesterday. The ceremony was held at a local church. Lady Seymore, Edward and Mary Rose, and my household staff were in attendance. Lorelai wore a white dress and flowers in her hair. Afterward everyone came to Cadwallader for an extravagant breakfast.

We leave for the coast tomorrow. I purchased a property with ocean views and a cottage, a house much cosier than Cadwallader Manor. Lorelai and I fancy the idea of painting seascapes and tutoring young people. We wish to open a conservatoire. Mr. O'Connor even offered to put in a good word with the Royal Academy's board.

"Farewell" seems crass, but I must conclude this pursuit so I can focus on the present. Not all loves end with *together*. Some last only a season or a day, but they matter—they have purpose. After everything that has happened, I believe the miracle I needed was not to find you.

It was to know you in the first place.

You are rare, my darling friend. So effortlessly your-self. Wherever you go in the world, I am certain people will adore your everything. Let others accept your brokenness like you accepted mine. Find someone who loves you the way I love you. And perhaps one day, after we conclude our separate journeys, I shall hold you in my arms and whisper against your lips, "My dearest Josephine, you were worth every second."

For a moment with you, I wait an eternity.

Yours ever,

Elias

Josie: Elias didn't finish the book!

Faith: What do you mean?

Josie: He left the partial manuscript in his study. Those chapters from Oxford weren't part of the novel. Someone else wrote them.

Faith: Who?

Norman: Ey up, Josie dear! I'm on the veranda. You and Oliver come inside. Too cold out. That blouse you're wearing looks much too breezy.

Norman: Don't let my grandson bother you, lass. Put him straight.

Norman: You can finish your chat at the kitchen table. Want to stay for tea?

Norman: My, you really do fancy that chat.

Norman: Proper kiss right there. The McLaughlin lads give fine kisses.

Faith: Okay. I must know. Who wrote the rest of the book?!

Josie: Someone who loves me.

Faith: Oliver? OMG. Why did he do it?

Josie: He wanted to give me a happy ending.

TWENTY-EIGHT
THE NOVEL

Elias and Josephine got married with haste. They resided at the De Clares' cottage, where Josephine schooled local children for a modest wage. Elias accepted a job from Mr. Heyworth and worked as a clerk. Although the position required much travel, Elias managed to spend half the year in Morpeth and help Josephine maintain the property.

Two years after their union, Josephine bore a daughter, whom they named Emilia. An undeniable beauty, the child possessed her father's curls and mother's face. She grew fast like a beanstalk, or so Elias claimed. He could hardly believe his daughter's height.

No family seemed more content with little than the Welbys. They found pleasure in their simple routine. Elias and Josephine took Emilia on long walks across the countryside. They gardened, read stories by the fire, and attended church each Sunday.

For five years they were satisfied with their income of one hundred pounds.

And then they received a great deal more.

$$\approx$$

"You look comfortable over there," Josephine said as she laboured in the garden. She yanked weeds and pressed seeds into the tilled soil.

Elias sprawled on the lawn while Emilia crawled over his chest. He lifted her small frame above his head, smiling when she laughed and squealed. "Mrs. Welby, I'm quite at my leisure."

"I could use a strong man to assist me." Josephine removed her wicker hat and dabbed the sweat from her brow, replacing it with dirt smears. She leaned onto her heels and watched Elias sway Emilia back and forth. "She may get sick on your face if you're not careful."

"Wouldn't be the first time," Elias said with a snicker. He rose from the ground and propped Emilia on his hip. "Come fetch her. I'll relieve you."

Josephine left the garden and moved toward them. She wiped her hands on her stained apron, then extended her arms to Emilia. "Would you fancy a jam tart?"

"Do you know how to make a jam tart?" Elias grinned. His wife struggled to bake and cook, for no one had taught her the skills. Mrs. Capers visited them once to offer instruction, but neither Elias nor Josephine could master the art.

Most of their meals consisted of stew and sandwiches.

"You think you're so clever," Josephine said with a scoff. "I do, in fact, know how to make a jam tart." She grabbed Emilia and pecked the toddler's cheek.

"Forgive me. How could I ever doubt you?" Elias hugged Josephine's waist and kissed the back of her neck. He closed his eyes to memorize the moment, how a warm breeze drifted over the hillside, the bleats of sheep as they milled about the pasture.

"Look. Someone's here." Josephine patted his wrist and gestured to a horse and rider now racing toward the cottage. She bounced Emilia to keep her calm, the child's dark curls bobbing in the wind. "Were you expecting company—"

"Excuse me. Are you Elias Welby?" the rider yelled once he reached the property's gate.

"Yes. How may I help you?" Elias approached the man with caution. He and Josephine did not receive callers except for the vicar, schoolchildren, and on occasion Kitty Darling, who lived nearby with her officer husband.

The rider dismounted and greeted Elias with a nod. "I bring unfortunate news, sir. Your father, Lord Welby, expired a week ago."

Elias flinched, his chest aching with an old pain. He hadn't spoken to his father in years, not since he married Josephine. "Do give my condolences to his widow."

"Sir, he named you his heir," the messenger said. "You're to inherit his estate."

"What?" Josephine hurried to Elias's side, their daughter jouncing on her hip. She gawked at the messenger as though he'd sprouted horns. "Are you sure?"

"Indeed, madam. You may occupy Windermere Hall whenever you please." The man smiled and tipped his topper. "Good day to you both."

"No, no, there must've been a mistake." Elias looked at Josephine, his mouth agape. "This cannot be possible. Father disinherited me."

Josephine laughed and touched his face, her eyes welling with tears. "You deserve this good thing," she whispered. "After so much loss, you deserve to know what it's like to *have*."

He kissed the inside of her wrist. "I have plenty."

∾

They arrived at Windermere Hall a fortnight later, after Widow Welby moved into a separate residence. Mrs. Capers and Anne joined the household staff. Emilia grew lovelier with each passing day, her countenance near identical to her mother's.

No family seemed more content with much than the Welbys. They found pleasure in their long walks across the countryside and intimate gatherings. They lived bright and waking, determined not to repeat their relatives' mistakes. And at the end they were together.

They were happy.

And they wanted for nothing.

TWENTY-NINE

JOSIE

June 8

Dear Elias,

Thanks for your letters. I found them at the right time, when my life was a disaster zone. A lot has changed since then. I attend a university in London and plan to move to Cadwallader full-time once I graduate. Rest assured I'll take care of your house. I want to turn it into a museum, perhaps teach at Atteberry's primary school.

My best friend moved to Italy a few months ago. I met her in Milan, and we drove a caravan down the coast. Oh, I wrote a biography about you. It's not published yet. I hope to see it in print before the museum opens. Who knows? Maybe your life will be a bestseller.

On a different note, I found someone who loves me like you loved me. He goes to school in Scotland, but we met here in Atteberry. He's perfect for me, always laughing and acting ridiculous. He'll be a doctor soon. I love him, and I love you.

There's so much I would like to tell you, but since you won't read this letter, I will do my best not to ramble. I suppose I just want to say thanks for giving me a safe place. Your home became my home. Because of you, I stopped waiting.

See you someday.

Yours ever,

Josephine De Clare

P.S. I'll put this letter in your desk drawer for safekeeping.

June 12

Dearest Josie,

When thoughts are inked on paper, they stand up and say to the world they're important enough to be preserved. To be worthy of something a person can hold.

You deserve important words, so I propose we begin a correspondence. I'll keep sliding letters under your back door until you return to London. Write back. Put your messages in the gorse alcove. I'll leave an old biscuit tin to act as a postbox.

It's time I tell you the story of why I wrote the rest of Elias's novel. I need to explain on paper because I cannot look at you without joking. One smile from you, and I turn into a clown. All seriousness fades into trolley races, bad dance moves, and singing at the top of our lungs.

~~That morning I brought firewood to Cadwallader.~~ I'll never forget the first time I saw you. Blimey, you were a mess, standing in the kitchen, waving a sword over your head. You wore fuzzy slippers. Your hair was matted and dyed a weird pinkish brown color.

And that was it for me.

From that moment, I lived for your chaos, how you phoned me to complain after talking with your mum, the way you screamed when I took you for a ride on Pop's motor-cycle. I wanted to debate with you about movies, tease you for not cleaning up after yourself. I liked assisting you with renovations because you got this determined look on your face as if painting was a life-or-death mission. My every laugh had something to do with you. Still does.

You pushed me out of my comfort zone. You got on with my grandparents so well. Better than well. I'm convinced they fell in love with you before I did. Speaking of which . . .

I realized I loved you, like very much head over heels, that night we watched *Dracula* in Pop and Granny's living room. You fell asleep on my shoulder with chocolate smeared in the corner of your mouth. You wore my blue hoodie, the one you stole after I misplaced it in your kitchen. And as I held you (while Dracula escorted a bloke up a cobwebbed staircase), I made a promise to myself to love you even if you never loved me back.

Your search for the end of Elias's book presented an opportunity. I decided to finish the novel because it's what you needed. During secondary school I dabbled in creative writing. My English teacher and I were close, so I read all the assigned classics. Did you have a similar experience? For some reason it's like every interesting person I meet was friends with their English teacher.

Anyway, I spent a solid month in my bedroom. I came up with the worst excuses as to why I couldn't hang out with you. Remember when I said I got the sheep flu? Yeah, there's no such thing as sheep flu, and shearing isn't half as difficult as I made it out to be.

Once I finished the book, my history-buff mate helped me polish the writing to match Elias's voice. I didn't want to give you the chapters, not really, because I knew you would believe they were from Elias and ~~you'd friend-zone me even more.~~

And because I thought my writing was literal rubbish. No pun intended.

Watching you fall for him was the hardest part. I almost told you the truth after the Halloween party, but then I remembered the promise I made to myself. You were my best friend, and being friends was great. I didn't want to jeopardize that.

My inspiration for such angsty martyrdom came from Elias. We both resolved to love the person we didn't think could love us back. We prepared to watch that person live without us. And look how it all panned out. Not quite as we planned. Not horrible either.

To be honest, I thought you'd be disappointed if you knew I had written the chapters. You didn't seem to like me *like that*, but I liked you *like that*, and the novel made it clear Elias liked

Josephine *like that*. So yeah, of course, you should've liked Elias. Made sense.

How in blazes can I compare to Sir Elias Catesby Roch?

I write all this not to sound insecure or pathetic, but to tell you I'm convinced everything—from start to finish to beyond that—was worth it. Elias set a high standard, and I don't plan to compete with him. We both love Josephine De Clare. He loved Josephine first. I aim to love *you* much longer.

For that reason, I can consider Elias a friend.

So many people waste time waiting for good things to happen to them. But sometimes we need to make good things happen. And when we finally start doing that, we often see there were good things in our lives all along.

I suppose I finished the novel to show you the good. I thought if you found hope in your own happy ending, then perhaps you'd fancy me. Of course, that seemed unlikely then. I just wanted to see you happy, to hear you laugh and dream about the future and know people loved you regardless of where they were in time. You're loved. That's all I really wanted to say.

You have a story, Josie De Clare. A flipping wonderful story. And I want to be a part of it for as long as you let me, because this—what's happening between us—is better than fiction. Real. This is real. Us sharing earbuds on train commutes. Going for seaside picnics with the knitting club. Staying on the phone well past midnight to chat about school and work and Pop's recent obsession with Harry Styles.

After reading Elias's work, I've decided there aren't ends, just beginnings. And I want every beginning in the world with you.

How's that for my first attempt at a love letter? Shall I write more? I can't be Elias Roch, but I'm here, and I choose you.

What do you say? Are you up for more of this?

Oliver

June 13

Dearest Oliver . . .

ACKNOWLEDGMENTS

(Credits)

Although novels don't end like films, I wish to roll credits and lead a standing ovation for the people who made this book possible.

Jesus. You are the reason I write. Thank You for not giving me what I wanted when I wanted it. Thank You for saying no in preparation for Your best yes. This book is a testimony to Your goodness, faithfulness, and unmerited, unrestrained love. For the rest of my days, I'll remember Bethel.

Kim Carlton, my brilliant editor and friend, who brought this story to life. You deserve your name on the cover for how much you guided this book. Elias and Oliver are who they are because of you.

Erin Healy, for magnifying Elias's and Josie's voices. You encouraged me more than you know.

Laura Wheeler, the mastermind behind this book's design. Amanda, Kerri, and the rest of my Thomas Nelson/HarperCollins family. Words cannot express my gratefulness for you. Thanks for believing in my stories and welcoming me with open arms.

Tessa Hall, my literary agent and beloved friend, who championed *Dearest Josephine* from the beginning. You've been at my side through highs and lows, prayed for me during seasons of trials, and never wavered in your confidence. I think back to when we first met—both young adults with a passion for writing—and I praise God for how far we've come and grown together. May you find your Elias Roch in this century.

Mom, for reading my first drafts and supporting me amidst impossible odds. No one has seen my writing journey as up close and personal as you.

My family, who tiptoed around me during Christmas and quarantine as I wrote this book. Thanks for putting up with my eccentrics—accidently calling our dogs Elias, speaking in a British accent, playing the *Pride & Prejudice* soundtrack on repeat. You let me be weird.

Mrs. Capers, my former middle and high school English teacher, and her daughter Jamie. Thanks for believing in me when I didn't believe in myself. Thanks for reading my first drafts, getting mad at my rejections, and celebrating when I received good news. You're the definition of true friends, and I'm beyond grateful to know you. Mrs. Capers, please consider this book proof of your impact—your legacy. Because of you, I pursued an author career. May the world see your spunk and kindness through Elias's Mrs. Capers.

Faith, my long-distance pal, whose communication inspired

the friendship within this book. May you continue to find your happily ever after.

Stephanie and Mozy, for being my spiritual and emotional support. The writing process involves a great deal of solitude. As an extrovert, I don't know what I would've done without you. Thanks for the late-night texts, phone calls, and gifs. I love you both so much.

Hannah, for letting me stay at her apartment during my business trips to Nashville.

The Merce Family, who stood at my side when I received a contract offer, who attended my contract signing and celebrated every little milestone. You've been a needed constant in my life these past few years. Thanks for your prayers, laughs, and friendship.

Last but not least, my writing community—the people who push me to learn more, write better, and do hard things. Whether we've met on Instagram or in person, thanks for being an integral part of my journey. You are precious to me.

For a moment with you, I wait an eternity.

DISCUSSION QUESTIONS

(Spoiler Alert!)

1. Josie and Elias struggle to move forward with their lives after grieving their fathers. They find comfort in the written word, their attachment to each other, and later realize they're using their correspondence as a crutch—a distraction from their pain. Do you believe their relationship is healing? What do you consider "crutches" in your life?

2. Letters bring Elias and Josie together. Do you consider the written word more impactful than verbal conversations? Have you ever received a letter that meant a lot to you? If so, describe that moment and how it made you feel.

3. Throughout the book, Elias views gorse as a symbol of his safe place. What are some items that make you feel at home? Do you think Josie finds her safe place in Elias?

4. Faith says the novel's conclusion will help explain Josie's situation. Although not explicitly stated, how do you think Josie finds clarity in the end?

5. Elias and Josie learn to embrace the loves already in their lives. They start to live fully in the present, realizing not all loves end in together, but all loves are important. Who are the loves in your life, and how can you be more present with them? Have you experienced temporary relationships that have shaped you for the better?

6. Near the end of the book, Faith chooses to break up with Noah and pursue her career dreams. Do you think she has a happy ending? How do you define happily ever after?

7. Elias gleans inspiration for his novel from experiences and people in his life. What are similarities you noticed between his reality and fiction?

8. According to Elias's letters, he met Josephine De Clare in an assembly room. Do you believe he somehow met Josie? What you do suspect caused the serendipitous circumstance?

9. Oliver plays an important role in Josie's life. Do you commend him for completing Elias's novel? How do his decisions reflect the book's message?

10. *Dearest Josephine* revolves around the power of literature, writing, and community. What are some books that have influenced you? Do you "get lost" within fiction? If so, how can you find a healthy balance between imagination and reality?

ABOUT THE AUTHOR

 Caroline George is a multi-award-winning author of YA fiction. She graduated from Belmont University with a degree in publishing and public relations, and now travels the country, speaking at conferences and writing full-time. A Georgia native, Caroline aspires to one day host *The Great British Baking Show* and delights in being best known for writing the phrase, "Coffee first. Save the world later."

❧

www.authorcarolinegeorge.com
Instagram @authorcarolinegeorge
Twitter @CarolineGeorge_
Pinterest @AuthorCarolineG
Facebook @authorcarolinegeorge
TikTok @authorcarolinegeorge